Magical Girl Raising Project

breakdown

II

Asari Endou

Illustration by
Marui-no

Nephilia

Can hear the voices
of dead people.

Love Me Ren-Ren

Anyone she shoots with
her magic bow will fall head
over heels in love.

Miss Marguerite

Can bend straight
objects.

Francisca Francesca

Fights with the
mysterious axes she
carries in both hands.

Dreamy☆Chelsea

Can freely
control stars.

Pastel Mary

Can materialize the
sheep she draws with
her pastels.

Clantail

Can transform the
lower half of her body
into different animals.

Tepsekemei

Can become one
with the wind to go
anywhere.

7753

Uses magic goggles
that tell her all about
her targets.

Rareko

Can fix things that
are broken.

Maiya

Fights with a magic
staff that beats liars.

Clarissa Toothedge

Knows the location of
any object she's bitten.

Yol

Touta Magaoka

John
Shepherdspie

Mana

Ragi Zwe
Nento

Agrielreymwaed
Quarky

Navi Ru

Magical Girl Raising Project

breakdown II

15

Asari Endou

Illustration by **Marui-no**

YEN ON

NEW YORK

Magical Girl Raising Project, Vol. 15
Asari Endou

Translation by Jennifer Ward
Cover art by Marui-no

MAHO SHOJYO IKUSEI KEIKAKU breakdown (second part) by Asari Endou, Marui-no
Copyright © 2021 Asari Endou, Marui-no
All rights reserved.
Original Japanese edition published by Takarajimasha, Inc., Tokyo.
English translation rights arranged with Takarajimasha, Inc. through Tuttle-Mori Agency, Inc., Tokyo.

English translation © 2023 by Yen Press, LLC

Yen On
150 West 30th Street, 19th Floor
New York, NY 10001

Visit us at yenpress.com
facebook.com/yenpress
twitter.com/yenpress
yenpress.tumblr.com
instagram.com/yenpress

First Yen On Edition: February 2023
Edited by Carly Smith & Yen On Editorial: Rachel Mimms
Designed by Yen Press Design: Liz Parlett

Yen On is an imprint of Yen Press, LLC.
The Yen On name and logo are trademarks of Yen Press, LLC.

Library of Congress Cataloging-in-Publication Data
Names: Endou, Asari, author. | Marui-no, illustrator. |
Keller-Nelson, Alexander, translator. |
Ward, Jennifer, translator.
Title: Magical girl raising project / Asari Endou ; illustration by
Marui-no ; translation by Alexander Keller-Nelson and Jennifer Ward.
Other titles: Mahâo Shâojo Ikusei Keikaku. English
Description: First Yen On edition. | New York, NY : Yen On, 2017–
Identifiers: LCCN 2017013234 | ISBN 9780316558570 (v1 : pbk) |
ISBN 9780316559911 (v2 : pbk) | ISBN 9780316559966 (v3 : pbk) |
ISBN 9780316559997 (v4 : pbk) | ISBN 9780316560085 (v5 : pbk) |
ISBN 9780316560108 (v6 : pbk) | ISBN 9781975358631 (v7 : pbk) |
ISBN 9781975386603 (v8 : pbk) | ISBN 9781975386627 (v9 : pbk) |
ISBN 9781975386641 (v10 : pbk) | ISBN 9781975386672 (v11 : pbk) |
ISBN 9781975335441 (v12 : pbk) | ISBN 9781975339098 (v13 : pbk) |
ISBN 9781975348014 (v14 : pbk) | ISBN 9781975348458 (v15 : pbk)
Subjects: | CYAC: Magic—Fiction. | Computer games—Fiction. |
Social media—Fiction. | Competition (Psychology)—Fiction.
Classification: LCC PZ7.1.E526 Mag 2017 | DDC [Fic]—dc23
LC record available at https://lccn.loc.gov/2017013234

ISBNs: 978-1-9753-4845-8 (paperback)
978-1-9753-4846-5 (ebook)

10 9 8 7 6 5 4 3 2 1

LSC-C

Printed in the United States of America

Contents

Illustration by MARUI-NO
Design by AFTERGLOW

Go ahead!!

ONE MORE PROLOGUE

Sataborn came into the world, a newborn.

His family had been wealthy for generations, so he never wanted for anything. At one month old, he was saying words; at three months, he cast his first spell; and before he was crawling, he'd become deeply engrossed in technical books. This amused his father, who gave him everything he desired.

And so Sataborn grew up surrounded by magic tools, spellbooks, and magical gems. One could say that this period of his life shaped the core of his character.

Sataborn's toddler period:

By this point, people were already calling him a genius and a prodigy, but the boy thought of the praise and extolling of others as no different from the unceasing sound of the wind, and he quickly came to find it annoying, even.

Hidden laws, unknown theories, and magical formulas that turned the unknown into the known welled up one after the other within Sataborn. Once he had his hands full dealing with all this, he became too busy to feel annoyed by the sound of the wind.

*   *   *

Sataborn as a young boy:

Now that he'd gotten to know himself for a long enough time, Sataborn had a general understanding of what did and did not suit him. He pursued his research using the methods that worked best for him. As a result, his reputation fell from "genius" or "prodigy" to "eccentric," although that didn't change anything for him.

By this time, Sataborn knew what he wanted. Just about all magics had failed to satisfy him; they were all missing something. There was something insufficient about them. If he could compensate for what they lacked with the ideas that were always welling up from inside him, those magics would regain their proper forms—they'd become beautiful.

Sataborn had things he wanted to do, things he wanted to make. Rest assured, he'd carry them out.

Lyr Sataborn as a young man:

He gained another name on coming of age, but that didn't change the actions he took.

Sataborn continued to be an active independent researcher. Pharmaceuticals, barriers, grants, alchemy, contracts, curses, magical girls—he tried everything that interested him, generating some results in every area until eventually people were calling him almighty.

But Sataborn didn't think anything of what others said about him. He focused on his research.

Lyr Cuem Sataborn in his prime:

Because he had completed whatever task was at hand to the best of his ability, he'd been granted another name in recognition of his contributions to the Magical Kingdom. The title of almighty mage was one with some substance, but the man himself was unconcerned about it, as always.

More apprentices showed up at his door. Sataborn treated them like air—that is, he taught them nothing at all. The only way to learn from Sataborn was to sneak peeks at his work, and anyone who disliked that method ended up quitting. It was very rare for an apprentice to stick around for more than six months.

Lyr Cuem Sataborn in middle age:
Whenever schools, departments, or the Lab sought his collaboration, he would respond to them all. It wasn't like he was seeking to contribute to society; rather, he jumped at the chance to take on any work he couldn't accomplish on his own as a researcher—work that involved producing confidential magics, such as for the military or the intelligence community. This was because the most important thing to Sataborn was actualizing the ideas inside him.

However, a lot of this kind of work wasn't supposed to be known to outsiders, and even though he headed the research, Sataborn himself counted as an outsider. In the most crucial moments, he often had the rug pulled out from under him. Right when he was so close to the next stage, when the project was about to become as it should fundamentally be, he would be shooed away.

After many such experiences, Sataborn had learned and transformed. At his core, his desire to pursue the mysteries of magic remained unchanged, but around that core, there arose some "workings of the mind" that had not been there before.

If he was going to be chewed up and spat out before he could finish his work, then he ought to arrange things so that the work couldn't be completed without him. People asked Sataborn for help in the first place because they couldn't accomplish certain tasks themselves, so if he planted pitfalls in those tasks that would prove ruinous for anyone but him, then he would need to stay and help until the very end.

No one could so much as guess the newest techniques that Sataborn was capable of, nor the traps he had set. He actually wished someone were able to figure it out, but nobody noticed that it was all intentional. Since no one was going to understand it anyway, Sataborn gradually became bolder with his methods.

These "workings of the mind" operated separately from the old Sataborn, not interfering with his core desire for research. But this wasn't a different personality. It was one necessary function added to the core of a man who was far too simple.

Lyr Cuem Sataborn, passing middle age:
His desire to make a plethora of hidden knowledge his own and actualize his ideas did not settle down—in fact, it swelled. The days, months, and years passed as he brought to life the ideas that welled up inside him. His hair turned white, and his skin grew wrinkled.

While Sataborn was immersed in his research, his apprentices got married and had children. Sataborn couldn't stand wasting his time with trivialities and always faked illness for ceremonies and other events. Eventually, his grown nephew kept hanging around and getting in the way, so Sataborn drove him off with some half-hearted scolding.

Sataborn's "workings of the mind" enabled him to deal with society as needed rather than ignoring it and ending all involvement. He didn't feel strongly about this either way, but simply carried on with his life, as indifferent as always.

And then Lyr Cuem Sataborn in his old age:
Age deepened his wrinkles and darkened his liver spots, but his mind was sharp as ever. Neither did his body provide any hindrance: Sataborn continued to produce as he pleased.

A new type of barrier, the development of which he'd been involved with for many years, had finally reached a certain stage of completion. And then, just as if they'd been waiting for that moment, members of the Osk Faction came to speak with him.

They were creating a magical girl who would serve as a vessel for the soul of one of the Three Sages, the great mages who had supported the Magical Kingdom since ancient times. The Osk Faction was going to work on an ultimate being, sparing nothing in funds, magic, or lifeblood, with no regard for cost. This magical girl had to be completely new in every sense of the word.

What an incredibly exciting theme for research.

If Sataborn added his existing research to any future endeavors and used the data from the Osk Faction, he should be able to create something interesting—a giddy voice inside him said as much.

He had them secure an island for him and put up a custom barrier there to create the ultimate research facility that none could enter without permission. He filled the island with flora and fauna for easy access as experimental material, while the actual residence was basically just cobbled together.

The Lab tried sending him a helper, which he declined because it was unnecessary. But it foisted a well-built middle-aged man on him, saying, "You can just use him for odd jobs," so Sataborn acquiesced and allowed his frequent visits. Chasing him off would be a waste of energy.

This man had to be a competent researcher, since he'd been dispatched by the Lab, but he merely did as he was told without a single complaint. Sataborn left him to it, treating him neither warmly nor cruelly. He didn't feel strongly about the man either way.

One day, when Sataborn had entrusted him with organizing the storehouse—a task that Sataborn would never do himself—the man babbled on about how this place had some amazing items and how this one item was a masterpiece connected to the First Mage. Sataborn, meanwhile, was always good at drowning out background noise, so he avoided trouble yet again by pushing the man's voice out of his brain.

Sataborn's mind was occupied with work he had to do. To complete the Sage incarnation's senses, he had to fill in each part one by one. A lot of mages would assume there was no great difference in senses between magical girls, so you could slack off in that area and put in an existing formula, but if you did it like that, the work would never be able to reach the point it should.

But then the man did something drastic—he grabbed Sataborn by the shoulders and shook him. "Are you listening, old man?!" he shouted, desperately trying to ruin Sataborn's concentration.

All that violent shaking caused a few pieces of paper that had been left on top of the table to flutter through the air. They were

Sataborn's will, which he'd made during an experiment simplifying will-issuing formulas for a government office. He'd filled it out with whatever came to mind, so it didn't matter if it got bent or dirty, but he figured the more of a mess was made, the longer it would take his helper to finish tidying up; he calmly removed the man's hands, pushed him aside, and returned to work, deep in his thoughts away from the man's voice.

By the time Sataborn had finished the sensory ability settings, the sky was already dark. He could have sworn the man had kept babbling on, but he must have left at some point. Sataborn cleared his mind of any thoughts of that man and seamlessly proceeded to his next task. He had to set a trap that only he would understand in the Sage incarnation's base. He obscured the way the formulas meshed so that anyone else would get burned were they to interfere, and then he created a secret hole in those formulas. He would not put this in the documentation. If Sataborn was chased off before completion, he would be called back—he was the only one who could revise the incarnation, after all.

At his core, Sataborn cared only for the further realization of his ideas; the workings of his mind knew nothing of self-preservation.

CHAPTER 11
FROM A CRISIS TO A BIGGER CRISIS

◇ **Dreamy☆Chelsea**

Chelsea, Mary, and the old mage were in the middle of an argument when worse came to worst: an ax murderer showed up. It was very sudden, as if this person had appeared out of thin air.

Among the many slightly obnoxious things that Chelsea's mother had taught her was "In an emergency, follow your instincts." That meant *"Don't take too long to think if you don't have the time"*—or that she shouldn't take pains to mull things over because it wouldn't do her much good. The fact was that things often went better when she left it up to intuition and took action, rather than exercising caution and thinking things through.

Chelsea acted on impulse. Intuition led her to figure out two things: *"This is an enemy"* and *"This is the one who killed Shepherdspie."* She flew right past the process of questioning or checking and went straight to attack. She'd made some stars beforehand by crushing a rock, and now she sent three of them flying from the right, three from the left, and another four skyward while she stepped forward, making peace signs. So cute. So adorably innocent.

Surprisingly, her opponent moved half a beat faster than Chelsea. The goddess did two vertical spins to leap backward faster than Chelsea's stars could fly before landing on a tree and lunging at her. She moved so quickly, you wouldn't think she carried axes in both hands. The tree did not break or snap—in fact, it didn't even drop any branches or leaves, just wavering slightly. You could tell that she wasn't simply used to using trees as springboards—she'd even mastered some kind of technique for it.

Chelsea was still not thinking. She prioritized action.

Dropping the double peace signs, she made a heart shape with both hands in front of her face. The heart, a symbol of friendship and harmony, was appropriate for a charming and kind magical girl. It gave off an even stronger impression of the magical-girl subculture than the simple, innocent double peace sign. And it was cute, of course.

The goddess swung her axes up. She was still far away; she must have misjudged the distance— No!

Chelsea ran toward the goddess without a thought. She ran like a peppy magical girl in an anime opening—she was thinking of Riccabel in particular. But the enemy wasn't too far away; she hadn't made a mistake. Chelsea was the one who had it wrong. The enemy's axes had a wider attack range than they seemed to. As the enemy swung them, the axes writhed, and their gray, rocklike texture turned into something red and rough like sand, and right as they were about to strike, Chelsea flung herself up like she was doing a high jump over a bar, puffing out her chest and spreading her arms wide as she emphasized her girlish brilliance. The sand axes didn't hit Chelsea, striking the ground instead and kicking up dust.

The sand axes instantly reverted to metal, and the goddess swung them so quickly that it looked like she was wielding ten or twenty instead of two. Such incredible speed. Using a flowing amalgamation of spin and natural turns as if she was waltzing,

Chelsea avoided the string of attacks, and, with a little jump after that, she landed atop her rotating stars and leaped some more. The axes were just so fast. It was difficult to follow them with her eyes. Chelsea had somehow managed to avoid that attack just now, but if she kept this up, she would make a mistake somewhere down the line. And that one mistake would spell game over.

She made up her mind. She would fight this enemy with speed and add irregularity. Chelsea set her ten stars on seemingly random trajectories and moved in a confusing way herself, posing as she hopped from star to star or switching to the ground in order to toy with the enemy—not avoiding her, but preventing her from keeping aim. Plus, she dazzled the enemy with her poses.

With a double axel and a triple toe loop, Chelsea leaped from star to star, slipping past the axes to get closer to her opponent. She struck the enemy's forearm with an arm movement chock-full of lyricism only to be sharply repelled. Her hand tingled with numbness. The enemy's arm was crazy hard, but not as if from a spell; her flesh was just abnormally firm, even by magical-girl standards. It was not cute.

One of Chelsea's stars, which she'd sent shooting through the area, shattered with a *pop*, smashed by the goddess's ax. She destroyed two more stars after that. The axes were speeding up. The blades became fine and sharp. Chelsea could fight back by speeding up her stars, but that would destabilize her coordination. There didn't seem to be a limit to how fast the enemy could swing those axes, plus it would be disadvantageous to turn this into a competition of speed. Chelsea gracefully evaded the next attack with a jeté en tournant reminiscent of a swan landing on a lake. When the axes came swinging after her, she grabbed them by the handles, spinning herself and the enemy around to swap their positions before leaping. She did all this in a beautiful stance like a rhythmic gymnast while shouting pleasantly like a vocalist; that way, what she was doing didn't appear violent, like grappling or scuffling. But although she was reluctant to take such measures, this wasn't an enemy she could immediately beat.

"Mary, run!" Chelsea yelled, and then she imagined Mary running toward Ren-Ren. Suddenly, a crazy thought struck her: She didn't want her to run away, she wanted Mary by her side. She almost cried out, *"Actually, don't run,"* but another part of her restrained herself. She absolutely didn't want Mary to be in danger. Just thinking of her getting killed like Shepherdspie gave her goose bumps.

"Run! Not toward Ren-Ren!"

That was good enough.

Remembering Shepherdspie made Chelsea's heart feel like it was going to get caught in her throat, but Mary quickly blotted that out. She was Chelsea's top priority right now. Everything Chelsea did was for Mary.

The remaining stars raced through the air, or wove through the trees in complex trajectories to gather in one spot. Had an ordinary pro been controlling them, there would have been one or two midair collisions. But this was none other than the master of star shooting, Dreamy☆Chelsea.

When Chelsea and the goddess got up, Chelsea was holding an ax handle in each hand, crossing the blades so the enemy couldn't swing them anymore—not forgetting to tilt her head with a smile for added cuteness. Her opponent was smiling, too. The anger hidden behind one smile and the hostility lurking behind the other clashed like locked blades, entwining, enmeshing. She would not avert her eyes.

At just the right moment, seven shooting stars rained down behind the goddess, passing through the trees or under the sun to strike her undefended back. Even if these were just makeshift stars Chelsea had solidified, they would still hurt. No—if she was a normal magical girl, they would do more than just hurt. One star after the other hit the goddess, but she didn't even twitch; she just let them slam into her back and head. All the while, her smile never faltered.

Chelsea tilted her head to the opposite side. Her opponent didn't seem to be just putting up a strong front. Chelsea's observant eyes detected that the enemy had taken only minimal damage. Just how thick-skinned could you get? What did you have to eat to get a body like that?

After landing the first hit, the stars turned around and flew over Chelsea's head to pelt the enemy's face. Chelsea made them faster than before and added a spin like they were bullets. She wouldn't have gone this far with a normal opponent, but she wouldn't have needed to then. One after another, Chelsea struck this fearsome enemy's face with the stars, using a destructive force that would send even a tough magical girl flying backward three times. The stars were unable to take the force and shattered, knocking the goddess's chin upward. She lowered her chin, revealing that same smile, although a little bit of blood oozed from it.

"Is the one you dropped the golden ax?" the goddess asked just like before, her arms slowly coming forward. She was straining harder into her axes. Chelsea's spine made a cute sound from the strain.

"Or is it the silver ax?"

"Hya!"

With a pretty call that carried the full strength of her body, Chelsea returned to a forward-leaning stance, pushing against the goddess.

Chelsea took a few steps and stopped there. Her toes dug into the ground, her knees shook, and, though she was trying to go forward, her legs just wouldn't move ahead. In fact, they were going backward. She retreated several steps.

Chelsea looked at the goddess, who was calmly smiling. "Is the one you dropped the golden ax?" the goddess asked again.

"You've gotta be kidding me... What is this?"

"Or is it the silver ax?"

"The hell are you?" The words that came out of her mouth felt lacking in cuteness, so she hastily asked, "What the heck are you?"

Chelsea wasn't as strong as her opponent. She couldn't fight this. She was built like a child in late elementary school or early middle school, while the goddess had the physique of an adult woman. But a difference in stature is no barrier to a magical girl. Some were strong even if they were small, and even if you were large, those who were weak would still be weak. As Chelsea backed up a couple of times, her lower body struggled to stay balanced. She fired some stars from the cuff of her sleeve.

Sensing that the goddess's left leg was tensed, Chelsea intuited that her foe was going to spin on that leg to launch a kick with her right leg, which was now in Chelsea's blind spot, since the goddess had that leg drawn back.

The stars Chelsea had fired went into position. They weren't ordinary stars; they were pieces of mirror cut into star shapes. By reflecting one mirror star off another, she could see what was going on even behind her head. Chelsea popped out her leg in a cutesy kick.

Huh?

She'd meant to adorably meet the goddess's boring, run-of-the-mill, ordinary kick with her own leg and knock her down, but she couldn't envision it succeeding. Chelsea suddenly released the axes and hopped to the opposite side. Chelsea's jump and the goddess's kick met in perfect unison, sending Chelsea's small frame high into the air. The goddess swung her now-free axes.

Chelsea was looking down from twenty feet up in the sky. Pastel Mary was already gone. Incidentally, the old mage was also gone. Relieved that they'd run away, Chelsea changed the angle of the two mirror stars to blind the opponent's eyes with light. At the same time, she moved a different pair along a star-shaped trajectory to repel the ax handles from below. The attack wouldn't be able to stop the axes from swinging down, but it would slightly disturb their balance when the goddess tried to lift them overhead. In the meantime, Chelsea pulled out her wand and grabbed the star taped to the tip.

She made the star move downward at an acute angle. It dragged her along with it, zipping to avoid the attack by a hair or two. The magic tape couldn't take the speed, and some of the pieces peeled off. Acrobatic flight gave her a sick feeling like a direct stroke to her innards, and she didn't want to feel this repeatedly, but it was far better than taking a direct slice from those axes when she was defenseless in midair.

Chelsea avoided the right slash in midair, then skimmed over the ground to make it through the attack from the left. Passing under the sand as it sprayed up like in episode thirty-six of *Help Me! Hiyoko-Chan!*—the surfing episode—she did three turns, now twenty-five feet away from the goddess, to land on her right leg. But something was wrong—as she slowly tried to step out on her left leg, spasming pain abruptly stopped her.

Her leg was numb where the goddess had kicked it. She didn't think she could move it for the moment. She could have sworn she'd leaped the moment it hit to reduce the impact, but she'd still taken quite a lot of damage. It hurt.

Chelsea struck a slightly silly pose, spreading her right hand and lifting her left leg. It wasn't to her taste, but she had to at least go through with it, for appearance's sake. Granted, no matter how she posed, the enemy would probably be able to tell she'd taken a hit.

The goddess slid her right leg forward. The movement was smooth, and it didn't seem like she'd been hurt at all. It was totally unfair that Chelsea had been injured and the enemy totally unwounded when they'd collided. This was less than egalitarian.

The waves of pain came endlessly, practically torturing Chelsea. She was about to lose to a foe who fought with pleasure. Was cuteness going to lose out? This would not do. That wasn't allowed.

The right ax turned black. The left ax turned red. The goddess came forward, and Chelsea hopped on one leg to back up. Unlike the goddess of the spring who appeared in fairy tales, this goddess only used her axes for violence. While she had such a fantastical and fairy-tale appearance—she was wasting it.

Chelsea's left leg was complaining harder. She needed a rest, not more fighting. More accurately, she couldn't fight any longer than this. It was a total pack of lies that a magical girl's true power came out when she was in dire straits. It wasn't magical girls who showed strength at times like that. It was those pseudo-magical girls who liked fighting. They were different from Chelsea.

Pastel Mary wasn't there. In other words, the one Chelsea had to protect was not there. There was no need to push through this. Cuteness would not lose. This was just a temporary retreat.

Chelsea clapped the star on her wand with her open right hand. Another cute sound. "Oh yeah, that's right. I did drop an ax. I totally saw that, yeah."

Still smiling, the goddess tilted her head. In this attitude, she did have a mysterious sweetness to her.

"But I don't think I saw the gold ax. I think it might've been an iron ax, yeah," Chelsea added, smiling brightly. Then she leaped backward, manipulating the star decoration in her palm.

The goddess started running after her with hardly a pause at all. The attempt to talk to her to try to create an opening hadn't really succeeded.

Chelsea had figured that if she ran into the forest, the trees would get in the enemy's way and slow her down, but she ran strangely, in a manner both forceful and light that made obstacles like tree roots or indentations in the ground no problem for her.

Okay then, Chelsea thought, and she changed the direction of her star. She shot it up into the sky at a sharp angle, scattering leaves and branches. Chelsea figured that since her enemy was not an angel or a fairy but a goddess of the spring, she shouldn't be able to fly. But the goddess immediately shot down that thought. There was an ear-bursting explosion, and then Chelsea sensed an object flying at her at the speed of sound—Chelsea changed the course of her flight at a forty-five-degree angle to evade the slice by a hair. The enemy was generating continuous explosions and using the blast of wind to fly. The hair on the back of Chelsea's head was sliced off, and a lukewarm fluid flowed from her head down her neck. Knowing it wasn't a magical-girl-like thing to do, she clenched her teeth. The hairdo she'd had all done up prettily was a mess, and this bleeding that wasn't appropriate for a magical girl was turning her head red. None of this was right for magical girls. It wasn't right for Dreamy☆Chelsea. It was not cute at all.

The goddess's axes increased their size with a *pop*. White and sharp, they looked just like wings. She flapped once to close the distance between them. With one more flap, she was even closer. They really were wings.

Agh, come on! Anything goes with this lady, huh?! No fair!

Chelsea pulled a sudden dive, and then, right before she collided with the ground, she changed direction to fly at a low altitude, parallel with the ground. The hem of her skirt swiped against the earth and grew dirty, and her injured left leg snapped off tree branches, the pain shooting to the crown of her head and making her cry out, "Yeek!" No matter how bad it got, cries like "ergh" or "gwagh" were out of the question.

There was an intense impact and the *boom* of an explosion behind her, and Chelsea slowed her star, lifting her legs up high enough to keep from knocking into things as she checked the situation. Clouds of dust were billowing up, and broken trees and branches were raining down along with clods of earth. Then the shape of a person rose, cutting through the dust, and Chelsea clicked her tongue and sped up her star. She didn't consider escaping high in the sky. The lack of trees as obstacles would just make it more dangerous.

This is not right! It's messed up, it's unfair!

The goddess wasn't just strong. Her reflexes were sharp in subtle ways, and most of all she was abnormally resistant to everything. Even being right beside the center of the explosion she'd created just got her a little dirty, and after falling from the sky that rapidly, she didn't seem like she was hurt anywhere, running after Chelsea like she was totally fine. When Chelsea looked back, the goddess's hands on her ax handles had the index and middle fingers sticking up. In other words, she was doing a double peace sign. Chelsea shivered. The enemy was even making to equip herself with both strength and charm.

"Don't copy me!" Chelsea yelled back at her, but even that was ignored with a smile.

Chelsea was finally out of options. One of her legs wouldn't move, the enemy wouldn't go away, even if she did attack her she didn't feel like she could do damage—there was nothing at all to be done. The only good thing here was that she'd managed to let Mary escape. That was the one area where she had been cute and capable.

When Mary rose in her mind, the next thing that came up was that irritating Ren-Ren. *Telling her not to run to Ren-Ren was a good play, if I do say so myself,* Chelsea praised herself, and she also thought that maybe Ren-Ren could manage this somehow. She seemed to recall that Ren-Ren had said her magic was to fire a magic arrow to control minds or something like that. Chelsea didn't want her own mind controlled, and she kind of thought that type of magic was too evil for a magical girl, but maybe mental attacks would be effective on an enemy who was seemingly invincible to physical attacks. Chelsea also seemed to recall her mother maybe saying something about how compatibility was important in fights between magical girls, though she wasn't sure. She'd ignored that stuff because she didn't really care about fighting, but she figured it had been something along those lines. Chelsea didn't think Ren-Ren was even worth paying attention to, but she did have a feeling she would be useful against the goddess. So she should head for the rocky area that Agri and the others were using as a meeting spot. Ren-Ren would probably be there, along with Nephilia or someone, and then Chelsea would work with them to beat the goddess. Then they'd make the goddess apologize and hand her over to the police.

Now it really did seem like a good play to have made Mary run someplace Ren-Ren was not. When a log came flying at Chelsea from behind, she kicked off it with her good leg to speed up the flight of her star.

◇ 7753

With Tepsekemei checking their position, Mana and 7753 were headed for the main building. After coming out of the brush, 7753 saw a shining streak of red on Mana's cheek and thought regretfully as she made her way along, *Ahhh, I should have held those pointy leaves away from her face.* Right now, 7753's head was too full for her to spare any minute considerations toward other people. Now she was regretting that she'd failed to make such considerations and was brooding over it.

They didn't show caution or exercise wariness as they traveled, emphasizing speed instead. "Let's hurry," Mana told 7753 and

Tepsekemei before rushing ahead. Mana had to be thinking about Marguerite. 7753 didn't object to Mana's decision. They were headed in the opposite direction from where Marguerite and the others had headed. If they ran into the enemy anyway, maybe they should just be coolheaded about it and consider themselves unlucky. They had to be somewhat cold about it, given the situation. 7753 started to remember the events of B City and shook her head to get them out of her mind. She really was brooding. And when she got like that, she remembered the past—painful, difficult things. 7753 of all people had to be clearheaded. She punched herself in the cheek to make it hurt. That seemed to energize her a bit more.

The area around the main building was well maintained, with the trees and grass being pruned and weeded and whatnot, making a bit of a garden. In other words, there was a better view here than inside the forest. When 7753 came out from the forest path, holding her hand up against the light of the sun, she heard a voice.

"Hey, you kids came here, too?"

A broad forehead, square face, and overall rugged and burly man—it was Navi Ru. He waved at them, the sleeve of his robe sliding down to expose the magical figure tattooed on his forearm. A mage's tattoo obviously had to have a magical meaning. But combined with his appearance, it came off less like something magical and more like the kind of thing you'd see on a member of a criminal organization.

Keeping such rude opinions to herself, 7753 waved back at him.

They'd finally encountered someone who was not an enemy. 7753 was about to rush toward him when someone held out an arm in front of her. She looked over and saw it was Mana's. Her expression was stiff. She seemed different from when she'd looked about to collapse in the forest. She was also different from when she'd brought up Hana's name and cheered up.

Holding back 7753, Mana went over to Navi very slowly—7753 was confused, but she followed. Mana stopped ten feet away from Navi, who was standing a slight distance from the entrance to the main building.

Navi didn't seem particularly suspicious about this, shoulders dropping as he let out a big sigh. "It's good to see an ally out here in this mess."

"Where is everyone else?" Mana asked.

"Clarissa is checking around. I told her not to, 'cause it's dangerous, but magical girls never listen. Yol and Rareko are hiding together in a safe place with the kid. Not like anyplace is safe, mind you. But it's comparatively safe. So what about you folks?"

"We encountered an enemy." Mana paused for a beat and continued. "It was a magical girl who carried two axes. Me, 7753, and Tepsekemei were there along with Mr. Shepherdspie and Marguerite, but we got separated from them when the enemy attacked."

"Was it the one who killed Maiya?"

"That seems highly likely."

"I see…" A corner of Navi's lips bent slightly. His expression looked terribly regretful. "I'll say first off that I don't blame you guys at all, but I'd like to say something, if ya don't mind."

"What is it?"

"Was that magical girl so strong that even three magical girls couldn't fight her?"

"…If you're asking me based on what I saw myself, then the honest truth is that I couldn't even tell what she did. Marguerite and a part of Tepsekemei drew the enemy away, but Tepsekemei said that part has already been destroyed—"

"Mei died," Tepsekemei offered.

"…So she says."

"Man, well…this isn't good." Both corners of Navi's lips bent, and his expression clearly darkened. That look made 7753 feel like her own uselessness was being shoved in her face. It was embarrassing to just stand there, but she couldn't go and hide.

"Do you think you could beat her if you had five or six magical girls?" Navi asked.

"I couldn't say."

Navi's gaze shifted from Mana to 7753, who realized that he was wondering if she had managed to measure the enemy's strength.

She hastily shook her head. If only she'd had her goggles, 7753 could have measured the enemy's strength precisely, but she didn't have them now.

Navi's gaze left 7753, and he glanced slightly upward at Tepsekemei.

"If there were lots, maybe we could win. Maybe we would lose," she said heavily.

"Well, of course."

"If Archfiend Pam was here, we could win."

"Stands to reason." Navi let out a deep breath and gave them a look featuring a slight wry smile. 7753 was grateful that Navi was easygoing enough that he gave Tepsekemei's answer no more than a slightly uncomfortable smile.

"Figures," said Navi. "If the situation could be judged easily, nobody would have run away, huh? Anyway, I get that she's a real strong opponent. Though that wasn't what I wanted to hear. Anyway, I guess we should gather everyone together. Let's meet up with Clarissa, for starters. She just said she'd come if she could, but she's the type to wind up showing up when you get together."

Navi took a step toward them, trying to come closer, and Mana held up a hand. Navi stopped. 7753 wondered what Mana was doing. Then she figured out that the hand sign meant not to come close, and she bit her lip. She almost said, *"What are you doing?"* out loud but managed to hold her tongue.

Navi didn't get angry—he actually seemed curious, tilting his head. "What's up?"

"We also ran into Dreamy☆Chelsea…," said Mana, "but it seemed like she was being controlled by someone."

"What the heck?"

"We somehow managed to make it through that situation, but she was being openly hostile. Oh, yes, and we haven't confirmed what sort of magic the enemy uses."

"Well, if you waited around until they used it, then you'd be in danger. Makes sense."

"It may be a magic that can twist minds or control people."

"I haven't seen it, so I don't know... Wait, are you saying I'm being controlled?"

"That is a possibility. After all, Dreamy☆Chelsea was indeed being controlled."

Navi scratched his head, at a loss. Since 7753 had been among those attacked, she'd seen the enemy. She'd seen the axes changing color, too. And she knew that after that, they'd exploded, and half of Tepsekemei had been shaved away. So then, wouldn't it be typical to assume that had been the enemy's magic? It didn't seem quite right to leap over such explanations and claim they hadn't seen the enemy's magic. It was true Chelsea had been acting strangely, but 7753 felt that was a different issue.

7753 wondered if she should say something, but after getting a peek at Mana's expression, she changed her mind. Mana looked just like an inspector as she stared at Navi: sharp and without weakness. Therefore 7753 shouldn't butt in.

"If you're sayin' someone's controlling me...," Navi said, "you got me there. But if you could check with the goggles..."

"The goggles aren't here now," Mana told him. "Chelsea probably stole them."

"That's not good."

"I'm fine just doing a basic check to ensure you have no hidden weapons."

"Now that sounds like a hassle. From where I stand, I don't know if you guys are being controlled, either."

"If we were being controlled..." Mana looked to 7753 and then Tepsekemei before returning her gaze to Navi. "Then we would have killed you or captured you."

Navi's eyes widened slightly, then immediately narrowed with a small smile. "Well, I guess you're right. There's no way I could fight two magical girls."

"Call it the nature of Inspection to be suspicious," Mana said, her tone the epitome of superficial and insincere politeness.

But Navi wasn't offended, raising both hands. "I can't fight a cop."

7753 approached Navi's side, more or less cautiously, and

Mana inspected his person more painstakingly than she'd said she would, confirming that he was not carrying any weapons.

Mana took her hat in her hands, placed it in front of her chest, and bowed. "No issues. Please forgive my rudeness."

"Oh, it's fine. More importantly, you came here for the same reason as me, right?"

"What do you mean?"

"I mean, didn't you come here thinking there might be something useful here to get outta this situation? I was lookin' for just that kind of great magic item."

Mana nodded and glanced at the main building. "That's the plan."

"Then you're outta luck." Navi approached the building and knocked on the wall, then gave it a slap with his palm. He seemed far more disgruntled now compared to when Mana had demanded to inspect his person. "I tried investigatin' the storehouse, too. There was nothing worthwhile. There were a few antiques that would fetch a good price if you took 'em to the right places, but there's no use for something like that now."

"Then I will look as well."

"Uh, I said I just looked."

"Our specialties are different. There might be something that only I would notice." Mana went straight inside.

Navi shrugged with a *"What do you do?"* look on his face. 7753 bowed apologetically. "I'm sorry. We're all on edge."

"No surprise there. I'm sure nobody thought things would wind up like this." He was always so easygoing.

7753 ordered Tepsekemei to keep watch at the entrance, then went after Mana. They walked briskly along, turning many corners, then went up a flight of stairs to arrive at a large door at the end. The door wasn't as heavy as it looked, and Mana opened it casually with one hand and went inside. 7753 followed her. The room was nine feet by eighteen feet at most, with shelves built in on all four sides. It looked like a storage room. There were a lot of things in here, and none of it was organized. Moving papers and piling books to the side, Mana dragged out an armful-sized box and slid the top open.

"Is there something here that could help us?" asked 7753.

"You wait there. An amateur shouldn't go touching these things." That meant 7753 couldn't do anything.

Then Mana turned back, having remembered something. She thrust a finger at 7753's chest. "Also—you can't trust Navi. He said there was nothing here, but don't just take that at face value."

"Huh? We really can't trust him?"

Mana faced the box again and pointed at the bottom. "Doesn't it look like something was here?"

7753 leaned over Mana's back and looked down to see a space roughly four inches square.

"I'd assume it was like that to begin with," said 7753.

"Look around it. There's dust in the box. But there's no dust in just that one spot."

7753 looked more closely. Now that Mana pointed it out, she did notice. It was true, it was as she'd said.

"It's already suspicious that he would choose to split up with his magical girl to come to the main building, given the situation. It's too reckless for an employee of the Lab—he should be used to danger."

7753 had sensed the air about Mana change when she'd seen Navi standing in front of the main building. Maybe this was what Mana was like when she was working. She wasn't simply steeling herself, she was working as an employee of the Inspection Department.

"At the very least, we should suspect him of being a looter," Mana continued.

7753 followed what Mana was saying and went back to consider everything in order. She scowled. "You mean you think maybe Navi took advantage of the commotion to steal some of the inheritance? And that's why you inspected his person? But he wasn't carrying anything, right?"

"He wasn't carrying anything that looked like the inheritance."

"So then, it's also possible that someone other than Navi went in during the confusion to steal it, right? Or wait, maybe it wasn't even stolen, but that, um—Sataborn, was it?—maybe he needed something, so he took it out."

"No." Mana cut 7753 off. "Navi is the most suspicious."

"How can you say that for sure? You inspected him."

"He just had a few grayfruit and one staff. He didn't have a magic bag, either."

"So then, he didn't steal it, right?"

"He was missing something he should have had before."

"Missing what?"

"He was using a magic carpet before. That's gone."

7753 recalled when Navi had showed up. That had left an impact. True, he'd had a carpet. Or rather, he'd been riding one.

"He could have given it to Clarissa," 7753 suggested.

"In this situation, I doubt he would give a magical girl who isn't with him a tool he could use for escape or retreat."

"That's true…but what about not having it makes him untrustworthy?"

Mana looked up, and 7753 followed her gaze. There was nothing particularly strange about the cream-colored stone ceiling. If anything, it was just a little dusty.

"How far up do you think the barrier goes on this island?" Mana asked.

"Who can say…? I don't really know."

"You don't think that if he put the item he wants atop the carpet and sent it up above the clouds, it wouldn't be found?"

7753 clapped her hands with an "Ahh." Then he would just have to retrieve it after everything was over. Since there had been no kind of catalog to begin with, nobody would even notice it had been stolen.

"I heard a story about how a long time ago, a robber stole jewels via a similar method," Mana explained. She pulled a pale-pink ceramic container from the box, then placed it down on the shelf more slowly than she'd picked it up. There was a chip in the neck. "It seems like…a lot of these things are broken."

"Did someone break them?" 7753 asked.

"No, it's probably simply due to age. These are the sort of antiques you'd find in a museum. Some people find historical meaning in even a single chip. You shouldn't repair them if you don't know how."

"So this means there are a lot of old things in here."

"I'd have been glad to find things that made use of new techniques, though..." Mana pulled a number of items from the box and carefully lined them up. There was energy even in those little gestures. She didn't look like a victim who had been caught up in an incident, but like an inspector who had found someone suspicious. This was unquestionably Mana.

◇ **Rareko**

Touta seemed worried about something—he was groaning to himself. He wasn't trying to hide that he was troubled, worried, and at a loss.

"If you can't hold it, I dug a hole in the back...," said Yol.

"No, that's not what it is. It's something else, Yol. I've been thinking about things a bit."

It seemed it wasn't that he wanted to tell them something. If complaints and whining had followed, then Rareko could say *"I see"*—for her, that would be straightforward and easy to understand. She wanted to keep on whining and complaining, too. The world was filled with misery—this island in particular.

Yol let out a sigh and looked down, seemingly lost in thought. Maiya's death had left her heavily disheartened. Her reliable bodyguard was gone, and she had been abandoned on an island surrounded by outlaws. She couldn't remain a mere carefree and pampered young lady.

Rareko adjusted her glasses with the tip of her index finger. Her setting them at this angle would make it difficult to read her eyes from Touta's position, due to the reflection of the light. As she spent some time observing Touta, he flicked repeated glances outside. It seemed he hadn't given up on his idea to leave the cave. That basically had to mean he was thinking about how to leave, how to change Rareko and Yol's opposition into agreement. Rareko doubted that he'd come up with an answer immediately, given his child's brains.

Rareko looked away from Touta.

Maiya had been killed. To Rareko, this was a bigger blow than simply losing her master. As a magical girl who had served for many years, Maiya had had a unique position in the house. She'd been given a position of responsibility in working for both the past generation and the current one, and she likely would have been responsible for the future generation—Yol—as well. Maiya had touched many secrets that couldn't be allowed out, and she had been able to make statements a mere servant could not. Rareko had only been employed because she was Maiya's apprentice. With Maiya gone, Rareko's presence in the household was at a terrible risk. Her position was going to get worse, even if this wasn't her fault.

Rareko twisted the hem of her apron in her fingers. Getting back safely was her absolute condition, and she had to think about after she got back, too. There was a single dripping sound in the back of the cave. The sound rang out, but she didn't look back toward it. She was so on edge, she'd been looking back there with every drop of water, but she'd gotten sick of that. Only magical girls like Maiya could accomplish the feat of always being alert to their surroundings. Even if Rareko couldn't do it, that didn't mean she was at fault.

Navi was trying to get into Yol's favor. Maiya had hated that. Navi failed to measure up to Maiya's standards in character, career history, skills, and appearance. With Maiya there, it had been difficult for Navi to even approach Yol.

With Maiya's guard so incredibly firm, Navi must have seen her as a tough nut, as before long he'd sought cooperation from Rareko. It wasn't dramatic enough to call betrayal—she was just sort of leaking information to him.

Rareko needed to have more than just one person she could rely on when something happened. She didn't view this as not trusting in others, rather managing to get by in the world—but she knew full well that wouldn't fly, socially speaking. If the information Rareko had leaked had caused Maiya's death, then Rareko would have no place to run. Even if she insisted, "It's not my fault! I didn't do anything," nobody would listen. Even if she wasn't really at fault, even if it wasn't because of her, that wouldn't matter.

Yes, perhaps Navi had been involved with Maiya's death here. Navi had said a few times that he wanted to convince Maiya somehow, but if this was the kind of convincing he'd meant, that would be disastrous. That would inevitably make Rareko an accomplice. Since coming to this island, she had been sending Navi information via notes—they were about comparatively trivial things like what Yol and Maiya talked about and the things they did. When Clarissa had brought her mouth to Touta's sleeve, Rareko had let that go, and when Clarissa had come over while being chased by Clantail, Rareko had run to help, even though that meant leaving Yol behind. Rareko had undeniably cooperated in everything. If Rareko's cooperation had led to Maiya's death, that would make it Rareko's responsibility.

Though 7753's goggles had denied his direct involvement, it wouldn't be a surprise for Navi to be up to something. Rareko saw him as a man who would do anything for his own benefit, and that worked out for him. He had a new face for every occasion and said whatever people wanted him to say. He would sometimes play a cheerful clown and other times a scary-looking but kind man, and he could also be an outlaw who made a reliable ally.

I'm going to get him on my side somehow, after all.

Even if Navi hadn't been the one to cause this situation, he would still try to use it. So the best thing would be for Rareko to actively cooperate with him. This was how you made it in the world. This was for her own survival.

Rareko had heard so many sad stories about what happened to magical girls when they lost their jobs, she couldn't count them all on the fingers of both hands. She didn't want to be a part of that statistic. She didn't want someone else stomping on her. She also didn't want to meet some miserable fate for unfair reasons. She was timid and no good at speaking her mind, and nobody saw her as important. That had never changed. Only Maiya had paid attention to Rareko. The words that Maiya had taught her—"Always think about the future"—lived on inside her. Times like these were when you most had to think about what might come next. She would live for the future. She would insist, *"It's not my fault."*

The problem was how to get in contact with Navi or Clarissa. She couldn't spew everything in front of Yol. She wanted an opportunity to speak in private. Touta aside, Rareko couldn't abandon Yol for a long time, and she just couldn't think of any good way.

"Hey, I was just thinking..."

That was Touta. Rareko looked up, and her glasses slid down.

Some people would use the preface "I was just thinking" or "I just had an idea" even when it was something they already knew or had noticed. If he was digging up what they'd already talked to death, it would end with "Drop it already," but if he made it so that he'd come up with a nice idea just now, then people would actually listen to him. He'd used a pretty cunning technique there, for a kid.

Expression a little brighter, Yol looked at Touta. Rareko kept her expression decently hard. She was showing her tension and caution at one quarter of actuality.

"So Clarissa...she was chased right up to us, right?" Touta said. "Then that means that the one chasing her, Clantail, would know that you're here, right? And Yol, who's with you."

Yol's lips opened slightly in an "Ah." About a second later, Rareko's mouth opened wide in an "Ahhh!"

That damn brat is too perceptive, Rareko thought, but she didn't let her true feelings show. Rareko had been doubting herself that Clantail's attack on Clarissa had been one sided, but she hadn't voiced her suspicions. If Clarissa had tried to bite Clantail's clothing to use her magic, but she had then been caught and made her mad... Well, that was a bit of a casual assumption, but maybe something like that had happened.

"I think it's a bad idea to be here after all, but what do you think?" Touta asked.

"Yes, you're right. I think it's not good for someone, um…violent who would go around chasing people to know where we are… Let's find a new shelter." Yol nodded, took her staff, and stood.

Rareko closed her mouth, opened it about half as wide as before, then closed it again and stood. Touta poked his head out the entrance, checked how things were outside, and then called back "Looks okay!" to the two inside.

Touta checked left, right, ahead, behind, up, and down, and when he looked up into the sky, he froze. Pointing above, he muttered, "There." Rareko came out from behind Yol and looked up in the same direction. She couldn't hear any sounds—but there were explosions. Was there a spell erasing the sound? But that wasn't all. Magical girls were chasing each other through the sky. One of them was a magical girl with a strange ax in each hand. The other was Dreamy☆Chelsea.

"Are those…explosions? It looks like someone is flying…," said Touta.

"They're zooming around…but the smoke from the explosions is getting in the way, and I can't see through," Yol said.

The two of them couldn't tell who the magical girls were—not because of the speed, but because of the smoke getting in the way. It was no surprise that they could only see hazily, with the eyes of a human and a mage.

"What's going on?" Yol folded her arms and tilted her head, making her curls sway.

Rareko stuck up the index finger of her right hand to adjust the position of her glasses, but when she glanced from side to side, they fell down again. "Magical girls…I think they're magical girls."

Rareko tried to make some kind of shape with both her hands, then dropped her hands like she'd given up. With a groan of "Hnn," she looked up, then moaned, "Ahh" and dropped her chin. She made it look as if she was so confused, it was even a little much. Pretending to be weak made it easy to gain sympathy. This was already deeply ingrained in Rareko—it was the way she lived.

"I think one of them was Dreamy☆Chelsea," Rareko said. "I don't know the other one. It looked as if she was carrying axes. I think it was some magical girl we don't know. The two of them were fighting."

"A magical girl we don't know...," Yol murmured. "So then, that means, in other words, the one who Maiya..."

"Yes...I think most likely..."

Yol's expression stiffened. "I'll go, too."

"You can't."

"It's too dangerous."

Touta and Rareko both spoke at the same time, and then they shared a look, and Rareko waved her right hand in front of her face as Touta aggressively shook his head.

Whether Yol was listening to them or not, her eyes remained pointed, unmoving, in the direction in which the enemy had vanished—she didn't even blink. "But we have to go help her."

"I said, it's too dangerous," Rareko repeated.

"Even if we did go, we'd just drag her down," Touta pointed out.

"Rareko is very strong," Yol offered. "She's Maiya's number one student."

Rareko couldn't say, *"Miss, this is the very person who just killed Maiya."*

"But look, if she were to be protecting you while fighting, then she wouldn't be able to put everything in the fight, right?" Touta helped out, and Rareko emphatically agreed with him.

Yol hung her head, twisted up her cheeks, and clenched her teeth. She slowly, slowly brought up her staff, and once it was over her head, it hit a tree branch, making Yol twitch and look up at it. She lowered her staff weakly with a little sigh. "But, but...we can't just let Chelsea die."

In a very timid manner, Rareko intervened. "Shall I go out alone to help her?"

Touta found himself yelping, "Huh?"

Yol also seemed surprised, as she covered her mouth, and the covering hand trembled slightly. "You mean that without a burden holding you back, then you can fight with all your strength...is that it?"

"Yes, precisely," Rareko replied. "Ordinarily speaking, I would be unable to leave your side. But, perhaps fortunately, we've learned the villain's position, so I believe my leaving this area would not pose much problem. Then, as for where we would meet after—"

Navi wouldn't want Yol to be hurt. Even after they'd gone into a state of emergency, he was still coming around persistently to check up with her. In other words, what Navi wanted from Rareko was for her to protect Yol—but if she was doing that, she couldn't make contact with Navi. So she would use going off on her own to get in contact with Navi or Clarissa. There had to be orders they wanted to give her directly, too.

Rareko tried to pull out a grayfruit, but she fumbled and dropped it. The grayfruit rolled over the fallen leaves, and Touta and Yol's eyes went toward it. She had her chance. Rareko reached out to Touta's robe and ripped off the fabric of his cuff and took it. If she took Clarissa's bite mark and went off somewhere, the odds were high that Clarissa would come to her.

Rareko bowed her head as she accepted the grayfruit from Touta. The situation was very unfortunate. But Rareko knew she'd been unfortunate since she was born, and she was used to it. She would contact Navi or Clarissa, avoid encountering the ax-wielding magical girl, and pray that Yol would remain safe.

Her course basically decided at last, she firmly reminded herself that this wasn't her fault.

◇ **Love Me Ren-Ren**

She felt like her head was going to spin, but she encouraged herself and returned to the rocky area at full speed. Agri and Nephilia were having some kind of intense discussion, and they only glanced at Ren-Ren.

Ren-Ren made sure that nobody but Agri and Nephilia were in sight before calling out, "Agri!"

The pair turned around, both apparently tense. Nephilia had never had an air of seriousness, often either looking dazed or smirking. But right now, her expression was unusually serious. Agri, on the other hand, seemed serious as she listened. There was nothing joking about the look she gave Ren-Ren.

"Did something happen?" Agri asked.

"It's strange—there's something strange going on," Ren-Ren told her.

"Nephilia said something similar." Agri let out a little sigh.

Ren-Ren looked at Nephilia, and Nephilia looked at Ren-Ren; they nodded at one another, and Ren-Ren drew her chin back slightly to prompt her to speak. Nephilia gave in her muttering way the explanation that she had probably also just given Agri. She said she'd extracted a large sum of money from Clantail and that she had also caught sight of battles that properly speaking shouldn't be happening anymore. Following Nephilia, Ren-Ren told them about how she'd also seen signs of battle. There was a fight going on that shouldn't be happening if Navi was controlling the situation— at least if he was managing to control his magical-girl ally.

This didn't seem to make sense to Agri. She was repeatedly tilting her head. "Is this really something that Mr. Navi's ally is doing?"

"There isn't anyone else it could be," said Ren-Ren.

"You did make the contract with him properly, right, Nephilia? You made no mistakes?"

"No…mis…"

"Yeah, of course. Then, assuming he's failed to control her, the initial contract aside, there's no reason for him not to be honest about that in our second discussion… If he spewed some nonsense and then it became a problem down the line, his whole fortune would go *pop*. It reeeally seems like there's something else going on here."

"Maybe…that…time…"

"Ah yeah, I guess you could say that maybe he'd been able to control her then. True."

"Now…also…"

"Mm-hmm, it also seems plausible that he thought he had

control over her, but she's been consistently getting out of control since the beginning."

Agri closed her eyes and walked around the area in a ten-foot-wide circle, muttering under her breath. At the end, she grumbled to herself, "Well, not bad, I guess," and nodded. "Change of plans."

"Yes?" said Ren-Ren.

"Let's be more proactive about sharing the grayfruit with the others. We sell them off at a cheap price. Instead of direct help, we offer them support so they can fight that person who's on the loose. But we should stay in hiding, someplace as safe as possible. We won't be actively attacking Mr. Navi and his happy friends, but we will just in case be assuming this is an emergency situation and making our personal safety the number one priority."

"I think that's a good idea. It's important to stay alive."

"Uh... It..."

"Mm-hmm."

Agri beckoned to Ren-Ren, and then she beckoned to Nephilia. The two magical girls sidled up to Agri, who slung her arms around their shoulders to bring them close. She'd done this a number of times since they'd first met. It was like a ceremony. Whenever they were going to try something and whenever something happened, Agri would embrace the other two.

"We've nabbed that surprisingly big payout from Clantail, plus if things go well, the contract breach fee from Mr. Navi, so I think that should be enough funds to live on. I'm fine with that this time around."

The sweet smell of the grayfruit lingered on Agri's breath. Looking up at her, Ren-Ren felt very troubled, and she was relieved to see Agri's eyes were fixed forward more firmly than she'd thought. Ren-Ren felt so happy, she buried her face in Agri's chest. The desperate daughter of a mistress who'd been willing to throw away her life for a money grab was now trying to get through this more safely. Maybe that was because she was dealing with not only her own life but Ren-Ren's and Nephilia's as well.

Ren-Ren looked at Nephilia to see her forcefully thrusting

her cheek into Agri's chest, seemingly enjoying the sensation. She was, to put it mildly, smirking with smug self-satisfaction. That reminded Ren-Ren how she'd pulled something like sexual harassment when they'd been in human form, too. Ren-Ren did find this regrettable, thinking it would be nice if she could enjoy this embrace with more pure feelings, but then she had a sudden realization that sent a shock racing through her like lightning.

Agri wanted to feel at ease. Nephilia enjoyed the sensation. Even though their behavior was the same, each party had different goals. Ren-Ren was feeling serenity from being embraced by Agri. She had felt this serenity somewhere before, but she'd been unable to put it into words. Now she understood it. It was the same as being embraced by her mother. Agri let Ren-Ren treat her like her mother, and that was why Ren-Ren wanted Agri to be happy.

"Mom," slipped from Ren-Ren's lips, and then her face jerked up. Agri looked back at her with a curious expression. "'Mom'?"

"No, um, that's not what I mean, sorry."

Agri laughed happily, shoulders shaking. "When I was in school, there was a kid who called a young teacher Mom and got laughed at until graduation... Ah, that really takes me back."

"Sorry..."

"Mom, huh? She caused me hardship, and I always resented her...but now, it's not so bad."

Ren-Ren felt her expression softening. The smile spread around her face. Agri hadn't rejected her for muttering, "Mom." When Ren-Ren had tried to somehow cover up that slip of the tongue, Agri had smiled at her—with that smile just like her mother's—and put a hand on Ren-Ren's head, mussing her hair and tangling it around her horns.

"Um, family...," Ren-Ren muttered.

"That's right, family. We're a family. Let's all find happiness together. I'd like to be happy."

"...Yes!"

They were a family. They were a family. Ren-Ren felt like tears would spill from her eyes, but she held them back. She shouldn't cry yet. She could do that lots after she was happy. A family would live together. It would be good to have a bigger apartment. Mom had come back. And Dad was here, too. Because they were a family, she would be happy. Her mother was alive. Ren-Ren hadn't killed her. There was no way she could kill her.

"So...then...," Nephilia said, and Agri relaxed the embrace, while Ren-Ren brought her face away as well. She was reluctant to let go, but they couldn't be hugging all day. This was in order to become happy. It was in order to make her family happy.

"I'd like to hear about Mr. Navi," said Agri.

"He's dangerous," Ren-Ren said.

"Why not have Chelsea go? She's strong, and worst case, it's fine if they get her."

"...So...then..."

"Mm-hmm, that's right. I think it would also be a good idea to send Mary's sheep as messengers. Goats are the ones who eat letters, so getting the sheep to do it is safe, and kinda chic—"

Ren-Ren nocked an arrow to her bowstring. Nephilia raised her scythe blade at a diagonal. The two magical girls stood in front of Agri, who belatedly noticed—"What's that sound?" It wasn't footsteps. It was the sound of hoofs. A herd of creatures were stepping on the earth, bounding off rocks, and cracking branches underfoot on their way to the rocky area. Ren-Ren lifted up Agri by sandwiching her waist between her thighs, and, with her bow still up, she flew about six feet. Agri cried out, "Ohhh!" in surprise, twisting around like she was ticklish.

"It's dangerous. Please stay still," Ren-Ren told her.

"What is it, what happened?"

The answer came quickly. Sheep were racing along, some covered in vivid green leaves and some dirtied by mud, while others had thick tree branches still caught in their wool. They came out of the forest one after another—seemingly endless—to come to a stop in the rocky area, then huddled in a group in the center of it. Ren-Ren and Nephilia went to the side to avoid the herd of sheep, watching them closely from behind the rocks.

The line of sheep continued on and on, in fact they increased in number and force, filling the area with the smell of sheep and pathetic bleats. Nephilia said something, but the cries of the sheep were so loud that they drowned her out. The mistress of these sheep appeared moments later. Riding astride a particularly large sheep with fine wool, a magical girl was furiously scrawling with her pastels. She tore one sheet, then another, off her sketch pad, the sheets billowing up to become sheep that were added to the herd. Basically, she was fleeing while dropping sheep, embiggening the herd.

"Mary! Stop!"

Mary wouldn't miss the sound of Ren-Ren's voice, and she would listen to Ren-Ren. Mary's chin jerked up, transmitting a tremble through her lips, shoulders, and legs to make her whole body shake, and she smacked the butt of her sheep to make it run toward Ren-Ren. She raced toward her so hard, she built up too much momentum, and when the sheep came to a sudden stop, she fell off the sheep onto her head to finally come to a halt. There was a little crack in the rock.

Mary bounced up like a doll on a spring and cried, "It's awful!"

Agri tilted her head in the same way Ren-Ren had seen before. "What is?"

"We were attacked! A magical girl carrying axes showed up! And Chelsea was fighting!"

Ren-Ren flying in the sky, Agri who was held in her legs, and Nephilia standing on the ground all shared looks, and then, after a pause of half a breath, Ren-Ren opened her mouth. If Agri asked the question, Mary might not listen. If it was the one she loved, Ren-Ren, that was something else. "You mean it was a magical girl you don't know?"

"It was someone I've never seen before. And Mr. Shepherds-pie... It was awful..."

"You mean he was killed?"

"Yes."

Nephilia huffed through her nose; she found this sincerely loathsome. Ren-Ren bit her lower lip. Something bad was happening—bad and unexpected.

"...And then?" Ren-Ren urged.

"Chelsea said to run, so I took the old man and ran, telling him we've got to get out of here... Ren-Ren, let's get out of here."

"The old man? Do you mean Ragi? Where is he?"

"Huh? Wait..." Mary looked right and left and then around the herd of sheep before face-palming. "Ah! I dropped him somewhere! It's always like this! Nothing but memory lapses and slips of the mind and stupid mistakes! Always! Always!"

Ren-Ren wasn't able to say anything to console her. Something rocketed in from the forest and snatched Mary away, and by the time Ren-Ren confirmed that it was Dreamy☆Chelsea, the next visitor had appeared. With a dirty red ax in her right hand and a black ax in her left, she was muddied, clad in a toga that had probably been white to begin with, and not even trying to sweep the dead leaves from her slightly wavy golden hair. Standing there was the goddess of spring from the fable.

"Is the one you dropped the golden ax?"

The sheep all stirred. Nephilia raised one heel. Ren-Ren was bewildered. How had they let the goddess get so close? It was obvious at a glance that she hadn't been creeping toward them silently, but they hadn't heard her coming at all.

"Or is it the silver ax?"

Ren-Ren decided to fly, and she ordered her muscles to move her wings. But before she could actually move, there was a streak of light. She had no clue what had happened. Before she knew it, she was blown away like dandelion fluff caught up in a typhoon. A comical number of sheep danced in the air. Dirt and dust flew in the air along with trees and even boulders that had been smashed to bits. It happened in slow motion, like a movie. Her ears hurt. Even sound seemed to come slowly. The sheep were bleating. Was Nephilia safe? Where had the goddess gone? Ren-Ren was alive. She could see and hear. She had her bow and arrow. She had both arms. Her legs kept a firm grip on Agri, and her wings could move. She regained her balance with a large flap of her wings, then recalled that Chelsea had grabbed Mary and run off. Sparing not a single thought, she undid the magic she'd cast on the two of them.

If Ren-Ren shot the goddess with her arrow without undoing the spell, then the goddess would fall in love with Chelsea. Ren-Ren didn't think making the goddess fall in love with someone who wasn't present would stop her from attacking Ren-Ren. Losing track of Chelsea was hard, not to mention losing track of Mary, but dealing with the imminent threat was more important than such regrets.

Below, the sheep that had escaped the danger were running and trying to get away. Nephilia and the goddess were nowhere to be seen. Everything that had been blasted into the air aside from Ren-Ren was falling.

"Are you all right, Agri?" she asked.

She suddenly noticed something—Agri, in her grasp, felt weirdly light. Ren-Ren looked down at her. The lower half of Agri's cream-colored robe had turned dark red. Her eyes were pointed downward, looking nowhere. Blood was dripping from her mouth. Everything below her waist was gone, blood and innards spilling out of what remained of her body.

CHAPTER 12
THE DESIRE TO HELP AND PROTECT

◇ **Dreamy☆Chelsea**

The world changed. Even though the intensity and cold of the wind hitting her cheeks and forehead were the same, the southern trees she'd left behind, the gentle light that filtered through the trees, or the star decoration Chelsea stood on—it felt like everything had changed.

Chelsea felt terribly disturbed, but she still kept on her feet and didn't fall from her star. Remembering that she held Pastel Mary in her arms, she looked at the girl to find her even more confused than she was. Mary was glancing around as though she was frightened and didn't know what was going on. Seeing Mary like that just made Chelsea feel even more rattled—but not because she was at the mercy of girlish love like before. Remembering how aggressively she'd been gluing herself to Mary made it feel like fire would come out of her face from embarrassment. Next Ren-Ren's face rose in her mind, and anger joined that embarrassment, and a surge of emotions that were difficult to express swirled around inside her in an ugly whirlpool.

Reaffirming that she'd been holding Mary in a bridal carry during the confusion added more embarrassment and anger, plus Chelsea's own unique sense of failure—she was treating someone else like a princess! The whirlpool of feelings became so vicious that she nearly tossed Mary away, but then she thought, *Wait, no, I can't do that* and grabbed her tighter, readjusting her grip. She just about let her feelings slip out as a yell, but that wouldn't be very cute now, would it? She somehow held the storm back inside.

And so, caught in anguish like this, Chelsea wasn't steering her star. Before she knew it, splintered tree bark was looming four inches in front of her nose. Chelsea tensed her toes over the remaining three and a half inches and then leaped right in a toe loop for a wafting jump off another tree to do a vertical spin, and then she figured that wasn't playful enough and so added another turn and a half, following which she bounced off a branch for a half turn in the opposite direction and landed.

She made her star decoration fly another thirty feet before returning to her hand on a heart-shaped trajectory, with turns and sudden rotations added in, and despite feeling jittery about Pastel Mary, she set her down on the ground on her feet. Though Chelsea did her best to set her down as gently as possible, when Pastel Mary saw Chelsea, her whole body trembled, and she hugged herself with both arms and retreated—neither what Chelsea wanted nor expected.

"Why are you reacting like that?!" Chelsea cried.

Mary shrank away from Chelsea's menacing look, frightened enough that you'd even feel bad for her, before looking around the area and muttering in trepidation, "I was worried you might glomp me again."

"I won't!" She grabbed Mary firmly by the shoulders. "I was being mind-controlled by nasty magic! You were being controlled, too!"

"But—"

"There's no butts here, or behinds!"

"Chelsea, that's such a dad joke. Only an old man would say that."

"I'm not an old man!"

Still grabbing Mary's shoulders, Chelsea shook her from side to side to keep her from talking. Since Chelsea couldn't get any more agitated now, she calmed down a little and looked at what she was doing objectively. She was grabbing Pastel Mary's shoulders and shaking her. Chelsea could feel the heat of her body through her thick clothing. Remembering how she'd single-mindedly clung to her in pursuit of that heat was just so embarrassing Chelsea couldn't take it anymore, and she lost her cuteness and presence of mind and howled, "Nooo!"

Chelsea tossed Mary aside, holding her head in her hands as she watched Mary shriek and land in some bushes. No. She'd just lost herself for a moment. Well, that wasn't quite it, either. This was Ren-Ren's fault. Mary rose, groaning, with a hand on the back of her head. Raising her upper body out of the brush, she pointed at Chelsea. "I mean..."

"What?"

"Your face is red..."

Chelsea touched a hand to her cheek; it was warm. She closed her eyes. At this rate, she was really going to wind up hopeless. She had to think about something else. *Anything else...*, she pleaded internally, and Shepherdspie's face rose in her mind. "Ahhh!" she yelped. It wasn't a cute cry, but Chelsea couldn't restrain it. When she realized that she'd been distracting herself with other things because she didn't want to think about Shepherdspie, "Mr. Pie" spilled from her mouth.

Mary's eyes widened, and immediately her whole face contorted. Seeing Pastel Mary's reaction, Chelsea knew it hadn't been an illusion or hallucination. Chelsea clenched her hands and opened them again. The feelings she'd been holding back by prioritizing her fake love, thinking, *That was bad with Mr. Pie, but May-May is more important*, broke through the dam to overflow. Though she'd only known him for a short time, the feelings were surging in strongly enough that she couldn't hold them back—was that because she'd been holding them back so hard? Or was the strength of feelings not proportionate to time?

When she'd destroyed his room and his house, burning it up and bringing down the tower, and gotten his cookies stolen by a thief as well as probably failed at a whole bunch of other things, Shepherdspie had always looked troubled, and with each failure, she'd thought she was sure to be fired, but never was. Chelsea had been a shut-in for ten years, hardly having contact with anyone but her family, and so she'd felt anxious about relationships in a new workplace, and she'd been relieved to have such a good person as her employer.

The last thing to come to her mind was Shepherdspie's exquisite and specially made cuisine. *Oh yeah, he never taught me how to make that*, she thought, and a single tear hit the hand touching her cheek.

Mary was looking down, her expression terribly sad. Chelsea clenched her teeth. If this were the world of a wholesome magical-girl anime, Shepherdspie wouldn't have died.

She felt her body getting hotter. Her heart was hammering. As a magical girl, Chelsea felt a responsibility to be cute. But Shepherdspie had died. The goddess had killed him. The goddess was strong. She was stronger than Chelsea.

No!

Her breathing became ragged. Her body felt like it would be torn apart. This feeling like a dam had burst inside her wasn't stopping. The cute Dreamy☆Chelsea and the Dreamy☆Chelsea who was thinking about Shepherdspie were standing there like two separate people. Mary was hanging her head and quietly muttering, "Mr. Shepherdspie," and that remark came with a shock that shattered everything to gather Chelsea's heart into one.

First, the grayfruit. Chelsea knew where Agri's cohort was storing them. If the spell on her had come undone, that might be because something had happened to Ren-Ren, fighting against the goddess. Ren-Ren was a bad person, but Chelsea thought it was better for her to be alive than dead. But Chelsea would take the grayfruit. It was kind of like compensation money.

She would get a full supply of grayfruit to fight a war of attrition. If she made good use of the sheep as a diversion as well as the mobility of her star to fight while running away, then the enemy's transformation should come undone first. Chelsea settled on her general plan. She would get back at her for Shepherdspie. She would have her revenge.

Pastel Mary lifted her chin. "Oh yeah…I forgot that I dropped the old mage."

Chelsea let out a long breath and pursed her lips in the process to ensure she looked cute.

◇ **Nephilia**

Nephilia's will to fight was quickly crushed. It broke with a light *snap.*

Dreamy☆Chelsea had zoomed through the sky, crossing over the rocky area to sweep Pastel Mary away. Nephilia didn't have to mobilize her logical thinking to figure out what sort of creature would come lumbering behind her. It was the enemy who was chasing off Chelsea. And chasing off Chelsea was not so easily done.

Having crossed blades with Dreamy☆Chelsea herself, Nephilia could say for certain that Chelsea was a monster. And that very monster was being forced to run. An unarmed human would see a grizzly bear, a tank, an aircraft carrier, and a space fortress all as opponents that couldn't be beaten, but there were clear differences in level among these opponents. Within the Department of Diplomacy, or among the graduates of the Archfiend Cram School or the toughs of antiestablishment factions, there was a hierarchy with some stronger and others weaker. No matter how strong a magical girl you became, you'd know there was someone above you.

That was why Nephilia fled without hesitation. If this was someone Chelsea couldn't beat, then Nephilia should never fight her. Nephilia always valued her own life.

"Is the one you dropped the golden ax? Or is it the silver ax?" a voice called from behind.

Nephilia turned back without slowing down. The goddess wasn't moving from her position, just standing there and looking at her. She was just like the goddess who appeared to show a miracle to the poor woodcutter who had lost his ax. If you took the illustration Nephilia had once seen in a picture book and made it a little dirty, it would be exactly like this. The way she had an ax in each hand was just in the style of that picture book, too, but seeing it in reality was eye-openingly bizarre. Seeing her hold a heavy-looking ax with each of her cute, delicate, and slender arms was so unreal, it made Nephilia's head spin.

When Nephilia ran a few steps, the goddess swung her ax. It wasn't that Nephilia actually saw her do it. The moment Nephilia thought, *Oh, I think she's going to swing*, she made a flying leap to the side. Right after that, there was an explosion. Shattered rocks flew everywhere, and earth and sheep fluttered down, and, pitifully enough, former sheep that had been shredded into meat and sinew also hit the ground as Nephilia rose from her knees.

You can do it. Don't give in. Stand up, Nephilia, she encouraged herself as she kept her eyes on the goddess seen beyond the dust and smoke. Even if Nephilia had lost her will to fight, the enemy was still there. It didn't seem like the goddess would let her get away because she didn't want to fight.

"Is the one you dropped the golden ax?"

The wind blew through, and the cloud of dust wavered and thinned. When Nephilia got a little glimpse of the goddess's face, she was looking off in the other direction. She wasn't looking at Nephilia. That attack just now hadn't been aimed at Nephilia, either, had it?

This is your chance, Nephilia, she told herself. Lowering her stance, she walked silently. Hidden in the dust cloud, she went a few steps to get away from the goddess, then stopped.

The goddess was sliding along in the opposite direction from Nephilia's route of retreat. Her lower body was hidden by the cloud of dust, so that was part of it, but she moved so smoothly, it was like her feet didn't exist. Did she not notice Nephilia, or was she ignoring her because she didn't see her as a threat?

With the utmost care to even keep from making the cloud of dust waver, Nephilia breathed slowly out her nose. The goddess wasn't looking at Nephilia, she wasn't paying attention to her, or she hadn't noticed her—that had to be because her target was someone else. And that someone else obviously wouldn't be the sheep. Since Mary and Chelsea had fled before the enemy came, it could only be Ren-Ren, or Agri, or both.

That guess—and the probability that two nasty people were being targeted—made Nephilia feel grim. She had the feeling she'd realized something she should not have.

Nephilia rose and stuck up one knee. She sucked in a deep breath of air and swung her scythe high up above her head. Roughly estimating, she was over a hundred feet from the goddess. Nephilia didn't even glance at the goddess, swinging down her scythe on the spot. This was just the scythe that was a part of her costume. She couldn't attack from a hundred feet away. She knew that better than anyone else.

Through her work—or, more precisely, through using her work to look for nasty people, Nephilia had become acquainted with many magical girls. Many of them had been highly athletically competent, and such people always had a sharp nose for danger, for attacks—if Nephilia was a human, their sensitivity was like that of wild animals or greater. Nephilia had trained a little, and she'd hired a special coach to learn how to swing and handle a scythe. However, that was no more than moderate study as part of an ordinary lifestyle. Learning law documents had been the far greater priority, and the difference between her and magical girls who took for granted that they would hunt and be hunted and risk their lives—it was obviously the difference between human and lion.

If Nephilia rose and swung up her scythe, even from a little ways away, the lion—the goddess—would notice. If she noticed, then she would read Nephilia's intentions. She would assume that Nephilia wasn't raising her scythe in the air for no reason.

A magical girl with a very ghostly-looking aesthetic swinging up her special item—a very lethal-looking scythe—from a hundred feet away. The odds were high she was going to use magic. Having investigated the group kidnapping incident Keek had caused, Nephilia knew that one of the magical girls who had been made to participate in that death game, Akane, had been able to cut anything she could see, no matter how far away it was. You couldn't ignore that there were people with magic like that. A beast would move without much consideration for the reasons why. Would the goddess dodge first, or would she attack? Judging from the way she handled things, from her trail of destruction, the odds of the latter were high. In other words, Nephilia could incite her to attack just by readying a swing of her scythe. Success was not guaranteed, though. She had maybe a 10 percent chance of success on this gamble. She couldn't count on her reflexes, and neither did she possess any technique or training in reading ahead. The most Nephilia could do was incite action, timing it half at random. But even so, she had no choice but to do it. Nephilia swung her scythe down with all the strength in her body, and right before the tip touched the ground, she jumped to the side.

She was struck with an intense sound and impact, and her body was flung into the air. Not just her—rocks, dirt, grass, trees, everything was flying. She'd seen something similar a moment before.

Certain that she'd succeeded somewhat in what she had been trying to do, she mentally pumped a fist in her heart with a silent *"Yesss."* She had lured the enemy with a pointless gesture, distracted her attention from Ren-Ren and Agri, and made her fire a shot. And having done that, Nephilia was still alive. In other words, she'd managed to control the enemy's movement.

So for my next move, she thought at just about the same time that her right shoulder was slammed into rock.

An impact that rivaled the total two explosions knocked Nephilia out—and when she opened her eyes, the dust was clear. The earth, the trees, the stones, and Nephilia herself were not flying in the sky. The quiet was chill, the sun was strong enough that it was annoying, and white clouds were flowing by high up in the distant skies. She was confused for a while as to why the situation had changed in an instant, but then she quickly got it. It seemed she'd been knocked out for longer than she'd thought.

She tried to inhale and reflexively coughed at the pain in her chest, and that made her whole body writhe with pain, clenched fists trembling. The pain woke up her hazy brain. Nephilia brought her shaking hands up to her face and confirmed that she was still in magical-girl form. If she'd gone back to human form, she would have died. But even as a magical girl, she was in agony.

She moaned in pain, but she confirmed that she hadn't lost herself and urged her protesting body onward. Moving and then stopping like a defective robot, she put her hands to her knees and then rolled to her side, and from there she sat up. She restrained the groan that was trying to free itself from the pit of her throat. Little stones that were stuck to her body pattered to roll off. She coughed a second time and spat out the saliva that was lingering in her mouth. It was cloudy with a thick redness.

She got to her knees and stood up. Looking back to where she'd just been, she understood the reason she had struggled to get up. The large boulder there was cracked and caved in, indented. It looked like Nephilia had hit the rock and made an indentation in it like she was being buried in it. She'd seen people getting beaten up like this in every kind of anime from slapstick to action, but she'd never thought to try it out herself.

She looked around. She was in a forest away from the rocky area. But even saying that, since the trees had been blasted away, the whole area wasn't forest anymore. Nephilia couldn't see the goddess. Ren-Ren and Agri were not there. She looked around a few times with her dizzy head and found her scythe lying on the ground. She thought, feeling haggard, that it was a good thing it was nearby, but worst case, she could have been stabbed by her own weapon. When she bent at the waist to pick it up, she felt a pain in her right shoulder like it was being twisted off, and she moaned in spite of herself. It made her want to cry, *"It hurts, it hurts."*

Nephilia didn't have enough experience with injury or medical knowledge to be able to judge if the bone was broken or if it was a torn muscle. Concluding that if she could move, then, well, things would work out somehow, she kicked the scythe up with her toe and grabbed it with her left hand. She thrust the scythe into the ground like a staff and dragged her leg along as she started heading into the forest. It was a struggle just being alive, but she had to do more than that.

Nephilia had only seen her briefly, but she had seen the enemy. She had been a magical girl with the motif of the goddess of the spring, right? The enemy's behavior had been strange enough that it was hard to just accept it. Had there been any meaning to that question about a golden ax or whatever? Nephilia had just been passed out—why hadn't the goddess finished her off?

The most unnatural thing of all was that she'd had no *smell*. In this case, "smell" didn't mean a body odor or some added scent. It was the presence of intellect. Nephilia would never miss a nasty person. Whether the goddess was going on a rampage on Navi's orders or her violence was at her own discretion or she was just abandoning herself to madness, it should come with some kind of smell. Was it possible that her violence was purely mechanical, with no feelings at all?

Even if that is possible…

The light filtering through the trees suddenly hit her face and made her scowl, and she sped up. Even if that was possible, Nephilia didn't like it. She felt more connected to the hopeless pair she'd gone and risked her life to save. The problem was where they were and what they were doing right now. Agri was a miser, but she understood the worth of the law, contracts, and Nephilia. Ren-Ren had the air of a psychopath but was very fixated on her relationships. If neither of them had come to save her, then she could conclude that they were in trouble of their own. She had a bad feeling about it, but she forced herself to hope for the best anyway. If that wasn't the case, then there would be no point in her having risked her life to save them. With the assumption that the two of them were safe, Nephilia scolded her aching body, *I have to meet up with the two of them right away.*

Her legs and arms wouldn't quite move the way she wanted them to. *Walking around in search of a miser and a psychopath when I'm this disabled, I'm a real piece of work, too,* she thought with a smile at the corner of her lips.

◇ **Ragi Zwe Nento**

Ragi sat up in the dim forest, rubbing his back as he confirmed that there was nobody else around. The thin trees and brush that had been kicked up by the sheep and the reminders of violence like shattered rocks and trees that had been snapped by something far stronger than a herd of sheep created a new path that cut straight through the forest, going as far as the eye could see. Ragi pulled a grayfruit out of his sleeve, bit into it, and finished it in five seconds. He refused to waste even a drop of the fruit juice stuck to his fingers, carefully licking it off, then wiping his fingers with a paper napkin. Choosing to settle his confused mind as much as he could, he thought back memory by memory on how he'd gotten into this situation. *Just as expected, if I do say so myself* was the resulting impression, but he was still angry. He crumpled the napkin and tossed it to the ground, stomped on it, and kicked it away.

Pastel Mary had grabbed Ragi and fled, and then she'd run off without realizing she'd dropped the person she'd saved. It made him wonder if she might have planned to toss him in front of their pursuer as a sacrifice—but Mary wasn't capable of thoughts that deep. But the conclusion that she didn't seem to have any ill will toward him just irritated Ragi all the more. Not all acts done out of goodwill were necessarily *good* acts.

He watched the crumpled napkin as it rolled along a tree root until it stopped at a rock. Suppressing his irritation, he crouched down, picked up the napkin, and tossed it into the sleeve of his robe.

He should be thankful. If he had remained there, not being a magical girl, he wouldn't have had any way to resist. Mary using what spare wits she did possess on the spur of the moment had enabled him to be here rubbing his back. He couldn't do that if he were dead. Fortunately, it seemed he had no broken bones.

And yet...

He had been left behind. Chelsea, Mary, the sheep, and the magical girl with the axes who had been after them had gone off somewhere unknown to Ragi, and he also didn't know what they were doing. His plan to manipulate Chelsea and Mary to try to escape the island had fallen apart.

Ragi looked around the area. He couldn't find his staff. Putting a hand to his still-aching back, he looked. He parted the grass and kicked rocks away, looking for places where it could be hidden, but he couldn't find it. His irritation built even further. His idea of using magical girls had been a mistake. Trying to use magical girls was no different from what that lot he'd cut off were doing. That which was magical girl was thoroughly incorrigible, and his idea that he would be able to control them had been nothing more than a mage's arrogance.

This wasn't just about Chelsea and Mary. There was also Clantail. If she'd just stayed back there, they could have worked together, but now he didn't even know if she was safe. The very person he'd meant to hire as a guard was now becoming a source of worry.

He couldn't find his staff. He'd be in trouble without that. Unlike the mental anguish from losing the hat that had been his favorite for many years, this was an actual problem. It was fair to say it was vital for Ragi's plan to open a basic gate. Magic cast without a staff was greatly reduced in both scale and accuracy.

While searching, he considered other things. He'd only seen that magical girl who carried two big axes very briefly, but he could tell she was not one he knew. There weren't that many magical girls who used an ax, and two axes meant even fewer. Just like magical girls with numbers in their names, there weren't many, so they stood out. If they stood out, he wouldn't forget them. In other words, he was certain there wasn't a record of her in the list at the Management Department. But despite that, he also had the feeling he'd seen her before.

She wasn't an acquaintance of his. He didn't have many magical-girl acquaintances in the first place. She also wasn't in the records he knew of from being the head of the Management Department. So where had he met her?

He couldn't find his staff. His thoughts wouldn't come together.

Irregularities were common in the field of magical girls, and some researchers even enjoyed generating "exceptions." Periodically, people with outrageous ethics would show up and ignore the will and rights of the subject and toss in new tech almost for amusement, leading some to say that even distinctions like "first generation" and "second generation" meant nothing. Basically, it was a hodgepodge situation of complete chaos.

He still couldn't find his staff anywhere.

That magical girl was clearly not an ordinary one. It was in the way she placed her gaze, unnatural for a living creature, and in the movement of her eyes. There was no hesitation or mercy in her acts of destruction, but it also didn't seem she was running wild out of sadism or was drunk with a sense of omnipotence. She was just mechanically attacking those she judged to be enemies. And you could catch a sense of humor in that phrase she said that contrasted with her robotic attacks. The inscrutable question she asked before attacking didn't seem to mesh with them at all.

Unable to find his staff, Ragi stopped and sat down on a broken rock.

It wasn't that he'd gotten tired and didn't want to move his legs anymore, or that he'd given up. An unsavory hypothesis had struck him. Even when he rubbed at it like stubborn red rust, it wouldn't disappear.

There were plenty of fools who would try to satisfy their desire for achievement or their curiosity under the banner of progress or making great strides. That was how the Osk Faction was now. Even working what was out on the fringes for a researcher, in the

Management Department, Ragi had heard plausible-sounding rumors that the present incarnation of Chêne Osk Baal Mel used a special magical girl as the base. And actually looking at the incarnation, anyone would agree that those weren't just rumors.

They were designing a homunculus with magical-girl abilities and preprogrammed with the stamina to endure long hours of labor. The designers would be thinking they needed an incarnation that could withstand the presence of divinity—even just a slight fragment of it. If it was a magical girl based on a homunculus, then you would be able to tinker with it a lot at the pretransformation stage. If Ragi were there, he would yell at them that they were lacking in reverence toward a divine Sage, but his voice would never reach them when he yelled at them from so far away.

Research on homunculi was older and deeper than that on magical girls. If you could divert that vast accumulation of knowledge toward them... But just technical prowess and knowledge alone would never do it. The relevant documentation to peruse, the facilities to use, personnel to gather, magic gems—all of these would require the power of an organization.

Ragi recalled Navi Ru's nasty smile and grimaced. If Sataborn was connected to the Lab, then it made sense that Navi Ru had been invited as an heir, even though he hadn't stood out as a student of Sataborn's. If they were cooperating with resources, technology, connections, or knowledge, then both Sataborn and the Osk Faction would benefit.

Sataborn had been an independent researcher—hadn't he been aloof and loathing of authority? It wasn't like Ragi had known him well enough to call him an acquaintance, but he could make some conjectures. He had not been fond of authority, nor had he despised it. Researchers tended to just see it as unimportant. If it was necessary for his research, he would work with authorities. That sounded very plausible.

But the thought that he might have figured out a sliver of the truth brought Ragi no happiness. If the magical girl on a rampage had been created by Sataborn and the Lab, this was not something to be glad about. A magical girl with axes had not been on the list of island security. In other words, this wasn't a defense mechanism that was going out of control. Then it was natural to assume that this tragedy had been caused by research to kill a magical girl and a mage, which couldn't be publicized, going out of control.

Ragi had been punted away from the mainstream, but he was still in the Osk Faction. He knew painfully and firsthand how the Osk Faction these days would manage such a situation. First, it would hush it up. Navi Ru in particular had a lot of experience in dirty missions like this, and he knew how it was done.

Ragi valued sticking to the rules. Even if there was a risk to his own life or something even more valuable, he thought adherence to the rules should be placed first. If a mage who wielded power over a certain level were to act as they pleased, that would pose a danger to the whole world. If everyone ignored the rules, then everything would fall apart. A mage could do everything: create order, protect it, and also destroy it and make a mess.

In order to keep the Osk Faction from hushing things up, first, he would capture the outlaw and, through the employee of the Inspection Department who was on this island, hand them straight over to the authorities, delivering this matter beyond the reach of the Osk Faction. Thinking to this point, Ragi shook his head. He clenched his fists tightly in his lap.

All this about incarnations and hushing things up was entirely based on Ragi's speculation. Even if things were just as he supposed, they didn't have the people, the tools, or the time to disable the magical girl created to be the incarnation, and because of the grayfruit, they even had a handicap on top of that. If things weren't as he supposed, then he would be risking his life pointlessly, and if it was as he supposed, this would be far too difficult. Either way, prospects were poor.

I should prioritize escape, after all.

After all that, he came back to this conclusion. In the end, he had to find his staff—using the extremely primitive method of haphazardly examining the places it could have fallen. Ragi stood up and swept from his rear to his thighs. Scowling at the coldness of his rear, he swallowed a curse.

Ragi looked up. The light that filtered through the leaves was flickering. No—the foliage the light streamed through was wavering slightly. Before Ragi could brace himself, a loud sound rudely shook not just the branches and leaves but even the tree trunks and boulders, and a sheep barreled through, followed by two and then three more, and Ragi ran behind a tree to hide from the herd of sheep, looking up at the figure that appeared.

It was Dreamy☆Chelsea, standing just on her right toe on top of a little star decoration. A few seconds later, Pastel Mary appeared astride a big sheep.

"There he is! Chelsea found the old grampa!"

"Who are you calling an old grampa?!" he yelled at Chelsea, but his eyes and head were moving. He had the vague sense that something was off about the two magical girls. Chelsea was riding a star, and Mary had appeared riding a sheep. Before they'd gotten split up, Chelsea had been practically hanging off Mary, who had been cringing away.

"What a relief... I really am so relieved...," Mary said.

"Yeah," Chelsea agreed. "It wouldn't have been strange for him to be hurt, or even dead."

"Watch your tongue!" Ragi snapped at her.

"Oh, I'm sorry. I mean it wouldn't have been strange for you to have passed away."

"That's not what I meant!"

Sheep were gathering around them. Ragi made himself small, but there still wasn't enough space. Gradually, his space to move around was being robbed from him. And then the star lowered into that and Chelsea landed, meaning he was facing her from so close that it was even difficult to move. He cringed away as she blatantly huffed out through her nose into his face.

He was about to really yell and let her have it when a twisted stick was held out to him. It was his beloved staff. "Sorry, Grampa... Ragi. Here, we wound up taking this with us."

Though Ragi indignantly snatched it away, he couldn't deny his private relief. It had been Mary's blunder that had separated him from his staff to begin with, so he judged that there was no need to thank her, but nevertheless the flames of his ire were quelled, and he calmed down somewhat. "...Why did you come back? To return my staff?"

"Well...um..." Mary hemmed and hawed.

"More than that, we didn't want anyone...to die," Chelsea told him.

Ragi looked back at the two magical girls. With her cheeks puffed up, it was quite difficult to call Chelsea sober-looking, but Pastel Mary's expression was fairly tense. But above all, they had come back for Ragi. He'd thought they'd been under mind control and hadn't had any consideration for him. They weren't running wild now like they had been before. Ragi nodded. Wanting to keep any more people from dying was a value he could share.

Chelsea adopted a strange stance, putting together the backs of her hands to bring them over her head as she looked at Ragi. Next she looked at Mary and then hurriedly averted her eyes, and Mary also looked down awkwardly. Ragi didn't have much of an eye for people, but even he could tell—their relationship was different from before.

Chelsea cleared her throat like she was trying to cover something, closed her eyes, and nodded. "Then we've made sure Grampa is safe, so let's punish the bad guys."

"Wait, no," said Ragi. "First we must escape."

"Chelsea and May-May were both controlled by someone called Ren-Ren."

So the mind control had been undone after all. And they still retained their memories from when they had been controlled.

"Never mind that. But—"

"Besides...there's Mr. Pie." Chelsea brought the backs of her hands apart, then brought them in front of her face like she was drawing a circle and clapped them. The herd of sheep, which had been bleating and baaing the whole time, quieted down, Pastel

Mary reflexively went on guard, and Ragi furrowed his brow in irritation.

"I absolutely won't forgive her," said Chelsea.

The herd of sheep pulled away from Chelsea, huddling close together and trembling. The sound of Pastel Mary swallowing rang through the quiet forest.

Ragi leaned on his staff and relaxed his brow. The way Chelsea moved her body and facial muscles, it was like she was trying to maintain her peculiar silliness. But her gaze was serious.

"Impossible," Ragi said.

"It is *not* impossible," Chelsea protested.

"That is not a magical girl. It's a weapon in the body of a magical girl that some foolish mages got together to create… It's like a demigod created to fight and win." Ragi could only guess about the creation of this magical girl, but he didn't have to tell them that. As a threat to keep her from fighting, it was best if it was easy to understand.

"I don't care." But Chelsea still wouldn't understand, shaking her head.

"Do you think you can win in a fight against something you do not know? How arrogant can you be?" Privately, he could understand how Chelsea felt, but he couldn't say, *"Let's combine our powers to defeat her."* He knitted his eyebrows together. *"No more foolishness,"* he seemed to be saying.

Ragi turned toward Mary. "What about you, Pastel Mary? You can't say you'll fight it."

She stared at her feet, neither confirming nor denying Ragi's accusation. If you were just looking at her slight trembling, it wouldn't seem like she was headed out to battle. But from her small hands, clenched until the ends of her fingers were red, he got a glimpse of something like determination she wouldn't put into words.

Ragi frowned beneath his beard. "Out of the question. Do you think you'll be able to win such an unwinnable battle?"

"It might be difficult…but there are other strong magical girls. Like the cookie thief," said Chelsea.

"Who's that?"

"And Marguerite. Honestly, she's real dangerous. Chelsea thought she was gonna die."

"I don't care in the slightest."

"And as for other strong ones…what about your magical girl, Grampa?"

"Clantail is strong."

"All right!"

"No, don't do it. What does it matter if they're strong? Abandon this thoughtless idea that you can win if you gather strong magical girls. It will only lead to more deaths."

"Umm." Mary timidly raised her right hand. "We have lots of grayfruit. So if we eat lots and fight…"

"That's right!" Chelsea agreed. "Yeah, we have grayfruit. We gathered a whole bunch."

"That's not good at all. You mustn't. Consuming grayfruit will only hasten your own demise."

"What do you mean?"

"This plant's nature is most likely to absorb and store up magic power on the island in order to bear fruit. The more grayfruit are eaten, the more your power is sucked away, making you have to consume even more grayfruit."

"Huh? What do you mean?"

"Listen, the grayfruit absorb magic power from their surroundings in order to bear fruit, and the power accumulates there. The fruit are the gathered consolidation of magic power. Do you understand this much?"

"Basically."

"The magic power they absorb from their surroundings includes the power of mages and magical girls—that's why the mages collapsed and the magical girls' transformations came undone."

"Ahhh, that's what it was! So it was because of that!"

"After that, we harvested a large volume of grayfruit, but the pace of fruit consumption—in other words the pace at which our magic powers were consumed—also went up. Of course it did—since the trees were trying to compensate for the amount they'd lost in the fruit."

"So it got sucked away since the fruit was gone, and 'cause it got sucked away from us, we ate some fruit… That's a loop."

"Exactly. That's why I'm telling you not to consume fruit pointlessly."

"So then shouldn't we just not waste them?" asked Mary.

"Yeah!" Chelsea said. "Yeah, we should just gather them up to use for the final battle."

"That's not what I'm talking about!"

He could feel his blood rushing through his veins. Even though he understood logically that he shouldn't allow himself to go red, the blood was rushing to his head anyway. Chelsea's understanding of the situation was so low it was on the floor, and Mary wasn't any better. If they were going to be like this, maybe it would have been easier to manipulate them if they were still being mind-controlled. He'd thought it so many times before, but now he felt it even more deeply: Magical girls were incorrigible.

"I won't forgive her. I'll never, ever, ever forgive her!" Chelsea wailed.

"What does you forgiving anything matter?! There are other things we have to do!" Ragi roared back.

"No! For Mr. Pie! I'm not! Forgiving her!" It seemed Chelsea had blood rushing to her head as badly as Ragi, or even worse. She was yelling and wailing and swinging her arms around, clenching her teeth as she declared her absolute unbending assertion.

Having someone in front of them raging in anger would actually make many people feel calmer, but this did not work on Ragi. "Enough of your nonsense!"

"This isn't nonsense!"

"Why do you want to fight so badly?! Magical girls weren't created just to fight!"

Chelsea's eyes opened wide, her whole face reddened and contorted, and she bared her teeth. Then she turned her face to the sky and yelled out so loud Ragi wanted to plug his ears, and then

she lifted her right foot, pausing a moment before stomping on the ground. The sheep all around, Pastel Mary, Ragi, little stones, and even boulders rose in the air to land with a slam. The sheep ran about in confusion, Pastel Mary fell over, the little stones bounced, and Ragi supported his body with his staff. Chelsea's face was still pointing to the heavens. He couldn't see her expression. When he'd sensed violence, he'd brought his staff close to his body. Maybe it had been reckless to get into a shouting match against a dim-witted magical girl out where he had no defenses. But even being aware of his tendency to be reckless when the blood got to his head, he couldn't stop himself. In the sense of being hard to control, Ragi wasn't much different from magical girls.

"Fine." Her voice sounded painfully hoarse, the word pronounced sharply and cut off at the end—like she was wringing out a drop of blood with it.

Ragi narrowed his right eye at her remark. Understanding her meaning, he slowly widened his right eye, looking back at Chelsea's face, which was gradually lowering its angle. Her expression remained angry. Her face was pale. Chelsea lifted the foot she'd stomped, scattering pebbles, and he saw there was a deep imprint in the earth.

Chelsea walked a few times over the imprint to even out the earth and turned back to Ragi. "Let's go."

He had no idea what had tugged on Chelsea's heartstrings and in what manner. His opinion that she was an incomprehensible magical girl was unchanged. But even so, he had to cooperate.

Ragi got onto Chelsea's back, a crestfallen Mary got astride a sheep, and Chelsea flew off, riding her star, leading the herd of sheep.

◇ **Navi Ru**

When Navi stroked his chin, he felt one hair from his beard that was longer and thicker. He'd never been the type to try to dress up nice to play the game, nor did he think he was capable of that sort of thing, but the single long strand felt wrong. He gave it a sharp pluck. When he brought it in front of his eyes, it was thick, after all. He blew it away with a sigh. Even if he didn't fixate on his appearance, it was best to avoid things that bothered him.

Clarissa had told him, "Wouldn't you seem a bit less dubious and suspicious if you took a little more care in your grooming?" But she was the only one who would say something like that. No matter how he tried to disregard how others found his appearance, nobody who knew about Navi's career history would trust him. His former superior had once lectured him with a measure of contempt, "Only a third-rate spy becomes famous from their deeds. A first-rate spy, an operative, would keep his past hidden and get the job done without anyone getting suspicious." *But isn't it way more amazing when people are suspicious, think you're fishy, and assume you could betray them at any time, and you finish the job anyway?* Navi had thought, but he'd never said that out loud, dropping the matter with a smile.

Navi tried to look up at the sky, squinting at the bright light as he shaded his eyes with one hand. He figured it wasn't yet noon, but it was past what you'd call early morning. Perhaps because he didn't keep a regular sleep schedule to begin with, he just never managed to get an internal sense of time. All he could trust was the level of his hunger.

He snorted. When he looked toward the entrance, Tepsekemei was biting into a brown object. She was fluttering there in the wind as she assaulted a piece of bread as big as her head. There was even a nice addition of butter on it. It hadn't been spread on—it was sitting on the bread as a lump. That much had to be unhealthy. But right now, his body wanted that sort of badness. He wanted fatty acids, cholesterol, and salt. Navi touched his right hand to his stomach. He was holding an empty stomach. That was unquestionably the case, without any need to reconfirm it. Right on time, his stomach rumbled sadly.

"Heyyy!" Navi called.

The tiny magical girl did not stop, crunching along and

scattering crumbs as she bit into the bread. From how the butter was not at all melted, you could tell how cold the bread was. On top of that, it even looked hard. If you saw it on a normal day, you would just say, *"That looks like it tastes bad,"* but right now it looked like a feast.

"Hold on there a moment," said Navi.

"Mei won't wait."

"Hold up. Stop eating and listen."

"Mei won't stop."

"Hold on—okay, okay, I'll give you something good, so stop."

An expressionless Tepsekemei turned just her face toward Navi. She showed no sense of superiority or joy in eating. She was even hiding the fear and cautiousness she had to feel from having had her part erased by Francesca. Or had she never felt such things from the start?

Amazing. Navi was deeply impressed.

He rolled one grayfruit out from his sleeve into his palm to hold out to Tepsekemei. "Look here."

Navi planned to offer the fruit for the bread, but before he knew it, Tepsekemei had bitten into the grayfruit. She'd swapped the bread into her left hand. Navi looked at his own right hand and confirmed that he was holding nothing, then looked at Tepsekemei. The little magical girl bobbed in the air as she finished eating the grayfruit before opening her mouth wide to go at the bread again, showing her rows of teeth.

"Wait!" Navi yelled. "Hey, you little twerp! You took the fruit, so give me the bread!"

"Mei didn't hear that."

"What?"

"Mei heard, 'If you wait a bit, I will give you something good.' Mei waited a bit and got something good."

"That's too mean. Just cruel."

"If you eat too much of the congee with sweet potato you were longing for, you'll hate it. So you should watch Mei eat."

"Goddamn, you little twerp... Aren't you a magical girl?"

"Mei is a magical girl."

"Then you don't need to eat."

"Mei eats."

"If you're a magical girl, then help people in trouble. That's supposed to be your job."

"Mei is saving Mei, who's in trouble."

It was less that he wasn't getting through to her and more that he was getting tricked and teased. She strangely exuded that aura, despite being completely expressionless. Or rather, Tepsekemei's personality came through when you talked to her. *Damn it*, he thought over and over again. Maybe her lack of expression was not a wall or shield to hide herself, but part of her inborn nature.

Navi pointed his spread palms at her in a clownish gesture, nodding a bunch. "Fine, fine. You win. Let's make a deal. An exchange of grayfruit for bread."

Tepsekemei thrust her right hand in front of her sharply and stuck up her thumb, index, and ring fingers. "Mei wants this much."

"You stick your fingers up in a weird way. One, two…three? Wait, you want three?!"

"Mei will give the same amount."

"A trade of three on three, huh?"

"Mei needs enough for the flock. Mei wants one each for Mei, Weddin, and Funny Trick."

"By flock, you mean your friends?"

"Family."

"'Family,' huh…? Then there's no helping that."

"No helping that."

"Give me some of the butter, too. If you can promise me that."

"Mei will endeavor to."

"Let's not make promises you can't keep."

"Mei will make the utmost effort."

"That's the same thing."

The two of them exchanged three fruits for three pieces of bread plus a two-inch-square butter lump wrapped in silver paper that Mei handed over to Navi. Finally, Navi had obtained some sustenance. The hard, cold bread and the butter that was just as cold were truly delicious. The flavor and nutrients spread from atop his tongue all around his body. It's difficult for an adult man to live on just fruit. He glanced from the corner of his eye to Tepsekemei, who ate half of a grayfruit and tucked the rest into her pocket, and saw again that she was expressionless.

"Hey—so is your family those two companions of yours?" Navi asked.

"7753 is Weddin, and Mana is Funny Trick."

It seemed she'd created her own little world. She was expressionless, but it came across through all their conversations that she didn't restrain her idiosyncrasies. She had little fear, even though her part had been killed by Francesca. *Maybe she's one of those*, he thought silently. When a creature that was not a human transformed into a magical girl, their lack of experience in making use of language and their inhuman mentality would often make them exhibit behavior that was difficult for others to understand.

Each and every day, a variety of magical girls were invited to the Lab, which Navi worked for. Methods like human trafficking and kidnapping were absolutely taken for granted; the Lab found aristocrats who'd fallen into dire straits and held their children hostage. There were battle enthusiasts who'd been tricked by canvassing that was essentially fraud, whereby they were told they would become strong magical girls, and members of the faction who had been dealt an execution sentence under the pretense of punishment for some error. Magical girls who had transformed from animals were particularly favored. No matter how you treated them, they had no family to complain to, the authorities wouldn't make a fuss about it, and no trouble came of it down the line. It was also thought that lots of them had powerful magic, since it was rooted in their instincts.

It seemed like this Tepsekemei also had powerful magic. From what Mana had said and the way Tepsekemei herself spoke, it didn't seem like her part had been killed without her knowing what was going on, so she had to have faced Francesca and done something before the part had been killed. Even if knowing about Maiya's murder had made her wary beforehand, she'd still pulled off something that even a hundred normal magical girls wouldn't be able to do.

As he was thinking, she suddenly launched a question at him. "What about your family, Navi?"

"I've got one," he answered impulsively.

It wasn't Navi's style to blabber honestly like an idiot about his family, even on impulse. Restraining the urge to click his tongue or grimace, he put on a smile like it was nothing. "Just one person."

"Clarissa?"

"She's less family and more like a relative. She's my little sister's daughter—my niece."

"'Mei niece'?" said Mei.

"What? I didn't say anything strange."

"Mei…"

Mei was looking off into the distance to who knew where. This sort of incomprehensible behavior was another characteristic of magical girls who were transformed from animals.

Navi wolfed down half the bread, continuing to watch Tepsekemei. Maybe they'd be pleased if he took her to the Lab, but the risks were higher than the potential benefit.

Then Tepsekemei suddenly narrowed her eyes, their outer corners rising. She slipped to the side and took up position in front of Navi, spreading her hands and bringing them forward. Was she going on guard?

"Coming. Hide."

"Nah, this one is…" He looked through Tepsekemei's half-translucent body and toward the forest.

A magical girl leaped out from between the trees up in front of Tepsekemei, scattering leaves as she moved with the nimbleness of a cat. Her big animal ears twitched, and her long tail smacked the earth. "Heya, heya. I came up here to report to ya. You've got something that looks good there."

"I ain't giving it to ya. Your name just came up, Clarissa."

"Huh? What? Were you making nasty remarks about li'l ol' me?"

Telling Tepsekemei that they had to have a private talk, Navi prodded Clarissa's back to draw her away from the entranceway, walking about twenty steps before coming to a stop. Walking over here where Tepsekemei couldn't see was really suspicious. It was not something you'd do if you were worried about being attacked—even though his guard, Clarissa, was there. When he turned back, Tepsekemei was looking toward the forest. But even if she looked like she'd been reduced to a third of her usual size, Navi understood that he couldn't be careless around her.

Navi activated his stone so the sound wouldn't get out and covered his mouth with one sleeve. "I doubt there'll be a problem, but hide your mouth, just in case."

"That thing can read lips at this distance?" Clarissa moved just her eyes to point toward Tepsekemei. "She doesn't come off as that sharp, does she?"

"She was apparently fighting pretty decently against Francesca. One part from her."

Clarissa's face contorted like she was sincerely repulsed, and her ears hung weakly. "For real? Clantail was crazy strong, too. Strong enough that I kinda can't beat her."

"The hell are you doing?"

"It just wound up that way, okay? It wasn't so bad, Clarissa can make excuses for it later. Also, there's some other strong ones, too. Two or three probably got away from Francesca."

"Hey, hey, hey."

This was not an ordinary situation. Never mind what was inside Francesca—the container couldn't be managed by any random magical girl. She was the best of all technology coalesced, a magical girl to surpass magical girls. That they had gotten away meant that she hadn't been able to win. There were magical girls on this small island, multiple magical girls even Francesca had not been able to beat.

"Whoa." His astonishment was sincere and brief. There was no need to play with words.

The lives of many mages and magical girls had been spent in order to create the single magical girl called Francisca Francesca. Though Francesca had not been completed in the end, it was still possible that she could become a vessel for the soul of one of the Three Sages in the future. Navi had assumed there couldn't possibly be more than one idiot who would bring an incredibly strong magical girl to a discussion about deciding the allotment of the inheritance, and he'd underestimated the magical girls, assuming Maiya would be far stronger than any of the others. But the world was large, and there were a lot of them. He could be arrogant and say he'd seen hundreds, thousands of magical girls in the Lab, but here they were.

"More importantly, Clarissa's got news. The old man ran away."

"If he ran away, then chase after him and catch him."

"He threw away eeeeverything Clarissa bit. It seems like he noticed."

Not everything would go well in life. Hard-core types, Ragi in particular, could sometimes mobilize their experience and knowledge to pull off things the young couldn't. Not to say that Navi had been taking him lightly and assuming he could toy with him easily, but still, it posed a problem to not know where he was. If Ragi ran into Francesca, then he would die. No matter how talented a mage he was, if he happened to bump into a magical girl who killed any passersby, he wouldn't stand a chance—and that went double for a custom-made one that could become a vessel for the incarnation. Even a magical girl who ran into her would die—or so he had thought, but Clarissa here was saying there were in fact on this island some magical girls who had escaped her. What with losing his magic power and passing out and the magical-girl transformations being forcibly undone, there had been too many unprecedented and unexpected situations.

The world was big. Navi was often entrusted with outside jobs for the Lab, and he didn't think of himself as naive in the ways of the world, but this situation was difficult, even in terms of his profession of dealing with magical girls.

"Change of plans," Navi said. "Since we've run into the

unexpected, it'd be perfect to hold back a little. I think we've managed to put the old man and Yol in our debt, and Maiya's gone. I've hidden the goods, too. Now we're just waiting for Rareko."

Mana had noticed something. She'd also surpassed Navi's expectations—she was a good inspector. But she hadn't tried to hide that she'd noticed something. In that area, she was still young. He should be grateful for her youth. He could resign himself to getting tied up as a petty villain who'd tried to swipe part of the inheritance like a thief during a fire.

"If the other magical girls say they're gonna beat Francesca, then you work with them. If Francesca's gone, that means the old man's safe. At the very least, while they're fighting, Francesca will be too busy to get the old man mixed up in anything."

"Yeah, yeah... Wait. Huh?"

"What's wrong?"

The tip of Clarissa's right ear moved twice, and then she slowly lowered the ear and stuck it up straight again. Her expression grew grimmer as it twitched around. "Touta's on the move."

"Now the kid's causing trouble for us, damn."

"He's going fast. A little too fast, whoa. That's not human. That's magical-girl speed."

"Rareko?"

"Probably... The way he's moving, it's not like Francesca caught him, or he got cut to pieces and just his clothes are caught on something, so relax."

"I can't relax. Why is Rareko moving around now when we went to the trouble of securing her safety? Now that she's left her cave, what if she gets attacked by Francesca?"

"Clarissa doubts Rareko knows how Francesca works, either."

"Go pop over to Rareko and poke 'er."

"Roger."

Not bad, old man, Navi thought, impressed that Ragi was causing surprises. But Rareko causing surprises just made him think, *Give me a break.* Navi didn't want someone he saw as an ally stirring things up by acting on her own. Nobody would like something like that. This was Rareko, so she was probably pulling this unasked-for move out of fear, or thinking that she was being useful.

When Clarissa was about to race off, Navi raised his right arm to call out, "Hold on." Yol and Rareko rose in his mind, and, finally, he thought of Touta. It looked like he and Yol were friendly. It wasn't bad for boys and girls to have the tie of common interests. If they could safely escape from this island, they'd probably get even closer. Navi imagined the heartwarming scene of a boy and girl smiling together before he dropped his fantasizing and looked at Tepsekemei. Her eyes were on the forest.

"It's best if Touta's gone, if possible," Navi said.

"Yep, yep. Clarissa'll tell Rareko if I can."

◇ **Miss Marguerite**

Agony rose from where there had been nothing. Agony brought with it cold and pain. She noticed that she couldn't move right, and she remembered that she was herself. Her chest and throat twisted and spasmed in succession, and though she made to moan, her voice wouldn't come out. She focused her feelings in her throat to get her voice out, pouring all the strength of her body into it, and then the air went through with a *pop* like some kind of stopper had come out. She coughed hard, and a lump of pain leaped out from the back of her throat, from inside her mouth. Her back bent and her body rounded, and she lay on her side to spit up something pulpy from her stomach. It was half-liquid and had the sickly sweet smell of fruit, which became the linchpin that hammered into her vague memories. It was grayfruit. The smell of mud and stomach acid mingled, making a stench she'd never experienced before that spread around her mouth.

She tried to open her eyes, but they wouldn't part. She patted her face with her right hand and realized mud had dried to harden in her eyelashes, and she rubbed her face to break off the mud. She was surprised by how cold her hands were, as well as how cold her face was.

When she opened her eyelids, next she was dazzled by the bright light. Every motion came with some awful pain. She coughed over and over, gradually pushing open her eyes and putting up with the light, and when she focused, she found the severe face of a girl looking down on her. Then the corners of the girl's mouth gradually relaxed, her mouth opened slightly, and she let out a breath. The two gazed at each other for a while, and then Marguerite remembered this girl was Clantail's human form.

Marguerite made her stiff body obey her, using her elbows to raise her upper body from her position on her back. The girl immediately came in to support her from the side, and by half leaning on her, Marguerite somehow got herself up. Instead of feeling thankful or apologetic, she felt disgusted by how the girl's body was so much warmer than her own. How had she wound up like this? She traced back in her memory. She remembered dying, or rather being in a situation where she could easily have died, but now she was able to move around decently.

"What—?" Though it was her own voice, it sounded awful. And she was coughing.

The hand that rubbed her back was warm. Accepting the plastic bottle that was held out to her, Marguerite rinsed out her mouth and then spat to the side. She coughed for a while more, then drew in a breath through her mouth and exhaled. She drank another mouthful of water, and this time swallowed without rinsing. When she felt like she could manage to get her voice out, she tried speaking again. "What...happened to me?"

"I found tracks...and followed them into the mud...and then..."

Marguerite started to grimace, but held it back. That explanation was shockingly incompetent. But it would feel bad to make a face at the one who had just saved her life, so she covered it by coughing, even though she could breathe. The girl stroked her back with care, which just made her feel worse.

Thinking she should just start by explaining, Marguerite told her, "I was being chased by the magical girl who killed Maiya, and on the way, the effects of the fruit ran out and I sank into the mud.

It was a magical girl carrying two axes…a magical girl like the goddess of the spring in the fairy tale. She asked me if I'd dropped the golden ax or the silver one, but it probably didn't mean anything, and she was just repeating it. I think her magic is to transform her axes. She made them explode and turn into magnets to pull iron toward her and things like that…and she probably also has exceptional physical abilities."

The girl's expression was serious as she listened, but she didn't say a word. Marguerite looked at the girl's face, and she realized why she hadn't recognized right away that it was Clantail. Marguerite thought she'd been wearing glasses before, but they were gone now. Her face seemed different.

"Tepsekemei was also with me, but she was probably killed," Marguerite added.

The girl's face darkened—or contorted, rather. She clenched her teeth. It wasn't fear or sadness she was smothering, but anger. The words "Cranberry's children" rose in Marguerite's mind.

"What about you?" Marguerite asked.

"I was attacked by Clarissa."

This time, Marguerite didn't restrain her scowl as she looked back at the girl. The girl didn't say anything after that, looking back at her. She still seemed angry. Marguerite thought that getting attacked by Clarissa was way worse than getting attacked by the one who had killed Maiya, who was a clear enemy, but the girl didn't add any information, reporting only that she had been attacked before falling silent.

Marguerite was forced to prompt her, "Why did Clarissa do that?"

"In retrospect…I think maybe it was just bad timing."

"Bad timing?"

"As we were talking, a broken-off tree flew at us, and Clarissa dodged toward me, and that was so sudden, I went on guard, and Clarissa reacted to that by attacking, and then we just slid into a fight…" She was doing her best to explain in her clumsy way, but it really was lacking.

"You were talking? What about?"

"She had Ragi's hat... She tried to hide it, so I asked her why."

Marguerite basically understood the flow of events: Clantail had spoken to Clarissa, since she'd been suspicious that Clarissa had done something to Ragi, and in the middle of that discussion, a tree had flown at them, which Clarissa had dodged, and that had brought the two close together, forcing them into a fight. If Clarissa had harmed Ragi in some way, his trying to steal grayfruit or something sounded like a plausible reason for that.

But Marguerite was more bothered by Clantail's behavior than her explanation. When Ragi's name had come up, the outer corners of her eyes had risen, her gaze wavering around slightly as her right hand trembled. Signs of tension appeared all over, and she was trying to hide it. Marguerite had thought Clantail loyal enough to Ragi to run into the forest alone for him, but this was not a reaction of concern.

"Also, Nephilia was selling grayfruit," Clantail said.

Someone who wanted to make money would even make danger to life material for business—even if their own life was included. Marguerite wouldn't deny that there was a possibility that Nephilia's very dubious behavior had been of her own accord, but it was reasonable to assume Agri was making her behave as she had.

"I bought some," Clantail continued.

Marguerite hated the idea of giving up money to a miser, but you couldn't accomplish a goal without some sacrifices. And nothing was more vital on this island than the grayfruit.

Marguerite was suddenly struck with doubt. She raised her palm to look at it. Her hand was covered in mud. It was a human hand. It was not the hand of a magical girl, unbefitting of mud. The one before her who was haltingly and clumsily explaining to her was also a human girl. Her school uniform was torn in places and even splashed with reddish stains.

"...Where are the grayfruit?" Marguerite asked her.

"I used up all the fruit I bought."

The dry mud cracked audibly over Marguerite's face, and she

was aware of the stiffness of her own expression. "There aren't any left?"

The girl started opening her mouth, then closed it, expelling a breath. Her lips were in a slightly twisted shape. She closed her eyes once more, and when she opened them again, her expression was apologetic. "When I dug you up from the mud, you'd stopped breathing, so."

"Ahhh."

As usual, the girl wasn't explaining enough, but from her face, Marguerite got what she was stabbing at. The girl had used up all the grayfruit when she'd dug up Marguerite and revived her.

"After removing all the mud and water with a water pipe, I sent the grayfruit directly into your body... I figured it would be easier to revive you if you were in magical-girl form...since you'd have more vitality, that sort of thing. You were in magical-girl form but wouldn't quite wake up, and then your transformation would come undone right away, so I added more, and the amount of grayfruit decreased rapidly."

It seemed like it would be best not to ask what organ from what animal had made that water pipe. Regardless, Marguerite had felt an intense pain in her chest and throat—they still hurt—and now she knew some of why.

If it was as the girl said, then she had used up an exorbitant amount of vital grayfruit on someone half-dead who she hadn't even known could be saved—should Marguerite call her foolish for having used them all up? Or should she be thankful that this girl had disregarded all else to save a life? Whichever it was, since she had been saved, she should express gratitude. Marguerite put her knees together to kneel formally. Laying her hands on her knees, she bowed her head deeply and said, "Thank you." When she looked up exactly five seconds later, the girl was in the same position, bowing her head back.

While Marguerite was going through the motions of gratitude, her eyes were cold as she gazed at the top of the girl's head and her two hanging pigtails. Marguerite and Clantail had only just met.

And Clantail was saying that she'd been attacked by Clarissa, with whom she had a similar relationship. Using up all her grayfruit to save Marguerite meant she was very much indeed overflowing with the spirit of self-sacrifice, totally disregarding her own needs. Would you do that much for someone just because you knew her face and name, in a situation where you didn't know who was enemy and who was friend?

Now that she thought about it, Clantail hadn't seemed very concerned for her own safety when she had gone into the forest for Ragi. But what didn't make sense was how tense she'd seemed when she'd brought up Ragi. Why was she hiding that? She was being oddly quiet.

Magical girls would sometimes sacrifice themselves to save others. But hadn't Clantail sacrificed others for her own sake? The term "Cranberry's children" rose in Marguerite's mind again, and this time it stuck around. She asked herself if these negative feelings that had been there from the start had turned to visible antipathy toward Clantail, but she got no answers.

Five seconds after her, the girl lifted her head, and however she interpreted the eyes fixed on her, she didn't say anything, just looking back. Compared to before, there was a harshness so minute that Marguerite couldn't even be sure of it. It would be more accurate to call it caution. Realizing her own feelings for Clantail were coming back to her, Marguerite wiped off the mud on her forehead with her palm, disgusted with her own lack of experience.

CHAPTER 13
BY OUR POWERS COMBINED...?

◇ **Nephilia**

Her body was throwing a fit, saying it didn't want to move anymore. A single step made her flesh and bones cry out. Her spirit was wailing that it wanted to get away from this dangerous place and begging to be far from the goddess. Nephilia coaxed her body through its persistent suit to escape and skip out, and she walked. She really didn't want to loiter around such a dangerous place, but there was no safe place on this island anyway. Besides, there were lots of things she had to do.

Of the large volume of hidden fruit, she retrieved all the ones she'd told Chelsea and Mary about, leaving the rest and praying it wouldn't be found. If something happened to Ren-Ren, her magic would be undone. She should prepare for the worst.

She was relieved that the fruit was as they had left it, but she was also disappointed that Ren-Ren and Agri hadn't retrieved any. Nephilia spat some bloody spit into the brush. The grayfruit that wouldn't fit into her pockets or the plastic bag in her hand she packed into her hood, and the ones that were still left over she tucked into her bone decorations. She was already fed up by the fruit hairs poking her in the back of the head, but the grayfruit were a greater priority now than her comfort. Taking a lesson from Agri's stinginess, she didn't leave even one known fruit behind. The grayfruit were important to keep her transformed on this island right now.

Since she had no idea what the situation was now, it was best to have as many allies as possible. And she didn't just want people who called themselves allies, but absolute allies who were bound by law and contract. The grayfruit would be needed in order to make those.

And if she was going to make her move, then she should do so as soon as possible, given the situation. There was no guarantee something wouldn't trigger this into turning into an extreme survival-of-the-fittest situation at some point. If they wound up in some *Lord of the Flies* situation where you could write off murder by saying *"It was to protect myself,"* then it would be no time for contracts. You couldn't make a contract with a beast. Nephilia would request protection for herself, Agri, and Ren-Ren while people still remained people, and she would hand over the fruit as compensation. Now she would leave aside the money that had been their initial goal. She wouldn't let Agri complain about it, either.

The problem was that Agri and Ren-Ren might be in such a bad state, they wouldn't be capable of even a single complaint. The grayfruit being left there meant that Agri and Ren-Ren hadn't retrieved any. Say what you liked about their character, neither of them was stupid. They understood the importance of the grayfruit. If they hadn't had to change location because Ren-Ren hadn't undone her magic, then that was fine. If that wasn't the reason, then things were bad. Things were very bad.

The people they had extorted for money using grayfruit—Clantail and Touta and the others—probably didn't feel favorably toward Nephilia, and Clarissa and Navi couldn't be trusted at all to begin with. As for Dreamy☆Chelsea and Pastel Mary, if Ren-Ren's magic came undone, their goodwill would drop to the floor.

Though she wouldn't describe this situation as "enemies on all sides," not many here would feel positively toward Nephilia.

And accomplishing her goal of negotiating with people while they remained people would be very difficult for Nephilia on her own. With her total forces of one battered magical girl, dragging one leg to walk, her prices would get beaten down to the floor. Depending on the goodwill of the other party—or rather, on their ill will—she might well wind up with not a protection contract but a slave contract. If she had Ren-Ren or Agri with her, the situation should improve a little.

Thinking this as she walked, she thought with some self-deprecation that it was like she was looking for an excuse to search for Agri and Ren-Ren, and she swallowed. There was a lot less red in her saliva now.

They had two locations where they'd decided they would meet in an emergency. One was a dip in the hilly section a slight distance from the rocky area, and the other was on the way to the main building, by the spring where they'd run into Navi before. If Nephilia were to choose between them, she would take the dip rather than the spring. Thinking about how their potential enemy could be described as looking like the goddess of the spring gave her no desire at all to go to the latter. Agri and Ren-Ren would be thinking the same thing. Surely that was what they would think, if they were alive.

Using humor and sarcasm to keep herself going, Nephilia made her way along. It was extremely difficult to tell who could be trusted and who could not. She couldn't say for sure that her wits hadn't been dulled by her injuries or that she wasn't confused due to fear, but more to the point, she had no information with which to make any judgments. Agri's belief that the string of incidents that had begun with Maiya's murder was all an unfortunate accident had been ridiculously off the mark. But that being the case, how much of this was out of malice from Navi? Or had it really been an accident after all? Even guessing based on the talks they'd had with him and what was in the contract was too much for Nephilia. A lawyer was neither a mystery novelist nor a detective.

A shrill cry made her come to a stop, and then she watched, sighing, as a brightly colored bird took flight. Nephilia didn't have enough energy to think right now, never mind consider these matters. She pulled a grayfruit out of her pocket and bit into it, then returned to her depressing walk. It was a mental strain to keep herself from breaking into a run when she wanted to. Her injuries just made her sadder.

Since Nephilia had enough good sense left that she wouldn't race off after getting a scare, she continued to walk along slowly. Having to jump a little every time she heard some noise was bad for her body and mind. It wasn't just that she couldn't run around. She couldn't take the shortest route to where she was going, either, and so she tiptoed along with the utmost anxiety as she chose paths where she could hide behind trees, grasses, and rocks, and when she somehow managed to arrive at the hills that were her goal, her nose twitched. A smell was flowing to her on the wind. It was the smell of something burning. The odds were high that the goddess was rampaging close by. Nephilia had to be more cautious.

She crawled along the ground up a hill, moaning in pain the whole way. She'd been using her scythe as a cane, but now she hid it in the grass. Even just carrying it was a burden now.

Whining of *Ahhh, it hurts, it hurts, ahhh, it hurts, ahhh, it hurts* looped in her head, and she lamented that she hated herself for doing her best even in this state, and when she heaved herself over the top of the hill to look down, she found one good thing and one bad thing.

The good thing was that Ren-Ren was there. The bad thing was that Agri was not there.

Nephilia crawled over the top of the hill, staying low until her head was lower than the peak, and once she was past that point, she stood up and waved at Ren-Ren. Ren-Ren was holding a sort of handmade torch that was lit—so that was the source of the burning smell—and was sharply alert to her surroundings. Ren-Ren noticed her immediately, giving her a carefree smile and waving an arm wide. She flew up too fast for the injured Nephilia to react, coming to her side to support her. Nephilia breathed a sigh of relief. At ease because she had someone supporting her battered body, Nephilia leaned on her, then flinched a bit at the heat of the torch and moved away. Why was Ren-Ren carrying that around in the middle of the day?

"T...tor...?"

Ren-Ren didn't reply to Nephilia's question, grimacing sadly. "What awful wounds!"

"H...ur..."

"I'm sure it must hurt. All I've got is a handkerchief, but let's rest over there."

With Ren-Ren supporting Nephilia, they walked out toward the dip in the hills. Ren-Ren was glad that Nephilia was in one piece— though Nephilia wasn't intact enough to call it that. Nephilia casually slung her arm around Ren-Ren's waist as she listened to her talk. Ren-Ren said things like, *"Let's rest over there, did that magical girl like a goddess get you? Thank you for bringing the grayfruit, what did you do with your scythe? If you left it behind, I'll go get it."* Agri did not feature among these topics.

Ren-Ren avoided touching on Agri to an unnatural degree, and when she brought up what they should do now, the subject of searching for Agri was not included. She never once mentioned the employer she'd been so attached to—it was as if she'd never been there.

The burning smell became even more pungent. Nephilia's gaze dropped to the torch that blazed high in Ren-Ren's right hand. She could hear fire crackling and popping. She looked up. Black smoke was blowing from right to left, and she could see the flickering of sparks dancing in the air. It was all burning—the trees of the forest.

"Thi...fire..."

"Mm-hmm. We have the advantage of having lots of grayfruit. But there might still be lots of grayfruit in the forest, and I figured if they find someplace where there are lots growing, then our numerical advantage won't be an advantage anymore. But if the whole forest burns, then nobody can find a spot like that anymore, right?"

Nephilia's eyes widened as she looked at Ren-Ren. Ren-Ren looked back at her with an expression that seemed to say, *"Is something strange?"* A muffled laugh bubbled up from deep in Nephilia's throat. Sometimes you had to laugh, or you couldn't go on.

The doubt that had been budding within Nephilia was turning to a certainty. Ren-Ren knew what had happened to Agri. And, knowing that, she wasn't going to talk about it. Either her heart refused to touch it, or the shock of it had caused a gap in her memory, but either way, Agri was no longer alive. And the fact of Agri's death was a spice too potent for Ren-Ren.

Nephilia prayed for Agri and breathed a sigh at her partner, whose mental state was even more dicey than her own, despite her injuries, and set her brain cells to work to consider what to do now. If Nephilia proposed to put out the fire, would Ren-Ren listen? There was no water nearby, so that might be difficult to do. Coming to the conclusion that if it became a problem afterward, they could blame it on the goddess, Nephilia offered up one more prayer— that there would be an "afterward."

◇ **Ragi Zwe Nento**

Chelsea was riding on a star that she'd made by gouging out a rock, Mary was astride a sheep, and Ragi clung to Chelsea as the three of them headed to the place where the grayfruit was stored. They said it was a primitive hiding spot, just a hole dug to pack the grayfruit in, with leaves on top. Ragi's eyes dropped to Chelsea's feet. She had to be holding back a little, but, being a mage, he felt they were flying at an unbelievable speed. This was not a carpet, protected by magic power to be absolutely safe, or even an airplane, which had some guarantee based on technology—two people's worth of weight was being supported by a rock ball one size smaller than Ragi's fist. Chelsea had to have chosen this method of travel since she was sure of her balance, but having only just met her the other day, Ragi felt nothing but doubt as to whether he should trust her to this degree.

"Hey," he barked at her.

"What's up?"

"Why would you choose to make such a small ball to ride on? You have your star decoration. Weren't you riding on that before? A flat star shape is more stable than a ball-shaped rock. And a magical girl's attached item will be more durable, too."

Chelsea gave him a sour look, and Ragi panicked. "Face forward! Just how many obstacles do you think there are in the forest?!"

Chelsea faced forward reluctantly, but her expression didn't change. "Well, that's not Chelsea's."

"It's not?'

"That should be obvious. If it were originally mine, I wouldn't have to put magic clear tape on it. It's because it's not mine that I used the tape to stick it on."

Ragi heard Mary mutter, "I thought that was just the aesthetic." It was loud enough for Ragi to hear, so there was no way Chelsea couldn't have heard it, but Chelsea didn't touch on that and continued.

"It was from a friend of my mom's, you know, and that generation are all such busybodies. Even though I don't really need it, she shoved it off on me, saying it'd be convenient to have. I figured I should just dump it in my closet, but my mom nagged me about it so much, saying, like, *'She got that nice present for you, so make use of it.'*"

Ragi could hear Mary mutter, "I think it was really convenient." Chelsea ignored her.

"Look, Dreamy☆Chelsea is a cute, fancy, and fantastical magical girl. Chelsea doesn't want to add in any elements that sniff so hard of real life, like 'a souvenir I got from Mom's friend.' That's why Chelsea"—she flashed the star decoration and put it back in her pocket—"wants to avoid using this as much as possible. It's okay designwise, so it's fine to take it out for posing and stuff, though. Also, Chelsea decided today to use it when things get actually dangerous."

"So you're using it in the end, huh?" Mary muttered a little louder than before—she must have thought the *whoosh* of the wind would make it so they couldn't hear—but Chelsea ignored that.

When Chelsea was being controlled, she'd reminded Ragi of a cat in heat. But now she made him think of a dog whose territory had been invaded. Either way, she was an animal. Chelsea's fixations were animalistic and foolish, but plenty of people couldn't abandon their fixations, no matter how petty they seemed to others. Ragi started to get a flash of insight, and he closed his eyes. Covering his vision made him feel the wind even more. He'd tucked his beard into his clothing, but his hair was still fluttering in the wind.

Fixation. That was it. Some people couldn't let go of their petty fixations. That was common for magical girls. It was also common for mages. A technical expert praised as a genius might incorporate inefficient formulas, despite how objectively pointless they were, puffing out his chest about their perfection.

Ragi thought of the major research projects Sataborn had produced. He hadn't been a thoroughly efficient worker at all, and he'd pursued hobbies in some areas. Society would forgive you for being an eccentric if you could produce results. And nobody would deny that Sataborn was a talented eccentric. Even if he had accepted support from the Lab, this place was Sataborn's estate. Sataborn's inclinations would be the top priorities.

So that means...

"Ahhh!"

"Huhhhh?!"

Ragi's thoughts were cut off by Chelsea's and Mary's shrieks. When he opened his eyes, the star they stood on had already come to a stop. It seemed that he'd been focusing so hard, he hadn't noticed that the wind was no longer blowing in his face. *Not many young whippersnappers these days would be able to concentrate like that,* Ragi thought with a snort as he fluttered his cape like a young man to land on the ground. The shrieks hadn't interrupted him due to a lack of concentration on his part. They had just been so shrill and painful on the ears.

"What's the matter?" Ragi demanded.

"What do you mean, 'What's the matter?' All the fruit we hid is gone," said Chelsea.

"I think…Ren-Ren and them must have taken them before we did," Mary said.

"Those jerks! Agh! They keep pulling nasty stuff over and over!"

The branches and leaves that had been placed over the hole had been moved to the side, and all that was left was the hole, with nothing in it. It had been plumbed right to the bottom, and not even a single stem or drop of fruit juice was left. Chelsea's shoulders dropped exaggeratedly like a caricature's, and Mary sighed sadly.

The width of the hole was one head longer than Ragi's height, while it was half his height in depth. It was a big hole, so Agri's group must have stored up quite a lot. They were probably still harvesting grayfruit as they found them, too. They certainly had to think it was a perfectly natural thing to do, eliminating the possibility that the fruit would go to others, while increasing the numbers they held. Ragi doubted that Agri and her attendant magical girls had realized that harvesting more grayfruit sped up the rate of consumption—in other words, that this was strangling everyone on the island. If they were all going to steal from each other and harvest to the very last, they were headed for mutual destruction.

He had failed to make an escape using the grayfruit. What should he do now? Should he push them to procure grayfruit regardless and fulfill his initial objective? Or should he change direction?

Perhaps because he'd been acting like a young man, it felt as if his thoughts were moving faster and more clearly. It was always times like this when good ideas came to mind. But for that, he needed material—in other words, information. If there was going to be a change of plans, then he would settle down to focus on this for now.

"There's something I want to ask," he said.

Chelsea, with her shoulders drooping, turned around, hands on her hips, with her cheeks puffed up. "I'm feeling down, so you should console me."

"This is more important."

"Okay. So?"

"Tell me what you two saw and learned while you were being controlled."

Chelsea turned to Mary, who folded her arms and tilted her head.

"Just talk to me," Ragi insisted. "About anything else. Oh, I know—tell me about when I was unconscious. I may already know, but my memory is vague around a certain time, so just tell me everything."

"You're kinda weirdly eager about this," said Chelsea.

"This is important. It affects whether we live or die."

The three of them sat down facing each other. Ragi prompted them, Chelsea talked, and Mary corrected. Or Mary talked while Chelsea pointed things out. There was a lot of information Ragi had been unable to acquire because he'd been unconscious—information about the land, magical girls, and events. He estimated just how far Sataborn had pushed through with his interests and how the Lab had interfered, sorting things out in his head. When Ragi prompted the girls to tell him anything they had noticed, Pastel Mary talked about how when she'd been going around to distribute the invitations to the heirs, many had voiced doubts about the conditions for coming to the island—the condition about bringing magical girls, specifically. It was indeed fishy, but Ragi had let it go as well, thinking, *Well, this is Sataborn.* But it was highly suspicious now. Was this also a part of an experiment for which they had wanted to get a number of magical girls as samples? That was an exceedingly unscrupulous idea, but he also thought the Lab was apt to do such a thing. But since magical girls were so rampantly unique that each one could be called a different type, even if you got a number of samples, you could never make statistics from them. There was no way Sataborn and the Lab would not know that, so it was difficult to imagine that the goal of this summons had been an experiment.

In between bouts of talking, they ate grayfruit, personally

experiencing that the pace of power consumption was accelerating. With the fruit harvested, the trees were sucking up power in order to make more fruit. Just how much did Navi Ru know about the side effects of the grayfruit? They said he had passed out as well, but still, you couldn't say for sure he didn't know. The girls told him that Chelsea's violence had caused a lot of fruit to fall from the trees, and it didn't seem like Navi Ru had had anything to do with that. Regardless, one should not make assumptions about the position or goals of that man. It was best to think anything was possible.

I must not give in.

He didn't know whom he was up against, or even if it was Navi Ru or not. But he didn't want to come out the loser. He'd been driven into a dead-end job, and even at that position he'd been unable to fulfill his duty and had information stolen. It was humiliation upon humiliation. His pride as a mage would not allow a third humiliation. That's what his intellect, that's what his magic was for.

The discussion shifted to stories of Mary's blunders. Chelsea avoided her own mistakes as much as possible, or tried to act like they hadn't happened, but she'd go into detail about Mary's mistakes. She became particularly emotional when she talked about the time a herd of sheep had swallowed up Navi Ru when he'd fallen to the ground, and he'd been jostled around—or, rather, she talked about it like it was a funny story, while Mary cried out in protest.

"It's not fair to act like I was the only one screwing things up!" Mary cried.

"But you did make a boo-boo there, right?" Chelsea teased.

Ragi wasn't sure if he'd heard about this before or if this was news to him. His memories of that time were terribly vague.

"B-but, well, look, it started because of you, right, Chelsea?"

"Ahh, here you go blaming it on others. So you're that kind of magical girl, huh?"

"Stop forgetting what you did yourself! It's because you ruined that wall!"

"That wasn't deliberate."

"Well, yeah, maybe that's true…but even if it wasn't, it's not like you should just get away—"

"Hold it right there." The mountain of information parted and light shone through. Ragi waved his right hand at Chelsea. "It started because Chelsea ruined the wall—what do you mean by that?"

"Chelsea destroyed the wall," Mary explained, "and then Mr. Navi was really disappointed."

"This is about the main building, correct?"

"A-ah, yes."

Chelsea made some protest, but Ragi wasn't listening. Chelsea had destroyed a wall, and Navi had been disappointed. Ragi couldn't see the connection. This was fishy. Why would he feel regret just from someone destroying the wall of the residence? It wasn't as if he were going to receive the wall as an inheritance.

Was there something there?

It was something important to Navi. Inheritance. Sataborn's research. Something Navi would know.

Sataborn was a hard-core research nut who had been so dedicated to his work, he'd never even taken a career position. He didn't want luxury or a social position. He simply wanted to do research. And on a research farm that had originally been there headed by that sort of idiot—in other words, on this island—he had made a facility where he carried out research that couldn't be made public. Of course the Lab would know where that new facility was. There was no way Navi Ru would not know. As he imagined Navi Ru getting swallowed up by a herd of sheep, the corners of Ragi's lips twisted up. Chelsea and Mary had stopped their quarrel, and both of them were looking at Ragi—Chelsea curiously, and Mary with bafflement.

"I see it," Ragi muttered.

"You see what?" Chelsea asked.

"That research nut Sataborn must have been thinking he wanted to put the research facility in his own living space. Getting there using a gate or carpet would take time. He wouldn't want to waste even that amount of time. It would also take time to transfer the things he needed for his lifestyle to such a facility. He wouldn't want to waste that time, either. He had the new facility made in the main building, which was his base…most likely in the basement. If one had an eye for security, one would never build it close to one's own home, but he had hardly a thought for security."

"Sorry, I don't really get what you're talking about," said Chelsea.

"It wouldn't be strange for Navi Ru to know where it is. It also makes sense that he would be shocked to see it fall apart. The facility was right underneath, or the collapse went right over the entrance… It's gratifying just to imagine how he must have felt."

Ragi wasn't certain this was true, but he spoke as if this had all really happened. He had to speak with confidence, or the magical girls wouldn't follow him. Ragi stood up and struck the ground with his staff. It made mud splash up, but he couldn't be bothered by that.

"We're going—back to the main building. There should be a hidden facility. Dig up the area that Chelsea made collapse," he declared, and he was about to look at their reactions when the girls' expressions suddenly faded. Not just their expressions—everything faded. His field of view flipped over, and then someone caught him, and Chelsea's shriek and Mary's cry made him want to plug his ears, but he couldn't, and then his vision worsened like pale ink had mixed into it, and shivers welled up from within him. His body remembered these symptoms. Thinking that he had to eat grayfruit, he remembered: *Oh yes, I've just eaten the last one.* Even the sun shining right overhead gradually faded and eventually went out.

◇ **Navi Ru**

Since Clarissa had found Rareko, Navi proposed that they meet up with them, for starters. Mana more or less accepted, and though she didn't hide that she was suspicious, it wasn't as if they had any other particular plan, and the group just sort of wound up heading in that direction in the end. Navi was walking in the lead.

Tepsekemei was bobbing along a foot over his head. Mana came behind Navi, and then 7753. The order was reasonable. If they were going to be walking on an island where there was an incomprehensibly violent person wandering around, placing magical girls with their excellent senses at the front and behind and having the mage in the middle of the line made it easy to protect. Making it so that you sacrificed the mage to let the magical girls live and take advantage of the opening when the mage was attacked so they could act might have actually been the best positioning, but being that very mage himself, there was no reason for Navi to suggest that.

This positioning was decent enough, but the biggest problem with it was that it made it difficult for Navi to make any moves. It was a quiet path, with just the sound of the dry branches and fallen leaves they stepped on, and aside from that, there was just the occasional cry of birds and insects. Having things this quiet made the other senses sharper, and he felt the gaze that was stabbing daggers into his back keenly enough that it hurt. He knew that Mana had her attention on him, but he did also think, *She can't be looking only at me.* Did she think that if an enemy showed up, then two magical girls would be enough to deal with it? Or was she thinking rationally about it, that her senses wouldn't amount to much when she was watching out for the enemy, so she should focus on the dubious mage in front of her instead?

"Hey, Mana," Navi addressed her.

"Please don't speak."

"It's fine. It's not the sort of thing that'll sneak up on you from behind, right? It seems like they're the type to just go berserk and cause chaos everywhere, right? So then the two of us whispering won't change anything."

There was no reaction from Tepsekemei. She was floating over Navi's head. No reaction from her also meant that his statement had not been rejected. When Navi popped around to look, Mana had a sour expression. 7753, behind her, seemed discomfited, if anything. He got the impression that Mana was jumping the gun a bit.

"Hey, Mana."

"Like I said—"

"Haven't we met somewhere?"

"What? Where?" Mana's eyebrows furrowed like she was seriously considering Navi's nonsense. It was funny to watch, but since laughing right then would ruin it, Navi also put on a serious look as he waited for her reply.

"I have no memory of that," she said.

"Oh, really? I feel like I've seen your face somewhere."

"But I have no memory of it."

"So, then…it might've been someone else with a similar face. Like your dad, or something."

"Ah, if that's what it is." Her expression relaxed slightly. "My father is the head of the Magical Girl Inspection Department. You might have met him through work."

"Ahh, I see. That makes sense."

The chief of the Magical Girl Inspection Department was ranked equally to the chief of the Magical Girl Management Department, but he was functionally far more important. If you were to express it briefly, it was the difference between the star of the department and the useless old man at the boss's desk.

Navi stroked his jaw with his right hand. In the roughness of his beard, he felt the passage of time.

Mana's manner of speaking had not included even the minutest sense of antipathy or rebellion toward her father. Judging from how foolishly upright she was, he could guess that the father was not an unscrupulous corrupt public official, at the very least in his daughter's view. This was not something Navi would be happy to deal with.

Mana pointed ahead. Navi faced forward and ducked under a thick branch. If he'd kept talking while facing backward for another ten seconds, he would have been hit right on the back of the head.

Even if Mana's father was also an upright character, if he was the same as Ragi, that would be easy to deal with. But being that the main job of the chief of the Inspection Department was fighting criminals, he would not be easy to deal with at all. It could create a bit of a hassle if he was just as uncompromising as his daughter.

Maybe I should throw a wrench in things.

He wondered if he'd be able to force Mana out, but then he had the feeling that going that far would just invite unneeded intervention instead. The more of an honest mage someone was, the more they would lose control of themselves when it came to family. The head of the Inspection Department had authority. Even being from the Lab himself, Navi couldn't ignore that. He would not eliminate Mana—he would compromise by giving her an appropriate-looking "souvenir" to make her feel good.

That was how he was thinking he would treat Mana. But he was aware he still felt sort of repulsed by her. Putting it into words to say he didn't like her or she irritated him sounded immature and unpleasant. But writing it off as just his imagination would be even more immature, so Navi considered the reason behind his feelings.

Nah.

He knew what it was, even without thinking about it. His antipathy was toward law-abiding upright types like Ragi and Mana's father. They valued ethics, hated veering off the path, and fulfilled their professional duties without ever falling into depravity. Navi felt a distaste for that kind of life. It wasn't like he didn't know the rumors about the Lab. And not just the Lab—how many individuals and organizations out there did unethical experiments while claiming it was for the sake of the Magical Kingdom? Ragi would just rage about it and be useless, and even Mana's father would never be able to expose them all. The backbone of the Lab was one of the Three Sages—organizations like that would never get cleaned up, even if you spent your whole life on it. The most you could do was tell them, "I have my eye on you" to pressure them to restrain their activities, and even if you did that, it wasn't like you could prevent everything. If they went full tilt and showed no mercy at all, their brutal deeds could be cut down by 30 percent at most.

The deaths would continue. Mages would die, and magical girls would die.

It was because Ragi wouldn't give up on his fixation on ethics and had stuck to his own path that he had been shoved into a dead-end job. Had he never considered that maybe the damage would have been lesser if he'd remained in the mainstream, even if it meant using methods that weren't of his choosing, dirty methods, to keep a position where he would have some say? Mana's father was the same. He just did what he did without caring how it looked, and he was sure to give up if that didn't work. But just because it was no good when you only ever worked within the rules, did you think that passed as an excuse for those who died, for their surviving families?

Everyone used dirty methods that people would avert their eyes from, trampling even the victims of the same circumstances, but you still had to push forward to accomplish your goal no matter what, smeared in slime with others talking about you behind your back, or you couldn't call yourself a great mage.

Navi rapped his middle finger on his forehead. Nothing good would come of getting emotional. But how many people in recorded history had ignored their feelings, tried to do the job, and failed? The key to success was not to reject feelings, but in fact to hold them in esteem to please yourself. Considering a number of routes to the place where he was going to meet up with Clarissa, he confirmed that one of them went right by the trash dumping ground. It would be interesting to go that way.

When he turned around, Mana was glaring at him as she stuck a round white pill in her mouth. It wasn't anything much—just an over-the-counter drug for stabilizing mood. Even if she put on a tough act as a great inspector, she must have taken a big hit mentally. She had no idea where the enemy might come from, and neither did she have an abundance of grayfruit.

Mana and 7753 had both been pretty tightly scrimping in an attempt to make the grayfruit last. The pace at which Mei was eating the grayfruit had clearly slowed down. If he made it subtle enough that they didn't realize he was taking the long way to buy time, maybe Mana would pass out, or the magical girls' transformations would come undone. If they did, Navi would stand to benefit. If they didn't, it wouldn't hurt or help him. So it was worth trying out.

Perhaps thanks to his deciding what should be decided, his heart, which had been headed in a glum direction, cheered a little.

◇ **Mana**

Mana had told 7753 to pay attention to how Navi Ru was acting, but she didn't know how seriously 7753 was taking that order. 7753 had the habit of getting into denial about malicious people—rather, Mana thought it was kind of a guiding principle in 7753's life. If 7753 were her underling or coworker, or maybe even her superior, she would have yelled at her, *"What's the point of saying something like that now?! If you want to be that soft, then do it at home,"* but 7753 was not her underling, coworker, or superior.

Instead, Mana was the one with thorns stuck in her heart. If she hadn't brought 7753 to this island, 7753 never would have gotten caught up in this incident. She was taking advantage of her and Tepsekemei's natures, since neither would say anything reproachful. It made Mana remember that time with Hana. If Mana hadn't been the team chief, then Hana would never have volunteered for the mission. And if Mana had been saved because of Hana, then wasn't it also because of Mana that Hana had died? Mana had wondered this many times, and had come to no answers. That was because she was afraid of the answer, and she cut off the thought without trying to take it to the end.

Tepsekemei had been reduced to one-fourth her size, and 7753 had lost her goggles. Mana didn't have the right to order them to try harder. The two of them had already made sacrifices.

Navi Ru was boldly walking in front as if he were showing off the greasy back of his head. With everything else going on as well, it irritated her. Maybe he was even doing it deliberately to cause her particular irritation. It had also felt sort of contrived when he'd brought up her father. Causing someone stress to draw information from them was a conversational tactic.

I won't let myself get taken in by him.

There were a lot of mages from the Lab whose names had been noted down as people to watch out for. They weren't in the same department as Inspection—it was just hearsay going around at the management offices and the Public Security Department—but it wasn't the way of the Inspection Department to shyly withdraw their hand once it was extended just because there was a fence there.

No way am I going to let him pull something funny, she thought as she glared at the greasy back of his head, and when the face occasionally turned back, she glared at that, too. Mana just kept walking on without ever taking her eyes off Navi Ru. She left it to Tepsekemei to keep an eye out for attack from external threats. Mana really didn't think she herself could handle those, even if she tried to respond.

She dropped a tablet in her palm and popped it into her mouth. It stabilized her mood. Marguerite was probably not alive. They were up against a magical girl who was capable of killing Marguerite. She felt nothing but regret about having brought Tepsekemei and 7753, but if she hadn't brought them, she might have been killed without even being able to resist.

Suddenly the tension between her eyebrows relaxed. It was because Mana and the other heirs had brought magical girls that they were in this situation. And the reason they'd brought magical girls was that the condition had been included in the will. That condition was nonsensical and suspicious. There was no reason for the deceased to ask for such a thing, aside from "because he was an eccentric."

Mana touched a finger to her chin. The will was protected by Sataborn's magic. You couldn't rip it or overwrite it. Something bothered her there. It was that—

"Hey, Mei! Calm down!"

She was drawn back to reality. Realizing that she was letting her focus slack as she indulged in speculation, she cleared her throat to cover her embarrassment. She was acting like a senile old person.

Tepsekemei was clinging to a tree about ten steps away. Grayfruit was growing there in clusters. Tepsekemei cut down a fruit and swallowed it in one bite, knocking off the other fruit one after another and catching them with her body.

7753 was about to run up to her when Navi held out a hand to stop her. "Whoa there, hold up. It's dangerous if you're not Mei."

7753 looked down to the ground. Half a step ahead was blackish mud that continued as far as the tree where the grayfruit were growing. It was mud all around—or maybe it was more like a bog. Long things that could be mysterious branches or antennae were sticking out all around it, and rusty cans were floating on it to aggressively generate an atmosphere that said *You can't step in here.* The place where Tepsekemei was, for a radius of just six and a half feet around the trees, had escaped the incursion of the bog, like it was floating there pop in the middle, like a separated little island. Then Mei disappeared. No, that wasn't it. Her transformation came undone. A small tortoise rolled on a tree root to get stuck in the bog and struggle. It was slowly being swallowed up.

7753 cried out. She crouched to spring in a wide leap, kicking off an antenna on the way to land beside Mei, scoop her up, and wipe off the mud with her hand—and then she changed form. She was no longer 7753. She was a human woman in her nightwear. Mana tried to call out across the bog, and right that very moment there was an intense blow to the back of her head and her vision flashed, and she was disoriented. Without even the time to wonder what had happened, Mana lost consciousness.

CHAPTER 14
NOW AS HUMANS

◇ **Miss Marguerite**

Exhaustion, hunger, sweating, heart palpitations, shortness of breath—even moving just a little brought all these troubles to her at once. Wiping the sweat off her forehead with the back of her hand, she looked up at the glaring sun and scowled, but it didn't look like the brutal rays would ease even slightly. They were burning her skin as the heat was muggy in her hair, making her feel even more exhausted and hungry, and most of all stressed. On top of that, fear was a major presence. Being in a situation where encountering the enemy meant death would most certainly torment anyone's spirit.

They did have a clear plan. They would look for the others who'd gotten separated, as well as trees where the grayfruit grew, all while moving stealthily around the island to keep the goddess from finding them. So basically, that made them a search party with the goal of rallying forces and replenishing supplies, but in actuality, they just meandered in a painfully difficult way, not even knowing if the allies they were searching for were alive, seeking grayfruit that could be anywhere, praying that those they had to protect were safe, all while frightened of the enemy. They could never even take a moment to rest.

They stayed hunched over, though Marguerite had doubts about how useful this was, hiding in the grasses to traverse a way with no path. They kept an eye on their surroundings as they walked through the forest, and when they discovered signs of fruit having been plucked, Marguerite clicked her tongue. Suddenly hearing the cry of a little bird, they trembled and threw themselves to the ground.

When it turned out it wasn't the goddess, Marguerite sighed, set her hands on her knees, and got up. The girl with her was already standing, short spear raised in one hand as she stayed alert.

Her rough and primitive spear was just a long branch with a pointed end, and her uniform was torn in places, with the dots of red sprayed on it giving her a more apparent air of violence. You might call her the wild bookworm type—her appearance was beyond contrastive and nigh surreal.

She was mostly expressionless, and just as silent in human form as she had been when transformed. But the girl didn't have a tail that moved with her emotions. That made it more difficult to see inside her than when she was Clantail, and she came off even more intensely, like an eerie person who could be thinking anything.

Marguerite felt eyes on her and looked up to see the girl looking down at her. Marguerite had sat down, so maybe the girl thought she was tired. Embarrassed, she hurriedly got to her feet, and some stick-shaped object was held out to her. It was store-bought preserved food that hadn't been unwrapped yet.

"What's this?" Marguerite asked.

"It was in my pocket."

The girl said nothing more. It seemed she thought that would get the message across well enough. She gave a little nod to prompt Marguerite and didn't say anything further.

Marguerite was actually hungry. The last time she'd eaten had been at the main building, and she'd hardly refueled at all since

then. She accepted the bar and opened it up, then broke it in half and handed half back.

She had the feeling that if she asked why the girl had brought such a thing, the girl would answer, *"Just in case."* The more of a veteran a magical girl was, the less she would prepare for when she was not transformed. 7753 had wound up humiliated in her at-home wear when her transformation had come undone, but Marguerite couldn't laugh at her. That was the laziness characteristic of a veteran magical girl, and Marguerite had been more than just close to embarrassing herself in the same way.

Even the training plan at the Inspection Department just about never touched on battle techniques for human form. If your transformation was undone in front of the enemy, you'd die helplessly. There was no point in preparing for it. Besides, plenty of people wouldn't even be able to handle human training pretransformation: pampered girls who'd never exercised in their lives, middle-aged women with flab in the gut, preschoolers who would fall over if they ran, old women who would stagger just from walking—it was unreasonable to gather up such people for combat training. That was why the Inspection Department never did it. You started with momentarily forgetting how you used your body as a human so you could learn to use the body of a magical girl freely.

But this time only, she could praise someone for being prepared. When Marguerite bit into the bone-dry preserved food, struggling to eat it without water, a plastic bottle was held out to her. The bottle label said OOLONG TEA, but the fluid inside was clear. Had the girl filled this at the river?

"Thanks." Marguerite accepted it and moistened her throat with a gulp. The lukewarm water slid down. Thinking that at this rate, she'd wind up drinking until it was gone, she kept herself to just three sips and tried to give the bottle back, but the girl raised her palm and shook her head. A different bottle was sticking out from a pocket in her uniform.

The girl put the preserved food in the pocket on the opposite side and stuck something like a piece of meat in her mouth and slowly moved her jaws up and down. It seemed like it wasn't raw meat, but Marguerite didn't know what she'd done to it. Clearly, this girl was ahead of her when it came to the outdoors, so it would be nonsense to advise her not to put something dubious in her mouth. Marguerite turned the oolong tea bottle upside down and stuck it in her butt pocket, holding it in place with her belt.

The two of them started walking again. Marguerite explained as best she could how strong and terrifying the goddess was. She thought she was getting across to the girl, who hadn't actually encountered her. At the very least, as she listened, her expression gradually stiffened up. If they ran into the goddess, they'd die—and to keep from running into her, they would find the others. With the goddess wandering about as she pleased, and the others hiding from her as they traveled the island, this would be very difficult to do as humans instead of magical girls. But regardless, they had to do it.

The girl stopped occasionally, closing her eyes, cupping her hands around her ears, and sniffing repeatedly. Marguerite thought it was weird, but now that she thought about it, she noticed belatedly that the girl had lost her glasses. Was she trying to make up for her poor vision with smell and hearing? She was also quite knowledge-able about plants and animals. As for Marguerite, she found a tree that bore grayfruit—though she couldn't even tell it apart from the other trees—and then, seeing the signs the fruit had already been plucked, she sighed.

She didn't feel like she could count on the girl so much as she felt creeped out.

Training yourself for activity as a human was going too far, for a magical girl. And preparing for if you lost your glasses was going beyond too far and entering the territory of madness.

Marguerite walked in the lead, and when they went over a rise in the ground, she turned back and held out her hand. The hand in her grasp was a little sweaty. She wasn't sure whose sweat it was. The girl's body felt hot. Her hand was soft, but there was a sort of callus that caught on Marguerite's middle, index, and ring fingers below the second joint. She was surprisingly light, and Marguerite was able to pull her up with just a gentle tug.

The words "Cranberry's children" reverberated in her chest.

The Musician of the Forest was the one to blame for that, not the victims who had been dragged into it. They were like child soldiers, born on the battlefield with no choice but to take up a gun. But even though she knew that, the echoes wouldn't disappear from her heart. Every time the girl displayed her abilities, her survival skills, her preparation for every situation, something unsettling crept over Marguerite.

As they were walking along the river to keep from leaving any traces, Marguerite went to stand on top of a big, flat rock, then pulled the girl up. The girl came to a stop there, putting her hands to her ears and closing her eyes, sniffed, and froze. Marguerite couldn't interfere or say anything to interrupt; she could only watch. The girl sniffed over and over, her face rising higher each time. She wound up standing on her tiptoes, and by the time Marguerite was wondering if she should say something and was reaching out, suddenly her face came down again and she went down flat against the rock.

Marguerite's brow furrowed. The girl was scrunching up her face, too. The girl looked up and back at her, and when Marguerite started saying something, the girl stuck her index finger up in front of her lips. Marguerite didn't see how the girl reacted after that. Rather, it was no time to be looking at her. A magical girl with a goddess motif was lumbering along on the other side of the river.

It was over thirty yards away, on the opposite side. She appeared suddenly. That was too close. If they had been transformed into magical girls, the encounter would not have been so sudden. They would have noticed before she got so close. Marguerite's heart made an aggressive leap in her chest, and all the blood in her body roiled up before withdrawing like the tide. Her knees felt like they would buckle, but she desperately held them up. She still hadn't let out her breath, and she couldn't breathe right. A goddess with a gray ax in her right hand and a red ax in her left was running—no, she was walking. Maybe a magical girl would call it walking, but seen from a human perspective, she was moving so fast it could only seem like running. Twenty yards. Fifteen yards. Their eyes met. The goddess stopped. They were dealing with a magical girl. But they couldn't transform. They were helpless. Marguerite immediately averted her eyes. The goddess turned her head around and pulled a little plastic case from her pocket, shaking it out to drop a bead into her hand. Marguerite had seen this before. Wasn't that a pill? It was difficult to tell from ten yards away, with human eyes. When she tried to look closer, her ears grew warm and started distracting her. The goddess leisurely put a pill in her mouth as if there were nobody there and swallowed.

Marguerite didn't inhale or exhale. The goddess turned her head around. She wasn't looking at them.

Our eyes met...but she isn't reacting at all...?

There was no way she hadn't seen. This close, it wouldn't be strange for her to have even picked up on the beating of their hearts. The goddess leaped high in the air like she was doing classical ballet, then spun around like a figure skater, swinging the axes in her hands around to match as she ran off. The hands holding her axes were making peace signs. Little pebbles scattered on the opposite shore to make ripples on the surface of the river, and then, a beat later, a spray fell like drizzling rain.

Why had the goddess ignored them? Marguerite remembered when she'd fought her in magical-girl form. She figured the goddess didn't rely on her eyes, but perhaps made use of some other sensory organ. Could that be the reason she had overlooked them?

Marguerite kept her eyes wide open to observe the goddess's every move. She moved differently from when they had fought before.

The goddess was going berserk and throwing all her absurd strength into this rampage. After some time, she had copied the way Miss Marguerite walked and done it herself, going from unsteady steps to an incredibly smooth pace. Now she was at a level even beyond that. She walked based on the style of the Inspection Department, with playfulness inserted at every opportunity, enchanting them with movements patterned off magical girls from anime. She performed martial arts blocks with a sideways peace sign, and also did eye gouges with a double peace sign. It was like the *xing yi quan* of Chinese kung fu, an idea that could be called a type of madness—and Marguerite had seen it before.

So she fought Chelsea.

Chelsea must have mastered that new concept for a fighting technique only from abundant talents and brutal efforts in training over a very long time, and her skills had probably been stolen easily in one fight. The odds were high that her life had been stolen at the same time. Marguerite could only pray that she'd managed to escape somehow, with the characteristic toughness of a veteran.

She let out a slow and gradual breath. The air that escaped her nose through her throat stung. The goddess left her field of view. Marguerite tried to move her head to watch her go, but her whole body was frozen. Her body trembling stiffly, she somehow managed to point her face that way, but the goddess was already gone. Marguerite's head swayed and her legs wobbled, and the disorder of her body told her of her deep relief. She suddenly felt a heat at her stomach, and when she looked down, the girl's head was there. She'd thought the girl had basically been on her belly, but now she was on her knees, head touching Marguerite's stomach as she held her spear at the ready. When the girl swayed like she was about to fall over, Marguerite supported her, embracing her with her right arm to bring their faces together.

"Um…the magical girl with the axes…," the girl began.

"That's the enemy."

The girl's lips bent, and she blew air at her own nose. Her bangs wafted upward, then fell. A crease formed in her brow, and she closed her eyes, and by the time she opened them again, the strength had returned to her expression.

With an anxious look that Marguerite couldn't interpret as anything other than one of concern for her, the girl asked, "Are you…okay?"

Marguerite couldn't bring herself to say, *"That's what I should be asking."* The girl was soaked with sweat from her forehead to her jaw, there were tear tracks under her red eyes, but her expression was still extremely serious, with not even the trace of being open to joking or smiling. Though she looked nothing other than completely exhausted, you could see strength of will and robustness of spirit in the light in her eyes.

"I'm all right… What about you?"

"I'm good to go."

Go for what, and how? The girl raised herself up and gazed in the direction the goddess had taken, which Marguerite considered to mean *"I can go after her."*

Marguerite shook her head. "There's such a thing as too reckless."

"If we follow her…then we can intervene if someone is attacked."

"That's what I'm saying is reckless."

"Why didn't she react to us at all?"

Clantail hadn't fought the goddess. She didn't know that incomprehensible terror of a creature that they couldn't even be sure was a magical girl. She didn't know her physical abilities, her magic— thinking this far, Marguerite thought, *No*, rejecting that. The girl's sweat-smeared face had even been stained with tears. It didn't seem like she had failed to understand how terrifying it was for a human to face a magical girl. Even if her heart rejected that understanding, her body was forced to understand, whether she liked it or not.

"If she didn't perceive us…there might be some way to do it." Unaware of Marguerite's thoughts, the girl wrung out a very clumsy attempt at persuasion. "I'll go alone."

"That's even more reckless."

"But…I think it will be dangerous…so…"

And then it clicked. Marguerite hadn't understood the principles behind this girl's behavior, but now she felt like she had it. This girl would try to prevent death, no matter what sacrifice it took. She didn't try to prepare herself for any situation so she could survive any situation. It was because she wanted to keep others from dying in any situation. She would use up all her grayfruit for someone she'd only just met and had hardly spoken with, and stand between her and the enemy with her spear raised, even as she gushed sweat and tears. She was throwing a tantrum like a willful child, saying she didn't want anyone to die—even though she should know whether that would work out.

Or maybe I'm wrong.

Was it less that she knew that, or rather that such knowledge had been forced on her, leading her to become like this? She knew she only had two small hands, she knew her desire to keep from letting go wasn't enough, but even so, she had to believe that a magical girl could do it, or she wouldn't be able to go on, was that it? How many times just that day had the words "Cranberry's children" risen and fallen in Marguerite's mind?

Marguerite bit her lip and took a breath, putting on a mature face to place a hand on the girl's shoulder. "You can't go alone."

"But—"

"I'll go, too."

The girl was surprised, her expression turning challenging, but before she could say anything, Marguerite told her based on her own experiences why she thought the enemy hadn't perceived them. While talking, she moved her feet, and they headed in the direction in which the goddess had disappeared. The girl's expression gradually turned serious.

Thinking that the girl had acknowledged her as not just someone to protect but also a partner she would at least allow to accompany her, Marguerite snorted as she acknowledged that she felt a little glad about that.

If heading into mortal peril was the life of a magical girl, then accompanying another to help them survive was also the life of a magical girl. So she thought with some cynicism, but the rough feeling in her heart had lessened more than she'd expected.

◇ **Pastel Mary**

Ragi had been talking about something that seemed incredibly important, and then, right when she had been thinking, *I don't really get it, so please explain things,* he had passed out. Mary really did need some TV drama–esque plot twist, but not in this way. She wanted to cry, but this wasn't the time for crying.

Before passing out, he'd had more energy than any old person

Mary knew. He'd been like an old master from a kung fu movie, that sort of mentor figure. She'd felt she could count on him.

Right now, Ragi was just lying limply on his side. He made her think of her maternal grandfather, who had passed away the year before. Just rolling over had looked painful for him, which had turned into not even being able to roll over, and then he'd grown so thin you could see the shape of his skull, and before long, he'd passed away.

"What do we do?" Mary asked. "This is probably because of that thing, right? The grayfruit ran out, right? If we can make him eat grayfruit, I think he'll wake up again."

"All right, then let's make him eat," Chelsea replied.

Chelsea took a grayfruit in her hand and did it the rough way: putting her hands on Ragi's upper and lower jaws and prizing them open by force. She crushed a fruit in her fist to dribble in the juice, then made him eat smushed remains of the fruit in an even rougher way: She just shoved it right into his mouth.

"W-will that be okay?" Mary stuttered. "It won't, like, get stuck in his throat like mochi at New Year's?"

"It's fine, it's fine. Look, he swallowed."

It looked painful, but the fruit in his mouth did more or less disappear down his throat—but Ragi still didn't get up.

Mary tilted her head. "Maybe…it's not enough."

"Then let's try giving him more."

"Hold on, Chelsea. How many should we feed him?"

"I don't know…"

"It'd be bad if we gave him all our grayfruit, right?"

"Yeah, that's true. If we make Grampa eat more grayfruit when we don't even know how many he needs, then we might run out, and worst case, he might not even wake up even after they're all used up. And then, if that happens, Chelmary's transformations will come undone."

Aside from that bizarre Chelsea/Mary ship name, Mary could get what she was trying to say. Ragi was passed out, but he was breathing for now. If his symptoms were the same as before, then they should have enough time that it'd be okay to leave him for the moment, and if something had happened to cause his magic power to run out like someone had said, even if he looked like he was going to die any minute, it shouldn't be a matter of life and death. But if Chelsea and Mary's transformations came undone, that would be a matter of life and death.

"Chelsea, how many grayfruit do you have left? I have four," said Mary.

"I have...two."

"So...isn't this bad?"

"Yeah...this is bad, huh?"

Ragi had passed out saying something about how to get out of this situation. Chelsea had caught him and laid him down on the back of a sheep, where he was sleeping and wouldn't wake up. If they used up the grayfruit to help Ragi regain his consciousness, then Mary's and Chelsea's transformations would be in trouble. Chelsea folded her arms with a troubled expression, but since she had both hands posed with her pinkie and index fingers out like Star Queen, it didn't feel very dire.

"Well, anyway...," Chelsea began, "Grampa was saying we should go to the main building, right?"

"Yeah, I think."

"He was saying to dig around the main building...um, where the wall was destroyed, right?"

Ragi had been enthusing vigorously like in an election speech. Mary had been so overwhelmed by all his vigor, she hadn't actually gotten what he was saying. She'd just been thinking, *Well, I should just go along with whatever he says*, and now they were in trouble. Pastel Mary bit into a grayfruit. The sweet juices didn't make her happy now. The number of fruit she carried had decreased by one more.

Chelsea maintained the Star Queen pose as she gazed at the grayfruit with a severe expression. Even Mary could predict that whatever she was thinking probably wasn't anything useful. And that was because Mary wasn't thinking anything useful.

Mary sighed and clapped a hand on Chelsea's shoulder. Chelsea jumped, and she looked back at Mary with surprise, cheeks red as she hopped back. "What're you doing?!"

"Aren't you going to the main building?"

"Oh…yes."

"Then let's hurry."

Ragi had won Chelsea over. There had probably been a lot of things she'd wanted to say, but when Ragi had preached to her about how a magical girl should be, she'd been convinced. And then Ragi had passed out. Chelsea could no longer argue back. She had no choice but to do as she'd been told, despite still feeling that actually she wanted to do something else. Even if she wanted to strike back at the goddess, even if she wanted to get revenge for Shepherdspie, she had no choice but to suck it up. From where Mary stood, the goddess magical girl and Chelsea were both so strong, they were ten levels beyond out of reach, with such incredible speed and power that Mary would say she'd never seen anyone else so strong. To her, it wasn't even about who was stronger—they were both strong. Who would win or lose seemed like it was just based on the luck of that moment.

But Ragi had said that Chelsea was never going to win. And Chelsea, who was always filled with baseless confidence, hadn't denied that. So that had to be true. Mary had experienced herself the phenomenon where someone with no practice in something would see a top-class amateur and a top-class pro as the same. But once you tried that activity yourself, you knew there was an unscalable wall. Those who enjoy art and draw whenever they have the spare time as well as art school students would all have found that wall to a greater or lesser extent.

Mary wanted Chelsea to fight. Mary wasn't used to cursing, but she wanted to yell four or five different words at the goddess magical girl, and she wanted Chelsea to beat her black and blue. There was no reason for Shepherdspie to wind up like that—Mary knew best of all how he'd devised his menu and worked to show the guests a good time. And while Mary had flubbed a lot, she'd handed over the invitations, cleaned the main building, and ordered the foodstuffs. Now that was all ruined. It had all been messed up. Shepherdspie could no longer sigh, or put a hand to his forehead, or look up at the sky, or wipe his sweat with a handkerchief.

Mary's head was swirling with doubts. *But... Still...*

It didn't seem that bad to have Chelsea fight for her because she herself couldn't fight. It's the obvious thing to request a specialist for something you're not good at rather than forcing yourself. But, but still, it was obviously better not to make Chelsea fight an enemy she couldn't beat. Ragi had been saying the same thing. Chelsea would know better who the stronger magical girl was, and Ragi would know better than Chelsea, so that business about it being the obvious thing to request a specialist held true here, too.

Noticing her sheep were bleating up a storm, Mary looked up at the sky to see smoke trailing over the trees. It was far away. But the stripe of smoke was dark and thick. Words that gave her bad feelings, like *violence*, *destruction*, and *unfairness*, rose in her mind one after another.

Mary poked Chelsea's upper arm, and Chelsea shrieked and leaped to her feet. "What're you doing?!"

"Chelsea, look."

When Chelsea saw where she pointed, her expression quickly grew concerned. "It's her! She's doing something bad again!"

"Hey, let's hurry to the main building... Since, um, if we don't make it in time...it'll be bad." Mary didn't come up with any specifics on how it would be bad. It wasn't that she couldn't think of any. She just really didn't want to confirm them by putting them into words.

◇ Navi Ru

This place had been made a waste disposal facility, but it was actually just a bunch of mud. It was just used for trash, since if you tossed in things you didn't need, it would sink down in the swamp. Being a pursuer of the academic, Sataborn was uninterested in anything he didn't need, leading to a crudeness in his waste disposal that would make even Navi grimace. Heedlessly creating a polluted area on the island where he lived himself was characteristically insensitive of the man, but even so, Navi could neither understand nor sympathize.

But this was the one time it was working out well for Navi. He had been giving the place a wide berth, thinking it was a bad idea to get close, but now he saw it as an unexpected fortune, bringing him such great results that he struggled to restrain his smirking.

"Ahhh! This place! Whoa!" 7753 cried out.

"Calm down! Don't move around without thinking!" Navi called back.

Putting on an innocent act by panicking and showing sincere concern for another was his specialty. He clamored loudly, letting himself temporarily forget that he'd been the one to cast that spell on Mana from behind to knock her out. He was also used to the acting trick of giving loud instructions in a clear voice even while he was panicking.

"Mana! What's happened, Mana?!" called 7753.

"I don't know! I have no idea what just happened!" Navi called back.

Having a yelling exchange across a bog with a woman in her nightwear and a tortoise was objectively extremely silly. If Clarissa had been a witness, she might have rolled around holding her stomach. His ability to act seriously in situations like these gave his act a sense of veracity.

Navi tentatively tried stepping into the bog, and when it started sucking him in, he hastily backed up. "It's no use! It doesn't look like I can go over to you!"

"I'm sorry! I can't, either!"

"Shit! What a disaster!" Hiding the joy in his heart, he plucked at his few remaining hairs and stomped in place with realistic acting.

The fruit Tepsekemei had eaten had not been a legitimate grayfruit. It was the same color, and had to smell the same, since a magical girl with a good nose had put it in her mouth without hesitation, but the stem area was shaped slightly differently. It had a curve that had been lacking in the original fruit. Had it changed from the pollution, or had Sataborn been developing a type that would grow well in polluted areas? Judging from how their transformations had come undone, it was no good. Navi was glad that

7753 had gone to that detached islet so thoughtlessly. If possible, it would have been even better if her transformation had come undone partway and she'd sunk into the bog, but you couldn't expect too much.

Well…

"Me and the little lady'll leave here for now!" Navi called.

"You can't! Please don't leave us behind!"

"Are you telling me to leave this unconscious lady lying here in a dangerous place?!" Given everything he had done, the lines, the acting, and what he was about to do, no words could be emptier, but 7753 hung her head apologetically.

"S-sorry…um, but I'd like you to save us, if possible!"

"Hold on there for a bit! I'll come back with Clarissa!" He took Mana's arm and raised her in his arms, then put her on his back, with her bags and all. She was light—but she was still almost one hundred pounds. She was carrying quite a lot, too. Just what had she packed in her backpack? The "seven tools of a detective" or whatever? Even a first-year preschooler would know you're not supposed to bring things you don't need on a field trip.

He went into the trees, and once he was out of 7753's field of view, he peeled Mana's backpack off and tossed it into the thicket. Now that was a little lighter. But an out-of-shape mage couldn't go carrying this for a long time. A tree hollow or a natural cave would be fine, or, worst case, he could dig a hole and toss her in there. There were a number of magical locks on Francesca. One of those was that she couldn't attack anyone inside a hole. A hole big enough to fit Mana's frame would be enough.

"Then wait there! You got that? Don't move from that!" Navi yelled the order at 7753, who was out of view, and started walking. He didn't relax his expression. He had things to think about.

He wasn't going to kill Mana or let her be killed. He wasn't going to go further than knocking her out when she wasn't expecting it. He wasn't going to let her father interfere. So long as he let Mana return home alive, then he could use the name of the Lab and the Osk Faction as a shield to keep those chumps at the Inspection

Department from meddling. The worst idea would be to make the man get desperate and not care about keeping his own skin safe. A cornered mouse would bite not just a cat, but even a tiger. And sometimes a tiger would catch an illness from that bite and die.

He would let Mana live. It could be difficult to calculate how the father would behave if he lost his daughter. But Navi also knew more than full well—at least double or triple that—just what a father with a daughter he treasured would not want done. While Mana could be a dangerous trigger, she was also his weakness. That's why Navi would let her live. He didn't really need to let anyone else live. He just wanted to keep Mana properly under control while she was on this island because she was a problem. And to that end, it was best to separate her from her fighters. With 7753, there was the issue of the goggles. Even if that was fine for now, it was bound to cause trouble later when she got them back. That was trouble that he could manage, given the current situation, but even so, trouble was trouble. It would obviously be best to get rid of them.

Navi walked along an animal trail for a while and came out to a more open area. The trees weren't as dense, and the sky was open above. Seeing trailing black smoke in the western sky, Navi narrowed his eyes. It was Francesca. It was good that she was being so proactive, but the fire was a problem. There were supposed to be installations in preparation for fire, including forest fire, but he wasn't sure how well they would be working in this situation. The initial fortune of Francesca and Maiya's encounter had been followed by the inexplicable misfortune of the magic power running out, and now that he'd been blessed with luck in the waste disposal spot, maybe the pendulum would be swinging back the other way.

But...I didn't expect a tortoise.

It was pretty rare for a non-mammalian animal to become a magical girl. It kind of stimulated what little remained of Navi's curiosity as a researcher. He drew back his chin, thinking that if things went well, he'd let it live. That would fulfill his debt for the bread he'd gotten. But that was just if things went well. Bad things happened when he got too greedy.

His greed would never run out. The trick to a comfortable life was to know where to make compromises.

◇ 7753

She immediately realized that she was no longer a magical girl.

She'd been 7753 until just a moment ago, but now Kotori Nanaya's swaying body was too much to handle, though she kept a hold on the tortoise anyway and immediately clung to the nearby tree to prevent herself from falling into the bog. Her shoulders heaved, and her palm felt like it would slip from sweat as she set the arm that carried the tortoise over it to support herself, bringing her whole body toward the tree, leaning against the trunk that was only thick enough for her to encircle with both hands. She wound up knocking her shoulder against the tree, and though it hurt, she was beyond worrying about it. She desperately hugged the tree, grasping it with no intent of letting go, until finally she let out a breath and turned back to see Mana with her eyes closed, being held up by Navi.

7753 got in a panic and tried to go back, and then the soft and sticky sensation she felt under her feet made her remember where she was, and she somehow managed to stop herself. This was a bog. A human and a tortoise were alone in a bog. She looked all around, feeling disoriented by this desperate fact. Since the area wasn't perfectly circular, some green was farther away and some was closer, but even the closer bits were too far to reach with a human jump. When she'd gotten here with 7753's legs in the first place, she'd bounced off something else halfway and made a second jump to finally arrive. And Tepsekemei, who flew in the sky, was now a tortoise that crawled on the ground. She was the round type, her shell about four inches in diameter—it seemed like it would break if Kotori squeezed a little too hard, even with the thin arms of a woman. She couldn't grab her too tightly.

After many exchanges, Navi put Mana over his shoulders and walked off. Kotori was left behind. She couldn't even converse with Tepsekemei. Her shell was cold, and there was no emotion in her eyes. There was a lack of humanity in a different sense from the usual Tepsekemei, who would confuse people by saying glib things with a straight face.

What am I thinking about a tortoise? Kotori thought, hanging her head. Of course she was lacking in humanity. She wasn't human. And when it came to becoming a different creature when you transformed, that was the same for all magical girls. Kotori Nanaya stayed 7753 as much as she could. Using the excuse that she could protect her heart if she had a magical girl's strength, she had continuously shaved down on her time as a human.

She crouched, leaning against the slim tree. She couldn't bring herself to sit on her bottom. She didn't like the idea of sitting down on this island in the bog in her pajamas. The bottoms of her feet were filthy, but that was fine. The bottoms of your feet are there to get dirty.

Kotori held Mei to her chest and looked at her face. The tortoise moved her legs like she was struggling and pulled her neck all the way in. Kotori sensed intellect in those movements and sighed. Right now, Kotori was weak. But there was still someone she had to protect. Right now, Mei was weaker than Kotori. Tepsekemei had always protected her, and now Kotori had to take care of her. Feeling this was kind of funny, she looked up.

Navi had said to stay here. But if she stayed here, she would stand out, whether she liked it or not. Her pajamas had orange and white stripes with KICK! in pink fuzzy font, making her stand out abnormally, smack-dab in the middle of this blackish bog as she was. She had to hide, at least, or she'd be in danger. But even if she dug a hole with a tree branch or her hands, she wouldn't be able to hide. Mana had carried off Mana's secret tools. 7753 had been thinking to keep Mana from being abandoned empty-handed if they got separated, but now her consideration had worked against her. 7753 had come along as a luggage carrier, so she should have carried Mana's luggage.

"Ah!"

Couldn't Navi have tossed over just some of Mana's things? Or wait, couldn't Navi have used his magic to help somehow? Kotori had been panicking, so she hadn't thought of it, and by the time she did, Navi was gone. Tears rose in her eyes, and Kotori looked up at the sky. The weather was pointlessly good. The sun was scorching her skin. *No, wrong idea*, she told herself. She'd just realized something that hadn't hit her before, so didn't that mean she'd calmed down a little? Then she could think. She might actually come up with a great way to get out of this situation.

First, she confirmed her situation. She was on an island in a bog. She had pajamas and a live tortoise. As for the rest, it was at most the elastic that tied her hair, the grass, and the earth. There had been grayfruit growing on the tree behind her, but they had been harvested by Tepsekemei and there were none left over. Those she hadn't eaten were in Kotori's pockets. Considering how Tepsekemei's transformation had come undone after she ate them, it would be best not to eat them herself.

"Why did you eat something funny, when your nose is so good?" she said to Mei with a sigh. The tortoise wiggled in her hands like she was uncomfortable and hung her head. Kotori didn't know how much had gotten across to her, but she kind of felt like they understood each other, and she felt relieved.

Couldn't she use the tree? It was a little over twice her height. If she climbed up to the top of the tree and jumped from there—she would get hurt and sink into the bog. No, maybe that depended on how deep the bog was. She should consider that maybe Navi had just been exaggerating. To test it, she tried putting her toe in, and then it felt like she'd be sucked in, so she panicked and drew it back. It would be no joke if she couldn't get back after a trial run.

What do I do…?

She felt like there was nothing she could do. In the end, was there nothing for it but to sit here and wait like Navi said? There were cans and some antenna-like things sticking out of the bog. The place looked to Kotori like it was for garbage disposal. If this bog was used for sucking up things people didn't need, then worst case, it was possible there was no bottom at all. This was a mage's island, after all, so it didn't have to obey the laws of physics.

But then, thinking about it the other way, because it was a

mage's island, what if some of the garbage had mysterious powers? She was about to put her right hand on her chin, and then she remembered she was holding Mei and put her left hand on her chin to consider.

Speaking of things on the island with mysterious power, for starters, there's the grayfruit, she thought, rolling the fruit in her hand with a scowl. Judging from Tepsekemei's current condition, these unfortunately weren't grayfruit. So aside from these. Fortunately, there were things around her.

"Don't move for a while," she told Mei just in case, though she didn't know if she'd understand. Then she got down on her knees on the green of the bog, grabbed some grass with her left hand, and reached out with her right. When her hand was just a few inches from a rusty can floating in the bog, the earth wobbled, and Kotori panicked and drew her hand back.

She wasn't even given the time to think about what had happened. The goddess, seen between the trees, rapidly got bigger. She was approaching. Before Kotori could even be surprised, the goddess was already there across the bog. Her heart leaped in her chest, and she tried to back up, but her back hit the tree. She was too panicked to even feel the pain. The goddess never stopped walking, coming closer. Kotori squeezed Mei, who was tucked into her clothing. She couldn't think. She had no mental space for anything. The goddess was drawing nearer. She was slower now. Even with her legs caught in the bog, she was forcing them through to walk.

Kotori noticed something strange. The goddess wasn't looking at Kotori. She was just walking as if she hadn't noticed her at all. Kotori timidly stood up and moved to the edge of the island. The goddess ignored Kotori's movement, continuing to cut through the bog, and then put her foot on the island. Could she not see Kotori? Or maybe she thought of her as the same as the trees and rocks?

A big branch was riding on the goddess's right shoulder. She'd just left it there and wasn't sweeping it off. The goddess took one step onto the island, and that impact made the ground shake. With the resistance of the bog gone, she continued to step forcefully on the land, so that single step was abnormally powerful. Kotori staggered and put her hands on the tree to stay up. The goddess paid no mind to that either, taking one more step forward.

Now?

She didn't even really get what "now" meant. She couldn't put this off. She'd either do it or she wouldn't—that was all. With a steady grasp on Mei, Kotori leaped onto the goddess's shoulder, the one the branch was not on. She didn't even know what her heart was doing anymore. She couldn't breathe, either. All she knew was that she was just desperately doing it. Though she didn't understand what she was doing, somewhere there was a voice saying that she had to do this, pushing her to move. The force of her leap started to knock her away, like maybe the way it would feel to body-blow a slow-driving vehicle. *No way, I'm not letting myself get knocked off,* she thought, reaching out, and her fingers caught the goddess's clothing.

She might die doing this. Because she was in human form, even just casually being swept to the side could easily kill her. But that didn't happen. Kotori put in all the strength of her body and soul and clung. If the goddess had been human, it would surely have hurt, but she ignored it. She crossed the bog like there was nothing on her shoulders, and when she got past the area in the ground that caused resistance, she sped up, and Kotori panicked and let go. She hardly caught herself and hit her back hard, winding up looking up at the sky and gasping.

The sensation of the impact she felt in her back gradually faded. She got up, and when she looked in the direction in which the goddess was going, there was already nobody there. It was just a line of muddy tracks. Kotori let out a deep sigh. The tears that had been building in the corners of her eyes flowed over her cheeks.

CHAPTER 15
SET FIRE TO THE HEART

◇ **Nephilia**

Everything was lit in orange. Nephilia once again looked up at the flame before her eyes. The phrase "heaven-piercing" seemed apt for the pinnacle blazing up high. It went over grass and over trees, and it had to be many times Nephilia's height. It extended over a wide range, with the wind blowing to spread its force even farther. When she touched her own face, it was hotter than body temperature, and she reflexively drew her hand away. When she touched her eyelashes, they'd hardened and were warping backward. Maybe she had been too casual about this, since magical girls were resistant to fire. She turned away from the fire to get a little farther from it.

"Little…furth…," Nephilia murmured.

"Yes, yes," Ren-Ren replied.

Nephilia buried her face in Ren-Ren's chest and clung to her, and by the time she felt that sensation of her insides floating, the fire was already far away. She put her chin on Ren-Ren's chest, and while getting a sense of comfort and ease from the softness that seemed to suck her in, she gently looked up at Ren-Ren's face. She was looking ahead with a serious expression. Her eyeballs were moving around rapidly. She was staying alert as she flew perfectly without Nephilia even asking, maintaining a low altitude and weaving among the trees.

Ren-Ren was mentally unbalanced. Nephilia had been thinking that she had to take care of her, even though she was wounded herself. But Ren-Ren was doing well enough that you could send her anywhere as a career magical girl and it wouldn't cause embarrassment. This had always held true—after the fire, before Agri's death, and after Agri's death. Ren-Ren was still Ren-Ren. That was a very frightening fact. While feeling the heat beneath her chin, Nephilia considered. If Ren-Ren had tried to deceive others, then maybe Nephilia would have noticed. But the one Ren-Ren had been deceiving was not others, but herself. That was why Nephilia had failed to notice it, and now Ren-Ren was still being Ren-Ren. Nephilia's nose had judged her "just right" as a nasty person, but just what about her was just right?

"…Ng…ah…"

"You don't have to force yourself to speak." Ren-Ren stroked Nephilia's head. That had to be a way of saying, *I understand even if you don't say everything,* but it made Nephilia shiver. It wasn't that she was cold from the oncoming wind she felt when flying through the sky. This was different from the chill that came up her sleeves and skirt while she skimmed the trees at high speed, making her hair stand on end. The chills she felt right now came from enjoyment.

The fire was narrowing the range in which living creatures could survive. The magical girls were also being pushed into a small area of land. With the trees being burned down, the grayfruit currently circulating would be the last of it. All of this would be convenient for them. This was their opportunity to negotiate. Since they had caused this situation for themselves, they would use it themselves. There was also the possibility that a safety system or something on the island would start up to put out the fire, but seeing as how the fire had spread this far, at the very least that was not a given. If there was a system, it would put out the fire manually, and if they were to use it, then it would be at the main building.

"Main...," Nephilia said.

"The main building, hmm."

The main building was near the center of the island. It would take some time for the fire to get that far. If a rational mage was alive—in particular Ragi, who had investigated the systems—then he would try to head to the main building. What would Clantail do? What did she think about Ragi? How were the seeds Nephilia had sown growing? There were lots of things to look forward to.

There was a cracking pain in her back that made her body spasm. It wasn't really that there were lots of things to look forward to. It was more accurate to say that she had to find even some small joys, or she couldn't go on.

◇ **Clarissa Toothedge**

Clarissa had a priority ranking for what to do. Number one was securing Rareko's safety, with protecting Yol very slightly behind that, and in an "if possible" position was eliminating Touta. She did think, *I'm not enthusiastic about doing stuff to a kid*, but that was no reason to oppose Navi Ru's will. She actually felt favorably about how thorough he was in removing anything that might get in the way. What was needed for success was neither mercy nor pity, and that was the truth.

After leaving the main building, she went off the path and cut across the forest. She chose to gracefully run among the tall trees, careful to keep from being found. Not just from Clantail. Even if it were someone else, having them say, *"Let's stick together"* would be a real hassle for her.

Fortunately, nobody found or questioned her, and Clarissa discovered what she was looking for. She always knew where Rareko was, after all. No matter where she went, the radar in Clarissa's head would tell Clarissa her position. While mentally cursing the damn girl for running around for no reason, Clarissa started calling out, "Hey wait" to Rareko's back as she was rapidly striding around the forest. Precisely speaking, she was only able to get as far as the "Hey." Clarissa's claws scratched at a transparent thing that whizzed through the air at her, which turned out to be the decoy for the stick thrust at her, which she evaded by a hair. Bending backward, she put her right foot forward and her left foot back, even putting her tail on the ground to support herself, maintaining this awkward position as she turned just her face to the other to glare at her and protest, "What're you doing?"

Rareko's tense expression contorted like *"I've screwed up,"* and she hastily folded up her staff and put it back in her sleeve, bowed at the waist, put her hand behind her head, and bobbed another bow. "I'm sorry... I thought I was being attacked."

"It's fine to carry a sense of tension, but, like, you've got to make sure to distinguish between enemy and ally." Clarissa ran a finger along her cheek to find a small amount of red fluid oozing there. *If I'd been careless and taken that hit, I'd be going to the hospital*, she thought, thanking her own reflexes.

Rareko chanted, "Sorry" as she reached out to the tree beside Clarissa and pulled out a lens—even if the glasses were part of her magical-girl costume, she'd cracked a lens from using it recklessly—and gave it a stroke. Just that little touch activated her magic, repairing the crack, and then she stuck it back in her glasses frames. She breathed a sigh. "I honestly am so sorry."

"Watch out next time, okay?"

"Yes, of course."

"Li'l ol' Clarissa will give you directions and advice, so make sure to do what you're told."

"Yes, of course. I'm sorry. I was just frightened... Um, it's, you know. I saw fighting. I thought there was no way I could win, and I was wondering what if I was attacked."

When asked, Rareko said that she had seen Chelsea and

Francesca fighting in the area and that then she'd left Yol, saying she was going to go save Chelsea. Now Clarissa knew that one of the magical girls who had fought Francesca had been Chelsea.

"What happened to Chelsea?" Clarissa asked.

"It looked like she ran away. I wasn't able to watch until the end, so I wouldn't know what happened after."

Telling her *"Watch them properly"* would probably make Rareko depressed, so Clarissa just said, "I see" and nodded. Rareko was usually mentally fragile to begin with, to say nothing of the current situation. If you were going to use her, then you needed to take that into consideration. It wasn't like she was completely useless. Her relating that Dreamy☆Chelsea was one of the magical girls they'd have to keep an eye on scored her a point. Clarissa decided to offer her some safety guidance—not necessarily as thanks for the information, but mental care and physical protection would be included. She was a little too unstable for Clarissa to order her to go back to Yol and protect the miss, so it would be best to have her be good and stay where she was.

Clarissa told her with an air of kindness that the magical girl costumed like a goddess would not attack a person inside a hole.

"Um, is that really—is that really true?" Rareko asked.

"What would be the point of Clarissa lying?"

But Rareko was still frightened and badgering Chelsea with questions. "Will that be okay?" "Is there really no problem?" Clarissa soothed her as she dug a hole in the ground with her claws and Rareko's staff and somehow got her shoved into it.

"This is okay, here? This is okay, right?"

"Clarissa told you to believe me... Hm?"

Rareko sniffed. Recognizing that weird scent was a burnt smell, Rareko immediately made a strange face and sniffed. Before long, a thin line of gray smoke came flowing in, and Rareko panicked and leaped out of the hole, and Clarissa glared in the windward direction. The volume and thickness of the smoke was rapidly increasing. Her excellent hearing even captured the crackling sound of branches bursting. This wasn't a fire in the middle of the wilderness. It was an island fire. It did sound kind of silly compared to an ordinary forest fire, since there was lots of water all around. But it was no joke at all for the victims who were caught up in the smoke and running around. The sound of the flames came even closer, and there was lots of smoke rising up, too. No matter how long a magical girl could hold her breath, enveloped by smoke while curled up in a hole, she would soon be a goner. Was Francesca the cause, or was it the magical girl she had attacked? Either way, they had to immediately abandon this safe spot that they'd made by digging up the earth. When Clarissa told Rareko that, she unsurprisingly panicked. She kept muttering under her breath things like "What's going on?" "Is this okay?" "Why is this happening?" Clarissa couldn't even tell if the questions were for her or not anymore. Rareko was looking restlessly around the area, head twitching around so much she was ignoring her footing. She stumbled over a root and started falling, and her own fall must have startled her, as she cried out and started to flee.

Clarissa hastily grabbed at the sleeve of her robe and reeled her in. "Calm down!"

"But! But this is—!"

Rareko really was pathetic. She was so incapable of adapting, you felt bad for her.

Her teacher had been so capable, she'd used events as an excuse to knock out a total of over a hundred people from the Archfiend Cram School, students and graduates. She'd had such a loyal and true character, she'd even get called a knight or a samurai, and she'd been showered with compliments in the vein of *diligent, upright, sincere, steadfast,* and so on. So naturally her master had held her in high regard, and she'd been entrusted status in the household beyond that of a magical girl. Even Navi Ru hadn't been able to lay hands on her so easily, and if he hadn't used the pretext of the will to call her over and set the experimental subject on her that had almost become a Sage incarnation, then her removal would have been difficult—she was just that remarkable a figure, and an imposing challenge as an enemy.

Yet as her disciple, Rareko had tragically failed to inherit her master's more abstract traits. She had so many things going for her: a powerful repair magic that Clarissa envied, staff and martial arts skills taught directly by Maiya, physical abilities that had been trained up, and an eye for tactics, and she wasted it with her personality. She was underhanded and cowardly and made others do everything for her, blindly following their lead. An opportunistic weather vane who firmly maintained that good things came from her own effort and bad things were other people's fault, she was cold to the weak, flattering to the strong, cynical, and a whiner. Clarissa hadn't known her for long, but even she could make out a long list of nasty things to say about her.

She really was impressed that Maiya had been able to deal with her. Would Clarissa be able to control Rareko perfectly right now? She felt like she could not. She told her to calm down and soothed her and stroked her back, and then she ran off in the lead to just get away from the fire for now. The sound of Rareko's footsteps followed.

Clarissa flicked a glance backward to look. Rareko was still glancing all around as she ran, and behind her, speckles of smoke were spreading in pale and dark gray. Clarissa faced forward again, and with the claws of her right hand she cut down a branch. She did it out of concern for Rareko, thinking that if she ducked under the branch to avoid it, it might hit Rareko behind her, but there was no word of thanks from that certain someone who was running scared behind her.

What do I do?

Beyond the mental burden of Rareko's presence, Clarissa really couldn't help but think that she was a bomb in the physical sense. To put it in Navi terms, this one could pull anything if she got freaked out. Even before the fire had started, she'd been so on edge, coming to attack Clarissa after hardly looking at who she was. Now that there was a fire, she had to be even more freaked out than before—was it a good idea to have her as an ally at this point?

Clarissa asked herself, *Is this an emergency?* and answered herself, *Yeah, it's an emergency.* Maiya was gone, and it was a good time to escape, once they'd had Rareko do her job. The only person you could say was definitely dead was Shepherdspie, who had gone completely still, and they couldn't read the situation on anyone else, which was a little scary. If Francesca continued on her spree, then fine, if the tables were unexpectedly turned on her, then fine—she'd done her job at this point. When you considered the number of grayfruit left as well as the pace of consumption, they couldn't be standing around doing nothing.

Clarissa bounced up to a ledge at a good tempo and casually avoided a branch that was jutting out in her way. Right after that, she heard a smothered shriek from behind, and she finally made up her mind. Rareko was dangerous. This magical girl trained under the devil instructor Maiya was so worked up that she couldn't even dodge a branch.

Clarissa started running again and looked back. The smoke was growing distant. The smell was distant, too. Rareko was the same.

Clarissa leaped over a tree root and changed direction to the left to leap again. She was headed for the main building.

◇ 7753

7753's heart was hammering so hard, it almost made her believe it was jumping up and down, but it gradually settled. Though she'd been feeling like her body and mind were too much to handle, now she finally had them back, and, still carrying the tortoise, she pushed herself into a sitting position. The goddess had been there until a moment ago, crossing over the bog, and Kotori had made use of that to escape from the middle of the bog. That had not been a hallucination. The footprints that continued from the bog indicated it was a fact. Kotori moved over the grass on her knees and brought her face close to the footsteps. The mud had still not yet dried.

She stood up and shook her head. Since suddenly turning back to human form and being so occupied panicking, freaking out, and cringing in fright, she couldn't quite remember what her surroundings had looked like. But she had to know which way Navi went or she wouldn't be able to meet up with him.

Kotori quelled her fear and examined the land around her once more. It was fair to call this a unique place on the island. A very toxic-looking swampy land spread out over the whole area, with a little islet all alone plop in the center that had one sad-looking tree and some grass growing around it. No matter which way she turned, all around the bog were rows of trees of varying sizes. Frankly speaking, it all looked the same.

On her first step, she trod on a pebble, cried out in pain, and held her foot. She should have at least put on some sandals. She'd taken it seriously and not doubted it when Mana had said a professional magical girl would never undo her transformation, and this was the result.

Wait, wait, no, no. Don't think that.

Give her a moment, and she was trying to make this someone else's fault. Was that because of her weak human heart? Or was she just shifting the blame for her own personal weakness onto all humans in an attempt to escape responsibility?

Kotori tensed her stomach, opened her eyes wide, and bit her lower lip to keep from missing any signs. With a will that it was fair to call decently strong for Kotori, she restrained her fear, her regret, and all other such negative emotions. It was kind of strange, but she felt like she'd gotten a bit of confidence. Up against the fearsome goddess who had made even strong magical girls like Marguerite and Tepsekemei flee, not only had Kotori touched her, she had tackled and clung to her, and yet she was still alive. She had managed to protect Mei. So she should also be able to protect others.

The forest unfurled over on the other side of the bog, and she caught sight of a bit of an area where the earth was exposed. That was the place. When they'd been walking on that path, Tepsekemei had found the tree in the center of the bog and had flown over to take the fruit. After that, Kotori had been left behind on the little island, and Navi, who had been talking with her, would have been basically around there, and then he'd turned exactly 180 degrees to head off into the forest, carrying Mana. In other words, wouldn't that mean the goddess had come from the direction in which Navi had headed? Though the goddess had ignored Kotori and Mei and they'd gotten through the situation without incident, she would not necessarily overlook Navi and Mana—no, she wouldn't overlook them, would she? Kotori didn't know what the goddess based her judgments on or what her sensory abilities were, but you didn't have to compare them to a powerless human and a tortoise—she probably wouldn't go ignoring mages.

Kotori ruminated on these facts she'd just realized, and as she came to understand just how fearsome this was, her face stiffened up, her shoulders trembled, her knees trembled, and she crossed her arms in front of her to hug Mei tightly to her chest.

Oh no!

Kotori started running off with Mei in her arms but immediately stopped. A slimy feeling caught her feet; they felt horribly heavy. When she looked at the ground, wondering what was going on, she was buried up to the ankles. She panicked and leaned backward, dragging her ankles out of the ground. She brought her face close to the ground to see what it was and found that the color here was slightly different from the place where her feet had been caught. When she tried touching it, the difference became even more clear. The place where she was standing was soft earth, while the place where she'd been caught was claylike bog.

She looked ahead. The trees and foliage kept her from seeing the ground, so she shoved some plants aside to bring her face close to it. When she touched the ground around here, it felt not much different from mud, but it was different from the bog. Plants grew from it, and it didn't look like mud at a glance, either. But it was nastier than mud that looked like mud. You couldn't tell from its appearance where you would sink.

Kotori stood up and looked around the area. She couldn't

go over there in a straight line. She took a slightly different path, figuring she should take a bit of a roundabout route, and then stopped. She squatted and looked down under the thickly growing leaves. The stems of the greenery before her were dense, with long, sharp thorns. Even if she did suck up the pain and keep going, she wouldn't be able to walk anymore with ripped-up feet, let alone run—though as a magical girl, she could have ignored these thorns and walked on.

Agh, good grief!

Even a roundabout route was fine; she just had no choice but to go. It made her really antsy, but right now the long way was the shortest route. Kotori walked the opposite way from her goal. If she could just reach the path, she could return to comparative safety. She prayed to God and to Navi that they would hide themselves from the goddess and somehow make it through.

She sucked up all the things that would have been better if she were just transformed into a magical girl—the worries that someone might die, the fear that she might be killed, the way her heart asserted itself just from running, the blaring sun, the gross feeling on the bottoms of her feet—and, telling herself that she could do this, with the hem of her pajama top fluttering, she ran as hard as she could.

◇ **Navi Ru**

There had been a number of accidents.

The first was running into Francesca briskly striding along. This wasn't a big deal. Navi knew how not to be attacked by Francesca—he knew how he should reply to her question. He wouldn't want anyone else hearing it, but fortunately Mana on his back was unconscious. No one was listening. With a few words, he got past Francesca, who was now harmless to him. Seeing her feet dirtied with mud, her mussed hair, and the burn marks on her toga, he thought with some sarcasm, *Sorry to cause you trouble*, and, seeing the little hole that had been dug in her forehead and the red body fluid oozing from it, he wiped away cold sweat, wondering, *What kind of monster did that?* Even just getting burn marks on her and cutting her hair was pretty impressive, but someone making her bleed was even more outrageous than what Clarissa's report had said. Francesca should have been able to take an attack that would cause a regular magical girl's face to fly off, shatter her skull, and turn her exposed brains to chopped meat. Francesca's skin would block it, and she'd take no damage. Navi hadn't been directly involved with her development, so he'd just memorized what numerical specifications he could, but he doubted the researchers at the Lab would write down the wrong numbers.

The world was really big. But this island was small. If he continued on down the path like this, there was no guarantee he wouldn't run into someone, just as he'd encountered Francesca a moment ago. And there was no guarantee it wouldn't be the magical girl who had injured Francesca. If said magical girl was alive, she would have to be pretty on edge from fighting with Francesca. If he ran into her, accidents might happen. That would be a problem.

After some walking, Navi took a turn into where plants and shrubs lay thicker, then walked thirty paces and hid himself in a thicket, bit into a grayfruit, and cast a spell. The soft earth warped like it was peeling up, ripping the roots of grass to make a big hole. Decently satisfied by the size, which was big enough that an adult man could sit in it holding his legs, he tried to lay Mana down inside the hole. He couldn't go throwing her in roughly; she might break something. He held her gently in a princess carry and slowly lowered her in. He gingerly and carefully laid her down in the hole, and, with a snort, thinking this was just like playing with dolls, he wiped the sweat off his forehead, set a hand on the ground, and stuck up one knee.

There was the sound of the wind rustling in the leaves and the cry of a bird in the distance, but nothing else. He raised his head more cautiously than when he'd lowered Mana and looked over the thicket to the path. Nobody was there. He breathed a sigh of relief, but of course this wasn't over yet. He pushed through the thicket and returned to the path, then went back the way he had come. He was stepping faster now that he'd unloaded one girl's worth of burden. He went off the path and returned to the bog where the stench wafted, and right as he was thinking, *Okay, what am I gonna do about 7753?* his brow furrowed. He narrowed his eyes and looked around the area. He could have sworn there'd been a tree growing on the island where 7753 and Tepsekemei had been stuck. Now dots of mud were splattered at the edge of the bog, and not just that—prints of bare feet in the mud continued into the forest—the opposite direction from the one Navi had come from—to disappear.

What had happened? What did this mean? If these footprints were 7753's, then that meant she'd gone across the bog and moved on, though he didn't know why. But that was impossible. Navi scratched around his eyebrows with an index finger. Even just touching them with his nails, he felt that they were greasy. He put his hands on the ground, and on all fours, he glared at the footprints that went across the bog. Not only were they in the mud, but they also went in deep. There had been force in the steps. These were not those of a human. These were from a magical girl—a particularly strong one.

Francesca?

7753 in her human form had been barefoot, but Francesca's costume didn't include shoes, and she was also barefoot. Navi recalled the position and the distance at which he'd encountered Francesca. She wouldn't have been just going single-mindedly in a straight line, but from this close, well, you would come to the bog. And those footprints had to be from Francesca coming out of the bog. When he looked closely, there were also broken trees and brush that had been kicked aside.

It seemed to him that being sunk into the bog by Francesca would be a fair ending for 7753. But even if 7753 was dead, Francesca lacked the consideration or care to finish someone off without spilling blood. From what he could see, not only were there no scraps of clothing, there wasn't even any fresh blood from the victim—wasn't that strange?

He stood up, and after he rubbed out the wrinkle between his eyebrows, something vibrated at his waist. It was his magical phone. On this island, there were limited ways to use the magical phone to make contact. Navi pulled his magical phone out of his pocket and confirmed that the caller was Sataborn. The punch line here was not that someone dead was calling him, or that Sataborn was actually alive.

"This is cute li'l Clarissa."

"Why is cute li'l Clarissa over there?" Navi asked her.

"Clarissa got Rareko to fix the place that Chelsea destroyed and went into the underground room."

A transmitter was installed in the underground lab that was far more powerful than the handheld type. Even if you couldn't communicate between magical phones, you could communicate from the transmitter—just like Clarissa was doing right now.

"You don't see any smoke?" said Clarissa.

"Oh, that." Trees arched overhead, hiding the sky from him. Navi took three steps back and looked up. There were more streaks of smoke than he had seen before. There were two. And one of those was thicker than before.

"D'you know the cause?"

"Nah. I figure it's either Francesca or her opponent, though."

"Clarissa got caught up in that smoke, then it seemed like it was probably a bad time to be hiding."

"True, there's no helping that, huh? But that's no reason to go to the main building."

"Clarissa figured I'd get Rareko to do her job right away. Clarissa made her repair the entrance to the underground and also lowered the carpet you sent up high to have her fix that thing."

"Whoa, whoa, whoa, whoa, that's more than you can do without consulting with me. Does the good little girl Clarissa pull that much on her own discretion?"

"It's 'cause Rareko was freaking out so hard about the fire that she could pull anything. Clarissa'll have her do the work we really need her doing for starters, and then get her to be quiet and toss her in somewhere. Isn't that the best way to solve things?"

He could easily imagine Rareko cringing in fear. Just as Clarissa said, you didn't know what she might pull, and that was risky. If something funny happened before he'd accomplished his goal, this would go beyond unforeseen and into failure.

Eliminating Maiya had gone well. Now there was nobody to get in the way of him getting close to the next generation of great nobles—to Yol. And then, if his second major goal went well—to acquire the relic of the First Mage from the inheritance and have Rareko repair it, then Rareko's job would basically be done, too.

There had been two full-time magical girls employed at Yol's house. Maiya and Rareko would both often attend the young lady while she went out. If you added, *"Come bringing two magical girls,"* that would generally lead to Maiya and Rareko coming with her. That was exactly why Navi had added such a condition to the will. It was absolutely impossible to falsify a will that had been bound by magic, but just sticking on a transparent film that had been developed in the Lab to add additional conditions that wouldn't contradict the others would not generate issues. He'd made the transparent film as thin as possible so that no magical girl or mage would notice, no matter how sensitive. He had invited Maiya in order to eliminate her. Rareko he'd invited in order to have her repair the gear on the island.

"...Fine, I get it," said Navi. "I get how competent you are. Make sure to put away that gear. It's not for me to use. A far, far greater idiot...whoops, honored personage wants it, so we can't have any dust or nicks on it. It's a special package going up."

"Aye, sir."

"So how are you gonna quiet Rareko down?"

"Clarissa whacks her in the head from behind and kicks 'er down, and then strangles her or whatever to knock her out, right? Then Clarissa ties her up and tosses her underground."

"Don't kill her by accident or something."

"Clarissa is making her finish the job first, so it'll be okay to kill her by accident."

That was logical. Navi did basically warn her, saying, "Don't kill her if possible. There'll still be ways to use her, even after leaving the island," and Clarissa answered, "I know that." She probably did actually know. But there had been a lot of unforeseen events in these past two days.

"Oh yeah, things have been tough on my end, too," said Navi. "I dug a hole near the waste disposal area and put Mana in it. 7753 and Tepsekemei are probably dead, but they might be alive. They have some grayfruit, but it seems like they're bad or poisonous ones, so don't take them and eat them."

"...What happened?"

"Lots of things happened, okay? Lots." Navi put a hand to the back of his head. It really did feel oily.

◇ **Touta Magaoka**

It was very hard to tell Yol that he couldn't trust Rareko. And what was more, given Yol's level of trust for Touta, actually winning her over would be really difficult. Yol and Rareko had an accumulated history together that Touta didn't know, and all Touta could say were things like *"I thought this"* or *"I felt that,"* and he had no tangible proof. He couldn't be all cool and resolute like a boy detective and say, *"She's the culprit, and here's why."*

So Touta took action. Rather than hiding where their meeting place was, behind a square rock standing right at the foot of a little hill, he probed around the area under the pretext of checking things out. He looked around, searching to see if anyone had left signs, or if there was something that could be a hint as to what to do.

While returning to Yol, he expanded the range of his search, and when he came out by the side of the river, he leaned out over a big rock to look around the area, and when he happened to look at his palm, it was wet. On top of the rock he'd just been placing his hand on, there was a wet spot in the shape of a circle. It was a little ring. When he considered about what size it was, it hit him that it was the size of the 350-milliliter plastic bottles they sold at the convenience store, and he cried out a little "Ah!"

It was the bottom of a plastic bottle. Someone had put a plastic bottle here, and it was still wet. Which meant that not much time had passed. He looked around once more and confirmed that no one was around. But the person shouldn't be far. If they went now, maybe they could catch up.

Touta went back and explained. A magical girl would not have to eat or drink, so they wouldn't need a plastic bottle, either. The one who had placed the bottle on that rock would be either a mage or a magical girl who was detransformed, so it couldn't be a bad magical girl who was being violent.

"It was still wet," Touta said. "Not much time has passed. Let's follow them."

"But Rareko's still not back," Yol said, sounding very pained. Touta could sense her feelings, and his expression became pained, too. If Rareko had beaten the bad magical girl and saved Chelsea, then she would have come back already—since magical girls were very fast to fight and to move. But he couldn't say that.

"Couldn't we—? I know…how about we leave something? We make a mark so she knows we came this way. If we do that, then if Rareko follows us, we can meet up."

Yol still seemed pained. But they couldn't miss this chance. They didn't know where the person they had to follow was headed, and that person was getting farther and farther away.

That was when a pungent burnt smell wafted their way, and by the time they noticed it, a thin line of smoke was trailing toward them. It was a fire. Most likely, the bad magical girl had set it. Touta panicked, and Yol panicked, too. This was very bad. He'd heard more than enough during fire drills that it was bad to inhale smoke. And he didn't need anyone telling him that it was bad to get burned by fire.

"Hey, are magical girls strong to fire and smoke?" Touta asked.

"They won't get burned by just a little bit of fire, and I don't think they can get carbon monoxide poisoning or things like that…but they do breathe, and they do need oxygen, so it's not as if they can survive in the smoke."

"Then that means…"

"Yes. Even a magical girl will try to run from fire and smoke." Yol wore a very pained expression.

Touta thought his expression had to be similar. Each of them could tell what the other was thinking. If magical girls needed to run from fire, then that bad magical girl would also run from the fire. And then Rareko wouldn't come to the place she'd promised— behind the square boulder that stood conspicuously at the base of the hill. Touta poked his face out from behind the rock and looked up at the sky. He felt like the smoke was closer than before. He felt like the burnt smell was getting stronger. If they kept hiding like this, they might get caught in the fire.

He pressed his chest. Bearing with the burnt smell, he took three breaths in and out. He took the biggest breaths he could. But he still breathed out slow. Yol took a bite out of half a grayfruit, then wrapped it in paper and tucked it into the pocket of her robe. She had been eating only bit by bit, saving what she had, and when they had come here, they had found three whole grayfruit. But despite that, now there was just half a fruit left. The speed at which Yol ate them kept accelerating. She'd noticed it herself. But there was nothing they could do about it. Touta didn't know why it was happening. There was just nothing for it but to eat so that she didn't keel right over.

"…I don't think we'll be able to stay here," Yol expressed, like it was painful to say.

Touta was privately relieved to hear that. Even if he wanted to be the one to say, *"Rareko isn't coming back, and it's hopeless to stay here at this rate, so let's just go,"* that would be hard to say aloud. Even as he felt relieved, he silently apologized for his relief and nodded. "Yeah. I think we'll really be out of luck if we get caught up in the smoke and fire. Like I suggested before…how about we leave a mark here that Rareko would recognize?"

With a feather pen and red ink, Yol drew a figure on a plain card that she said was "a crest passed down for generations in our family" of a circle, triangle, and square combined, and then she set the card on a rock and cast a spell. The rock dented in with a crack-ing sound, and that figure was carved on its face. An inch away, she also carved an arrow that indicated the direction in which they were going. Touta cried a sincere "That's so cool!" and applauded her. Yol seemed shy as she urged, "Let's hurry and go." Maybe the magic was simpler than Touta thought.

Touta considered whom they could rely on most right now. That seemed like the most important thing for him and for Yol. With him alone, or even the two of them together, it was difficult to protect themselves. Touta wanted to be cool and say he'd protect Yol, and he did mean to do what he could to protect her, but he doubted he would be able to do that if an enemy showed up. He figured his aunt would say, *"If you can't do it even if you try, then there's no point."*

"I think…I'd like to meet up with Marguerite," said Touta.

"That's the magical girl who accompanied you here, isn't she?"

"She's really strong. I've heard she's beat up lots of bad guys."

Yol went, "Hmm," touching just the index finger of her right hand to her chin. "Rareko might look unreliable, but she's strong, too."

"Oh, um, I don't mean at all to speak badly of Rareko in saying this. Um, I mean I can trust Marguerite."

"We can trust Rareko, too."

"Ah, yeah…"

"And if you're talking about trust, we can trust Uncle, also."

"By 'Uncle,' you mean Navi?"

"Yes. Our families know each other, and he's always treated me well."

"Ohhh."

"It was just for a brief time, but there was apparently talk about making him a fiancé."

"A fiancé? For who?"

"For me."

"…Huh?!"

"Surprising, isn't it? It's such a large age gap, one would normally refuse. But you know, he was so considerate of me, saying, 'Only if you'd like.' Since he's such a kind man."

"Uh, yeah…oh…mm-hmm."

Yol chuckled, putting her hands to her hips and lowering her head to peer up at Touta from below. There was a mischievous smile on her face. "My late great-grandmother and Maiya were very against it, so the talk evaporated, but… Ahhh!" Yol cried out and ran.

She didn't hear Touta's call of "Watch out!" trying to stop her, either, and she did a baseball slide into the thicket. Touta tried to follow her, saying, "What are you doing?" but then as she was coming out, her forehead struck his, and Touta arched backward. That had been a pretty loud *clunk*. But he sucked it up somehow, touching his hand to his forehead as he looked at Yol.

Yol wasn't bothered by her reddened forehead, her eyes on what lay in her palm. There were four grayfruit.

"Four?! What the?!" said Touta.

"I could see they were growing right close to the ground on the other side of the brush." She seemed happy.

Touta was also glad. He *was* glad, but he paused a moment to consider. He tried looking around the area again. Touta had also gone by here on the way to the river. But he hadn't been able to find any fruit. He considered, *hmm, hmm,* for a little while and realized, *Yol is shorter. So then if she's crouched down, moving slowly as she pays close attention, she'd find fruit somewhere you wouldn't find it just from normally walking around with your eyes up high.*

It's important to look at things from a different point of view, huh? he thought with a little embarrassment as they kept going, reaching the river. Though it had dried a little, the mark that looked like it was from a plastic bottle was still there.

"But…," Yol wondered, "which way did they go?"

"Well, you know. We find that out now. We don't have time, so let's do it quick."

He'd thought that it would be hard, but they easily found signs of people. There were a lot on the opposite side of the river—shattered boulders, pebbles blasted away, exposed ground—whoever would do this was probably the one on a rampage. They had to have been stomping hard, as they'd left many footprints in the shape of bare feet, with even the shape of each individual toe made clear. The toes were pointed downstream, in the opposite direction from the fire.

Touta considered. The one who'd left the wet plastic bottle and the violent one were probably different people. There were no signs at all of destruction on this riverbank. It was very strange that the plastic bottle had been set down gently, while on the other side there had been a lot of violence. If they were different people, what would happen then? What would they do?

The one they wanted to follow was the one with the plastic bottle. The violent one, if anything, they wanted to avoid.

Touta narrowed his eyes. He would change the way he thought. He would change his point of view. If the person with the plastic bottle had headed upstream, then after seeing this smoke, they would have turned back the other way. But they hadn't come back. Had they headed someplace with no connection to the river, or had they gone downstream, or neither way? It was worthwhile to proceed downstream.

The problem was that the person on a wild rampage was also headed downstream. But from how the one who had left the plastic bottle wasn't lying here and from how there were no marks of blood anywhere, you could tell it wasn't like something had happened to them right away. It wasn't like something had suddenly been dangerous.

Touta shared his thoughts with Yol. She gave a, "I see, I see," as she listened, but when he suggested they go downstream, she tilted her head. "Wouldn't that be dangerous?"

"But if you look at it from a different angle, I think it might not be. If she's doing all this while traveling"—he glanced at a boulder that had been completely smashed—"then she'll be making a lot of noise, right?"

"That's true."

"So then if we sneak along quietly, then even if she does notice us, wouldn't we notice her first? So long as we don't slip up and pop out in front of where she's headed, I think it would be safe to follow."

"Magical-girl ears are good, but…it's true, you have a point." Yol looked at a fallen tree and nodded. "I actually think perhaps we should run in the opposite direction."

"Mm-hmm."

"But in the other direction is a fire."

"Yeah, huh." To use a sort of adult expression, he thought they didn't have many options. Touta thought that if they were to choose from the few they had, then this was a good one.

Yol waffled a little and then bit off a third of what was left of her half of a grayfruit and nodded one more time. "If the time comes, I'll protect you."

"Hey…I'll be protecting you."

They looked at each other and both burst into giggles at the same time.

◇ **Rareko**

Rareko had spent her life worrying about what other people thought. To someone who lived at the bottom of society, such observation skills were a lifeline. Without them, you would die. That was why she polished them. No matter how Clarissa tried to cover it, Rareko noticed that she was agitated about the fire. Clarissa had tried to hide it. She'd acted like it was nothing and put on a smile like it wasn't a problem at all. And Rareko had panicked.

She couldn't let it show. If Rareko were to go against Clarissa because she couldn't count on her anymore, then Clarissa would think of her as disadvantageous. If someone who operated based on what was most advantageous to themselves were to consider her disadvantageous, then she'd get cut off. Rareko operated based on what was advantageous to herself, so she was sensitive to subtleties like this. Even if she was a mess inside, she would make sure to follow Clarissa's instructions. Clarissa was still her only hope, just like before the fire.

But despite assembling such logic in her head, she couldn't stop her illogical areas from getting upset. Navi should have been able to keep a handle on this mess—Rareko had done all of this because she'd assumed he would. So if they were going to tell her at this point that he didn't have a handle on things, she was stuck thinking, *What do I do?*

Clarissa said they were going to the main building, so Rareko followed her, watching that small back run in the lead. She was so focused on that, she failed to dodge a branch, and it hit her in the forehead, and she got even more upset. But nevertheless, they somehow got back to the main building and, following along the outer wall from the front entrance, they circled to the side. They headed thirty yards to the right and came up to the wall that Chelsea had brought down. Since she had completely destroyed it, you could see the hallway from the outside.

Clarissa stood in front of the broken wall and muttered, "I think it was here," then spread her arms wide and stared upward. Rareko wouldn't say she was imitating her, but she looked up, too. Clarissa muttered a spell, and a little dot gradually became bigger, and by the time Rareko realized it was a carpet that flew in the sky, it had already come down to within arm's reach.

Clarissa picked up the wooden box that was placed on top of the carpet and handed it to Rareko. Rareko accepted the rectangular, face-sized wooden box on her upturned right palm, and Clarissa undid the purple string with just her index finger and thumb, gingerly opening the lid to show her the contents.

"Put this back how it was, 'kay?" said Clarissa.

"This gear, you mean?" Had she noticed Rareko's voice was trembling?

Rareko narrowed her eyes right up until she almost couldn't see anymore, then slowly opened them and looked into the box. The gear was old, old enough that she couldn't tell how old, snapped in two and sitting diagonally in the wooden box. Rareko swallowed. She was feeling overwhelmed by a mere object, and a broken one. She wondered what it was, but she clenched her teeth, thinking it was surely a bad idea to ask.

She timidly reached out and touched it. It just felt like metal. But goose bumps stood on her skin. She wanted to let go of it right away, but she also felt like she wanted to keep touching it forever. With a single stroke of the two parts, Rareko repaired it. She let out a big sigh. She didn't even need the time to blink before the old junk was the original gear again. "Your magic is amazing, no matter how many times I see it," Clarissa said, but Rareko didn't know how to react to the praise, and shook her head vaguely.

The gear that had been repaired with magic went back into the original wooden box to be sent together with the carpet high into the sky. It shrank into the distance with a muttered spell from Clarissa, just the opposite from how it had arrived. Rareko felt lonely to see it go, flying into the air, and that feeling frightened her. What was that, really?

After the gear, she repaired the crumbled wall. She didn't feel any spiritual pressure from this task. But there was earth stuck in between some places, and she had to properly sweep it clean so that it wouldn't get in the way. She had Clarissa help as well, and they got the earth and dust out of the way. She prodded the wall with the end of the broom used for cleaning, and with a *clunk*, the crumbled wall was reassembled in an instant. The hallway that had been visible from the outside was hidden, and the wall was safely back to how it had been.

"Here, this is your reward for now," said Clarissa.

"Oh, yes, thank you." Five grayfruit were rolled toward Rareko, which she hastily accepted.

As for why she had to bother to fix the wall, Clarissa showed her the answer to that question. She muttered a spell just like before and shoved at one brick in the wall, and then the ground swayed. The grating sound of rock rubbing against rock rang out. As was her obvious right, Rareko panicked, readying her staff as she looked all around, and then her eyes stopped at the ground at Clarissa's feet. A spot that had just looked like ground shuddered and opened up, splitting right to left, making a square hole of about two and a half feet by two and a half feet, and then the shaking and sound stopped. Clarissa's lower body dropped into the hole. Though Rareko was so shocked her heart could stop, Clarissa slipped on inside without explanation. From inside the hole, she called out, "Wait right there!" and Rareko timidly approached and looked down. Inside was dark, but a magical girl would be able to see. The walls of the hole were not natural, but smooth as if they had been filed down after being cut. There was a metal ladder that went downward.

Rareko wasn't sure if she should follow, and then, as if reading her mind, a voice called to her, "Clarissa's gonna contact the mister, so keep watch!"

Rareko turned her face to the sky and blew out the breath she'd kept stored in her chest. It wasn't like she didn't feel dissatisfied about being put on watch after having been used for all that, but maybe it was better than being ordered to follow Clarissa into a suspicious underground room.

She turned away from the underground entrance. Since the forest was right there outside the main building, it wasn't like there was a pleasant view. Rareko did not let up in her mental readiness to leap into the hole immediately should anything show up, and, while standing there, she bolted down one of the grayfruit she'd just received, and then another without a pause. Breathing a sigh of relief, she stuck up a finger to lift the arm of her glasses and fix its position.

She sighed again and looked up at the sky. It was shining bright. She didn't want to have to do work that required standing outside in this weather. She vaguely thought, *If they'd made the entrance inside the building, then I would have been able to keep watch indoors.* Though there was smoke rising beyond the forest, it was far away. She was physically distant from it, and also psychologically distant. Now that she was more at ease, she felt like she'd become able to see herself more objectively.

She was scared of fire. Smoke was frightening. The mysterious magical girl was even more scary and frightening. But she was preferable to Navi Ru. That man was really scary and terrifying. She'd thought so all over again when she'd been shown that incomprehensible but incredible gear. Why had Maiya died? How had Clarissa gotten the information that said magical girls couldn't attack people in a hole? If you considered all of that as well, it became clear that it would be best not to oppose Navi Ru. Hugging herself, she happened to look up.

She thought she'd heard something. Should she tell Clarissa? She had to tell Clarissa. Rareko turned around, and she was face-to-face with Clarissa, who had her fist raised. Before she could even be surprised, Clarissa punched her. Rareko twisted around and took it on the shoulder—she tried to pull out her staff, but Clarissa's tail was wrapped around her sleeve, keeping it shut. Clarissa restrained her other wrist as well, and Rareko struggled, trying to keep from falling over. Then Clarissa wrapped her arm around Rareko's neck, and without even the time to think, *Oh no*, she was about to be strangled.

Someone yelled out, "What are you doing?!"

Something flew across the corner of her vision. Clarissa bounced off Rareko's back to leap, and Rareko rolled on the ground, coming out of her roll at a run to race toward the main building. Whamming her shoulder into the wall she'd just repaired, she destroyed it and stepped into the main building, then repaired it with her magic without stopping and kept running without even looking at the wall behind her, which was right back to how it had been. She raced through the hallway at full speed and came to the courtyard, where she still didn't stop. She couldn't stop. She was confused. What had happened? Clarissa had attacked her. Had someone saved her? She'd just heard a voice—a girl's. A magical girl's voice? She felt like she'd heard it before, but also maybe not. If they were going to save her, then shouldn't they save her? But she didn't know just how much they could help. Navi Ru was a fearsome man. There was no way Clarissa would try to kill Rareko based on her own judgment. Obviously Navi Ru had ordered it.

She was confused. She had to rely on someone, but she didn't know whom to rely on. She couldn't trust anyone. She threw herself into any walls or doors that were in her way to destroy them, and then, after passing through, she instantly fixed them. She wouldn't let anyone follow her. From hallway to room, room to hallway, the bottom of the stairs, the kitchen, all she could do was just run. She couldn't stop anywhere. She had to get someone to help her. She could no longer hear the voice of the one who'd barged in on the scene, or of Clarissa.

She broke a wall and fixed it, continuing to run through the main building in a zigzag pattern, and then she thought, *Oh* as Yol came to mind. If Rareko was out of luck with Navi, then she should just go back to her. Was Yol still waiting at their meeting place? Rareko was still confused. Her feet didn't stop. After breaking through a number of walls she'd lost count of, she took a step into bright light and reflexively narrowed her eyes. Sunlight. In other words, she was outdoors. Had she cut through the main building and emerged outside? After running around aimlessly all this time, even Rareko didn't know where she'd wound up.

"Is the one you dropped the golden ax?"

She turned her head to the right. A magical girl who carried a giant ax in each of her hands was standing at the rear entrance. She smiled at Rareko—she was ten yards away, with a voice that carried well. Rareko felt like her knees would crumple, but she desperately recovered her stance to face the magical girl. Rareko had watched from below as she had pursued Chelsea. Just seeing that little bit from a distance, she'd thought, *No way.*

Clarissa had said that Rareko wouldn't attack if she was in a hole. But after being attacked by Clarissa, Rareko's reason to believe that was gone. She didn't even have the time to dig a hole in the first place. She pulled her staff out from her cuff. With a rattle, she slid out the three sections, extending it from a little over twenty inches to one yard long. It was very portable compared to a normal staff, which made it more of a hidden weapon. It wasn't as strong, but it was strong enough that she could cover for that by using her repair magic. Rareko swung the extended reinforced alloy rod to smash a wrecked wall, sending into the air fragments that she smacked at the enemy, three shots in succession.

Rareko let out a short breath and backstepped, retreating inside the main building, then stomped on the floorboards to break them, thrust up to bring down the ceiling, and readied her staff horizontally—it was a defensive stance called "the eight-armed stance" in magical staff arts. She let out another short breath and struck the wall to send fragments flying.

The magical girl leaped to the side to evade the remains of the wall with a balletic turn, and when Rareko shot more rocks at her, she struck them aside with her axes. Rareko broke the door with her back and bottom, backstepping to escape into the room behind her. She kept her eyes on the enemy and never faltered.

Taking the most fundamental stance, she looked down the staff at the enemy and let out a short breath. She had completed the full course of her combat breathing routine, which was for concentrating the mind. All confusion was already gone from her heart. It wasn't that she didn't understand the situation—she sincerely didn't want any of this—but she was ready to fight.

"Or is it the silver ax?"

She stopped breathing. Her body temperature dropped. Her heartbeat slowed. Rareko was standing inside the main building, at the entrance to the room. The enemy was standing in the area that had been opened up from the wall being destroyed. The sun was at her back.

The enemy magical girl went from a turn to a leap, closing in suddenly. Rareko immersed herself in a mire of concentration. She looked at her opponent. There was a tangle of information. She had killed Maiya. The way she moved was freewheeling and hard to figure out, and also too fast. It was the most Rareko could do to just follow her with her eyes. She couldn't even see the swing of her axes. She wasn't much different from colored wind. Rareko immediately came to a conclusion. If she allowed the enemy to attack,

she would die. Rareko couldn't block the attacks, and even if she dodged, she'd lose an arm.

Maiya had been strong. A strong magical girl would impose her own strength and try to win. She would throw her trained skills, her physical strength, magic, everything at the opponent in an attempt to wrest a victory from her. Rareko was different. She wasn't as strong as Maiya. If she did the same thing, she would just die. If she really wanted to be victorious, then she had to win, to kill with cheap, cowardly tricks. It was kill or be killed.

The magical girl stepped on the crumbled floor, and Rareko focused on timing it just right. The moment her opponent's body weight was on the floor, Rareko repaired the broken floor without even a split-second lag, making the place where the magical girl had stepped out no longer crumbled footing but good as new, capturing the enemy's foot below the ankle in the floor. At the same time, Rareko closed the distance between them, coming into range before her opponent could right her stance.

When chasing Chelsea through the air as well as in their current fight, the enemy had shown an abnormal fixation on moving acrobatically. So then Rareko would stop her first.

Rareko brought her left hand in for a *honte uchi*, or normal strike, followed by a pulling-hand sweep in which she moved the staff over her palm and made use of centrifugal force for a hit to the left knee; from there, in a basic *hanmi* stance, she struck the top of her enemy's foot with the return swing in a "dropping snap."

Those were the fundamentals, a combination that was in her katas. "Foundations are important" had been one of Maiya's mottos, and she had never allowed Rareko to slack off in her practice of katas. Rareko stayed in motion through the attack, flowing with sliding feet from the enemy's left hand to diagonally behind her. Rareko further combined her magic with her staff work, repairing the fallen remnants of the ceiling in the hallway, and the fragments of ceiling banged into the enemy's body and face as they shot up to their original positions, and when the enemy staggered, Rareko kept on striking at all her joints. The sensation in her hands was not that of flesh. It was far harder than that, thicker. Her hands on her staff just about went numb. And forget hurting the enemy; her exposed bare feet weren't even red, and hitting her thumbnail didn't even crack it. The enemy was unfazed by Rareko's attacks, swinging up her axes to hit the floorboards.

She was too resilient. Her physical capacity was on another level. It would be impossible to grapple with her for a clinch or to restrain her, and if Rareko tried hitting her with her hands or feet, she was bound to hurt herself. The technique that Maiya had taught her, the technique her body had absorbed, made the optimal choice on its own.

Rareko canceled the repair of the floor and undid her magic. The floorboards that had been catching the enemy's feet as they tried to restore themselves suddenly lost force, and, as she lost her support, the magical girl's upper body was flung backward. Rareko moved behind the enemy at the rightward diagonal. After moving, she used a "pull-down" that spun her staff around the axis of her own knee to strike the enemy's ankle, and then, after spinning the staff in a half turn, she raised it vertically and thrust it into the ground. Her other hand moved like a different creature to pull out the second staff tucked into the back of her robe. It was colored like a bad joke, with stripes in passion pink, white, and blue, and was not to Rareko's taste. But for destruction in particular, this staff was more reliable than anything else.

Rareko pulled the staff close, lowering and widening her stance. Maiya had been in the habit of saying that all staff arts rested on how smoothly you could handle the weapon in your palms. Even if the skin of her palms tore and spurted blood, Maiya had not called an end to training, and Rareko had cried as she drew in her staff. Now Rareko's palms moved like running water over the staff Maiya had loved. She clearly felt the presence of the staff, Maiya's presence as she became one with the weapon. The enemy was still unable to face her. Rareko's awareness was heightened. She would focus on the single point of the staff in her hands. The basics of her staff technique were in capture and suppression, and it was one of the few techniques with the goal of destruction. It had been named from how it had pierced one and a half of Archfiend Pam's wings. Rareko threw her whole body into this "Fiend Piercer," going for the end of the enemy's chin, which she'd just gotten a glimpse of diagonally, and to the right at her rear.

There was the satisfying sound of a knock on her jawbone. The enemy whipped her head around to face the other way, as if she'd been repelled. If this were Maiya's Fiend Piercer, then it wouldn't have just taken her jaw, it would have blasted away everything over the neck. But this was fine. Rareko had already calculated that it wouldn't be as strong as Maiya's. If she knocked her opponent out, then it would be the same thing in the end. Rareko swung up the staff and retreated a step for the finisher, and at the same time, the enemy swung her ax.

Huh? Rareko thought. She had struck clean through her jaw and rattled her brain. You couldn't block that just from being tough or hard. No matter how solid a magical girl she was, it wouldn't prevent a concussion. On top of that, she was still facing away. Rareko had moved into her blind spot, so there was no way the enemy could instantly know where she was like that. There was no way, but the ax in her right hand flashed. Rareko couldn't see her face, but she felt like she was being *looked at*. She could tell that the enemy who hadn't been trying to see her until now was clearly *looking* at her.

The ax was coming closer. Strangely, it looked like it was in slow motion. But she knew she could absolutely not avoid it. She suddenly understood why the enemy had *seen* her. She'd had her attention on the floor and ceiling, and she'd turned it to Rareko instead because she'd judged that Rareko's attack, the strike that had gone through her jaw, was more of a threat than the floor and ceiling. That was why the enemy had *looked* at Rareko and attacked.

Rareko cursed Navi Ru, Clarissa, and the ax-wielding magical girl in order, and when finally Maiya's face rose in her mind, she cursed her with *"Damn woman, teaching me garbage staff technique that isn't useful,"* and then her world went dark.

CHAPTER 16
WE WON'T GIVE UP

◇ **Pastel Mary**

As soon as she reached the main building, she was dragged into a fight.

Pastel Mary didn't like kicking, punching, hitting, throwing, shooting, jabbing, or anything like that, and she wasn't good at those things. But even from where she stood, it clearly looked like Clarissa was attacking Rareko in front of a big hole. The air of violence made the sheep wail and bleat, and Mary froze up, and Chelsea, standing beside her, was fuming.

Chelsea yelled, "Stop it!" to try to put a halt to it—this was Chelsea, so she probably meant to use force, but by the time she reached out, Rareko had already run away. She jetted off so fast there was no time to call after her. Chelsea's extended hand wouldn't reach. Left behind were the confused Mary, the angry Chelsea, Clarissa smiling shyly, Ragi, still unconscious, and lots of sheep.

"No, no, don't get the wrong idea." Clarissa's ears were stuck up sharply as she waved open palms at them. Aside from her long and sharp claws, her hands looked the same as a human's.

Chelsea put her hands on her hips, stepping up to Clarissa like a mother scolding her children, and Clarissa stepped quickly backward, keeping the space between them at fifteen feet, neither widening nor narrowing. Clarissa nimbly backing up was apparently not what Chelsea had been looking for, as her cute nose crinkled.

Seeing that, Clarissa waved her hands even more aggressively. "Like Clarissa *said*, you've got the wrong idea."

"What do you mean?"

"When you think about our positions then, it might have looked like Clarissa was attacking Rareko."

"That's exactly what you did."

"No, no, that's not what was going on. It wound up like that, look, since cute li'l Clarissa was stronger, so it got to the point where I was trying to take her down by strangling her, but that doesn't mean Clarissa was the one who attacked first, right? When you see a police officer trying to restrain a criminal, will anyone think the police was the one to attack—that he's a bad cop? I don't think so, absolutely not." Clarissa battered her with these questions, and she sounded kind of convincing.

Chelsea scowled and brought her hands from her waist to fold in front of her chest, tilting her head to the right. "Aren't you just trying to make yourself look good now, since the person you were fighting is gone?"

"No, no, that's exactly what proves Clarissa's legitimacy. Look, if you're right, then you don't have to run away. You should just run straight to the people who came to save you and be like, '*Oh, this person is so awful!*' You run if you've done something nasty. Is Clarissa wrong here?"

That sounded reasonable. Mary recalled how Rareko had madly dashed off. She'd looked panicked, and also as if she was frightened of something. Clarissa's hands were in constant motion as she talked on and on in a way that sounded like making excuses but also explaining, and her gestures were so funny and giggle-worthy, they were too silly to come from a bad person.

The harsh look on Chelsea's face seemed to have eased a little. She put her hand to her brow to massage away the wrinkle as her other hand pointed to Clarissa's feet. There was a hole there—or more like an entrance. You could see a ladder. A square was cut out in the earth, making a hole where you couldn't see the bottom. It looked like either the kind of secret passage to an underground room that would appear in a horror movie or the entrance to a dungeon in a computer RPG.

"And hey," Chelsea said, "what's that hole? That wasn't there before, was it?"

"Who knows?" Clarissa replied. "I wonder about that myself. Not that I actually know. I wonder what it was. How strange. Maybe Rareko knows, but she ran away."

"You're just trying to shove everything off on someone who isn't here, aren't you?"

"She's not just absent, she ran away. It might seem similar, but it's subtly different, since she left of her own accord. Clarissa just said before that you wouldn't run without a reason."

Mary noticed that she was starting to be won over, but she was really shockingly unsure about her own powers of judgment. *What do I do?* she thought, unable to give instructions to her sheep, who were looking at her from every direction. At times like this, you should look to the judgment of someone who had powers of judgment. That was always the right thing in life, and in magical-girl activities.

She was very much reluctant to call Dreamy☆Chelsea a magical girl with powers of judgment, but at the very least, when it came to areas that smelled of violence, she had more experience than Mary.

"What do we do, Chelsea?" Mary asked her.

Chelsea opened her mouth like she was about to reply, but then loud sounds came from the other side of the main building—the sounds of something crashing and something breaking—and

Chelsea and Mary looked over there, and before they could even be surprised, Clarissa had slipped past Mary. By the time Mary looked back, Clarissa was already out of reach, disappearing right away into the woods.

When Mary panicked and turned back to Chelsea, she found she had already raced off, too. She didn't give so much as a glance to Mary or Ragi, leaving them behind with a "Wait there!" as she spread both arms wide for a magnificent leap to lightly land on the star that zoomed out from her pocket, and then she crossed over the spire that decorated the top of the main building to vanish over to the other side. Mary had even less ability to stop her than to stop Clarissa.

Pastel Mary still couldn't have any confidence in her own powers of judgment. But the only ones there were her, the sheep, and the unconscious Ragi, and the only one with powers of judgment was Mary.

The sound had come from the direction in which Rareko had run. If Rareko was a bad guy like Clarissa said, then she might have attacked someone. Maybe that wasn't it, and Rareko had been the one attacked. Either way, Mary thought that Chelsea would try to go save her.

Mary looked at the hole. Her sheep were gathering around the edge of the hole and wiggling their noses. From how it was cut in a square and you could see the top of a ladder, it was clearly man-made, and it didn't look like it had been made just now, either. If this had been set up in the main building to begin with, then Shepherdspie would also have known about it, but Mary hadn't been told, and, from the looks of it, Chelsea hadn't heard about it, either. Right before Ragi had passed out, he'd tried to guide them to the main building. Had the old man known about this hole?

Mary pushed aside the head of a big-horned sheep and shoved back the rear of a large sheep, gently addressing her flock as it continued to bleat shrilly, shooing off a sheep that was wearing goggles. While soothing the sheep, Mary desperately racked her brain. What would lead to the best outcome? Just standing out here with nothing around made her really anxious, and it was really dangerous. If she went into the hole and then put a lid on it so you couldn't tell it was there from the outside, then even if that magical girl did come, Mary might be ignored.

Mary audibly swallowed. The one to make the judgment, the decision right here and now, in this place, was nobody else but Mary. She had to choose what to do.

◇ **Ragi Zwe Nento**

Even just opening his eyes was quite laborious. Ragi dug his nails into his palms and clenched his fists and confirmed that his body would move—at the very least somewhat. He opened his eyelids even wider, but the darkness didn't change much. In the dim space, there was a cold, hard sensation on his head and back. As soon as he tried to inhale through his nose, something awfully irritating came up his throat to his nose to make him choke fiercely.

He coughed, suffered, and writhed. The coughing gradually subsided, either because he was used to the aroma or because it had faded, and he heard other sounds that had been drowned out by the coughing before. The shrill laugh of a girl would have been quite grating even if he hadn't been in such a situation, and while he was coughing, Ragi's anger rose to carefully simmer on a low flame. When the pungent smell and his coughing had both died away, he put his hands on his knees to push himself up and glared at the source of the laughter.

"What is the meaning of this?" he demanded.

It was dark. There were no lights. It seemed like he was indoors. The cold, hard sensation under his bottom had to be stone. He hadn't just been coughing, his eyes had been watering, too. Even without the darkness, he wouldn't have been able to see straight. And with the smell receding, he finally noticed the pain with a throbbing heat to it that spread from his forehead to his nose.

"Oh, don't misunderstand, I'm sorry, I didn't laugh because it's funny." The voice sounded familiar.

"Pastel Mary?"

"Yes, it's Mary. Or wait, can't you tell from looking? Are your eyes all right?"

"Don't assume I'm like you. You're a magical girl. How am I supposed to see in the dark?"

He heard a surprised clap of the hands. "Oh, that's right. I'm sorry, but I didn't bring any lights."

"Where am I?"

"It's a secret underground room nearby the main building. Oh, by secret, I mean that I didn't know about it, either, and I was surprised that when I came to the main building, there was a hole in the ground."

"...How long was I unconscious?"

"I don't think it was that long... I wasn't looking at a clock, so I'm not sure exactly."

"What happened to Chelsea?"

"Umm, well, Clarissa and Rareko were fighting. When Chelsea came and said, 'Cut it out' and stopped them, Rareko ran away, and Clarissa made excuses. And then we heard loud noises from the direction Rareko ran off in, so Chelsea went to look. And then, Gra...Mr. Ragi, I took you and took refuge in this hole."

He went back over everything that had happened, one thing at a time. Based on the way Navi Ru had acted, Ragi had figured there was some kind of facility underground... Ragi let out a cry of "Ahh!" Wasn't this very place where he and Mary were right now his goal? Ragi moved his fingertips to cast a spell and create a ball of light over his palm. It was just barely larger than a fly, but it was enough to light the area. They were in a little room, about ten feet square. Three sides of it were covered by metal shelves, while the remaining side had a wooden door. It was half-open. Glass bottles lined the shelves. It felt like this place was made of rock, unsurprisingly. The light illuminated Pastel Mary's expression of surprise from below. The shadows were deep.

Ragi blew out a breath and let the hand that held the light fall to the floor. "Why...have I regained consciousness?"

"Yes, that was it. I was laughing because I was glad about that." A smile came to Mary's face, and she thrust one of the glass bottles she had in her hands at Ragi. The pungent, stimulating scent was what had irritated Ragi's throat before and made him cough so hard. Ragi's expression contorted distastefully, and he turned his face away, but Mary was unfazed, shoving the bottle in his face. He accepted it reluctantly, and when he looked down at the label, GARGLE MEDICINE was written in an ancient language beside a picture that showed a human shape drinking a bottle of medicine.

When he inferred what that meant, Ragi's expression twitched in fear and anger. "It can't be...you made me drink this?"

"I didn't exactly—rather, when I was carrying you and wondering where to put you down, I staggered and just about fell. I crashed right into the shelf. And then bottles came spilling off the shelf, and the contents splashed right on your face."

Mary laughed gladly, saying, "I had no clue what was written on it, and I was wondering if maybe this was something bad, but it looks like this was good medicine, and you were saved, huh?" An icy feeling came right from the very bottom of Ragi's heart. That which was magical girl was truly incorrigible.

There were more than a few things he'd like to say to her, but for the moment he swallowed his complaints and stood. While it had just been an accident caused by Mary's lack of attention, nevertheless, in the end, he'd regained consciousness. Even if this was medicine, it was unquestionably a magical drug, and so it must have granted him some magic power. It had acted like smelling salts or shock treatment—it really had been too powerful, but whatever the case, it had managed to revive Ragi. He couldn't let this chance slip through his fingers.

Medicine and pharmacology were not his specialty, but he was still far more knowledgeable than Mary. And he could read the labels, at the very least. Ragi stretched and stood on tiptoe to peek at the rows of bottles. Illuminating the shelves, he selected a bunch of medicine bottles that seemed like they would be of use, then opened one to drink it down. It felt gentler going down his throat than the gargle medicine, drawing a sigh from him before he turned back to Mary.

"We're going to search this place. This time, be extremely careful not to trip and fall, and help me out."

◇ Navi Ru

Navi had thought Clarissa had contacted him from underground in the main building, but for some reason, she was now on the other side of the road, waving her hand. Navi narrowed his eyes and held up a hand to shade them from the sun, but Clarissa still didn't disappear, waving as she ran up to him.

"Why are you here?" Navi demanded.

"Stuff happened." She sounded tired. Her expression showed that she was sick of this, too. It even seemed there was disgust in the way she moved. She put out her right hand like she really didn't want to and pointed to Mana on Navi's back. "What about you, old man? Why do you have her on your back?" she asked, peeking behind him and twitching her ears.

With a big sigh, Navi replied, "I was thinking I should dig a hole and put her in, but you know. What with the fire and smoke coming close, that won't work. Just tucking her in a hole while she's unconscious is one thing, but taking all that extra annoying care with fire retardant and ventilation and all is too much for me. I don't have the facility or equipment here."

"It'd sound like you're a really nice person if you just heard that part."

"Shaddap. More importantly, talk. What do you mean, 'stuff happened'?"

All the "stuff" Clarissa described was, across the board and without exception, bad news that brought down his mood. Absolutely none of it was good. Clarissa had tried to strangle Rareko, but then Dreamy☆Chelsea and Pastel Mary had suddenly shown up, and she'd gotten away. What's more, the entrance to the underground facility had been left open, and they had seen it. Clarissa had taken advantage of a loud noise and gotten away, but if that loud sound was Francesca, then Rareko was no longer alive. Chelsea and Mary had been carrying Ragi, who'd seemed unconscious, and Francesca being close by meant that Ragi was in danger, too. If they would go in the hole for the time being, they could survive Francesca's passing, but if that happened, of course that would mean they'd seen the underground facility.

"We also talked about doing in the boy Touta, right?" said Clarissa. "Right now, it looks like he's at the river."

"Never mind him now. This isn't the time for that."

It was best for Mana, Ragi, and Yol to stay alive. It was best for Touta to die. But there was a priority ranking there. The number one priority was Yol's safety, with Ragi's next, followed by Mana's safety and then Touta's elimination. Worst case, he could get rid of Touta after leaving the island. Mana would also be a real task, but since he had her on his back now, it was comparatively easier to secure her safety. And Ragi's situation would depend on the two magical girls.

"What's your view on Chelsea and Mary?" Navi asked Clarissa. "Strong or not?"

Clarissa's face contorted like she wanted to deal with that even less, ears lowering flat to her head. "You're telling Clarissa to fight them?"

"I don't mean that. And judging from that reaction, I take it they're trouble to handle."

"If Clarissa's allowed to use the secret weapon, it's not like Clarissa couldn't fight 'em for you, but still…"

"Like I said, I'm not telling you to fight 'em."

"Mary can't throw a punch, but Clarissa thinks her magic is pretty unique. You don't see magical girls who can produce that many animals often, even at the Lab. Chelsea, on the other hand, is insanely powerful. She's got a weird service spirit, and Clarissa has got a bit of a whiff of Pam, so maybe she's an Archfiend Cram School graduate. Clarissa heard she had a fight with Francesca, but she's still totally fine."

"I see." Maybe it could be an option to leave Ragi to those two troublesome magical girls. But there was no guarantee they'd win against Francesca. Navi turned back to look up at the sky. The amount of trailing smoke had increased—and it was coming closer. He had to do something about that, too.

"Hey, old man." The tugging on his sleeve made him look at Clarissa. She was looking toward the forest with terribly serious eyes. Drawn over there, Navi's eyes met those of a beat-up magical girl who was supporting herself on her scythe as if it were a cane.

◇ Nephilia

Some crazy magical girls out there would bluster about how "a magical girl shines brightest when she's on the edge between life and death." But Nephilia knew that what those types were in love with was being on the edge between life and death before carving out a new path at the end. Less than one in a hundred were real deals who would say with terrifying sincerity, *"Man, that was fun"* as they slid over the brink into destruction. (In this case, "real deals" did not have the positive nuance of "real magical girls" but indicated a more negative view: "real crazy in the head.") Having heard the voices of the dead countless times, Nephilia could state this fact with confidence.

Was Nephilia the real thing, or was she a fake? Since fortunately she had never experienced destruction, she had yet to say either way. But right now, she was still enjoying the tightrope walk between life and death. Partly this was because she had to or she wouldn't be able to go on, and also this was surprisingly not so bad.

"...Hey," Navi greeted her.

"Long time..."

"Are you okay? Ah, it doesn't look like you're okay."

"Actually...good...but...Agri..."

"Is that right? Sounds like rough luck for her."

Nephilia was consciously trying to slow her speech. When she tried to speak as a magical girl, she would always rush it and wind up mumbling. Speaking slowly got her intentions across clearly, and this also made her speech a measuring instrument that showed if she was anxious or not.

Navi Ru was smirking. Maybe the way Nephilia felt was making it seem like he was smirking. Clarissa stood a half step in front of Navi, twitching her ears just like a cat. Her balanced stance was very much like those of the carnivorous beasts of the savanna. Her smile was highly aggressive, her gaze centered on Nephilia but alert to the whole area.

She was fifty feet away. If this turned into a fight, Nephilia, being injured, would be killed in an instant. She drew in a deep breath and let it out. Shallow breathing would only heighten the tension in her body and mind.

"We've...terrible..." Nephilia leaned against her scythe laboriously.

The index finger of Clarissa's right hand moved slightly. Seeing the two of them thus far, Nephilia made an initial judgment. From their reactions, Clarissa was more likely to snap than Navi. She had fearsome boldness for her apparent age while human, but she obviously had less experience than he did. Also, being in the position where she had to be prepared to fight at any time, she would be more tense.

From their gestures, looks, expressions, tone of voice, breathing, and everything else, every element, Nephilia read the feelings they were trying to hide and their goals. She would say that they wanted to keep from being discarded as useless, but also to avoid being eliminated for being too dangerous. She'd make herself someone they would think wasn't bad to associate with.

She could do it. She had to do it. Negotiations were Nephilia's bread and butter. At the very least, she hadn't been instantly killed on showing herself. She had passed the first stage. Nephilia inhaled a long breath and let it out. Not just all her joints, but her neck, chest, and stomach all hurt.

"Have...lots of grayfruit... Don't you want...?"

"Oh-ho, that'd be great."

"If you cooperate…then."

Navi and Agri's contract to organize their cooperation had made both their fortunes collateral. Even if Agri was dead, if Navi betrayed it, the magic would still activate. That held true even if the goddess magical girl who had killed Agri was Navi's ally. But the contracts that Nephilia had tucked under her costume had not yet activated, and no punishment had been dealt to Navi.

Well, then, was Navi purely a victim? Nephilia didn't think so. Before the goddess magical girl had shown herself, Agri had divulged her guess to him—that the goddess was rampaging under the belief that Navi's allies were under attack—and Navi's reaction to that had been suspicious. Though he'd said he didn't know, that had not been the answer of someone who actually didn't know. Wasn't that exactly the reason Agri had gotten the wrong idea?

He knew some things and was keeping silent about what hadn't been asked. When he'd rejected the possibility that Navi was a pure victim, this had also seemed likely. Also, the goddess magical girl was not affiliated with Navi's camp. At most, Nephilia figured that he knew some method to deal with her.

Agri had died because she had misunderstood the relationship between the magical girl who was out of control and Navi. Nephilia wasn't so cold that she could see it as Agri's error or fault, and she also didn't think that it wasn't Navi's fault because he hadn't lied. It was hard to say Nephilia was a very loyal person, but even she hated him enough to think, *I'd like to whack him one, step on his smirking face, and grind it in.* Navi Ru and Clarissa were both nasty, but they weren't nasties of the type that was worthwhile to Nephilia. They were different from Agri.

But she couldn't tell them that she hated them. The wind blew, and the pungent burnt smell was wafting thick. Nephilia looked up and breathed a sigh. "The fire…strong."

"That's a problem. What idiot pulled that one?" Navi asked.

Nephilia had no obligation to tell him, *"It was my idiot."* Looking at Clarissa's ears, she saw they had stopped moving. It was fair to assume she already knew where Ren-Ren was hiding. But it was nevertheless worthwhile just to have her hiding and watching them. Being forced to protect Navi kept Clarissa from being calm and made it easier to see her reactions.

"As I…said…before…don't you need…grayfruit?"

"Yeah, we want them." Like always, Navi's attitude was consistent. He didn't waver. But now he was seeking to settle things with that one remark. He didn't want a drawn-out conversation with Nephilia. Navi wasn't as calm as he was putting on. It would be fine for him to be a little irritated. But Nephilia could not emphasize from her end that he was in just as much trouble as she was. There was no reason that she absolutely had to be on top here. Depending on their mood, she could be killed. It would make it easier if they thought of her as being like a child who was overreaching herself to try to be equal.

"The contract is…still valid…should…cooperate…"

She had learned about Navi Ru's fortune when they'd made the contract. It was a fair sum. Agri had said jokingly, "If you betray me, then it's all mine, huh?"

But Nephilia thought that if necessary, this man would even throw away his "fair sum" of a fortune. Nephilia's history as a magical girl was not short, and she'd seen a few people like that—mages and magical girls. Some had been drunk on self-sacrifice, and others had had personal desires that were difficult to understand. Navi was one of those types, although not entirely. From what she'd seen of his actions and behavior on this island, his goal didn't seem to have anything to do with money. Agri might have assumed he and Navi shared the same values, operating within a profit-and-loss framework, but that was nowhere near the truth. Navi just wanted others to see him as materialistic. He wasn't simply trying to make himself look bad—it was malicious, and he was giving people the wrong idea about his character to try to pull the rug out from under them.

That was why Nephilia would have him assume that she was still relying on the contract. Because that made things easier for

Navi Ru to control. Even if Navi didn't think much of his fortunes, she would use the contract as a shield.

"Fire...strong."

"Yeah, we just heard."

"Dangerous..."

"For sure."

"Chelsea...and Mary...working together..."

Clarissa blinked. Chelsea and Mary had already escaped from under Ren-Ren's control, but there was no need to tell them that. She should actually conceal that it was just Nephilia and Ren-Ren. It was best to have as many cards as possible.

"No...contact...saying...encountered...survivors..."

Clarissa's face looked slightly stiff. There was no change in Navi, but when it came to him, you should assume he simply wasn't showing his emotions.

"If you're...not a magical girl...fire...very...dangerous..."

"Mages aren't to be underestimated, though."

Clarissa blinked twice. Navi's sentence had gotten just a bit louder at the end.

Navi Ru hadn't been ready for a fire. There was no way he'd have been able to predict Ren-Ren setting it. Navi was acting like the fire was nothing, which probably wasn't just a bluff, but what about Yol? Even if Navi had done something to protect her from the goddess, she couldn't escape a fire that way. Judging from Clarissa's reaction, the protection Yol was under wasn't perfect. Navi's desire to protect Yol was clear in how he'd placed that restraint in the contract with Agri's faction. There would be no point in incorporating not interfering with Yol into the contract as a bluff or to try to mislead them. Even if he planned to trick them down the line, there would be no point if Agri pulled one over on him before that. It would be a problem for Navi if Yol died, and while it wasn't a great thing for Yol that her safety was uncertain now, it was a wonderful thing for Nephilia.

"Should...deal with..."

"Mm."

"So…more…cooperation…"

"You mean putting out the fire?"

Nephilia slowly shook her head. "No…defeat…magical girl like a goddess…after…put out fire…"

She clearly said "goddess." She was absolutely not going to make accusations like *"Don't you know her?"* but she did make her existence explicit. Nephilia being as beaten up as she was made it look undeniably convincing that she had encountered the enemy magical girl. She'd made contact with the monster, and she'd only gotten badly hurt. She wasn't pitifully ailing from her wounds, she actually looked strong, as if her injuries were badges of honor.

But Nephilia played pitiful and leaned on her scythe. She didn't say anything out loud, but she communicated implicitly, *"If I fought you I'd die. But I'll do my best to hold on with just one arm. So let's negotiate."* She'd let them figure it out. Navi, the rough-looking middle-aged and bald mage nailing her with his vicious and tenacious gaze, would surely figure it out.

Nephilia wasn't saying anything wrong. Getting attacked in the middle of putting out a fire would just be dangerous. They should extinguish the fire after they'd dealt with the biggest danger.

Now Navi's expression changed for the first time. He touched his left hand to his jaw and stroked his five-o'clock shadow. His expression looked pensive, eyes pointed at the various trails of smoke hanging in the sky. Clarissa's eyes didn't move from Nephilia. Her eyelashes were trembling slightly.

"…Sure." Navi nodded and smacked Clarissa's back.

Clarissa's smile didn't falter as she spread her hands and stepped up to Nephilia in an utterly casual manner. Navi was behind her. From the way they were both acting, Nephilia sensed that their tension had eased. If they were thinking it was kill or be killed, Navi never would have approached along with Clarissa.

Nephilia approached them as well, but she was still ready to die at any moment as she held out her right hand. When Navi's palm reached out past Clarissa's, Nephilia clasped it, relieved at the meaty and reliable-feeling palm, and then she laughed quietly at herself.

◇ **Dreamy☆Chelsea**

Her body moved before she could even think, and as she leaped over the spire of the building, she wondered to herself, *Is Dreamy☆Chelsea managing to act calmly right now?* She was surprised that she was thinking that. Dreamy☆Chelsea would never mope, and she never got fussed about any sort of troubles. She would act resolutely and without a thought, resolving things cleanly. That was Dreamy☆Chelsea. That was what a magical girl was. Smart people should handle things like thinking.

Pushing through the wind blowing in her face, Chelsea pointed her star downward.

But Chelsea didn't consider it a failure that she'd just been thinking. She had to think. She needed to think, even if it meant going against the moves she should originally have been making. Because it wasn't just about her. The warmth of Mary's hand on her back. Ragi's face, constantly angry like the face of an uncle of hers. There were other people on the island, too. Shepherdspie was gone. She was clenching her teeth. She couldn't help but think that if she'd thought a little more, not just about herself, but even half about other people, maybe things would have wound up differently.

That's why she would be calm. She had to be calm. Even if Chelsea acted without thinking, she would be okay. Because Dreamy☆Chelsea was a magical girl. But even if Chelsea would be okay, not everything and everyone would.

Was it true that Clarissa hadn't meant to kill Rareko? If she was going to kill her, then it would have been way faster not to strangle her but to slice with her claws instead. But it was clear they had been fighting. Whenever there was a survival scenario in anime, manga, or novels, it was pretty common for allies to steal food-stuffs from each other, even when it had nothing to do with the main thread of the story. Not everyone could be like *Deux Ans de Vacances*. The world was always *Lord of the Flies*.

That was precisely why magical girls, why the cuteness of magical girls was needed.

Chelsea floated downward to hang there in the air. As the hem of her skirt slowly came fluttering down, Chelsea glared at the scene spread out before her. She'd had a feeling about this. She'd thought maybe things would wind up like this. But she hadn't wanted them to.

Pieces of the ceiling were clunking down to hit the floor. There was also the *tik, tik* of red fluid dripping. It was dripping everywhere—from the ends of the axes, the branches of trees. The goddess magical girl was smiling like she was very happy. At her feet was a maid outfit, soaked in red. The head and neck were gone down to the middle of the chest, so you couldn't tell who it was, but the outfit was familiar.

Chelsea took her star decoration in hand and spun it like a yo-yo, making it skim along the ground to snap back the other way, then caught it with her left hand. Her star was hot. There was heat in it.

The goddess swung her arms like a swan about to flap its wings, spinning as she approached Chelsea. She spread both arms with axes in hand, puffed out her chest, and looked up at Chelsea from where she was kneeling. Her white costume was dirty, but her movements were elegant enough to make up for it.

"Is the one you dropped the golden ax?"

On hearing that question, Chelsea put her arms together for a spin the opposite way, facing the goddess in a pose with her hands in a heart shape, her star decoration sandwiched between them. The two magical girls held their stances as they gazed upon each other with the greatest smiles. When the wind blew through, stirring up dust, Chelsea didn't even blink.

The goddess had learned to move in a cutesy way. It was purely superficial copying, but you couldn't look down on that. Everyone started with copying. It was admiration for her predecessors, like Miko-Chan, Riccabel, and Hiyoko-Chan that had made Dreamy☆Chelsea who she was now.

Chelsea couldn't win in a competition of strength. She was even inferior in speed and the power of her magic. And in cuteness, the one area where she'd been winning, the goddess was rapidly catching up. Chelsea wanted to run away, but she didn't like the kind of magical girl who would run away now. She spun her star and brought it overhead. At the same time, she brought the heart shape under her chin and to the right. The goddess rose, closing her opened arms to cross them, overlapping her axes. Just her face peeked out between her arms and axes as she watched Chelsea, sharp and alert.

"Or is it the silver ax?"

What Ragi had said was right. Magical girls weren't made for this. That was exactly why Chelsea had to stop the goddess. Comparing their strength seemed like cause for despair. But she had to win. So then what would she do?

Chelsea lightly bit her lip and wetted it. "Prepare to be wowed by a cuteness you've never known."

She only had one option. She dropped the heart shape and shifted to peace signs, then fired off a pose before crossing her arms as she pointed to the other girl and yelled, "Leave it to Dreamy☆Chelsea!"

Under the light of the sun, her star shone black. When the goddess jumped, Chelsea leaped into the air.

CHAPTER 17
STARS AND A GODDESS

◇ **Dreamy☆Chelsea**

A pitiful-looking corpse lay in the main building, in the hallway—where the hallway had once been. Beside it lay a staff that looked like candy. Part of the wall had been destroyed, there were holes in the floor, and the ceiling was dangling down. If you looked from the broken wall to outside, a tract of earth of roughly seventy square yards had been dug up, probably with an ax. Grasping the whole scene in a glance, Chelsea decided on a theme.

She evaded the blade's trajectory on a zigzag path, doing a little jump on top of her star decoration as it rotated at high speed—bringing her elbows in, she flapped her open hands like a little bird—by doing this, she made it past the second ax. The sound of cutting through air reached her ears long after the slice. Ten hairs were torn off her head, and it hurt as they flew off. It wasn't that she'd been cut by the blade. The pressure of the wind had pulled them out by the roots.

But Chelsea still maintained her stance on tiptoe. As they passed each other in midair, she locked eyes with the goddess magical girl. She was beaming a smile at Chelsea. Chelsea didn't even have enough time to smile back. After that momentary crossing, she leaped to avoid the slice that came at her as she was flying away, then clapped her hands twice under her chin to the right. It wasn't a provocation. She did it to get in a rhythm.

Spinning more and more, she moved her star right and left. Red spray flew through the air. She noticed the pain half a beat later. She'd failed a dodge, and some flesh had been shaved away. It was a little over her right elbow. It hadn't reached bone and tendon. It had also missed the thick blood vessel. Chelsea covered the damage and fear with a smile and clapped her hands.

Dreamy☆Chelsea's fundamental concept was "freewheeling," and she wouldn't change that, even if her mother pushed her on it, using snacks as a shield. But she did often settle on a direction before she did anything. She would choose a theme depending on the moment and situation, like courage, or purity, or the good old days of the Showa era. Her freedom was not chaotic; rather it gave her a flexible universality.

The theme this time was rhythm and tempo. She would add charming movements on top of that.

Her mother had scolded her about rhythm and tempo. She said that her movements became monotonous, and it made her easier to read. And then, to prove her point, she'd taken Chelsea by the wrist and thrown her down without any struggle, locking her elbow joint to push her to the ground. When Chelsea tried to kick her away, her mother got that leg in a lock as well, and when she tried to struggle with her shoulder and head, those were held down, and she was kept from moving at all. With her arms and legs all tangled up, she had no idea what was going where anymore. There was nothing but pain and suffering. Caught in an original joint technique that was less magical girl and more superhuman pro wrestling, Chelsea had wailed in protest that "this isn't like a magical girl," which her mother had coldly disregarded, saying, "So then, do it properly." That wasn't something a mother who'd forced her daughter into an unwanted sparring match should say.

Since then, Chelsea had stopped making rhythm and tempo her main thing.

Now she was breaking out the focus on rhythm once more.

As she landed, she stomped the ground forcefully. Countless pebbles bounced up from the impact, from which she picked out a number that she could accept as stars, poking at them with her fingers to send them circling around the area. Chelsea jumped atop them, bounding off one pebble star to jump to another, evading an attack as she clapped twice under her chin to the left, and, judging that it was all right to add in something a little uncouth as an accent, after somersaulting, she cutely smacked her own bottom at the enemy a couple times. The important thing right now was just rhythm and tempo, and evasion by means of that.

The goddess was different from her mother. Unlike her mother, who would restrain her and try to quiet her, the goddess would follow Chelsea's movements. And just as the goddess read her, the goddess did as Chelsea had foreseen.

With her first condition being avoiding any serious wounds, Chelsea moved around, just barely treading that line. She had already verified that kicking and hitting would hardly hurt the goddess at all. On the other hand, one touch from the ax and Chelsea would be fatally wounded. Right now there was nothing for it but to continue to evade while getting chills in her heart over each and every swing. Chelsea was sure she was right to judge that she wouldn't get anywhere with a frontal attack.

The goddess's ax cut through the sky to slice fiercely into the earth. The body that was probably Rareko's bounded like a broken marionette. The goddess used the momentum of her swift dodge to move into a roundhouse kick, and Chelsea relaxed her whole body like liquid to grab that leg, only to be shaken off in an instant. When the goddess's toe was thrust at her, Chelsea evaded by bending into a back bridge, then, after bouncing up again with the strength of her neck, she hopped from one rock to another at a good tempo. She clapped her hands over her head to the right and left, then crouched down for some cute continuous bunny-like hops. She didn't let you feel even a hint of the sweaty straining implied by this particular exercise, and was actually observing the movements of her body calmly. Her right pinkie finger joint had been crushed. It had broken when she'd gone in to grab the goddess's leg and been flung off just from the speed and momentum. But her right hand would still move.

Her hands went from imitating a bunny's long ears to her waist, and while still bent over, she shifted gears to comical movements: wiggling her butt to the right, then to the left, then she turned around and stopped. Chelsea was in the upper position, the goddess below her. Looking down, Chelsea smiled. Thanks to fixing rhythm and tempo as her main axis, she had somehow managed to keep avoiding hits. Frighteningly enough, the marks the axes had made ripping through the earth had drawn the pretty shape of a star. Of course this was not a coincidence. The goddess had made it look as if she were wielding the axes haphazardly, while she was actually expressing creativity over the earth. She'd done better than Chelsea, who'd had her hands full with running.

Even though privately, Chelsea was in a cold sweat, she never let her smile falter. If she lost her composure, she would also lose the rhythm.

When she looked closely at the star drawn on the ground, she saw there were six inches missing on the last side. She made one of her stars fly out to dig into the earth and connect the two lines to complete the pentagram. As the dug up soil was tossed into the air, the goddess's gaze never left Chelsea, a smile on her face.

The goddess stood on her hands and swung her legs around as in capoeira or break dancing, then spun vertically in the air three times to land in the center of the star she'd drawn. Then she spun to the side, carving into the ground with the axes in both hands, drawing a circle all around the star to make a pentagram. It was just like a magical sigil. Looking up at Chelsea with her hands spread, the goddess looked proud. Chelsea stuck up her index finger in front of her face to reply with "Tsk, tsk, tsk." She was telling her that it still wasn't enough while also ticking out the rhythm with her words.

Chelsea leaped onto her star decoration.

She clapped her hands twice under her chin to the right, and twice to the left, and the goddess answered that by smacking her axes together with a clanging sound. Chelsea ordered the star decoration she stood on to fly at full speed toward the ground. The goddess readied herself. So much earth had been dug up, the smell of earth hung over the whole area. The burnt smell of the fire started to join that scent as the star ripped through the air. Chelsea could feel the heat below her feet.

She dived in from high in the sky, then came to a sudden stop with the dust sweeping up around her before immediately jetting off again. With both axes raised overhead, the goddess approached rapidly. Even just the aftershock from the axes swinging would send Chelsea flying—worst case, she'd die. And if the aftershock was that bad, then a direct hit would shatter her whole body, crushing her into ground chunks in meat sauce. Chelsea smiled wide. She approached the limit, close enough that any more and she would be out, and then turned at a sudden angle. The goddess's axes pursued her but didn't hit. She resisted the pressure of the wind, turning the path of her star at a right angle. She changed direction in an attempt to get the goddess from behind, but the goddess twisted her back impossibly to meet Chelsea's strike as Chelsea was just getting behind her, and Chelsea leaped down from her star and cartwheeled over to step on the broken floor of the main building. While watching from the corner of her eye as her star decoration kept going to fly into the forest, Chelsea readied herself for escape using her own body. Her rhythm was coming faster and faster, indicating that the final stage was approaching.

The goddess swung down, swung up, swung down, swung up, swung down, and swept horizontally. Her combination looked like a sphere with the goddess in the center, attacking Chelsea, and the walls, door, and roof of the main building were torn to shreds. Chelsea leaped and jumped, and the bottom of her right shoe was torn open and blood spurted out, and the flesh of her cheek was gouged deeply, and the hem of her skirt was ripped. She ignored all the pain with the utmost focus on the goddess as she continued to move. Occasionally she clapped her hands or struck her heels on the floor as in a tap dance, all while humming her Dreamy☆Chelsea original insert song, *Fancy and Brave*, and the goddess's axes followed her with their rhythm and violence. As if she were a giant white termite eating wood as it went along, the goddess's destruction carved a large hallway through the main building.

Thus far, Chelsea had emphasized rhythm and tempo to the utmost. Just like an ensemble playing off a single score, the goddess and Chelsea combined and overlapped to create a harmony. Of course, the goddess was reading Chelsea's movements. Chelsea was falling into the state her mother had described—her movements becoming monotonous and her aim easy to read. When Chelsea's fingers touched a frying pan, she whipped it at the goddess, and the goddess struck down the lump of iron that came flying at her at high speed without even a glance. A little pause passed between them, just briefly, for less than a split second. In the half-destroyed kitchen, the two magical girls glared at one another.

Chelsea felt a cold stone wall at her back. Mingling with the smell of the powder from the shattered stone wall, the familiar scent of soup reached her nose. It was the soup Shepherdspie had made for them.

Mr. Pie…lend me just a bit of strength.

Chelsea thrust her hands in front of her. Sticking out her fingers, she touched her middle fingers to her thumbs. The goddess swung up her axes. There was a little pause there. Was she wary because of this new gesture from Chelsea? Or had some working of her mind considered the opponent with whom she'd been making this melody and hesitated because of the thought that this attack would be a waste?

The axes swung down. Chelsea's eyes widened. Everything

started lagging like it was in slow motion. She leaped to the right along the wall, snapping the fingers of both hands at the same time. The ax destroyed the wall, blades turning to Chelsea and coming after her. Chelsea set one hand on the traditional charcoal stove and leaped up, flipping around to put her feet on the ceiling, and ran. She dodged the axes as they pursued her but failed to avoid the rubble and took a hit on the rib. Hearing a rib cutely cracking, she jumped back to where she'd been before and faced the goddess. With the wreckage thudding down around her, she hit the timing perfectly. Her rhythm was also flawless. The ideal actions for Dreamy☆Chelsea in her mind overlapped with those of the real Chelsea.

She'd learned from Shepherdspie that when you snapped your fingers in the main building, things would come flying in from somewhere.

The goddess's smile twitched. She sliced at the plastic gas container that came flying at her from behind to knock it away, and clear fluid with a strong scent scattered around her. Next, a stool came flying, which she knocked away with the other ax, but by the time she was facing Chelsea again, it was already too late. Chelsea had taken a soundless step forward, without giving notice of her presence, to touch the goddess's wrist with a casual gesture. The way this girl advanced without revealing any rhythm or tells brought trouble. There was no malice in it, and it was crazy and sudden, her body acting on its own before her brain could think, so it couldn't be predicted at all, and nobody could stop her. It was just the way Pastel Mary moved.

In her head, she said to the goddess, *Shepherdspie's magic is amazing, right? Things come flying just by snapping your fingers. The way May-May moves is amazing, right? Even Chelsea can't stop her.*

With incredible strength and speed, the goddess tried to peel off her hand, but Chelsea wouldn't let her. With her mother's techniques, she could even overcome someone stronger than herself. With rhythm, tempo, timing, and a little force going from her palm to the goddess's wrist, Chelsea got the goddess off-balance and staggering forward.

The number one reason Chelsea had placed the most emphasis on rhythm and tempo was in order to avoid attacks. The second reason was to make the rhythm break down at the very end and land an attack.

With entirely calculated, perfect timing, she broke the window, and her star decoration flew into the room. It had separated from her right before she entered the main building and left the goddess's view, and Chelsea had given it enough of a run-up and enough acceleration, as well as spin on the max setting. This was the result. Spinning with intense momentum, the star zoomed past the goddess's side to destroy the wall, breaking it to bits and going about ten yards too far before stopping. Chelsea let go of the goddess's wrist and, with a combination of backflips, cartwheels, and somersaults, leaped over what was left of the wall, and, with a final three and a half twists, she landed in the air atop her stopped star decoration.

The goddess tried to swing up her axes, staggered, and stopped. A second later, her neck, which had been sliced open in passing—the wound was so large you'd want to avert your eyes!—fell open, and then it spurted blood like a broken faucet, high enough to wet the ceiling.

Chelsea could never have beaten this opponent on her own. She had been able to win because she wasn't alone. By borrowing things like Shepherdspie's magic, the way Mary moved, and her mother's technique, she'd finally managed to win.

Thanks…everyone.

Chelsea leaped down from her star decoration, spread her legs shoulder-width apart, and lightly clenched her right hand and put it to her waist while she thrust her right hand forward to stick her thumb in the air. The goddess was still spraying blood. She swayed to the right, to the left, and then, after a beat, she slowly fell forward.

◇ Navi Ru

He had the feeling there was even more trailing smoke. Was there really more, or did it just feel that way? If it was the former, then the fire was getting worse. If it was the latter, that meant Navi was feeling pressured by the fire. Either way, it was a problem.

Turning away from a puddle of rising steam, he did up his belt. Lately he'd been wearing it a notch or two looser, mostly because of aging, but now he stuck his buckle in one hole tighter than usual to get motivated again. He couldn't forget that he had to brace himself in a situation like this.

He pushed through the thicket, and when he came out to where the sunlight hit, Clarissa was alone there, waiting for him. To be more precise, Mana was also there, on Clarissa's back, but since she was unconscious, it wasn't like she was waiting.

"It must be nice to be a magical girl. You don't need to spend time on this stuff," said Navi, gesturing toward his clothes.

"You mean like it takes too long when you get old or something?"

"Oh, stop it. I don't wanna talk about that stuff." Navi casually glanced around.

Clarissa seemed to notice that, as she raised her right hand and said, "If you're looking for Nephilia, she went flying off with Ren-Ren," then breathed a little sigh.

"Where are they?"

"Moving toward the main building, cautiously but clearly. She wasn't lying."

Clarissa had put a bite mark on the bottle of medicine that he'd handed the pair. She had their locations precisely. In other words, that meant that Nephilia's offer to work together to eliminate Francesca had been sincere.

With a "Righto," Navi took Mana back from Clarissa and put her on his back, and then he nodded at her. Clarissa smiled at him and nodded back, then turned around to run off, leaving a cloud of dust as she went out of sight.

Francesca was a magical girl made to be an incarnation candidate for the great Chêne Osk Baal Mel. But things were different now. She was not an incarnation, just a vessel. Navi understood and had a grasp on her specifications and abilities. So long as they had the proper preparation and Clarissa to use it, that would be enough to deal with Francesca. And there were other magical girls helping out, so that was more than enough.

It was fair to say that his initial goal had basically been accomplished. Though there were a few remaining people he wished would disappear, he wasn't so fixated on it as to put in the labor and take on the risk to finish them off while on this island. Yol would be a stepping stone down the line, and he wanted to make Ragi a public-facing vehicle for his advancement, so their safety should be prioritized over the elimination of such people. While walking, Navi spat on the side of the path.

Had Ragi seen the underground facility? Though the important parts of the service manual had been removed, Navi wasn't happy about this at all. If matters were resolved while Ragi was searching the area, then it shouldn't turn into too big a problem, but it seemed quite possible that the old man would figure out what Francesca really was and try to come up with a way to deal with her. Even if the old man looked as if he were out of the scene, he was still in service. All the rumors Navi had heard said the old man was possessed of a rebellious spirit unbefitting his age, and there were some researchers who would be gladdened each time they heard that. Whether Sataborn or Ragi, a talented eccentric would have a lot of fans unbeknownst to him.

Navi wanted to put out the fire. He was already done with Francesca. Though the kid and the old man would be safe if they just went quietly into some holes, neither of them would settle down. Given the circumstance, it was fair to call Nephilia's offer a boat when he was at a river. That was how it looked from Navi's end, at least.

As they talked, he'd been observing all Nephilia's movements, all the way to the littlest gestures and trivial turns of phrase. Her eyes were on the dry side, and it looked like she was swallowing a lot. She was aware her situation was critical, but despite that, her core, her heart never bent. That girl was taking a gamble. Nephilia had come to Navi prepared for the possibility that they still needed

Francesca and that they would casually finish off someone like Nephilia on sight and figure out what to do with her then.

He thought she had quite a lot of guts to do that when she'd had the crap beaten out of her, but he also felt she could be dangerous. It was in her eyes. She seemed like she was zoning out, yet focused. Her gaze wouldn't let you figure out what she was fixed on—though it was the most crucial thing to know what she held dear.

He'd be glad if she would be a capable underling for him, but if she wasn't that, she might be an avenger with no consideration for danger. This was one thing that he would have to figure out while he was on the island.

◇ **Dreamy☆Chelsea**

The thumbs she'd stuck up gradually lowered before being tucked into her fists. Chelsea put both her fists together to place them under her chin and tilted her head cutely.

Though she needed to hear the *thud* of falling, she couldn't. She narrowed her eyes. The goddess had clearly been defeated. But she couldn't hear that sound. It was baffling. Chelsea bent at the waist, putting her hands on her knees and lowering her head. Bending her head over to peek at her from below, she cried out, "Ah." The goddess had not fallen. She had stopped flat four inches over the ground, only her hair dangling to touch it. It just looked as if she'd fallen.

Before Chelsea could wonder why, the goddess rose suddenly as if yanked by an invisible crane and invisible wires. The blood that had been gushing out so dramatically had now come to a stop.

Why...?

Brown earth was piled over the wound on her neck. The earth was connected to the handle of her ax, which was swinging, dangling off it. Realizing that she had turned the blade of her ax into a fast-drying, sticky earth to stop the bleeding, Chelsea went on guard.

But then the goddess thrust out a palm at her. "Please wait one moment."

That single remark became a frightening amount of information that inundated Chelsea's brain. Various thoughts rose at once, like *So she can say things other than that stuff about gold and silver axes?* or *Why would she think I would wait in this situation?* or *Why is she so calm?* and her head basically went blank, and by the time she figured she had to do something, the goddess had pulled out a plastic case and rolled what looked like medicine into her palm.

As if in response, Chelsea pulled out a grayfruit and took a bite. She picked up the pot that was sitting at a diagonal over the broken charcoal stove, tilted it over her mouth, and swallowed it with an audible gulp. Next she bit into the grayfruit, and though both should have tasted good, she didn't taste anything at all.

While she took one bite, two, her gaze never left the goddess. The goddess was entirely unmoved, boldly putting the medicine in her mouth as if confirming that Chelsea would not attack in the middle of this act. Her throat, covered in cracked earth, undulated, and you could tell from the outside that she had swallowed down the medicine.

It was just the briefest moment in real time, no more than a few blinks long, but as felt time, it was long enough for Chelsea to experience enough hesitation to grind her teeth and writhe around as she let her chance to attack go by.

She knew she could not let this person get away. That was why Chelsea had done things that were not magical-girl-like, why she sought un-magical-girl-like results. But her limbs just would not move. The goddess believed that Chelsea would not attack. To attack then without a word would not be Dreamy☆Chelsea.

She stretched, bending her knee joints. She'd taken many attacks so far, but no direct hits. The total damage wasn't beyond what she'd anticipated. She somersaulted and landed on her star decoration. Spreading her legs to the front and back, she crouched and lightly spread her hands like a surfer on a surfboard. Her opponent was incredibly tough. Even after gushing blood from her neck, she didn't pass out. You had to fight with the intention of popping her head off cutely, or you wouldn't be able to take her out of the fight.

Chelsea considered. She couldn't use rhythm and tempo anymore. But even if she had closed the wound, it wasn't like the blood would come back immediately. Bleeding that much would slow you down. And now, since she was using her weapon to stop the blood, she only had half the axes to wield as weapons. And since she'd piled a whole bunch of earth on herself, she looked ugly, too. The enemy's fighting power, cuteness included, was way decreased.

...All right, let's do it by force.

Chelsea remembered what her mother had said. Feelings would make magical girls stronger. Chelsea was forced to agree with that. If she hadn't been able to defeat the goddess, even after borrowing power from Mary, Shepherdspie, and her mother, then she would get more feelings. First she would add in Ragi, who had preached to her about how a magical girl should be. There should be lots of other people you should add to Chelsea's camp, too.

Just from a shared look, she and Miss Marguerite had acknowledged each other's cuteness. They were basically frenemies.

Ever since Nephilia and Love Me Ren-Ren had been fighting over Mary, they'd been working together as allies. The same went for Navi and Agri. Those relationships were kind of like something out of a shoujo manga.

Her connection with Tepsekemei was something of a cat-and-mouse game, like a thief and a detective. That sort of thing could be a bond stronger even than friendship, at times.

That meant it was fair to treat Clarissa the same way, since she'd just run away from her. And that would make Clarissa's boss Navi Ru the same.

Rareko and Maiya had been killed by the goddess. They would have died feeling regrets. They would be cheering Chelsea on, telling her to *"Do your best, don't give in."*

The two kids were Chelsea's friends—since children were always friends to magical girls.

She could go ahead and count Mana as a child, too. And 7753—yes, she'd been in her pajamas, so they were friends. She'd been standing in basically the same position as Chelsea in a bathrobe. They were sleepwear friends.

One more, yes: Clantail was an animal. Magical girls and animals were highly compatible. If you counted her as a mascot character, then she would fit in the partner position.

The goddess readied her ax in her right hand. Her left hand was lightly open, idle near her chest. Chelsea readied herself as well. She drew in a deep breath and blew out another. Power circled to each and every hair, crackling as they rose around her. It would be okay. She was the greatest magical girl. She gradually backed up her star decoration, securing the distance for acceleration.

"Here I go!"

The bottom of her star decoration skimmed the floor. It scattered rubble. She made her star run in a low-altitude flight that was inches from an accident. Chelsea was not alone. She had accepted everyone's feelings. Ragi, Marguerite, Nephilia, Ren-Ren, Agri, Tepsekemei, Clarissa, Navi, Rareko, Maiya, the two kids, Mana, 7753, and Clantail stood at her side. Pastel Mary and Shepherdspie were firmly pushing her from behind. A mysterious energy welled up from the pit of her stomach, her body temperature rose, and the feelings she'd jumbled together by force became a power that enveloped her.

The goddess's free left hand came to sit alongside the handle of her ax in a natural movement, and she raised her ax in a stance pointing toward the eyes. In terms of just her bearing, she looked like a master. It was a dramatic way to hold the weapon after swinging it around too much with just one hand. Then the goddess laughed clearly, in a voice like tinkling bells. Chelsea had never heard the sound before. But it was cute. She felt the power. It gathered at one point. The blade transformed, shifting smoothly to become a giant battle-ax with a blade five feet long and over a foot wide. Maybe it was too crude to call a battle-ax. Chelsea would believe it if you said that this weapon was going to be carved into the shape of an ax.

Chelsea narrowed her eyes. It wasn't just the size and shape. The color of the blade was dark, and it had become black. It was not a black originating from a mineral. It was a black deeper than black and shadow. Chelsea had seen this before. Her mother had once had a friend with multiple wings that were a color like this. She remembered that person because her mother had used polite language with her, though a lazy version with casual language mixed in it—something indescribable ran down Chelsea's spine, something that made her shiver that you couldn't even give a name to. With the hem of her tattered skirt fluttering, she did an emergency stop, standing her star perpendicular to the ground, and extended her bent knees to kick off the other way.

At just about the same instant, Chelsea was blasted away. The star decoration, floor, ceiling, rubble, everything was scattered, whizzing through the sky. All sound stopped. Even the wind slowed. An intense impact slammed Chelsea's whole body.

She saw the goddess coming right after her faster than even the speed at which everything was flying away, and Chelsea clenched her fists. She ordered the star in her palm to try to get away, and a beat later the goddess did a horizontal sweep.

Though she thought she'd evaded a direct hit, Chelsea's body flew horizontally. Something hit her back, and she didn't even have the time to realize that it was the wall of the main building before she broke through the next wall and the one after that, then hit her shoulder on the ground and bounced, rebounded, and rolled, breaking through a door to hit something hard, rolling along as she scattered multiple stars in all directions. Mary and the others should be somewhere in the main building. She had to warn them. She had to tell them to hide.

She couldn't hear any sound, but it was like energy was firing wildly in her brain. When she exhaled, bubbles mixed with blood blew out with her breath. Pain pierced her whole body. Her blood was flowing away. It wouldn't stop. She tried to stand up. Just trying to move her arms and legs made pain run through them. Something hot welled up from deep in her throat, and she spat it up. It wasn't vomit. Syrupy, thick blood was mixed in it. The blood wasn't just coming from her mouth. She had been completely sliced open, from her right shoulder to her chest.

She shifted her bottom away from a broken mop, kicking away a bucket, putting her hand to a broom to stand up using it as a cane. Her field of vision was misting pink, and on the other side of the door that was creaking and breaking, the goddess was raising her weapon.

◇ Ragi Zwe Nento

As soon as he opened the door and looked into the room, Mary let out a little shriek and sank down weakly in place. Even Ragi felt some fear, but his curiosity was greater, and a powerful ire was even greater than that, which kept his limbs moving. He went around Mary, who was still sitting there trembling, to push open the doors, lighting the room with the magic glow he made on his palm.

There were rows of transparent containers two sizes bigger than a normal human. This in itself was not unique. These could be seen in any research facility in the Magical Kingdom. They were mainly used as cultivation tanks, and also like the ones in this room. These containers had indicator lights on them, with cords and hoses connected as well. Greenish, translucent fluid filled the vessels, and the bodies of magical girls floated within. The forms floating there with full hair and spotless white togas met the description of the wild magical girl who was on the loose on this island.

Ragi's eyes swiftly ran from one end of the room to the other. There were ten containers in total with nine magical-girl bodies floating there. One container was empty. Ragi approached it, placing his palm against the glass, and when he was close enough to touch his forehead to it, he looked inside. Fluid—probably cultivation fluid—was accumulated at the bottom. The inside of the container was also damp. It was fair to assume that there had been a magical girl here until recently.

Ragi turned back and called out to Mary. "There's no need to be afraid. The bases here haven't been set up for operation."

Mary let out a deep breath, leaning against the wall as she rose to her feet, and then she let out another deep breath. Her eyes were bloodshot, and her lower lashes were wet and stuck to her face. "Um…one of them is empty… Is the person who was in there…?"

"It's natural to assume that it's the ruffian who's on a rampage outside."

Mary's eyes flared wide open. The hand she was resting against the wall tensed, and the wall made a nasty sound and cracked. A little piece fell down to bounce off the floor, where it rolled to Ragi's feet. "So then doesn't that mean…if we use the…um, nine people in here, then we can restrain the one going crazy out there? If it's nine against one, then they couldn't lose, right?"

"I just said they haven't been set up for operation." Ragi turned away from Mary, who was visibly disappointed, and toward the room. Pointing his light from one corner to the other, he searched the room. Aside from the containers and what came with them, there was just a cabinet in the corner, seven feet high and fifteen feet wide. The doors of the cabinet were all open. It was not locked. It was packed with a variety of stacks of paper that looked like records and data. As he picked some up, Ragi's eyebrows furrowed. It was written in an ancient script. He pulled whatever didn't look useful and tossed the rest aside, stirring up dust as he made piles on the floor, and at around halfway through, he discovered some writing that looked like the same script. The book seemed like a service manual.

"…Francisca Francesca," Ragi muttered.

"What's that?" Mary asked him.

"The name of those things over there, apparently."

The spelling and grammar were in the style of the later period of ancient script. It was the same as the label on the gargling medicine— did that mean it had been written by the same person?

The wrinkles between Ragi's eyes deepened. This place looked very much like a secret research lab, which fit perfectly with

Sataborn's boundlessly childish character. Ragi also felt an immature provocation in how he'd made use of a minor ancient language to write documents in, as if to say, *"If you're a researcher, of course you should be able to read this."*

Ragi broke the seal on a bottle labeled STOMACH MEDICINE and drank down the thick, viscous liquid. This one was also labeled in an ancient language. Judging from how the styles matched, Sataborn had written this. Sataborn must also have been the one to do the compounding and effects, as well as the adjustment of the ingredients. Even if a store-bought gargle medicine had the hidden effect of awakening a passed-out mage, would it have such an immediate efficacy? This was Sataborn, so it had to be specially made, with excessive labor invested to show off.

Ragi capped the half-drunk stomach medicine and tucked it into his robe. He would like to bemoan his hardship in having to rely on Sataborn's dubious pharmaceuticals, but he had something more important to do.

"Mr. Ragi."

"Wait a minute."

He flipped through the pages. He got the gist of the main points. This document was, as it said, a manual. It detailed just what sort of thing the completed item was. Ragi put a finger between his brow and rubbed out the wrinkles. There was almost certainly no mistaking it. This was the magical-girl base that had been made to serve as an incarnation for one of the Three Sages. He lightly bit his lower lip. This wasn't something natural magical girls could beat once it was activated, even if no spirit had been summoned into it.

Is there no way to bring it to a halt? There should be a stopper for emergencies.

He flipped to the end and clenched his teeth. There was a page with a piece torn out. It was the part that related to Francesca's weakness. Had someone ripped it out?

Along with rising rage and despair, he also had a feeling something was off. He flipped again from page one, rereading the manual apart from what was missing, and assembled a hypothesis. It

"Oh yeah, Leon just asked me if I'm into cross-dressing," he recalled.

"Would you like to try? The employees here would gladly lend you a makeup kit," Zem said.

Nick felt stares and looked up to see the men behind the counter looking at him with great interest.

"...How about it?" one of them asked.

"Not today," Nick replied.

"Aw, that's a shame. Let me know if you have a change of heart, hon." The employee laughed and set down a plate in front of Nick.

It was a stew consisting of passenger pigeon meat, onions, and broad beans seasoned with tomatoes and chili peppers. This dish had come from abroad over a century ago and had become a staple in Labyrinth City. Many who mistook it as local cuisine called it Labyrinth Stew or Labyrinth Chicken, and the fact that it was from another country was all but forgotten.

Nick often made it with wild birds they caught when they camped for their adventures. He used the recipe he learned from his parents when he was young. His party members liked it, and Tiana was fond of bringing the leftovers home to eat later.

"Hmm...this is pretty good," Nick said.

"Isn't it, though?"

"I'm so happy you like it!"

The employees voiced their joy with sugary voices.

"Don't get me wrong, though. My version is better," Nick added.

"Why do you have to make it a competition, Nick?" Zem asked.

"Sorry, can't help it." It truly was delicious. It was too spicy to eat regularly, but it made for an enjoyable meal at a bar. "You know, this place is nice once you get used to it," Nick muttered.

The employees took great interest in Nick as a first-time customer, but they were not being pushy with him. Many hostess clubs tended to be predatory and have the girls pressure the customers into letting them serve them; that was true of the hostess clubs Nick had been brought to, at least. This bar gave the customers space to enjoy themselves in their own way. It was surprisingly comfortable.

"Isn't it? It is quite relaxing," Zem agreed.

"I thought you preferred restaurants with female servers," Nick said.

The former priest smiled. "To be perfectly honest, women scare me."

"...Oh yeah. You're mostly scared of girls in their early teens, right?"

Nick remembered Zem's story well. A young girl had ruined his life by spreading a lie through his sanctuary that he'd raped her—he couldn't forget that if he tried.

"What I feel toward young girls is more than fear—it is trauma. And that is true of women in general."

"Oh, okay."

Nick was surprised, but it made sense. Zem went to hostess clubs and other restaurants with waitresses often. A female had ruined his life, while another had saved him from the brink of despair. It would be easier for him if only one of the two had been true, but both happening in rapid succession gave him a feeling of powerlessness around women that he couldn't escape. Despite his fear, he was doing his best to enjoy the presence of women and become comfortable around them. Nick figured he went to hostess clubs for the thrill of overcoming that fear.

"You're right. Women are terrifying," one of the employees said.

"We may have been born male, but we're women at heart. Tee-hee," another added.

"There's nothing wrong with you all being women at heart. I mean, some creatures are genderless. Some are male and female at the same time. It's up to you to decide who you truly are," Nick said. The employees looked at him wide-eyed. "Wh-what is it?"

"...I see why Zemmy brought you here. You have promise, Nick. Here's my business card," said the employee who looked mysteriously androgynous. He sat down next to Nick, produced a business card from his pocket and kissed it, leaving a bright red kiss mark. He then tossed it at Nick.

"I'm not making any promises about becoming a regular, though..."

"Come now. We're going to be working together, you know?"

"Whuh?" Unsure what he meant, Nick looked down at the business card. He was flabbergasted by what he saw. "You're a lawyer?! Wait, don't tell me..."

The business card said, SOUTH GATE LAW FIRM. REDD CHAMBERS, ATTORNEY AT LAW.

"That's right. I'll be defending Leon. I look forward to your assistance with this case," Redd said with a wink.

"Wow." Nick was stunned and unsure of what to say. "...Uh, this card says, SOUTH GATE LAW FIRM."

"Oh, this is a two-story building. The first floor is a bar, and the second is a law firm," Redd explained.

"Is that allowed?!" Nick exclaimed.

"I have a permit, so it's perfectly fine," Redd said, showing his collar. There was a badge sewn onto it, designed after a balance scale. Only lawyers certified by the kingdom could wear it. "I am defending Leon, but I plan on having his victims be reimbursed in full. Let's aim for a win-win outcome."

"S-sounds good," Nick responded.

"You can count on me. The trial isn't for some time, though. We'll discuss the details at a later date. Just enjoy yourself for today," Redd said before returning to the other side of the counter. Nick watched him go in stunned silence.

"Are you surprised?" Zem asked.

"Of course I am… I totally forgot what we were talking about," Nick said.

"Hmm… Oh, yes. We were discussing my fear of women."

"You know, I think I agree with you, Zem. Women *are* scary. And men, too."

"You are right about that."

"You're pretty scary yourself, Zem."

"I am? How so?"

"You've saved a lot of people in your life with your treatment. Lawyers help a lot of people, too. There's no way a person can have that much power and not frighten others."

Zem looked hurt by Nick's words. "D-do I really scare people?"

"Think about the people you heal and give medicine to. They don't want to anger you because they're afraid of getting rejected. You're their only source for treatment—if you cut them off, they're toast."

"No, I would never think like that when…," Zem began, but stopped. There was no way for his patients to know his true intentions. What's more, he had been using his healing talents for his own benefit since coming to Labyrinth City. He had even used them to threaten wicked hostess clubs that tried to swindle their customers. "…I see your point. People with power are frightening and cannot be opposed. No matter how pure of heart they may appear."

There was no guarantee they would never have a change of heart. Neither Zem nor Nick voiced that possibility.

"It is impressive you are able to think that way, Nick," Zem said.

"Really?" Nick responded.

"You were swindled, too. By Claudine."

"Don't bring that up." Nick glared at Zem.

"Ha-ha, my apologies," Zem replied with an awkward laugh.

"Now that I think about it, she and Leon were probably scared of us on some level. That was why they targeted us."

"...I see."

"Do you disagree?" Nick asked, and Zem shook his head.

"I cannot say whether that is true. I am sure you know better than me. What I can say is that picking a fight with someone just because they terrify you would not be particularly smart," he responded.

"You've got a point there."

"On the other hand, speaking to someone who frightens you takes courage. You could consider what they did an unlucky gamble."

"Gambling sure is scary. I'm sure Tiana would have something to say about that, though."

"Most likely. At least I was able to get my thoughts in order. It appears as if I have an inclination toward gambling as well, but different from hers."

"Go easy on the flirting, man," Nick said, and Zem grinned.

"That is enough about me. I wanted to ask if anything was bothering you."

"Eh, I'm fine. There's one thing I'm worried about, but it's not a big deal."

"I can tell it is important to you. What is wrong?" Zem urged. Nick made a troubled expression. After a lengthy silence, he forced himself to speak.

"...She's taking a break."

"A break? Who?"

"Agate, my favorite idol. She's taking a hiatus from all idol activities."

The Decision of Belle Huggins (Agate the Idol)

"How would you like to be an idol?"

Yet another shady customer. I started working at this bar three months ago and thought I had gotten used to handling the difficult ones. That was naive of me. This man looked so suspicious, he made me want to quit my job.

He was a large man dressed all in black. He was bald and had a neatly trimmed beard. Everything about the man's appearance screamed dangerous. I couldn't see him working a respectable job—if I had to guess, I'd have said he was an assassin.

"U-umm...I'm sorry, but it's against the rules for people from other bars to headhunt here."

"Oh, I see we have a misunderstanding, Belle. I won't deny that I am recruiting you, but I am not from another bar. Would you mind giving me a few minutes of your time?" he asked.

"Huh...," I gasped, frightened. He handed me a business card, and I took it without thinking. It said, JEWELRY PRODUCTION PRODUCER—JOSEPH COLEMAN.

"Hey, Belle. How many times do I have to tell you to chase away any weird customers?"

"Ah, s-sorry, Donny!"

Donny appeared from the kitchen. He must have sensed

trouble. He probably wanted to go ahead and close the restaurant, but he couldn't start cleaning up as long as there were customers around. It always put him in a foul mood when customers continued chatting right up until closing time, delaying when he could leave. His irritation was even stronger toward those who came to see me. His temper wasn't nearly so bad when he first opened the store, though.

I'm Belle Huggins—a singer at this bar and also Donny's girlfriend. I was happy to see him jealous, but there were elements of his behavior I wasn't okay with. It was for his sake that I sang and tried to grow the restaurant's popularity. I wished he would think of protecting me before he got mad at me, but I knew how busy he was.

"So what do you want?" Donny asked the man curtly.

"Apologies for the intrusion. Are you this bar's owner?" the man asked. His apology seemed to improve Donny's mood.

"Yes, but you don't seem like a customer."

"I want to recruit this girl as an idol."

"An idol?"

"That's right. Technically, she will be a candidate for an eventual debut as an idol."

"That sounds interesting," Donny muttered, apparently intrigued. I glared at him to hint not to trust this shady man at his word, but he ignored me. "That's wonderful. This is a chance for you to make it big, Belle. You shouldn't pass this up."

"I've never even seen an idol before," I protested.

"Then how about you consider it after going to one of their concerts?" Donny suggested.

The man in black clothes—Joseph—smiled in response to Donny's advice. "That is a great idea. I would love for you to come to one. How would you like to come backstage after the show? The staff will let you through if you give them my business card."

Joseph forced a concert ticket into my hand along with his

business card. He told me that the town hall in the southern side of Labyrinth City held many singing and dancing events, and he pestered me to come while saying that he "respected my intentions." He quickly left the bar after his business was done. Dressed like an assassin with the bearing of a salesman—curious.

Honestly, I didn't expect anything of the event at the time. I was too busy worrying that I was falling into a trap.

"...Hey, Donny. Why were you so eager about his proposal?" I asked him when it was finally time to leave after cleaning the kitchen and closing the shop. I immediately regretted my critical tone, but it was how I felt. It didn't feel good to be treated as expendable when I was working so hard to help the restaurant.

"It'll be fine. Customer traffic isn't bad right now. There have to be better places for you to sing than here," he replied, not picking up on my tone.

"I guess so, but..."

The reason I was working as a waitress and singer here was to help grow its popularity. I wasn't going to say this out loud, but my singing was well received, and many customers came specifically to see me. I wasn't sure if the bar would be able to survive if I left to become an idol.

"I know how hard you're working to support me. But I opened this bar to serve food and alcohol... I don't want to cheat my way to success."

"Are you calling my help 'cheating'?!"

"Don't get me wrong, *I'm* not saying that. I just hear that from customers sometimes."

"...I don't think it's good to take what customers say at face value."

"Trust me, I know how hard you're working. It's just...I'll never be able to pay you back if I keep relying on you all the time. I want to grow the bar through my own ability."

"Well…if that's what you want, I'll respect your wishes."

He should have just said it outright if he didn't want me around anymore. He should have never asked for my help in the first place if he thought any profit I brought to the bar was "cheating."

Rather than voice my complaints, I gripped the ticket and decided to go to the idol concert. I had no idea how much my life was about to change.

I went to the town hall alone. We couldn't both leave the restaurant, and Donny didn't seem interested in attending. The south side of Labyrinth City wasn't as dangerous as the east side, but it still wasn't a good idea for a girl to walk the streets by herself. I felt anxious and vulnerable and confused by the strange air of excitement around me. It didn't help that the other spectators were all filthy-looking men.

I almost turned around and left multiple times on the way, but I ended up encountering two girls at the venue. I felt like I had been saved. They seemed a little overwhelmed by the atmosphere at the town hall as well, and we hit it off immediately and decided to watch the concert together.

One of the girls had long blond hair and an easygoing manner. "This place is crazy. Can you believe this crowd? I was worried I came to the wrong place at first, so thank you," she said. She was pretty enough to be an idol herself but quite absentminded; I was worried she was going to get abducted if she wasn't careful.

The other one was a cheerful girl with short hair. She looked the most afraid out of all of us when we found her, but joining us seemed to restore her confidence, and she took the lead in our group. "W-well, there's no point in getting all flustered. We were given these tickets, so it would be a waste to leave now," she said. The way she was constantly trying to encourage us had me a little worried about her, too. She didn't seem like a bad girl, though. She found a nice spot in the venue to protect us from the jostling crowd as we watched the concert.

"Yeah, you're right. We might as well give the concert a chance," I said to convey my thanks to the two. I likely would have lost heart and left if I hadn't met them.

I ended up very glad that I didn't leave. I was enraptured the moment the concert began. The idols shone as they sang. It was scintillating. I had no idea that such an exciting stage existed for singers to perform upon.

I rushed backstage to see Joseph after the show, still flushed from excitement. For some reason, the two girls I was with were allowed entrance as well.

"That was incredible! I was blown away!" I exclaimed.

"It was really fun!"

"Yeah, I loved it!"

The other two girls agreed with flushed faces. Joseph's stern expression relaxed slightly. He studied each of us in turn and spoke slowly.

"I am glad you had a good time. Now…on the topic of becoming idols—"

I interrupted him with a shout. "I would love to be an idol!"

"Wonderful. That's a yes from you. How about you two?" Joseph asked, turning to the other girls.

"I want to be one, too!" the blond-haired girl said.

"I was all in from the start," the short-haired girl claimed.

I looked at them both with surprise. I hadn't realized they had been scouted like me.

"You're both idol candidates, too?" I asked.

"Huh? Did we not tell you?"

"…I thought you would've noticed. You were sitting right next to us."

They were both surprised I didn't realize it, and I looked down, blushing. Joseph spoke again to change the mood.

"Oh yes, I never told you. I invited all three of you. You will be idol trainees together. Let's give this our all," he said.

""""Okay!""""

The next day, I was given the name *Agate*. With my new name came a new life. I started to take vocal training and dance lessons. I even received free soap and perfume.

I became friends with the girls I'd gone to the concert with. The absentminded girl with long hair was named Topaz, and the cheerful one with short hair was named Amber. My pre-debut training was always with the two of them. I was good at singing but bad at dancing. Amber was the opposite—she was great at dancing. Topaz wasn't particularly good at either, but she had a fervor you never would have expected from her absentminded appearance.

It was a new experience for me. I had gotten into arguments with friends my age before, but never through the pursuit of a shared goal. We pushed each other to dance in sync, to sing energetically, and to learn how to fire up an audience. We strove to be the best we could be.

I had never had female friends like them. My parents had died a few years back, and after being evicted from our rental home, I supported myself by moving from one live-in job to another. I did make friends at those jobs, but we never had a shared goal. We comforted each other by complaining about our work, men, customers, and our own failures, but we didn't spend much time wishing for each other's happiness. Our days were hard and dark; we didn't have the mental leeway to do so.

That was why I came to love Donny. He spoke of his dreams and asked me to help him achieve them. I respected him for trying to find light in the darkness. I worked as hard as I could to support the bar, and no matter how tired I felt, all the exhaustion left my body when he thanked me for my efforts. I had only ever latched on to other people's dreams—it wasn't until I began training as an idol that I realized I could pursue my own.

It wasn't all sunshine and rainbows, of course. Some idols and trainees grew jealous and antagonistic toward me. But that just showed how serious we were in our efforts to reach the stage. The girls didn't just curse their rivals' names in bed at night; they would pick fights and use words that cut like a blade.

I didn't want to lose. That was the first time I realized how competitive I was.

"You haven't been helping out much lately," Donny said.

"S-sorry," I replied.

"No, it's fine. I'm the one who said you didn't have to, and I feel bad for not being able to pay you enough. It's just...I really could use you on the weekends when it gets busy."

"I don't mind that, but... Wait, where's Rose?"

"She quit."

"Huh? Why?"

Rose was a waitress at Donny's bar. We weren't close because our shifts didn't overlap very often, but I thought she was a good worker. Her bright and friendly personality made her a nice fit for serving customers, and she had worked at the bar since day one. I thought she had an attachment to the place, even if not to Donny's extent.

"...I kinda snapped at her. She was getting greedy."

"Greedy...? Wait, were you paying Rose poorly, too?"

"A-anyway, I'm counting on you!" Donny said evasively before withdrawing to the kitchen.

Looking back, I think we should have discussed the bar's future at that point. I was preoccupied with my idol work and a little too excited to think about anything else. It had been determined that I would open for the popular idol Garnet—who belonged to the same agency—and debut a song. I was concentrating all my efforts into practicing for the event.

Even if the concert hadn't been a factor, though, I was already thinking in a corner of my mind that my help wouldn't change a thing. Donny's customer traffic had only decreased after I stopped singing there regularly. He had apparently hired some girls to fill the hole I had left, but none of them lasted long. I thought his low salaries and the irregularity of his business hours were the biggest reasons the bar was failing, but I didn't say anything. It was clear he wouldn't listen to anything I said. Whenever I asked him about finances, he would just say, "I have a plan," and refuse to give me any details.

So I just devoted myself to my work. Part of the reason I worked so hard on my idol activities was because I didn't want to think about Donny. But whatever my motivation, my performance was well received. Garnet praised me onstage, and a rumor that there was a promising new idol spread among the fans.

Not long afterward, my official debut was set. Topaz and Amber congratulated me. They also admitted their regrets that I had surpassed them. They trained really hard and debuted after me, but I was the first among my contemporaries. If I had been overtaken by one of them, I would've been too jealous to sleep.

But they didn't want me to fail. They didn't curse my success. They might have done so out of my sight, but they both did so much to support me. They gave serious consideration to what I could do to stand out onstage, what I should do with my hair and clothes, and how I could survive as a new idol.

All Donny said was, "Wish I could be so lucky."

Donny's bar grew quieter and quieter. His closing time came earlier in the day, and he took an increasing number of days off.

"Can you lend me a little money?" he asked me one day.

"Is the bar doing that poorly?"

"Y-yeah... The interest will be really bad if I borrow from moneylenders again. So please?"

I was unable to refuse him in the end. I wasn't against the idea of lending him money. I wouldn't have minded doing so if he was going to use it to get through this difficult time and turn the bar's situation around.

I saw no sign he was going to put in the effort, though. He blamed customers for not coming, he chewed out his part-time workers, and he cursed the world for his troubles. Just being around him made me feel depressed. Eventually I started just giving him money and rushing to work without a word. I felt most relaxed when I was napping on the sofa at the office during my breaks between training and other odd jobs.

My time was filled with concerts, introducing restaurants and magic item shops, and being interviewed by newspaper reporters. My fans gradually increased, my songs spread, and I became famous. For some reason, Donny's behavior only grew worse as I achieved greater success. We were like light and shadow. As I devoted myself more and more to my idol work, my personal life had me exhausted. It was hard being with Donny.

It was around that time I witnessed something terrible. It happened when I was trying out a bunch of different cafés, desperate for some alone time. Donny had never taken me to a café before, but I had been to a few with producers and other idols from my agency, and I started going by myself as well.

There was an especially nice one called Fromage. It wasn't a high-class restaurant, but it wasn't noisy like a bar, either. I thought of it as a pleasant place where people like me who were becoming famous could relax. Until I heard the conversation at the table behind me anyway.

A young man was being threatened by a beautiful girl and two imposing men. It seemed like the girl was deceiving the young man into supporting her financially, and she dumped him after learning that he'd quit his job...or something like that. I just went to the café to enjoy some delicious cake, but every piece of their conversation I heard made the cake taste bitter.

"You were super good at finding bargains on accessories from street vendors and peddlers, Nick. This talisman has been very useful. I'm grateful for that, truly... But I'm done with you."

They weren't speaking loudly enough for me to hear every word from my table, but I could tell the girl was taking pleasure in her wrongdoing.

"Urgh..."

I almost spat out a mouthful of cake. This kind of situation was far from rare. I saw it all the time at restaurants I used to work at, and I had even gone through a similar experience. Someone might lend money only to never be paid back, or have their purse stolen when they weren't paying attention. I wasn't raised in the best area, so you would think I was used to seeing these kinds of petty crimes. Despite that, I couldn't help from getting nauseous.

What scared me was the thought that I might have been headed for the same fate as this young man. Donny was different, wasn't he? I wanted to ask but was scared to. The young man left, and before I knew it, I was walking through the city looking for him.

He was in a bad state when I found him. He was dripping wet in the rain, looking like a stray dog on the verge of death. I pretended our meeting was a coincidence, and I talked to him.

"Leave me alone."

He rejected me coldly. I supposed that was a natural reaction. I probably would have run for my life if someone had addressed me with no warning like that. But I didn't give up. I kept talking to him and ended up giving him a concert ticket that was meant for family and friends. I had an extra that Donny had refused.

I was happy when I saw him at the concert. That was just according to plan. He was dressed like a novice adventurer, so I immediately recognized him from onstage. The enthusiasm of the idol fans drew him in, and he enjoyed the concert to the fullest.

It wasn't long before I started to feel guilty that I might have pulled him in too deep. He bought a coat and a magic glow stick set, came to every concert, and even frequented fan club events. Just when I started to worry about how much money he was spending immediately after being swindled by his ex-girlfriend, he disappeared.

I was worried that something terrible might have happened to him, but I had no choice except to press on with my work. I was overjoyed when I next saw him on my day off. He had cleaned up so that he no longer looked like a stray dog—he must have been working hard. It was even better when I talked to him as he was stressing out over a trivial matter involving one of his party members. It was an endearing problem to have when compared to what he had been through.

I gave him what advice I could, then told him to take care of himself and keep working hard. He said that he would. I was glad that I had become an idol.

One month passed. My relationship with Donny was collapsing after I discovered that he was wasting the money I was lending him on gambling instead of using it as working capital for the bar. I happened upon him with a shady-looking man when passing through the area. He was closing for the day and leaving for a gambling parlor even though the busiest time of day for a bar was just getting started.

We got into an argument. I told him I couldn't lend him money anymore, and he lost his temper like never before. He told me that it was my fault he was in this predicament and that it was my responsibility to help him. I watched in horror as Donny was obviously taking what the shady tigerian said at face value.

After realizing he was now incapable of hearing anything other than flattery, there was nothing for me to do but leave the bar.

The next day, I had my third meeting with the young man. This time, I ended up turning to him for advice. That said, I couldn't tell a fan that "I'm stressed out because my boyfriend is a freeloader and gambler," so I gave a vague explanation. I told him clumsily that a friend of mine had lost their confidence and was in a dark place.

The young man looked at me like I was stupid and said, "Aren't you forgetting something?" I started to get mad, but his next words caught me off guard.

"You said it yourself, remember? It's an idol's job to make people happy and give them courage."

He was right. That was why I was working as an idol. People could change, just like the young man before me. If he could turn his life around, maybe Donny could, too. I at least wanted him to come to one of my concerts; I thought it might make him feel something. I believed that idols had the power to make people happy. I wanted to test that one last time.

"Urgh, what a goddamn pain..."

It wasn't easy, but I got Donny to begrudgingly promise to come to one of my concerts. He had one condition: I had to accompany him to a casino. I reluctantly accepted, and we made our way to one through a light rain.

"I know you think I'm a slob. I admit I've let you down many times. I'm sorry for that. But I'm not going to the casino without a plan," he said.

"...What's your plan?" I asked.

"You remember the tigerian you saw at the bar the other day?"

"Yeah."

"He was arrested for match-fixing, fraud, and a bunch of other stuff. He was a crook."

"...I don't understand."

"Huh? What do you mean?"

"If he was arrested, you should lay off the gambling... Weren't you a regular at his gambling parlor?"

"No, you don't get it. He tricked me. I'm a victim of his."

"Then why—"

"He had to fix my matches because he knew how good I was at gambling. I'll be able to win at a legitimate casino like this. Don't you see?"

It went even worse than I could have imagined. I wished I hadn't come. Anyone could see that Donny was an easy mark. He did occasionally get lucky and win at cards, but only when the dealer allowed it to rope him further in. I was sure he had fallen for this trick many times already, but he was totally oblivious.

The dealer and the other guest at the table praised Donny profusely. They complimented him on his "manly wagers" and said he was the "type of player who shows his true skill when the game is on the line." It was obvious flattery, but he fell for all of it. They even said things to me that set my teeth on edge. They realized I was his source of money. I tried hard not to glare at them.

I was fond of Donny's dream. I don't mean to speak ill of those who fight to make a living at casinos, but I thought Donny looked so absurd, I wanted to cry as I saw him throw away his dream in favor of delusions of fleeting success. I watched the cards dance across the table, wondering where things went wrong.

Eventually a woman joined the table and upended the entire situation. I've never played cards before, so I didn't know how exactly she did it, but she dominated the table. She was taking all the coins for herself before anyone even understood what was happening. By the time the game was over, the dealer, the other guest, and Donny were all despondent. Donny likely realized he was nothing more than prey for truly skilled gamblers like her. He slumped his shoulders dejectedly.

"A true gambler plays with their own money. If you can't do that, you're little better than an overgrown child," she said to Donny, driving the final nail into the coffin. Her words may have been meant for me as well.

She flipped her long blond hair and walked gallantly away, and I chased after her without thinking. I pressed her for her name and introduced myself. For some reason, I told her all about Donny and our relationship. I didn't tell her about my work as an idol, but I shared much more of my embarrassing situation than I needed to.

The woman, whose name was Tiana, gave a cold reply. "What if you just dump him?" she said. "Actually, you probably wanted to hear me say that." Her reaction made sense, though. As we talked, I began to question why I was dating Donny in the first place. I felt like I had obtained something to help myself live another day.

My memory of everything afterward on that night was hazy. I hadn't forgotten what happened, but it was all so absurd that I wasn't confident any of it was real. The only thing I remembered clearly was a beautiful knight protecting me from a tiger monster.

"We have paid the entire debt you owed to the casino. We will also shoulder all loans you accepted on verbal promises. You no longer have to worry about pursuit from debt collectors."

Three people were sitting in a small room divided by a partition. One was a bald man in black clothes—Joseph, a producer at my talent agency. He was dispassionately rattling off a long and tedious contract to the man before him. I could hardly believe my ears—he was assuming the man's entire sizable debt.

"However..."

Joseph paused and looked hard at the man sitting across from him. The man was Donny. He had a bandage on his arm from the night in the casino, but that wasn't nearly as conspicuous as the loneliness and frustration visible on his face.

"Your relationship with our idol ends right now. You must never speak to her again, and if you happen upon her by chance, you must stay away. You must also keep quiet on every detail you know about her, no matter how trivial. If we discover that you let something slip…"

Donny trembled in fear.

"We will ask you to repay the debt we assumed. We will entrust that to a professional collector, of course. If anything you do has a negative impact on her idol activities, we will bill you for any loss of profit. Are you aware of what that would mean for your life?" Joseph asked.

"A-all right, I get it…," Donny said without meeting Joseph's eyes. He turned in his chair uncomfortably and looked at the third person in the room—me—pleadingly. "I-I'm sorry, Belle. I never meant wrong. So—"

"Enough, Donny." I shook my head. "I'm Agate. I'm not your Belle, and I never will be. Forget about the past."

Donny hung his head. I felt a bit of sympathy well up inside me. I liked this man. From the bottom of my heart, I wanted to support him. It was hard to watch him fall so low.

The day that strange monster attacked the casino, Donny abandoned me and ran. It was over for us at that moment. I decided to break up with him, then told Joseph everything and asked for his help. He did not take the news well. He was furious, in fact. He told me I was a danger to myself, that I needed to act like an idol, and that I needed to "break up with him right this instant." It pained me, but I had no choice but to do as he said.

I also told him about the mysterious knight who had saved me at the casino. They were like a hero out of legend. I was relieved he seemed to react well to that part of the story. In any case, I had no choice but to move forward. That was why I called Donny here today. It was time to end our relationship once and for all.

"Donny…I wanted to support you forever. But I can't. Do your best without me. I won't ask you to help me anymore," I declared, looking Donny straight in the eyes.

He opened his mouth to speak but closed it and hung his head in silence. He then signed the document that Joseph gave him. It was a contract laying out the talent agency's proposal. The agency was going to release him from his gambling debts in return for his silence on my identity as the idol Agate. From this day on, Donny and I were going to walk completely separate paths.

"…I'm sorry," Donny muttered so quietly, I could barely hear it as he exited the room.

I sighed with relief when Donny left the office. I was finally done with all the problems I had been ignoring for so long. But this wasn't an ending; if anything, it was a new beginning.

"I am so sorry for the trouble," I said.

"Don't worry about it. Just pay me back with hard work," Joseph responded indifferently. He was probably still angry, but he wasn't the type of person to lose his temper at someone. He helped me out of my situation with Donny so that I—or rather, the idol Agate—could continue to work. That meant there was one thing I needed to do.

"About your next job—," he began, but I interrupted him.

"I want to write a new song, Mr. Coleman," I said.

"Oh?"

"I want to write the lyrics, too."

I had been proactive with my training and idol activities, but when it came to more fundamental parts of the job like planning and deciding what songs I would sing, I had only ever done what my producers told me. I could make the excuse that I was too occupied overcoming more immediate hurdles, but I hadn't given any thought to what kind of idol I wanted to be.

Until now.

"Do you know what you want to sing about?" Joseph asked.

Idol songs all had a theme. Minstrels, from which idols descended, did more than just sing. Their original purpose was to tour the lands and convey the beauty of nature and the preciousness of love they observed on their travels. They entertained people with the imagery their songs inspired, transporting them to places they would never see and telling them of people they would never meet. Minstrels didn't just rely on their beautiful voices—it was an important mission of theirs to use their skills to inform people of the beauty of the world.

But minstrels had another theme that was just as important for them to handle.

"Yes, I do," I answered resolutely.

After that, I temporarily suspended my normal idol activities and withdrew from the concerts I was scheduled to participate in. I spent an entire month writing a new song and training to perform it. My anguish-filled days as a writer and my path toward becoming a true idol were just beginning.

The Idol Stan Who Dreams of Being an S-Rank Adventurer

After a long break, Agate was finally about to take the stage once again.

Many rumors circulated among Agate's fans during her mysterious hiatus, some of it being terrible gossip. Only a small number of fans ceased to support her, however. This went without saying, but Nick was one of the fans who believed in her and waited. When a concert schedule posted on a park bulletin board included a solo Agate concert, her fans lost their minds with excitement. The rumor that she had retired was unfounded. Nick was as ecstatic as anyone and decided to get in line at the ticket booth early—so early that he camped out overnight.

He was one of dozens of adult men lining up at the ticket booth, which was so unusual that a stray dog that had wandered into the park turned tail and fled at the sight of them. Karan happened upon Nick on her way to breakfast when the sun rose that morning. She was taken aback when he told her he had been there all night, and she bought him a coffee with a warning that he would catch a cold. Nick accepted it gratefully but felt embarrassed when the other fans looked at him with sharp, accusing glares. They assumed Karan was his girlfriend.

Fortunately, he wouldn't have to put up with that much longer. It was almost time for the ticket booth to open.

"Hey, Nick," the man sitting next to him said.

"What's up, Willy?" Nick responded.

Willy was an adventurer who frequented the Fishermen Adventurers Guild. Nick approached the man after seeing him at both concerts and the guild, and they became concert buddies.

"...There's a rumor going around about a guy who makes his girlfriend wait in line for him to buy tickets, and another about a freeloader who wants his girlfriend to work as an idol so he can live off her earnings. So don't take their glares personally," Willy said.

"Sounds like you're trying to enter me into a competition for worst boyfriend of the year among idol fans. You know full well she's not my girlfriend," Nick snapped.

"Sorry, I'm joking. Anyway, have you heard? People are saying the legendary paladin who protects Labyrinth City has reappeared."

Nick shook his head, having no clue what he was talking about. "Who's that?"

"There was once a time when Labyrinth City was even more dangerous than it is now. Theft was so common that people couldn't walk the streets without constantly watching their own back."

"Hmm."

"Legend has it that there was an S-rank adventurer who made it her mission to eliminate the wanted thieves who threatened the citizens' safety. She was said to be beautiful, but because she always left without giving her name after saving the day, people could only call her the 'Lovely Paladin.'"

"Huh."

"Something wrong, Nick? You don't seem interested."

"No, it's just...I don't know where you're going with this. It's hard for me to focus on anything other than Aggie's concert right now."

"Trust me, it's related." Willy smiled and continued, "You know the casino that was attacked? People are saying the Lovely Paladin appeared and saved Agate."

"Cough, cough."

Nick began to choke.

"Huh? You okay, Nick?"

"Y-yep! I-I'm fine!"

"If you say so…"

Nick had been too preoccupied during the fight with Leon to register what was happening around them. It was only once they'd defeated Leon that he realized the girl Tiana was protecting looked like Agate. He had encountered Agate three times off stage. He thought it might be her, but he didn't have time to confirm.

Nick asked Tiana about the girl later, but apparently her name was Belle. He figured he must have been mistaken; there was no way Agate would go to a casino anyway. It turned out his bad feeling was right, though. He did his best to keep a neutral expression as Willy continued talking.

"…A-anyway, that's an old legend, isn't it? Do you really think it was the same person?" Nick asked.

Willy grinned. "No idea. She could've been a legendary race with a long lifespan, like a high elf or a dark elf."

"Seems unlikely."

"I agree, admittedly. Some people are saying she's been reborn, but I don't believe that, either. One thing's for certain, though— she did leave the scene without giving her name or accepting a reward from the casino or the Sun Knights. Her fame is growing rapidly."

"W-wow…"

"The paladin also looked androgynous. Agate thinks they were a woman, though."

"Huh? Did Aggie say that?"

"It's a rumor. She was apparently stunningly beautiful, too. But who knows if that's true," Willy said.

Nick was about to ask for more details when the ticket booth opened, and their efforts paid off in the form of front-row seats.

Nick looked at the ticket and breathed a sigh of relief. He thought Agate might have been injured at the casino or that the shock of witnessing such a fierce battle up close had caused her to shut herself away. Essentially, he was terrified that he had ended Agate's idol career. Her name and the concert date on the ticket put that fear to rest. He was sure she would show herself to be safe and sound. With that expectation in mind, Nick headed to the concert.

His apprehension turned out to be totally ungrounded. Not only that—the total opposite turned out to be true.

"Good evening! Thank you for coming today!"

""""Good evening!!!""""

Agate's fans responded to her greeting with hoarse screams. Nick was one of the many cheering her on. Despite the size of the crowd, he felt a strange sense of pride that he was at the center of it—that he had been more worried about her than anyone else. This kind of viewpoint was common among dedicated fans.

"I had to deal with a few things in my private life. The rumor that I was injured and retired is completely untrue. As you can see, I'm fit as a fiddle!"

"Yeeaaahhh!"

"I was so worried!"

"I'll always support you!"

Agate waved in response to her fans' cheers. She'd looked depressed when Nick saw her at the casino, but there was no hint of that now. She was brimming with energy.

"Thank you! It's true that I was involved in a dangerous incident, though... I could've easily died."

The venue grew noisy. Everyone sounded worried about Agate.

"But a woman saved me. It is thanks to her that I am alive and well." Her voice was quiet and mellow, projecting a charm different from her usual stoic attitude. "She was a virtuous person, just like a paladin of legend. She inspired me to want to save people and give them courage... So I am going to honor her heroics not as an idol, but as a minstrel. This is a brand-new song!"

The audience went wild at her sudden announcement of a new song. Nick glanced at Willy before cheering. He was smiling suggestively. He must have caught wind about the new song somewhere. Nick was jealous and surprised, but what Agate said next astonished him even more.

"I want to show my thanks through this song! It's called 'The Lovely Paladin'!"

Agate had suspended her idol activities with no warning and withdrawn from the concerts she was scheduled to participate in. The decision of her talent agency not to publicly announce the reason for the hiatus invited doubt. Some wondered if she had been badly injured in the casino incident. They also questioned what she'd been doing in a casino in the first place.

Agate put all rumors to rest by explaining at her concert that she had taken the break to write a new song. She'd devoted herself to its composition and trained for the performance, knowing her disappearance would spark rumors. She'd ignored all the noise and had written something truly incredible.

The quality of the song had caused quite a controversy within the talent agency during the process leading up to her performance. The disagreements concerned its theme and direction.

Singing songs with this type of theme was important for minstrels—you could even call it a mission of theirs. It was risky for an idol, however. The song was a hero's tale.

A glorification of one person was near to a taboo for idols. They were supposed to convey their love to all; singing of heroes may have been expected of a minstrel, but it wasn't a good look for an idol.

Some in the agency argued she should abandon the project. Others wanted her to go forward with it. Arguments on both sides were presented in countless meetings. In the end, the company president stepped in and made a decision.

"Eh, the song is about a woman. I think it'll be fine."

A rumor was circulating through Labyrinth City of a "Lovely Paladin" who protected the city from the shadows. She was said to be a beautiful woman, and some even said she saved Agate's life. This rumor worked in Agate's favor and her talent agency's. If the person who saved Agate had been a man, or even a woman whose identity was known, a significant number of fans would have left her upon hearing the song. Deciding that a story about a woman shrouded in mystery would be received positively, the president gave Agate his full support.

Careful consideration was given to the lyrics. The first half of the song praised the beauty and strength of the paladin, while the second half inspired the listener by likening all courageous people who carried out justice to paladins. The latter part especially resonated with male adventurers. It inspired them to be the kind of person Agate respected.

"Hey, this song is really good."

"I'm getting fired up."

"It's so beautiful."

"I wish they would auction off Agate's original draft. I'd pay any amount of money."

"All right, I'm gonna go catch some bad guys."

These were some of the thoughts that the song inspired in the adventurers among her fans. The song's live debut was a massive success, and her fans went home with the greatest sense of satisfaction yet.

All except for Nick.

"Why...? Why...?"

Nick was wallowing in sorrow on a bench by a street corner. He was happy about Agate's return and her new song. He couldn't have imagined the subject of the song, though. She had written a hero's tale about him...or rather, Tiana. The mage had done nearly everything to save Agate at the casino, and Nick thought Tiana had been mostly in control during their fight with Leon as well.

It was difficult to tell whose thoughts were whose while combined with someone else using Union; that was true when he was combined with Karan, at least. When he combined with Tiana, however, her will was stronger than his. He ended up simply aiding the actions she decided to take. Nick was mostly in charge of moving the body, but he felt like Tiana took charge of speaking, spell casting, and strategy.

That said, he had no more than vague memories of Tiana's thoughts from their Union. Bond told him, "Your partner's thoughts fade quickly due to a safety feature. Remembering everything from their mind would place too large a burden on your brain."

This all resulted in mixed feelings for Nick. He should have been happy about the song, but he felt as if the credit for saving Agate had been stolen from him, or as if he had stolen it from Tiana.

"How should I behave at her concerts...? I guess I could just not worry about it," Nick muttered to himself.

"That's right. There's no need to worry about it."

"I suppose… Huh?"

Nick heard a familiar voice and agreed without thinking. He sighed and turned around to see Agate wearing casual clothes.

"Hello, stray dog. This is the fourth time we've run into each other, huh?" she said.

"…Stop calling me that," Nick retorted.

"What else can I call you? I don't know your name. Oh, you don't have to tell me. You can call me whatever you want, too."

"I already know your name, though…"

"I'd rather you not use it. I could get in trouble if anyone overhears you."

"I get that, but why'd you speak to me in the first place?"

As an idol, Agate had to be careful to avoid making people think she was getting too friendly with any individual fan. Doing so could harm her popularity.

"I can't help it. I thought we might be getting too close, but I don't know where else to look for a lead."

"A lead? What do you mean?"

"Who was that person who appeared out of nowhere at the casino? And what happened to you and Tiana?"

"Grk." Nick flinched back from Agate's accusing gaze.

"How did you two do that? That tiger didn't really seem like a monster, either. I can't make any sense of it, but I'm sure you could tell me something."

Nick's greatest fear was close to being realized. They would be in big trouble if it was discovered that they were hiding the Sword of Bonds and using it for their own benefit. He needed to throw her off the scent.

"I—I don't know anything. Isn't this conversation backward? You sound like the idol fan right now with all these questions," Nick said, desperate to change the topic.

Agate giggled. "All right, all right. We both have our secrets the curtain of dust was faster than Marguerite's reflexes, but she had seen it coming. She was already evading, having placed her body in a safe zone to avoid it. Then she readied herself in a low stance, holding down the hem of her skirt with her toe to keep it from flipping up from the impact.

Dirt pattered down on her from above. Droplets of blood dripped from the goddess's hair to stop in her eyebrows. Her expression was fixed in a smile. The end of the ax thrust into her sash wriggled like an amorphous creature—it looked like it was slowly trying to make a blade again.

It's trying to make a full ax again... If it goes back, then we'll be the ones at a disadvantage.

Marguerite swallowed her remaining half of a grayfruit in one bite.

It was just as she'd predicted. The goddess wasn't as frightening using the stick as she was with the ax.

Her rough sweeps had come from simple attack instinct and not from any combat theory; with her magic axes that she could transform according to the situation, her strikes had been extremely difficult to evade. Even just dealing with each individual attack had whittled Marguerite down body and spirit, and, even focusing on evasion, she'd taken hit after hit. She'd been unable to predict what the goddess would do next, and then, while caught in surprise, she'd been driven further, until, before she knew it, she was just running.

Maiya and Rareko's staff skills came from a highly systematized technique, but they were based on an art for humans. It wasn't suited to a monster—or a goddess. Defense-based stances were overly sensitive to the enemy's actions, and blows meant to be blocked were far from full power strikes. With the goddess's tough exterior and reflexes, there was no need for her to be so defensive, but she was intently devoted to the basics of staff technique.

Marguerite lightly stepped aside to avoid a low jab, then timed a sweep of her knees with a thrust of her rapier, and then, right before the goddess's stick slammed in, Marguerite drew back her sword, shifting to the right with footwork that mixed in feints. With every swing and thrust of the staff, dust swept up, trees broke, and branches and leaves scattered. Marguerite clasped her left hand and opened it. Even if it wasn't healed all the way, it was enough if she could move this much. Her powers of regeneration were greater than normal—that had to be thanks to the grayfruit.

Marguerite responded to a sudden backflip from the goddess by kicking a rock at her, which she repelled by spinning her staff, but Marguerite closed the distance all at once to attack, thrusting in with her rapier. The spinning staff became an impediment that slowed the goddess's reaction, but she still escaped with three continuous cartwheels followed by a somersault. The full-body thrust from Marguerite skimmed the goddess's torso but only sliced away half of the sash at her waist.

Acrobatic movements didn't suit the goddess, either. Though at first Marguerite had been overwhelmed by how she mimicked Chelsea perfectly, once she was used to it, it was nothing more than a show. What point was there in an overwhelmingly powerful lion bewildering a rabbit with flashy movements?

There was a menace in the way Chelsea moved. She packed a single peace sign with her faith in magical girls from the ends of her fingers to each one of her nails, with enough apparent madness to make Marguerite hesitate to attack. The heart was a powerful weapon for a magical girl. If you were just going through the motions superficially without the conviction, it made them nothing more than half-baked *xing yi quan*. It was actually hindering the goddess.

The enemy pulled back for a slam and a thrust, both of which Marguerite evaded. With the dust scattering everywhere, even if it got in her eyes, Marguerite fixed her unblinking gaze on the enemy, rapier at the ready.

Staff work was a very popular martial art among magical girls, and lots of people used it. In other words, an instructor of the Inspection Department would have to assume it would be used by one of the potential enemies she'd have many opportunities to fight. Even someone like the goddess, who was incredibly physically powerful, wasn't such a fearsome opponent if she only used basic moves. The problem was the ax. The handle of the ax hanging from her waist continued to writhe in an attempt to restore its blade. She had no idea how long the one hanging from her neck would stay like that, either. The magical girls on this island had continuously whittled down the goddess's forces bit by bit, and, as a result, they had managed to make her fight with staff techniques, which were not suited to her. This was their chance. She couldn't let it go by. Rather, if she did let it go by, then things really would be hopeless. She would finish this before the ax went back to normal.

She slithered from tree to tree, the Inspection Department's style of footwork making smooth movement possible even if the footing was in ruins from fallen trees and dirt dug up. The goddess followed Marguerite with the same manner of walking, and Marguerite evaded her and thrust, at which the goddess slashed back, and Marguerite bounded off the trunk of a tree that had been blasted down in a two-point jump, bending the tree at a right angle to make it a throwaway launchpad, and, with splinters of wood scattering around, she dodged the staff that came thrusting toward her eyes, landed, and, after preparing for the goddess's next attack, kicked a fallen tree in half and stepped forward to slice at her. She skimmed the place she'd cut before a second time.

With a flutter, the goddess's sash was sliced off and hung in the air. Without even an instant's pause after that attack, Marguerite swiftly went facedown on the ground in one movement. The horizontal sweep of the goddess's counterattack cut through the air.

Hands on the ground like a four-legged beast, Marguerite slid backward, watching the handle of the ax lying there as she stuck out her tongue. She wetted her upper lip.

She had cut the sash and made her drop her ax. How should she set things up from here? Should she wait for Clantail's support? But if she wasted time, the effects of the grayfruit would run out. Marguerite was unable to make decisions on her own. She had struggled this much just to reduce the enemy's fighting power—in this case by one ax. But now that she was at this step—thinking this far, Marguerite narrowed her right eye.

The goddess drew the staff in with her palms, lowered her stance, and spread her legs. This stance was different from before. Marguerite sidestepped and then backed up, raising her rapier in front of her face.

What the goddess was doing was not a defensive stance. Her eyes were fixed only on destruction via attack. It was a Maiya-original unorthodox move, opposed to the staff technique ideal that both the wielder and the opponent be unharmed. Its name came from the time it had once pierced the wing of Archfiend Pam—Fiend Piercer. Since it was piercing a devil, you could say it was a technique fit for a goddess.

Marguerite had been letting her body move as it would, but now she stopped. She wasn't sure what to do. Maiya had used this attack to pierce Archfiend Pam's wing. Just what would the Fiend Piercer become when it was executed by someone far stronger than Maiya? Would it even be possible to read ahead of it, or evade it? She couldn't even imagine the scale of the destruction, or the force. Marguerite licked her bottom lip—it was entirely dry.

◇ **Ragi Zwe Nento**

No mage had failed to hear the rumors that the Osk Faction was a group of villains who didn't care about the law and treated magical girls like trash, with the Lab being the greatest example. But true evil lay in hiding your own evil as much as possible while putting on a face like you wouldn't kill a bug. Many of the nasty rumors about the Osk Faction and the Lab were propaganda.

"Do we take this, too, Mr. Ragi?" Mary asked him.

"Of course."

There was already an underlying shared perception of the Osk Faction being a frightening group, but using fear as transaction material helped close negotiations smoothly—such was the MO of organized crime. Having solved disputes this way meant they started off by spreading their own bad name themselves, and then they just let other factions say whatever nasty things they wanted and didn't deny them. Ragi would wail that such tactics were irresponsible, childish, and an abandonment of magely pride, but nobody in the upper ranks would listen to his lamenting, and even if they did hear it, none of them would be ashamed.

"We don't have enough sheep," Ragi told Mary. "Make more. Strong physiques suited to carrying are best."

"I told you that too much customization makes them hard to control."

Now he realized those tactics had changed not only the perception from the outside, but the perception of the organization from within. Hadn't the twisted idea come about that it was okay to go a bit too far because this was the Lab—that in fact you had to go too far? They believed the Lab was such a fearsome organization, nobody could look down on them, and a strange sense of pride had grown from that idea.

"It's really okay to move these?" Mary asked him. "They won't wake up while they're being carried?"

"Of course they won't. Dolls without souls in them are just things."

This had turned to arrogance, and they'd assumed that no one could be so imprudent as to ignore the Lab's requests and insert specifications not written in the documentation, and so they'd overlooked an eccentric researcher called Sataborn going out of control. Thinking about it like that, everything made sense, and that irritated Ragi all the more.

"I'll have you assist in the ceremony," Ragi said. "Make sure to have your sheep back off then."

"Wait, huh? Me? No way, I can't do that," Mary protested.

"The assistant need only handle one technique that even a simpleton could do. Even if you don't understand what it means, you can just chant it as I tell you."

"There's just no way!"

"Find a way!"

Now that he was thinking about it, he could picture Sataborn being somewhat prepared for murder, too. Ragi was not only not a blood relative but hardly connected to him at all—hadn't Sataborn indicated him as an heir because he wanted someone from inside the Osk Faction to stab it in the back, someone who would also be able to understand what he'd arranged? In other words, it had to be a mage with enough ability to protect him as well as someone to brag to when the time came—thinking that far, Ragi was so infuriated, he slammed the end of his staff into the earth.

But it wasn't just Ragi. Parties involved with the Inspection Department and their connections had also been invited as heirs. If he was thinking that when the time came he would have them act how he wanted—

"Mr. Ragi. Mr. Ragi!"

"Mm, yes. I can hear you. What is it?"

Was he overthinking this? Not as far as he was concerned. He had the feeling Sataborn would have been bound to do it. But he also felt like these thoughts were influenced by Sataborn's strong personality. But Ragi still thought that when Sataborn had found out that he would literally get to spend as much as he wanted to research and develop what he liked how he liked it, the old mage must have been happy like a little boy. It wouldn't at all be strange for him to place his own life as second or third place in importance after that—in fact, that would be very like him.

"The entrance is too small, and I can't get the cabinet outside, though," said Mary.

"You're a magical girl. If the entrance is too small, then just make it larger."

Even understanding this, Ragi did not sympathize, and he just became more and more irritated about it. In the first place, the situation indicated that Sataborn had not been murdered, but rather that he'd simply died accidentally. If it had been murder, then they would have made up some reasons to put off the distribution of the inheritance. Shepherdspie didn't have the guts to ignore such pressure.

But now Ragi could not preach to him about how a mage should act, or yell at him to consider the trouble he caused others, or entreat him to consider how he did things, or just whack him a good one. Sataborn had set out on a journey to a place beyond Ragi's reach. That was also quite vexing.

"That's crazy...," Mary whined.

"Even if it's crazy, do it!"

◇ 7753

It was easier once she reached a path, but in no way was it easy. Kotori occasionally looked down at the tortoise hugged to her chest and thought, *If she wasn't an Egyptian tortoise, but a Galapagos tortoise, would I be able to ride her instead?* which made her aware that she was also mentally exhausted, and she scolded herself with a *No, none of that*, and hurried onward.

When the main building came into view, she let out a deep breath and drew in another deep breath and walked farther. She held herself back from hurrying as fast as she could, but she also stayed alert to keep from feeling like this was a casual stroll, paying attention to her surroundings as she swiftly circled around to the front of the main building. When she saw that the scale of the destruction was much bigger than she remembered, her shoulders slumped, and she prayed that everyone was safe.

She swore to herself that no matter what awful sights she saw, she would not be rattled, and she would not cry out or fall on her bottom, and then she took a sneak peek through the cracks in the collapsed wall, where she found another pair of eyes. They weren't human eyes. She blinked a few times and drew away. It was about twenty inches away, and she realized what it was. It was a sheep.

Kotori circled around the crumbled area, and when she leaned forward to look inside, she saw three sheep grazing on grass. They just glanced at her and didn't seem bothered by her presence.

If there were sheep, then there was Pastel Mary, and speaking of that girl, she'd been suspected as the grayfruit thief. Kotori wouldn't be very glad to run into such a person. Or would they actually come to an understanding if they talked? At the very least, you'd be able to reason with her more than with the goddess.

I was even able to fight with Pythie Frederica. Compared to that...probably.

She could think about it, but there was nobody else to ask about it. Kotori Nanaya had no doubts that she was personnel to be used, and she thought herself completely unsuited to giving orders, or operating a group, or positioning people, or putting together overall plans. When she worked as a magical girl, it was almost never on her own authority, and her decision was basically never needed. There was always someone who was better at thinking than 7753, like her boss—on this island, that would be Mana—and she knew that it was best to follow the order of that someone.

Kotori's eyes dropped to the tortoise. Seeing her look up with round eyes did soothe her heart, but a tortoise wasn't very qualified to ask advice from. She didn't have the time to hesitate and wonder what to do. There was also no time to think. There was nothing for it but to go. Talking, she could manage, and if she told Pastel Mary the information she'd learned, maybe she would change her mind and come to cooperate with everyone instead. Given the situation now, she had no choice but to hope for that. She nodded and stood up.

Kotori heard the sound of striking some big metal thing, some fine things spilling, the cry of a girl, and then, loudest of all, a man yelling, "What are you doing?!" and then it went quiet.

She definitely remembered the voice of that old man. She only knew of one old man on this island to begin with. It was Ragi. Kotori ran out, passing by the sheep that only glanced at her, heading for where she'd heard those sounds. Her impression of Ragi was all bad—he was a stubborn old man, a complainer, he was always mad, and he got exhausted easily. But he was a mage of high enough status that even Mana respected him, and her way was to immediately snap at anything she didn't like. And even when Ragi got angry and yelled, it was for serious reasons.

At a time like this, what Kotori trusted was not someone who was friendly or easy to get along with. Someone who would never cheat or deceive would be better, someone stupidly overserious to the point of rigidity. She couldn't imagine the old man betraying others to get some grayfruit—in fact, it seemed like he would be more likely to scold Pastel Mary for stealing fruit.

Kotori went straight from that corner, and while she began to doubt if she was really going the right way, she squashed those feelings and walked instead, racing out, leaping—by the time she heard someone yell, "Watch out!" she was already tumbling over.

She found someone on top of her, and when she looked up, their eyes met. An airheaded-looking magical girl with a soft and fluffy costume—it was Pastel Mary. Before she could wonder what had just happened, there was a call of "What are you doing?!" and, on all fours, Pastel Mary turned around and called back, "It's all right."

Kotori still hadn't figured out what had happened. She accepted the hand extended to her and was pulled to her feet to look around. Was this the courtyard? In the open space were Ragi, Mary, and a few sheep—and when Kotori saw a bunch of goddesses lying down, she swallowed a scream and started falling backward. Mary tried to catch her, but her feet slipped and she couldn't do it, and the two of them fell in a tangle, and Ragi huffed at them, "What are you doing?! Honestly!" striking the ground with his twisted cane.

"I'm sorry," Pastel Mary said.

"Sorry." Kotori added her own reflexive apology. Despite apologizing, she still didn't understand the situation, though. "Um… just what is going on here?"

"There's no time to explain," said Ragi. "Just get away from there. You're a disaster waiting to happen."

Mary helped Kotori get up, lost her balance, and fell, and Ragi yelled, and with the help of two sheep, once they were a couple of steps away and looked back, Kotori noticed what she had failed to see before. The grass looked vaguely faded over an area of about one yard in diameter. When she looked closer, she saw it wasn't that the grass had faded. There was a translucent tray—a strange object like a tray—floating on the ground.

"What…?" Kotori started reaching out, and then, at the yell of "Don't touch it!" she turned around to find Ragi glaring at her with his eyebrows furrowed. Now that she thought of it, she didn't recall what he looked like when he wasn't grumpy or angry.

"Um, what is this? Is it dangerous?" Kotori asked.

"Assume that if you touch it, you'll die."

Kotori automatically backed up, and the back of her head hit something. Mary's shriek and Kotori's shriek came at the same time, and then Ragi was yelling, and as Kotori crawled along, in her confused mind, she thought, *I have to get as far away as possible from the dangerous thing.* Holding her head, she tried to stand, and then a goddess magical girl lying there in peaceful sleep entered her field of view, and Kotori shrieked again and reflexively backed up, and her back hit something. Mary's shriek and Ragi's yell rang out. Mei wiggled leisurely under Kotori's clothing.

◇ **Love Me Ren-Ren**

It took Ren-Ren a few seconds to understand what had happened. Maybe it was longer, maybe it was shorter. Clarissa's body flew through the air, scattering gradations of red, and when her back hit the ground, time finally started moving for Ren-Ren. Thoughts of the enemy flew out of her head. Ren-Ren's head was full of only Clarissa and Clarissa's family as she pulled a dive without a care for what would happen. After Clarissa bounced and was about to land a second time, Ren-Ren caught her from the side. Leaving two trails on the ground from her right and left legs, she backed up until her back hit a thick trunk and she finally stopped.

Ren-Ren was about to say, *"Are you all right?"* but the words evaporated before they could come out of her mouth. Blood continued to flow endlessly from Ren-Ren's arms as she held Clarissa, dirtying her chest, stomach, every place she touched. Her transformation had come undone. She was a very ordinary-looking girl.

The old-fashioned outfit of a white shirt with a suspenders skirt suited her small frame surprisingly well. Broken bones were sticking out here and there, her whole body was limp, her warmth was seeping away, her pulse and breathing were already gone. Her body did tremble slightly, but Ren-Ren quickly realized that was just the trembling of her own arms.

Everything that went around in Ren-Ren's head was difficult for Ren-Ren herself to explain or describe. There was a little girl who had been trying to return to her mother, and she was now still and unmoving in Ren-Ren's arms. Something that should not take shape was gradually taking shape. The little girl was Ren-Ren. She was Ren-Ren herself, who had become a magical girl in search of a warm family. She was none other than Ren-Ren, unable to return, fallen without accomplishing her goal. Even though this was whom she had to protect most of all, the girl slipped from her arms and landed on the ground.

She staggered. Swayed. A frog-like sound leaped from her throat. The trembling wouldn't stop. The scenery contorted, the forest became covered in rainbows. She heard voices that she shouldn't be able to hear, and a wind that shouldn't blow was whistling along, and, as Ren-Ren's body and mind were about to be blasted to pieces, a smack rang out on her cheek.

She locked eyes with a magical girl. She was expressionless—no, there was something there. She was holding Ren-Ren's collar in her left hand, while her right was open and raised. The psychedelic scenery returned to normal, and the incomprehensible sounds disappeared as well. There was a stinging heat on Ren-Ren's cheek, and she realized belatedly the magical girl had struck her.

"Snap out of it. It's not over."

Behind the magical girl, dirt and trees were flying. Even if it seemed like a joke, it wasn't. There were no lies or jokes here. The magical girl raised her horse front legs and lowered them. Her hooves stamped on the ground and left prints. Ren-Ren opened her mouth. She couldn't breathe right. Warm liquid flowed down her cheeks. She hugged the cooling body of the girl to her chest. The thick smell of blood flooded her nostrils.

"But she…she wants to see her mother, her family," Ren-Ren protested.

"I do, too. I'm going to survive and go back to my family. You too." Clantail's speech was faltering, and it was like she was trying to speak as quickly as possible, making the words very clumsy and hard to catch. But every single one of her words rattled Ren-Ren's brain, her insides, her core. A little flame lit in her body that had been chilled to the bone, making to warm her from the inside.

"Run or fight. Pick one. It's not good to just stand here." Saying just that, Clantail turned around.

"Wait." Ren-Ren called her to a stop. She shoved at Clantail an amount of grayfruit that overflowed from her palms and, before she could say anything, flapped her wings and flew into the sky. The scenery that she had only been able to see vaguely was now clear and crisp. The blue of the sky and the white of the clouds made a vivid contrast, and even with earth and trees flying into it, it never lost the sense of being connected to reality. Nephilia's face rose mistily in the clouds, giving her little *ksh-shh* giggle. It was going to be okay. Ren-Ren fully understood just what was what. She'd managed to properly distinguish who she was, what she should do, and what she should not do. The sight of Clarissa enjoying a chat with her mother rose in her mind. It was a happy and precious picture that she would never see again.

The next time, she would absolutely not fail to protect those she had to keep safe. She would fight in a place that gave her the best of odds of succeeding. Love Me Ren-Ren was the protector of love and families: She had to protect the love of the family with her life.

Ren-Ren had gotten ahold of herself again. She even realized that she had been out of sorts until now. She thrust out her right fist, opening and closing it, and inhaled from the bottom of her lungs, drawing in breath to every corner of her body.

The memories that had become twisted returned—clearly this time. Her mother and father fighting. Her young sister crying, trying to cut between them. The little body that had been impulsively flung aside to bounce against the wall and stop moving. The screams of a girl had drowned out her mother's cries and her father's yells. And then her memory cut off there, and she couldn't see any more.

Never...again...

She would not repeat the same thing. She would not let it be repeated. Ren-Ren would stop it.

Her parents were facing off, her father with a stick and her mother with a rapier. And then her little sister was racing toward them. At this rate, her little sister would die. Many times, she'd thought of her as annoying—all she did was follow her calling, "Big sis, big sis," but she was still her cute little sister. Even if she was bounding off the ground with the lower body of an animal, she was still her little sister. Ren-Ren had to protect her. Even if it meant shielding her with her body, even if it meant sacrificing her life, she had to protect her.

Her head was clearer now than it had ever been. Ren-Ren grabbed over a dozen arrows at once from her quiver and nocked them to her bow. She could see the flow of the wind. She could even see the weight of the air. Even before firing the arrows, she could see their trajectories. She had the feeling that right now, she could do anything. Thinking about resolving everything to live together with her father, mother, and little sister, Ren-Ren had a faint smile on her face.

◇ **Nephilia**

Swapping her scythe for Rareko's staff made it a little easier to walk, but it was still painful. But she put up with the pain and walked, just as she'd put up with the sick feeling to touch the corpse and gain some valuable information. The rest would depend on how accurate Nephilia's guesswork was.

She could constantly hear sounds coming from the other side of the estate. It made her wounds ache. It was hard on her mentally, too. Was Ren-Ren doing well? Had Clarissa carried out what she had said she would? Even if they were close by, emotionally she felt like a soldier's family, worrying far from the battlefield.

But what she had to do was far from pretty, and far dirtier and more underhanded than what people did when fighting on the front line. The way she was poking at dead bodies like this, she was no different from a hyena or a vulture.

She went through the entrance, which had been widened from the destruction, to enter the main building. She could hear the sounds of battle coming from the other side of the main building, so there wasn't much point in exercising wariness here, but even understanding that, she didn't relax her guard, perking up her ears to sneak from shadow to shadow as she followed the trail of destruction. When she came to a place that looked like it had originally been a kitchen, she lifted a pot off the ground and drank down the soup inside before gently setting it down on a broken traditional charcoal stove. Even to someone in magical-girl form, Shepherdspie's specially made soup was still good.

Coming out from the kitchen into the hallway made Nephilia scowl. The destruction here was particularly bad. Before, no matter how badly things had been wrecked, there'd still been enough remains that she could guess what had originally been there. Here there wasn't even debris left, and the whole floor had been dug up from the foundation, with carving extending into the earth below. It looked like an underground tank with a drill on the front had been going full speed straight across the main building—the fallen ceiling parts and pillars were shyly trying to hide it, but they didn't hide it at all. They were like pale snow piling on top of footprints.

When she looked up, she could see the ceiling of the second floor. The fact that it wasn't completely collapsed was impressive.

She hopped down from the floor into the rubble, and the shock that ran through her knees made her clench her teeth. As she felt heat seeping through the bottoms of her feet, the scowl on her face deepened. The path of destruction was hot. It seemed that it had not been an underground tank that had caused this, but a beam weapon.

When she followed the destruction, gradually its path narrowed. Sighing with the thought that if it was going to be like this, she shouldn't have bothered coming all the way down, she went up onto the floor again, and eventually the path of destruction ended. Nephilia narrowed her eyes. This wasn't enough to call destruction, but there was the mark of something having hit the floor. There was a trail of dots, making her think that it had been rolling along while hitting things.

She followed it farther. Red blood was sprayed all over, not just on the floor and walls—there was even some on the ceiling, indicating just how badly the victim had been wounded. Running into things, falling, sliding along the floor, it led to a destroyed door. Nephilia swept aside the remains of the door with her staff and stepped into the room beyond.

Someone was lying on the ground. For some reason, she was wearing a bathrobe. Wearing this incongruous attire was Dreamy☆Chelsea, pretransformation. She was leaning against the wall, head weakly hanging. Nephilia approached her, crouched down, took her wrist, shook her head, then put her own hands together and bowed.

Looking up at the wall Chelsea was leaning against, she sighed. There was a dark-red person-shaped mark on the wall. The wall was cracked deep and wide at the parts that corresponded to hands. She'd probably slammed both hands in when she'd hit. In other words, she'd caught herself—while getting wounds bad enough to make a human shape in blood.

Nephilia opened up the chest of the bathrobe and inspected the body. There was a broad slice on her front from shoulder to stomach, and she was bleeding enough for it to pool around her seat. But the cut was sewn up with little stones carved out like arrowheads, which were holding it shut like staples. Chelsea must have used her "stars" to stop the blood.

The marks left by her catching her fall and dealing with the bleeding told Nephilia that Chelsea had done everything she could to survive until the very end, but that fact just deepened Nephilia's gloom. When someone fought and fought only to die in the end, it hit the observer hardest. The athleticism to avoid instant death and the spirit to never give up brought about a painful end.

Right then.

Nephilia touched Chelsea's foot. It was still warm—indicating that she'd been alive until just a little while before. The freshness was nauseating, but right now she wasn't in a position to complain. She just rubbed the foot.

The sound that came out of her mouth, or rather her nose, made Nephilia squint one eye and tilt her head. It took her a moment to realize that this series of sounds was a song. It was fragmented and hoarse, and weaker than a katydid in the winter. It was very close to humming, and not a song Nephilia knew.

Singing right before death. She had to be deranged. Even veterans would sometimes become deranged when about to die. Nephilia didn't think it meant anything. She started rubbing a notch faster to move past it. When the proper noun "Chelsea" came out during the tune, Nephilia realized what kind of song it was. This was an original theme song or something. It was difficult to bear, but she had to continue.

"There's always trouble…but she's sure to come…'cause she's a magical girl… Save me, Chelsea…"

The voice stopped. Her voice wasn't coming out, as if there was something caught in the back of her throat. Nephilia put a hand to her throat and cleared it a few times. There wasn't anything strange here. Why was her voice suddenly not coming out anymore? When a hand reached out to her, she became even more confused. The young woman leaning against the wall was extending her hand, grabbing Nephilia's arm.

Nephilia's breath caught. The woman's expression was ghastly as she squeezed her hand. Pale lips trembling, her words almost trailed off, but they never faltered.

"Heard…that voice…"—her voice was a mutter that eventually became a whisper, then turned quieter than a mosquito's buzz to vanish—"asking…Chelsea…for…help…" She dropped her head, unable to finish.

Nephilia released the foot and smushed up a grayfruit she'd pulled out of her pocket, then began pushing fruits into the woman's mouth one after another.

She's...!

She had been dead. Nephilia was in the business of making contact with the dead, and she would make no mistake there. Chelsea's life had definitely come to an end. Everything about this was crazy. It was crazy, but you could say that magical girls were like that. Maybe it was her faith in magical girls, her mental fortitude, her experience, and the physical elements in her favor—how she'd broken her fall, stopped her bleeding, her strong body and incredible endurance just barely keeping her soul tethered—and then the final push of calling her by name to ask for help had enabled her to return—maybe.

Whatever the case, if she was back, there was no reason to send her off once more. If she could work, then Nephilia should have her work. The woman's skin gradually regained its color. Her fingers twitched.

◇ **Clantail**

Clarissa was beyond saving. Clantail knew better than anyone that her wish to keep anyone from dying wasn't going to come true. Living things would die. But still, she didn't want them to die. She didn't want Marguerite, Ren-Ren, anyone to die. She swallowed a grayfruit in one gulp. The fruit juices welled up almost to her nostrils and stung a little.

Marguerite remained stone still, facing off against the goddess. She wasn't able to attack. It was probably because of some technique or magic the goddess was about to use. Clantail would distract her, ruining her move and providing Marguerite with an opening to attack.

Clantail formed a route in her head, and, changing her lower body from a quarter horse to a springbok, she accelerated. Marguerite cried, "Don't!" She must have noticed the sound of Clantail's hooves. Heedless, Clantail rushed forward. In order to create an opening, she had to attack. With her toughness, the flexibility of her magic, and her ability to evade, Clantail was the one most suited for that role.

But she was still glad that Marguerite had been worried about her. It made her heart even firmer. Clantail would go first. It was settled.

She transformed from a springbok to a cheetah, using the change in height to throw the enemy's aim off, and accelerated. The momentary burst of speed was too fast for Clantail to handle. She landed on the ground and leaped up. Branches, leaves, and dirt slowly fluttered down. She headed to the right, aiming for the goddess's flank—but their eyes met. The goddess was turning back toward Clantail.

That reaction was more than expected. But Clantail wasn't about to take any hits now. Clantail saw herself as the best choice to play shield or bait simply because it was objectively true that she was—she hadn't done this out of a spirit of self-sacrifice or a suicidal urge. Even if the road to victory was a narrow one, it wasn't like it didn't exist.

She didn't want anyone to die. Clantail herself was included in that. Her life was important to her, as her friends had saved it. She would never waste it.

Then the goddess's gaze shifted slightly. Not to Clantail—behind her, to the right and diagonally upward. Leaves rustled. Branches broke. The goddess came out of her stance to use her staff to knock down the arrow that flew in from above. Clantail transformed into a puma and leaped high, and in midair she turned into a spider monkey, and with her long, agile tail she grabbed the arrow that was shooting for her back. Arrows rained down everywhere like hail, on the ground, tree trunks, and leaves. They hadn't been aimed somewhere. They'd been fired all over the area.

With a running start, Clantail reached the treetops in one bound, getting her long claws into a branch to get ahold of it and turning herself around, and on the way she checked behind her. She could see Ren-Ren nock multiple arrows.

Clantail moved from branch to branch, and when Ren-Ren fired more arrows, she grabbed another with her tail. For some reason, Ren-Ren was aiming for Clantail. The goddess smacked the arrows down while Marguerite rolled on the ground. The area where the two were fighting was stuck with arrows like a hedgehog. Ren-Ren was attacking all of them. Clantail couldn't understand what was happening. She couldn't understand the point of what Ren-Ren was doing right now.

"Ren-Ren! Stop it!" Marguerite yelled, but Ren-Ren didn't stop.

She swooped in a sudden dive from ten yards up to skim the ground, all the while continuously firing arrows without pause. This was different from when she'd unleashed a wild barrage over the whole area, and each and every shot carried the threat of death as it aimed for the magical girls. The goddess swept her ax to knock the arrows down, and Marguerite jumped along the ground while Clantail raced through the trees as she struck an arrow aside with her tail. A second shot was hidden by the first, and Clantail grabbed it with her monkey hand while she struck aside a third shot with her own hand. They were fast. She'd get hit if she let her guard down even slightly.

She moved along a branch to hide from Ren-Ren, and arrows *thunked* continuously into the trunk.

Marguerite was confused. She had her hands full just dodging. Clantail was harder to hit due to where she was, but it was only that she was less pressed than Marguerite, and she wasn't any less bewildered. Even the goddess, who had seemed unruffled no matter what, now appeared confused. None of them could understand what Ren-Ren was doing.

Ren-Ren was all over the place, flying from the sky to between the trees, even skimming right along the ground. For some reason, she was smiling like she was glad. Had she lost her mind? But she was moving too skillfully for that. From a low-altitude flight, she circled around behind Marguerite and fired an arrow. From what Clantail could see, it was close to a miracle that Marguerite managed to avoid it. That had been a fantastic shot.

Marguerite went down on the ground like a lizard. The arrow zoomed through where she had been a moment ago and headed straight for the goddess, who swept up the hem of her skirt to knock down the arrow right before it hit. This whole sequence of events all happened in less than a blink.

Ren-Ren had aimed at Marguerite while also using her as cover to aim for the goddess. It had been a nasty move, unpredictable to Marguerite, who should have been an ally, and even to the goddess, who you'd assume would be her enemy. That move had caused the goddess to falter. Her casual defensive motion—keeping her lower body relaxed as she struck the arrow aside with the staff—didn't make it in time, and she was forced into an emergency evasion that left her unbalanced.

Clantail still had no idea what Ren-Ren was trying to do, but she could take advantage of this. Clantail switched from a spider monkey to a leopard, staying in Ren-Ren's blind spot as she raced down a tree trunk to turn into a giant crocodile, using the massive change in size to close the distance to the goddess in an instant and swung her tail.

Marguerite worked with her. From her awkward position face-down on the ground, she threw a rock. Though the goddess was off-balance, she still swung her staff to repel the rock, then swiped back the other way to smack down an arrow. With her free hand, she grabbed the crocodile's thick tail and squeezed as if she were going to crush it through its thick scales. Clantail's body rose into the air. Even just her tail was over six feet long, but the goddess was going to swing this dinosaur-like saltwater crocodile around in one hand.

Clantail turned from a crocodile into a hagfish, using the mucus she secreted to slip from the goddess's fingers and escape her grasp. This caused the goddess to lose her balance further. With incredible force, Marguerite went from her knees to stepping inward to thrust and was blocked by the staff.

Clantail turned into a tiger and attacked the goddess. With the hand that was still smeared in mucus, the goddess grabbed the handle that was dangling from her neck and pulled it out, along with the earth. Blood spurted from the goddess's neck, but the bleeding was mild, given the depth of the wound. It was already starting to stop. Marguerite sliced at her, then swept her blade outward, and the goddess responded with a swing of her staff, but it lacked power. She was off-balance, sandwiched from front and behind, and with arrows coming at her. Her focus had failed. If they were going to do it, now was the time.

Clantail would literally get her from behind. She'd rubbed mucus on the goddess's free hand. Maybe needles wouldn't pierce her tough skin. Maybe she would even be resistant to poison, but no matter how tough her body was, smeared in mucus, she would slip. Even if they couldn't beat her when directly slicing at each other, if the goddess was struggling just to hold on to her weapon, that was something else. Clantail reared up on her tiger back legs. The goddess was tightly clenching the handle of her ax. The earth clod had formed a steel-colored blade and had gotten a lot larger. Her hand on the handle slid a bit. It was slipping. She couldn't hold on.

This is it!

They both locked on. Right when they were both about to attack, Ren-Ren fluttered down soundlessly.

Clantail was stunned and unmoving for less than a third of the blink of an eye. Ren-Ren spread her hands in a completely nonchalant manner to embrace the tiger torso. Clantail didn't even have the time to ask what she was doing. The goddess's ax swung down, and blood spurted out. White wings splattered with red fluttered down in pieces.

Ren-Ren was smiling. Her back was cut open and blood flowed from her mouth, but she was still smiling. "Don't... Family..."

Clantail leaped backward, cradling Ren-Ren. Held in her arms, Ren-Ren no longer moved. But she was still smiling. Marguerite swung her rapier, and the goddess turned back to her.

Even if Clantail didn't want to acknowledge it, she was forced to acknowledge that Ren-Ren had protected her. She still didn't know what Ren-Ren had been trying to do, but that wouldn't change the fact that Ren-Ren had protected her.

It was just like her friends. Nonako, who had always been getting mad at Rionetta and calling her "Fucking doll!" had died protecting her. And Rionetta had said, "I shan't forgive anyone who'd hurt Pechka's hands. I promised as much," and had been true to her words and died defending Pechka. Pechka had died guarding Clantail. She'd looked so strangely satisfied as she'd been betrayed. Ren-Ren's smile now was just like that.

The earth shook. Marguerite went for the goddess. The goddess raised her staff at her side. A voice leaked out. It took time for Clantail to realize it was her own voice. The voice was gradually getting louder. She didn't want anyone to die. Who was it who had attacked so aggressively and used Ren-Ren as a shield?

The voice became louder. It made her want to plug her ears. Marguerite's eyes flared wide. The goddess turned back to Clantail again. Clantail howled. Rage, hatred, sadness, everything was all mixed up and being scattered outward in a big whirlpool. The whirlpool had a lot bigger to get.

She transformed into a polar bear, swinging her arms around to slam at the goddess, heedless of the ax striking her, slamming her sliced-up palm on top of the goddess's head, and when the goddess went down on one knee, Clantail swung down with the front leg of an African elephant.

CHAPTER 20
UNPLANNED, UNEXPECTED

That magical girl did not have a single hair on her head.

Bald magical girls were unusual, but not completely unheard of. There were various situations that might make them bald: having the motif of a certain religion, or having been hit by a magic attack that had burned it off or made it fall out, or shaving it off to keep from being attacked by a magical girl who used the hair of others as a weapon. And there was one more case where they might shave their heads—to indicate an apology.

The first magical girl had the logo of a famous cake shop printed on the bag hanging from her hand, the second magical girl had a square box done up in wrapping paper from a famous traditional sweetshop dangling from her hand, and the third magical girl carried under her arm a manila envelope with *Written apology* on it in attention-getting block script, and all of them hung their heads with somber expressions, quietly proceeding down the hall like a funeral procession until all three stood in a row in front of a door.

The trio eyed the plate on said door and either scowled or clicked their tongues.

"What's this supposed to mean, he's temporarily out of the office?! Inheritance? Island? I don't care! Know when not to head out, old man!"

"Just how long do you think I had to line up to buy the seasonal limited Mont Blanc from Athena Wave?"

"This is bullshit! I wrote today's date on the written apology!"

Either taking off the bald wig to fan herself with a hand like she was hot, or smacking the wig like she was annoyed, each of the three cursed the owner of that room for a while, the expression of their anger gradually toning down until eventually their faces and voices became calm and cold and they put their heads together in the empty hallway.

"Well, whatever. It's not like our strategy has failed. We're just still not done."

"It really was a great plan to pretend to be remorseful and visit the office of the Management Department chief to create an opening from the inside."

"Old men are weak to the tears of young women, after all. Even if he puts on a tough face as the great chief of the Management Department, he's the same on the inside. If this goes well, then we'll be the ones who succeeded at extreme information theft, and we can get as famous as the Magical-Girl Hunter, and we'll get so many jobs—"

The three magical girls were so engrossed in their secret criminal discussion that they failed to notice that the door of the department chief shone blue and twisted up, opening a hole the size of a human head, and before the magical girls could even react, they were drawn toward it and sucked in to be absorbed, screams and all, and then, with another twist, the hole disappeared as if it had never been there, and nothing remained but the single bald wig that fell there, all alone.

The magical girl who had been sneakily watching from behind a pillar trembled, and the faceless puppet on her right hand also trembled, just like its owner. "Terrifying...the Management Department is just as scary as the rumors said."

The freckled magical girl who'd been leaning forward from behind to witness the entire thing shook her head. "There's nothing to be afraid of. That trap will probably only activate for those with bad intentions. We have a sincere desire to be on good terms with the department chief, so nothing should happen if we approach… but, well, there's no need for us to choose to approach the room while he's out." Saying just that, the freckled magical girl turned away from the door to the department chief's office and started walking back the way she'd come.

The magical girl with a puppet on her hand rushed after her. "Are you going back?"

"If he's not here, then there's nothing we can do. Let's get an appointment before we come next time. I wanted to at least see him as soon as possible, though."

"It sounds like he's gone to an island or something—if you're in a hurry, then how about we just go over there?"

The magical girl with the freckles looked at the ground as she walked, then touched a hand to her chin and considered awhile before looking up. "He's got a temper to begin with, so let's not do anything to offend him. Look, if he hates impropriety just as much as the rumors say, then he'll accept Magical Girl Resources, now that the puss has been taken out."

"Yes'm. Well, let's do that, then. By the way, will the girls sucked in be all right?"

"Before, when a bunch from the Archfiend Cram School were taken in by the dozens, they were apparently released in three days."

"That's pretty unbelievable…"

Muttering quietly to each other, the two magical girls left. The bald wig that had been abandoned there lay there as if in protest.

◇ **Touta Magaoka**

Marguerite had told him to head to the main building—so he would go there as fast as he could.

Pulling Yol's hand, he ran as fast as possible. Things he would normally be worried about, like that his arm might get cut by sharp leaves or his cheeks stabbed by pointed branches, he completely ignored, and he only thought about running fast. To be more accurate, he didn't even think. He just let his legs move.

The first thing he saw was not the main building; it was sheep. A bunch of sheep were gathered to bleat *baa baa* and lackadaisically eat grass. If there were sheep, then there would be Pastel Mary. Touta hadn't heard about sheep being kept on the island, so he figured these had to be hers.

He'd hardly had anything to do with her and had only ever spoken a few words with her, and he only remembered her name because she'd been brought up as the number one suspect in the grayfruit thefts. And actually, considering the situation then, she was the only possible culprit. If those suspicions were correct, that meant she was a good-for-nothing adult who only thought about herself.

Touta did understand that, but he still didn't slow down. Even if she was a thief and a good-for-nothing adult, right now Pastel Mary was the only one he had to rely on. It was like the saying he'd learned from the manga dictionary of proverbs in the school library, "A drowning man will grasp at straws."

Passing by the sheep, they went through an area that was filled with branches and leaves to come out to an open space. Suddenly under the light of the sun, Touta squinted. Before he could check around him, someone yelled, "Watch out!"

Someone leaped in from the side to scoop up him and Yol, and they rolled over the ground, and the someone who'd grabbed them came to a stop when her back hit a tree. Though his eyes wanted to spin, he somehow got them facing forward and looked. A magical girl like an Arabian dancer was floating in the sky with an old mage underneath her, and beside them was the fluffy-wuffy Pastel Mary, and there were lots of sheep around them, as well as tools and glass bottles and strange objects placed everywhere. Patterns he'd never seen before were painted on the earth in red and blue, and even just at a glance, there were enough lines there to make his head hurt. Mage, magical girl, and all were looking at Touta and Yol in surprise.

The magical girl in a school uniform rubbed her back with an "Ow, ow" as she stood up, releasing Touta and Yol. "The thing right there like a translucent tray is dangerous, so you can't touch it."

Touta looked where she pointed. It was right there. A vague something about five feet wide was floating about a foot and a half off the ground. Touta didn't reply to her, instead rushing to tell her what he had to say right now.

He told her that there were people fighting with the goddess magical girl close by and that he wanted them to go help. There was a mountain of things he was curious about, like why everyone was here and what they were doing, but this was more important than asking those questions. Yol added her part along the way, clasping Touta's hand hard enough it hurt as she spoke along with him. Touta squeezed back just as hard as spittle flew from his mouth, and he didn't even apologize for it as he talked, talked, and talked.

He wanted them to go help Marguerite and the others. He wanted them to beat the bad guy together.

Right as he was talking, there was a loud *bang* and the ground shook. Touta and Yol supported each other, hastily looking behind them. They watched as trees were blasted away and then fell. There was another loud sound, and shaking. They were the sounds of trees falling.

"Mei will go," the dancer-style magical girl muttered with a stone expression, looking toward the sound. "Nobody follow," she added, and then she vanished too fast for anyone to intervene.

The old mage stomped on the ground in aggravation. "They're too close. We have no time."

Pastel Mary moved her head uneasily, turning to the old man. "Wh-what do we do? Do we cancel preparations and, um, run? There are the children, so."

Being brought up as a reason to run, Touta told them, "Don't worry about us," which Yol followed up with, "If there's anything we can help with, then we'll help."

"Besides…" Touta moved his face to look up at the sky. Black smoke was trailing. It was closer than when he'd seen it before. "There isn't really anywhere for us to run to, either." Pastel Mary seemed startled, and she lowered her head slightly at Touta and Yol.

"We need all the help we can get right now," the mage said with a nod. "I'm thinking to make an impromptu gate to escape from the island. Preparations for that are complete…somewhat. We're about to have the ceremony for it. Oh, we have essentially no more concerns about energy. Make sure to stay away from there. If you touch it, you'll be sucked in."

Pulling Yol's arm, Touta moved away from the translucent tray. The mage nodded, beard swaying. "There is a silver lining. I have another mage assistant. Girl, you remember what you learned at school?"

Yol stuck her hands in her sleeves and popped them out again. Those cards with characters or patterns on them were stuck between her fingers. "Please leave it to me, Master Ragi. I will show you even more than I learned at school."

The instant after declaring that coolly, she just about fell over, and the magical girl in a school uniform supported her from behind and brought a glass bottle to her mouth, having her drink the thick purple liquid inside. When Touta asked what it was, he received the response, "Hair growth formula."

◇ **Miss Marguerite**

Tree trunk–like elephant legs were swinging down with such bloodthirst, she wanted to look away. They stomped mercilessly in one strike, two, putting the full body weight into it. The first stomp hit the goddess's right shoulder, the second her right upper arm, and then Clantail's elephant legs rose one last time to crush the enemy.

But even as she was under assault, the goddess was getting into a ready posture. She took the first strike hard on a shoulder, and with the second she stopped using her arm as a shield. The force, weight, and magic power on top of that would have crushed a magical girl, and only a goddess could have met those foot stomps with guards. Never mind breaking bones, they didn't even break skin.

Clantail's rage-filled attacks were powerful. At times, a magical girl's anger was power. But Marguerite thought that Clantail's strength lay not in powerful attacks but in versatility and flexibility. In that sense, the way Clantail was putting disproportionate emphasis on attack power now was extremely dangerous. She was probably even forgetting how important it was to replenish, that she needed grayfruit.

Marguerite aimed for the moment when the right arm, which held the ax, was tensing, and ran. She slipped smoothly between Clantail's legs to make an ultralow thrust, which the goddess dodged with a somersault, and, a beat later, Clantail's stomp shook the ground.

The goddess backstepped away. Clantail turned into a lion and pursued her, and Marguerite followed, leaping from tree to tree while maintaining a distance from which she could intervene at any time.

Marguerite went along a tree branch and bounded off a tree trunk. She made it seem like she was trying to get behind the goddess to get her in a pincer with Clantail, making the enemy worry about it to suppress her movement. She was actually going for something else. Marguerite crouched deep a moment before leaping off a tree trunk, flying at Clantail on a sharp trajectory. She caught an arm around her waist to bring herself to a sudden stop, and, astride the lion's back, she faced the goddess.

"Here." Marguerite shoved a grayfruit in front of Clantail's face. Even without the damage, having transformed at will so many times running around against the monster, she would run out of strength.

Clantail moved just slightly from the neck up, looking at the grayfruit that was held out to her.

The voltage of her anger decreased a little—not much, but a little—and the small light of reason lit in her eyes. A drop of cold calculation joined her passionate and strong desire to fight, to defeat the enemy. It was telling her that to win, she had to be calm and eat the fruit.

Clantail absolutely needed the grayfruit right now, as a symbol of calm as well as simple replenishment. That was why Marguerite held it out to her. But this also created an opening for the enemy.

Right as Marguerite held it out, the goddess stopped. She twisted her back as if copying Marguerite's form from when she'd thrown the rock, and, with a swing of her arm, she threw Maiya's stick.

Marguerite kicked off Clantail's back to leap upward. The fruit she'd failed to hand to Clantail she chomped in one bite, tossing the stem into the grass. Clantail transformed from a tiger into a snake that shone black, making use of the height difference to avoid the staff.

The form of her throw had made it look as if she'd just given the staff a very light toss. But Maiya's staff drove through the air faster than the speed of sound, blasting away branches and leaves. The throw was powerful like an automatic cannon shot, breaking thick tree trunks, sweeping up an intense cloud of dust where it landed.

Evasion was the only possible correct answer. But now Marguerite couldn't give Clantail the fruit, and the most she could do was escape into the trees. Clantail had no resupply.

In a flowing motion, the goddess went from the throw into a bash. Clantail slithered her snake tail to swipe at the goddess's feet, and the goddess did a little jump to avoid it. Marguerite threw broken branches at her from up in the trees, and the goddess repelled those branches in midair. Clantail whipped her snake tail at the goddess from behind, and the goddess brought her right ax behind herself to block it, but Clantail was cut by the blade of the ax, still making to strike her back.

The black snake tail became grayish-brown, and its shape changed as well. Large fins moved as if trying to swim in the air. Yet again the goddess swung her ax, and blood flew, slicing open gills. And then a shudder ran through the goddess's body, and she stopped moving for just a second.

Clantail had transformed from a snake into an electric eel, sending an electric current through her.

The goddess landed from her jump. Marguerite leaped down after her, and Clantail transformed again.

A scorpion's giant pincers went for the goddess's legs. The goddess kicked away the right pincer, scattering shell, and stomped the left into smithereens, meeting the poison stinger with a head-butt that shattered its shell as well, knocking Clantail far into a back arch. When the goddess was about to swing her ax at Clantail, Marguerite thrust in, aiming the weapon toward her overhead.

But Marguerite had no intention of attacking or being attacked. Her thrust was a feint. Before the ax could swing, she tugged on a vine with her right hand to soar back into the trees above.

The ax swung down. Even though it just cut through air, the pressure of its wind and the shock wave blasted away the trees, branches, and Marguerite. Clantail switched her transformation, turning from a scorpion to a bee to spray poison from the end of her stinger, but the goddess brought the flat of her ax in front of her like a shield to block it.

As Marguerite was being blasted away, she grabbed a branch and slid down the tree trunk. Weaving between the trees, using the Inspection Department style of walking to cross obstacles, she aimed for the goddess's back.

Clantail transformed into a tiger, leaping backward to land, then went down on her knees like all strength had left her. Putting her right hand on the ground to support her body, she somehow managed to avoid going face-first into the mud, but, unable to get up right away, she looked at her palms with disbelief.

She was looking at a human girl. Her transformation had come undone. It hadn't lasted.

◇ **Navi Ru**

The broken gear that was a relic of the First Mage had been managed by the Magical Kingdom, along with the ruins where it had been enshrined, but it had been lost to tomb robbers.

Sataborn had acquired it through a dubious pawnshop. If this became public knowledge, there would have been an obligation to return it. Sataborn had not reported it, and neither had he let go of the item, using it as research material.

Some scholars would call this the height of blasphemy, or at the very least a matter to report to the authorities. But the one to acquire the relic had been Sataborn. In the face of his research, any faith or reverence for the First Mage was trash.

Navi Ru had only recently learned that Sataborn had this gear. If not for a bunch of small strokes of luck—Sataborn's carelessness, his ignorance in the ways of the world, his cooperation with the Lab, Navi Ru's position, which enabled him to visit the island frequently—he would never have found out about it.

If the presence of the gear was made public due to Sataborn's death, the gear would be retrieved and it would be over. There would be nothing to be gained then.

Navi sought out gain. That was his specialty.

He could hear the intense sounds of destruction. Navi Ru stopped his casting for a moment to look toward the main building.

Clarissa had a grasp on Francesca's patterns of behavior as well as that sword he'd brought out from the treasure vaults, so she wouldn't lose. Things would work out better if Navi Ru's accompanying magical girl would eliminate Francesca, rather than his having to use commands to stop her. Since he couldn't kill everyone on this island, he would make events unfold here as naturally as possible.

Sounds of destruction followed. A shaking in the ground came up from the bottoms of his shoes.

The waves surged toward him, and, after spraying the smell of salt and white bubbles, they receded.

He felt strangely unsettled, like something unforeseen was about to happen. In his head, he carefully examined each piece of information and came to the conclusion that there should be no problems, but that uneasy feeling still wouldn't go away. Navi Ru rubbed a grayfruit with his sleeve and took two bites. The juices started to dribble from the corners of his mouth, and he wiped himself with a paper napkin he had on hand before balling it up and tossing it into the reef, but the wind blew the trash back at him to hit his shin and fall to the ground. He clicked his tongue, scooped up the garbage, and shoved it in his pocket.

He turned to the south side of the island. Trails of black smoke hung in the sky.

There was more than a little that was unforeseen going on. It had started with not being able to use the spare gate anymore, and the fire popping up for some reason had been another thing, and the situation where they had to keep eating grayfruit to keep from passing out was another. There were more survivors than he'd anticipated. That boy Touta Magaoka had made friends with Yol, and Nephilia had come to negotiate with him—the fingers of one hand wouldn't be enough to count it all up. But he was still keeping things under control.

Navi heard a moan and looked over toward it. Mana, lying on the ground, wore a pained expression as she stirred. Her presence had also been unexpected.

"She's tough," he muttered absently to himself. She wasn't an investigator in the Inspection Department just for show.

Her eyelashes fluttered up and down, and, gradually, her eyelids opened. Navi knelt down beside her to give himself the air of *"Look, I saved you,"* and, once she was conscious, he brought a grayfruit to her mouth. Before long, Mana's eyes opened and she moved her face from side to side, and as soon as she noticed the grayfruit, she bit into it. Just like an animal.

She finished eating the grayfruit, then put a hand on Navi's knee to raise herself into a sitting position. "How… What happened…?"

The ground rocked again. The two of them looked to the main building.

◇ **Nephilia**

Of course there were emotional reasons that she had tried to nurse Dreamy☆Chelsea, but it wasn't just that. Nephilia—rather, freelance magical girls in general—would always and at all times seek to benefit themselves. Dreamy☆Chelsea was someone she could use.

While feeding Chelsea grayfruit just like a mother bird feeds its chicks, Nephilia considered.

The first time Nephilia had run into Navi Ru on this island, the man had been sitting on a magic carpet that floated in the air. Since then, he'd generally come as a set with the magic carpet, but when she'd seen him earlier, he'd been walking on his own two feet. Despite having the added burden of Mana, he hadn't been using the carpet. He hadn't even been carrying it.

There was some reason Navi Ru had let go of the magic carpet. Nephilia didn't really get the sense that it had been due to a sudden accident. There was no dirt on his robe, and she couldn't sense any panic in him, either. And, combining that with Rareko's final words, Nephilia started to understand something.

Coming to the conclusion that he'd used his flying carpet to send some kind of item he needed high in the air to use the sky as a safe, Nephilia realized what she should do. Nephilia could not fly in the sky. Ren-Ren could fly, but she was with Clarissa. It would be difficult to get in contact with Ren-Ren right now and get her to get the item.

So here she had Dreamy☆Chelsea. This crazy magical girl could make star-shaped objects fly and could even ride on top of them to fly herself. In order for Nephilia to acquire that thing Navi Ru needed and stand in an advantageous position over him, she needed Dreamy☆Chelsea's ability to fly.

Chelsea raised herself on her elbows and reached out for the grayfruit, grabbing one to put into her mouth herself. Her color was a lot better than back when she'd been entirely a corpse. She was in magical-girl form, and the strength had returned to her eyes as well. But still, these were serious injuries that would ordinarily have sent her straight to the hospital—but these were not ordinary times.

After that, she devoured five more grayfruit before coming to sit with her legs to the side and letting out a *phew*, and after Nephilia wiped the grayfruit juices off her hands and mouth, Chelsea looked ahead and cried out in surprise, pointing at Nephilia. "You... Why... Huh? Could it be you saved me?"

Nephilia giggled. If she understood, that would make things faster, so she explained.

She told Chelsea that she had been dying—in actuality, she'd definitely been dead, but since if she started talking about that, things would go on too long, and it wasn't as if Nephilia fully understood it herself, she just made it like she'd been dying—and Clarissa and Ren-Ren had headed out to beat the goddess magical girl.

At this point, Chelsea tried to leap up, but Nephilia wrapped her arms around her waist to stop her. "If you fight...you need..."

"Where? Where is it?"

"Probably...hidden...sky..."

"Then I've got to go get it! We have to go, now! Show me!"

Clarissa would finish off the goddess. There was no reason Chelsea had to work so hard. But just like there were no hairs on Navi's head, there were no reasons to tell her that.

☆ Pastel Mary

They got more people. First, there was a woman in her pajamas and a little tortoise, 7753 and Tepsekemei. When they made the tortoise lick some gargling medicine, she transformed into a dancer-style magical girl. But she was two sizes smaller than when Mary had seen her before. Making a fuss more than a hundred times louder than the tortoise as she plugged her nose to somehow drink down the gargle medicine was 7753, who seemed to be lacking something. Her motif was a school uniform, so with her school cap and *gakuran*, you wouldn't think anything was missing, but for some reason, it didn't feel right. But Mary couldn't remember what the missing component was. She had the feeling like it was important, but also like it wasn't.

Anyway, she didn't have the time to be worrying about it. Even at the best of times, using her head took up time. When things were busy, she should just do her work, and if she got some spare time later, she would think.

They'd also added the two mage children on top of that. Now Pastel Mary could avoid the absolute worst, that she would have to be the assistant in some ceremony. She understood herself better than anyone. It wasn't an issue of confidence. Pastel Mary was startlingly unsuited to a situation where errors would not be permitted. She knew she would absolutely blow it.

She did feel like that was pathetic of her, at a time like this, but it wasn't like she could change herself right away. Mary would do what she should do. In other words, she would continue to draw and draw sheep to set them to work, and she would make them shields if needed.

She shut out all the discussion being had around her and the sounds of explosions she could hear from the forest and put her energy, strength, and magic into drawing sheep so that she would have no regrets, even if her life as an artist were to end here, and when she had a spare moment, she drank the hair growth formula or the cough syrup and stuff. She ignored the taste, how it felt going down, everything.

After drawing a particularly large sheep, she happened to look up. She had a feeling she could hear Dreamy☆Chelsea's voice. She immediately shook her head and resumed drawing sheep. She could remember Chelsea later. Right now, she should do her best to make it so there would be a "later."

◇ **Dreamy☆Chelsea**

She was made to wander all over the sky, like *"Maybe it's over here, maybe it's over there."*

Normally, carrying Nephilia on her back as she rode a little star-shaped rock flying through the sky would be an easy task. But right now, Chelsea was not the usual Chelsea. She'd been sliced open so bad, her cuteness had been dramatically reduced. It was really the most she could do to just move. And on top of that, the higher she got in the sky, the colder it got. Chelsea wasn't cut out for going up high right now.

But Nephilia pushed her hard anyway. And though she acted full of confidence, like she totally knew where it was, when it actually came down to looking for it, she got lost. This caused problems.

Nephilia pointed like *"Maybe it's over there,"* and Chelsea complained as she headed over there, and then Nephilia pointed like *"Maybe it's over this way,"* and Chelsea whined as she went over that way, and after repeating that a few times, they finally found something that seemed like it. The one to find it was not Nephilia. Chelsea found it. Nephilia was really not useful. She was very close to a villain to begin with, and if Chelsea hadn't owed her for saving her, she'd have been fine ignoring her.

But Nephilia had found her, and that changed things.

On top of a carpet that floated above the clouds sat a little wooden box. Opening the lid, Chelsea cried "Wow!" in mixed surprise and joy.

At a glance, it looked like just a gear, nothing special about it. But the clear cuteness hidden within did come across. It was such intense cute-pop, equivalent to that of a few dozen magical girls who'd gotten made into anime. Chelsea's cheeks had gone white from lack of blood and from the cold, but now pink rose in them.

Nephilia laughed. Maybe that *ksh-shh* sound could be considered cute.

◇ **Miss Marguerite**

The half-beast magical girl who had been fighting head-to-head with the goddess was gone. A small-statured girl in a tattered school uniform was clenching her teeth at her own powerlessness, holding to her chest the rage that she was no longer able to put in a swing, her breaths coming weakly as she knelt in the mud.

Marguerite let out a long sigh. This wasn't the absolute worst outcome she'd imagined. In fact, this was on the better side. If Clantail's transformation had come undone right in the middle of a bladed exchange, or even when she'd been racing or fleeing, then at best she'd be heavily wounded, and worst case, she'd have become mincemeat.

The goddess twisted her body toward Marguerite and pointed the blade of her ax at her. This killer could not perceive magical girls who could no longer transform. In a sense, you could say Clantail had escaped to a safe zone.

Marguerite bit into a grayfruit and leaped backward. The axes swung in pursuit, blasting away trees and dirt, and the girl in the school uniform who was behind the goddess was also flung away. Even if it was just the wind of the strike, a human wouldn't be able to stay on her feet after getting hit with that. There was nothing for it but to pray that her landing would be soft enough that she wouldn't die.

Marguerite finished the rest of the fruit in one bite, shaking off the juices that were stuck to her right hand.

The goddess still wasn't able to fight at full power. She was injured, she only had one ax, and it was slick with mucus and hard to hold. But even so, it would be incredibly difficult for Marguerite to win on her own.

Marguerite dealt with each tree-breaking attack carefully, one by one, and in the process her skin was peeled off, flesh shaved away, and bones broken, her fighting capacity gradually eroding while the enemy was gradually regaining hers. If Marguerite fought without a plan, then she'd just repeat what had happened before.

The more time she spent on this, the greater a disadvantage she was at. She just had to go.

Marguerite held her breath. While stepping to the right, she tensed and released—

"Hold it right there!"

Marguerite staggered, and the goddess's head turned to the voice.

Even with the branches and leaves in the way, she could still be seen. She was hovering about thirty feet off the ground, riding a misshapen starlike object about six inches in diameter, hand on her waist as she looked down from her imposing stance. "Repeated unfairness and violence! I absolutely won't forgive you now!"

"Stop," came halfway out of Marguerite's throat, but she held it back and swallowed it. Even from where Marguerite was standing, having surpassed her limits to fight while smeared in blood, the way Chelsea looked, it was hard to believe she wasn't dead. She'd bled so much that not just her face but even her limbs were pallid like the terminally ill. Her costume was shredded and awkwardly repaired with rocks as pins. The flesh underneath was probably also in shreds. Her face and her attire all the way to her socks was dirtied in dark red, and her bangs were stuck flat to her forehead. She wasn't carrying her wand, and her shoes were gone.

"Leave it to…" She paused a full ten seconds, using that time to raise up one leg and put her hands together in a pose. "Dreamy☆Chelsea!"

The goddess's mouth contorted. Was that a smile, or was that a sneer?

The star at Chelsea's feet hummed as it started to turn, then plunged straight at the goddess.

The goddess raised her foot a couple of inches to stomp on the ground. The shattering force made the ground shake, and Marguerite lowered her stance to withstand it. Next, the goddess spread her right ax to the side like a bird about to flap, then immediately drew it in, held the handle with both hands, and readied it vertically in front of her face.

Grimacing from the wind of the ax's movements, Marguerite groaned at the explosive impact that came next. The color of the ax blade was deepening endlessly. It was a black that drew the eye. Marguerite had seen this before. It was Archfiend Pam's wing.

Chelsea blew up dust and blasted away trees as she dived in. The goddess readied herself in a high guard, stepping so hard that her feet sank in the earth to the ankles. She was bracing to block.

It didn't look like Chelsea had a plan. The star rotating at her feet just looked like a makeshift, handmade object, and overall she seemed like someone at the end of their rope going out of control. As the goddess's stance widened, the ax spread as well, becoming even blacker, wriggling and writhing as if it would swallow everything. With stickiness, sharpness and sturdiness all together to make destruction, this was exactly like the wings Archfiend Pam had used to pulverize her enemies.

Caught right in the middle of a situation where things were moving with dreadful speed, Marguerite felt her sense of time was strangely relaxed as she thought about what she should do.

For the goddess, this change of the ax, the form that could be called a morph of the Archfiend wings, had to be part of a special move she couldn't use all the time. She hadn't shown it even once in all the fights she'd had with Marguerite. If she had, then Marguerite would not be standing here now. In other words, there was a reason she hadn't used it.

Did she have some fixation on not using it on weak enemies? No. Having seen the goddess repeatedly copy and reproduce moves in a wild frenzy all this time, Marguerite didn't at all think she would have a strong fixation like that.

Did it have some kind of backlash? But the goddess was reckless enough that she would fly by causing explosions with her two axes, so why would she fear damage to herself?

Was it because it consumed too much energy? On this island, magical girls already consumed power fast, and if they used it all, they could no longer maintain their transformations. The level of power consumption had to be different for turning her axes into things like iron and gunpowder than for making them into Archfiend Pam's wings.

It seemed the most likely thing was that the goddess wanted to avoid energy consumption. If that was the case, it was highly likely that right after clashing with Chelsea, the goddess would be completely exhausted. If they attacked her then, maybe they could land the fatal strike.

Despite all of this, Marguerite's lungs and throat were crying out, "Chelsea! Stop!"

CHAPTER 21
UNBENT, UNBENDING

◇ **Nephilia**

Basically trusting Chelsea when she'd said she would return it properly, Nephilia had entrusted the gear to her. She wasn't about to push for the unreasonable with a magical girl who might do anything if she didn't listen.

Chelsea leaped on top of the unshapely star-shaped plate that she'd just made by carving it out of concrete, and Nephilia hugged Chelsea's waist, riding behind. It was just barely big enough for two to ride.

With two magical girls aboard, the star zoomed through the air. Nephilia was badly injured and her whole body hurt, but her excitement was even greater than her injuries.

Riding together on the star, they flew out the window of the main building toward the forest behind it, in other words to where the fight was happening.

They circled to get to where the noises were coming from,

sneaking over quickly in a low-altitude flight, and as they saw what was going on from a distance, that excitement receded and pain came to the fore instead, torturing her whole body.

Nephilia doubted her eyes, but no matter how she doubted them, reality would not budge. Even though the goddess was injured, she was still moving, and Clarissa, who should have been dealing with the killer, couldn't be seen anywhere. Ren-Ren was gone, too. Yes, Ren-Ren was gone. Looking down from the star, Nephilia clenched her right fist hard. Even trying to squeeze with all the strength she had, she hardly felt any pain.

She'd lost all her cool. She felt more pressed than even this situation called for. Chelsea told her, "I'm going over there to help Marguerite," so Nephilia panicked and jumped off, then looked around. She crouched down as low as she could to keep the goddess from seeing her, using her arms like the front legs of an animal to move as she searched for Ren-Ren.

Ren-Ren's arrows were thrust in all over the place, in the ground, the trees. The vivid signs of battle only gave Nephilia more bad feelings about this. How had things come to this? She asked herself if she'd gotten duped by Navi Ru, but she'd just concluded that couldn't be. Given that, there was no reason he would send only Ren-Ren to a deadly situation.

Navi Ru was definitely trying to bring the situation under control. Nephilia didn't doubt that the mage from the Lab was deeply involved in the incident. That was precisely why Nephilia had tried to negotiate with him. The man had also been confident about the goddess. That hadn't been the baseless confidence of the reckless. That was the confidence of a rotten man who had survived the Osk Faction: treacherous, deeply suspicious, and surrounded by schemes.

Had something happened that even Navi Ru could not predict? If that was the case, then there was no way that Nephilia, who had even less information than he did, would be able to predict something he couldn't.

Nephilia went from bush to bush, behind one tree to behind another, freezing and going flat on the ground each time the ground shuddered. Her heart felt like it was going to burst. Death was not far away. Pressing her heart with her right hand, she prayed that it would not stop yet, and, smothering her fear, she got moving again. The fighting was still far off, but there was no way to know when Nephilia's location would be attacked.

Without falling to the ground shaking from fear, Nephilia made her way along, and behind a particularly tall tree, she discovered someone had been laid down. Nephilia bit her lip hard. She couldn't even fake a smile. It was Clarissa, now in a pitiful state. Her transformation had already come undone. Her body had suffered enough damage that Nephilia didn't feel the need to check her breathing. Even the miracle that had woken Dreamy☆Chelsea could do nothing about this.

There's no mistaking it.

Something unexpected had happened. But even if Clarissa had died, what about Ren-Ren? Nephilia slowly lifted her head and turned to the epicenter of the explosions and rumbling.

If Ren-Ren was anywhere, it would be at the center of the fight. With various obstacles blocking her field of view—tall grass and shrubs, broken trees, a little mountain of earth and sand—it was difficult to see far. But heading to the center of the battle now would be nothing other than an act of suicide. Miss Marguerite was fighting with the goddess. To Nephilia's eye, they were both so fast, she couldn't tell what either of them was doing.

It didn't seem like she could interfere with the fight. So, then, should she try to get some more information? She hunched over to try to touch Clarissa, but a loud noise made her look up again. It was an explosion. Something was being blasted away. A girl in a school uniform was flung up high in the sky.

The moment Nephilia saw the girl, she pushed her injured body and raced out.

She figured out where the girl would land and slid toward her like hitting a base, catching the little body in her arms, moving a few more yards from momentum before turning them both around and letting her own back strike a tree trunk.

Moaning in pain, she looked down at the girl. Her transformation had come undone, but Nephilia hadn't forgotten that face. It was Clantail. Her eyes were closed, with an anguished expression. She was unconscious. Nephilia wondered if she should give her grayfruit to eat, and she was about to put a hand in her pocket when she reacted to a voice that carried well and looked up.

Dreamy☆Chelsea was floating in the air on that star-shaped plate. After making some kind of statement, she made the star at her feet fly straight at the goddess.

◇ **Miss Marguerite**

Chelsea came out of her pose, raising a palm to hold back Marguerite when she tried to stop her. Marguerite came to a reflexive halt. Chelsea's whole body, star decoration included, shone like a star in the sky, and, a heartbeat later, there was a tremendous explosion.

Marguerite's back broke a fallen tree, and her shoulder hit a boulder to bounce off. Tossed up in the air along with the dirt, she turned in midair to grab her hat as it made to fly away, wrapping her cape around a tree trunk to slow herself. She made a light landing with just her right toe on a branch, pulling down the brim of her hat to shield her face from the dirt that rained down as she turned back toward the area of the explosion.

Chelsea was flying through the air headfirst. Like a mass fired out of a catapult, she went a few dozen yards in a clean parabola before disappearing beyond the trees. She'd passed out, moving along with the kinetic energy and not trying to fight it. She had a satisfied smile on her face.

Marguerite stopped her feet from trying to rush after Chelsea and pointed her toes toward the explosion—seeing what was there, she found out why Chelsea had been so satisfied. She had done her job. Marguerite had still not done hers. It began now.

◇ **Nephilia**

After Chelsea made contact with the goddess, there was an incredible explosion.

Nephilia went down on the ground with the girl underneath her. Branches, earth, and stones hit her back, and, while moaning yet again, she lifted her face to find now it was Chelsea flying in an arc. Though her transformation wasn't undone, she didn't seem conscious. While inwardly cursing, *Why is it always me?* Nephilia ran out to catch Chelsea, rolling over the ground even more awkwardly before somehow slowing their momentum to stop faceup on her back.

Bearing the pain, she tried to get up, coughing, with her right arm around a tree trunk. The sensation in her palm made her right eyebrow go up, and, raising her upper body, she brought her right palm before her face. She was holding a bird wing dirtied with mud. Nephilia's brow furrowed as she glared at the wing. It had to have been white to begin with, but now it was smeared with the dirty color of earth.

It was a large, imposing wing. The birds she had seen on this island were all small, and none had wings like this. Nephilia's heart had been in disarray for a while, and now it made a particularly loud thump. She bit her lower lip, wetted it with spit, opened her mouth, and let out a breath. Her heartbeat didn't seem to want to calm down.

She put her hands together and rubbed them with the wing between them.

"Don't... Family..."

Ren-Ren's voice, her words, came out of Nephilia's mouth. Rubbing Ren-Ren's wing had activated her magic.

Nephilia tightly clenched her jaw. Had she been in peak condition, she might have managed to break her teeth. But right now, she had no such strength left.

◇ **Miss Marguerite**

The goddess stood in the center of a thirty-foot-wide crater, all trees and earth blasted away. The corners of her lips curved up, and a single drop of red fluid dripped from her mouth, followed by a second and third drop, along with red bubbles that came burbling out, overflowing from even deeper within to come dribbling out of her throat and down her chest.

Just half of her ax blade remained, completely cut in two. Though what was left of the black blade writhed, its movements were sluggish, and the black color was slowly fading. The goddess leaned forward and coughed, and blood spurted from the gear stuck in her shoulder.

It was a gear. Firm and sturdy, it sliced deeply into the body of the goddess, which hadn't been affected by the stomp of an African elephant or Marguerite's stabs, breaking her collarbone to stick out from it now.

It was clearly a magical item, but that wasn't all—it also had a strange presence. Even when it was seen from a distance, just that one place was in focus, while the area around it was fuzzy.

Marguerite understood now. Chelsea had accelerated the star-shaped concrete, striking the goddess with the gear buried within it. She had believed that the gear would get through the Archfiend Pam wing, the goddess's physical strength and toughness, everything in order to pierce her, and she'd pulled it off.

Marguerite didn't know what that gear was. But her body moved before her brain, and she ran, jumping off a branch to the ground, brandishing her rapier to cut and even the fallen tree where she landed to make it straight, propping a leg up on it and using her magic to bend it to use it as a launchpad. With the combined strength of her leg and her magic, she leaped at the goddess.

The goddess spat blood and twisted around, swinging what was left of her ax at Marguerite.

It was slow. She was swinging slower than she ever had before. Though a hit would still kill her, Marguerite could deal with this well enough. She turned sideways to avoid the strike, squatted to evade the second attack, then managed the thrust of the ax handle with a small hop. With dirt coming down around them like heavy rainfall, she glared at the enemy.

The enemy was not faking. She had definitely weakened. She was on her last legs.

The goddess reached out to the gear that impaled her so painfully, and Marguerite matched that movement to thrust inward. A desperate slice made to swipe away that thrust, which Marguerite avoided by jumping to the right, then dodging to the left, slicing fallen trees as she went. While she was moving, her toe skimmed a fallen tree that had been sliced up, and she activated her magic. The fallen tree that had been cut to be straight bent at ninety degrees for a direct hit on the back of the goddess's head, then scattered into splinters.

It was far from being a fatal wound, but as the goddess was now, the impact was enough to make her lose her balance. Marguerite stepped on the goddess's knee with her right foot, using that to start a run-up to her shoulder and, at the end, forcefully stomp on the gear that impaled her collarbone.

She felt the flesh through the bottom of her foot. It was still hard and strong. Her flesh held the gear in place, stopping it from going in any farther. Even though it should hurt, you couldn't see that in the expression of the goddess—a vague smile that clashed with the situation.

On the rebound from stomping on the gear, Marguerite jumped and grabbed a branch. The goddess staggered, unable to even counterattack, and landed on her back in the thicket. There was the sound of rustling leaves as she continued to move around in the thicket without getting up.

Marguerite couldn't let her get away. They wouldn't get a better chance than this. This was the time to attack and keep attacking. Marguerite went from branch to branch, trying to catch what the goddess was doing from above. She wasn't going to attack carelessly, or with the assumption that she had the upper hand. No matter how weakened the enemy was, she couldn't let her guard down with this one.

She read her movements from various factors—the swaying of the grass, the flickers of white toga or golden hair that came up above the thicket. While moving around, the goddess put her hand into her clothes, pulled out something, and put it in her mouth. Was it grayfruit, or something else that was equivalent to it? She wasn't even looking at Marguerite. She must be doing her best to try to confuse her, as she frequently changed which way she faced and which way she went.

Marguerite was about to take a bite of grayfruit and stopped herself—she put it back in her pocket and slid down from the tree as she was. On landing, she stomped hard on the ground with her right foot, and one of the pebbles that bounced up from the impact she placed on top of her foot and kicked at the goddess. While crawling, the goddess turned back, swinging her ax in an awkward position to smash the pebble. With the pieces of the rock scattering around, Marguerite stepped in before the ax could swing back the other way. She thrust first, and when the goddess tried to meet the attack with her left fist, Marguerite fluttered her cape and took a step back to evade.

Through that step back, she bent her legs low to stomp forward even harder. She controlled the movements of her ax by putting the goddess on guard for rapier thrusts, and, stepping in again, once she was close enough to feel her breath, she raised her right leg.

She kicked the gear like a stomp. While it wasn't so much as a fountain, blood did shoot out as from a water gun to speckle both their faces. The goddess rose to her feet while kicking, and Marguerite immediately backed up, getting away from her to make her kick through air.

Feeling a sharp pain, Marguerite looked down at her right foot. A blade like a butter knife had pierced through her foot. It was buried deep in the earth from the handle to about halfway along the blade, sticking out of the ground with the blade part up. Marguerite had put her foot on top of the blade of that weapon, which was sticking about a foot out of the ground. Right after the pain, questions surged at her.

Marguerite was capable of bringing her foot back the moment it touched a blade, even if she was in the middle of battle. But she actually hadn't managed to do that. The blade was just too abnormally sharp. This wasn't normal. It was strange even for a blade coming from a magical girl. So then what was this?

She was confused for the briefest moment. She knew what

weapon the enemy used. She had let go of Maiya's staff just earlier. Aside from that, she only had her own ax, and Marguerite could have sworn she had never had this weapon. So that would mean she had used something lying in the thicket. Had she been moving through the thicket in order to use this? How had she known that this was lying here?

The slightest opening could be fatal in a battle between magical girls, to say nothing of when you were up against a creature beyond common sense like this goddess—even if she was heavily wounded. You could die three or four times.

The goddess stood up and swung her ax with part of its blade missing. Marguerite looked up at her. Eyes fixed and unmoving on the goddess, she saw something like a vague shadow quietly sneaking up behind her.

It had the form of a dancer wafting in the wind—by the time Marguerite realized it was Tepsekemei, she had approached the goddess from behind, from her blind spot. Expanding and contracting her body like smoke, she slid her hand toward the wound the gear was stuck in, but before she could reach, the goddess swung the ax blade that had just half of it left behind her. The blade became flame and blazed up red, licking all over Tepsekemei's body, and the form of the dancer instantly vanished.

Marguerite calmed her breathing and heartbeat, fixing the enemy with cold eyes as she went into her stance. The wound in her foot emphasized its presence with heat and pain, but she ignored it. What she should be thinking of was not the negative influence of the wound. She didn't have the time to pray for Tepsekemei's safety, either.

◇ Nephilia

Nephilia looked to the center of the explosion. Marguerite had her sword at the ready, the goddess was swinging her ax up, and the dancing girl–style magical girl was sneaking up on her from behind—that was Tepsekemei. Nephilia slid out the three sections of Rareko's extending metal staff and threw it at the goddess like a throwing spear.

She didn't have the time to watch and see how it turned out. Nephilia flattened herself to the ground, hiding in the grass while holding Chelsea, then moved to where she had left Clantail, and from there she skittered back to the place where Clarissa's body was, laying the two down behind the tree and lying down beside them.

Rubbing Ren-Ren's wing had activated Nephilia's magic. In other words, Ren-Ren was no longer alive. Nephilia should have been able to anticipate this, since Clarissa had been killed, but her heart was hammering anyway. She pressed her chest, taking ragged breaths in and out like a hen clucking as she suppressed the urge to vomit.

What she needed was not sadness or mourning—not even anger or a desire for revenge.

She consciously evened her breathing. What Nephilia needed now was calm. Calm would lead to coldheartedness. She would do all the things that needed to be done.

From Clarissa's body, she plucked one nail from the pinkie of the right hand. She could use it as material for her magic. There wasn't the time for her to use her magic now, but she would definitely need it in the future. She didn't want to damage the body of a child, even just by taking a single pinkie nail. But even if this wasn't what she wanted, it was no time to be turning away. Even if it was cruel, she would do all the things she had left to complete.

◇ **Miss Marguerite**

The goddess was about to turn back to Marguerite when from over Marguerite's head something stick-shaped flew in, which the goddess smacked down. The three-piece sliding metal rod was struck away, bounced off tree bark, and then thrust itself into the ground. Marguerite didn't wonder who had thrown it.

Marguerite came forward. The goddess twisted around.

Marguerite lightly rounded her left hand and pointed the back of her hand at the opponent. It would look like she was hiding her palm. She was, in fact, hiding something in her hand. Marguerite had pulled the butter knife–like sword that had pierced through her foot from bottom to top out of the ground, and was holding it, hiding it with her hand and arm.

The goddess hadn't been focusing her gaze on any one thing but on broadly capturing the overall picture, but now that shifted slightly. She became more strongly aware of Marguerite's upper body on the left side. Feeling that increased awareness, Marguerite spread her left palm at the enemy, letting the sword slip from her palm, and spun in a half turn to take the handle.

She still had yet to identify what this sword was. But it seemed her judgment that it was special had been correct. It was a special enough item for the goddess to be particularly aware of it.

The two magical girls stepped forward at the same time. Of course Marguerite wasn't shaking the ground as she stepped forward, but neither was the goddess now, taking a delicate step forward like a leaf falling on a spring.

Marguerite thrust in with the sword in her left hand. The goddess went into a sideways stance for that, and the sword thrust into her shoulder. The blade sank into her flesh with just about no resistance.

It was less that it stabbed her, and more that she'd taken it in. It wasn't anywhere near her vitals.

Even as the goddess was being stabbed, she swung her left fist up. Marguerite released the sword. That had not been her original goal. She circled around behind the enemy and thrust her rapier at the goddess's eyeball.

The goddess followed the rapier with her eyes, then shifted her head to one side to avoid it by a slim margin. A few golden hairs were sliced off to fly away. There was no distance between the two of them. They were close enough not to use rapiers or axes, but to grapple. The goddess moved along with momentum and tried to grab Marguerite, and Marguerite abandoned her rapier to touch the goddess's ear with the thumb of her right hand.

The sword was easy bait. It was because she figured it would be effective on the enemy that she'd decided to use it to draw particular attention to it. She'd used it as such to go all in on the thrust to the eye—which had also been bait. Avoiding that attack had put Marguerite's right hand close to the enemy's head.

When Marguerite's thumb touched the enemy, she did not draw it away, using her index, middle, and ring fingers as well to grab the goddess's ear. The goddess ignored this gesture from Marguerite and tried to grab at her—then lost her balance and staggered. Her fingers, which had started to touch the goddess's collar, swiped through air.

In the instructional unit of the Inspection Department, a number of techniques had been passed down through generations— such as the Department's method of walking, breathing, and tying. The technique of grabbing an enemy's ear and controlling their movements was one of those. Marguerite, who had worked as an instructor, had of course learned it.

The enemy's state was communicated through the ear in her fingers. Marguerite had a hold on the thickness of her flesh, the unnatural feel of her body's make, and everything else as she read the enemy's movements based on the minutest changes, forestalling them to make her own moves. She didn't actually have complete control over the enemy. But she handled and subdued the enemy just as if she did.

The goddess pitched forward, stumbling as she swung about one arm, trying to thrust in an elbow and drop in a knee, trying to rip off her own ear, and Marguerite dealt with each one of those movements, gradually throwing the enemy's center of gravity further and further off.

This alone would not be the clincher. That started now.

She captured the goddess's ankles with her cape, twisting it, and then spun her own body, twisting her waist even farther in midair, grabbing hold of her falling rapier. Sticking close to the goddess, she landed on her right foot. Any pain she felt was numbed by adrenaline as she ducked under the goddess's backfist and slid to avoid her elbow.

It looked as if she were just letting her body move, but it was actually calculated. The goddess was also restricting Marguerite's movements to keep her from taking the butter-knife sword that was stuck in her left shoulder. If that was how she would play it, that was no problem. The butter knife would play the role of bait from start to finish.

When the goddess dropped a fist, Marguerite avoided it and let her pitch forward, dodging to the right. From a stance that made it look like she would fall over at any minute, the goddess lifted up a leg and tried to slam her shin into Marguerite's stomach. Marguerite timed her evasion with that movement and dodged to the rear this time, slightly squeezing the hilt of the rapier in her left hand. Just like an assassin who circled around behind someone to bury a knife in their target's throat, with a gentle movement she turned the blade around in her hand and thrust it into the wound where the gear was still embedded.

Her rapier was buried deeply in the wound. She could feel the goddess's pain and shock from the ear she'd grabbed.

The goddess swiped her foot downward. She got Marguerite over her shoulder and tried to throw her, but Marguerite circled to the front and shoved at the blade. She buried the blade into her, going through the gaps of that firm flesh that was hardened like armor, avoiding the bone, which was even harder than the flesh.

Blood spilled from the goddess's mouth. Marguerite released the rapier, making a fist to whack the hilt, and, right before coming away, she stroked the blade and activated her magic.

The sword bent inside the goddess's body. The strength resisting her weakened. The goddess's left hand came forward and clenched at nothing.

The end of the sword, bent at a ninety-degree angle inside her body, had hit its mark and sliced into her heart.

Blood overflowed. The goddess swayed from side to side and front to back, her chin came up, and she vomited a large volume of blood like a fountain. The blood she vomited upward dirtied her face and flowed down to her ears, and since now it was too hard to hold on, Marguerite kicked the goddess in the face and leaped backward.

Marguerite took in a deep breath and exhaled. Her whole body was crying out. The slice on her leg might have permanent effects. Her right hand, which had grabbed the goddess's ear, was cracked in places. And aside from those wounds, she was covered all over with bruises and fractures, and it seemed her left eardrum was also broken.

Even if every part of her body was covered in wounds, she would still be able to finish off the goddess. You couldn't let your guard down with this one until she was completely taken out. Marguerite came a step forward. The goddess swung her ax up, then down. She wasn't swinging at Marguerite. She swung the ax down at her own body.

Marguerite opened her mouth slightly and immediately closed it. She understood unbearably well that this opponent was beyond what she could have imagined. Nothing could suppress the shock she was feeling.

The toga was already so heavily splotched with crimson that it was difficult to find any white parts. The gear, the rapier, and the sword like a butter knife were still stuck in her. Now one more thing—the ax that she had just swung down—was stuck right under the gear, about one fist's length down. It had turned black and was moving at fixed intervals. It was pulsing.

The goddess had thrust the blade into her own body to replace the lost function of her heart. She was not only sending the blood all around her body as with a pump, this probably also stopped the bleeding, covering the internal injury. The blood on her face that she'd vomited up might also have been intended to get Marguerite's hand off her ear.

Marguerite narrowed her eyes. She brought every cell of her body back to battle. She reflected on her failure to finish, having misjudged the enemy even at this point, and sent orders from her brain. The time needed to get into a stance to challenge her again was zero seconds, when rounded.

The goddess smiled with her face covered in blood, taking one step forward in the walking style of the Inspection Department, then switched to the shuffling feet of magical girl–style staff technique, sliding closer to Marguerite, and then at the end she spread her legs and leaped like a rhythmic gymnast.

Marguerite didn't move from where she stood, waiting for the enemy, hands on her thighs. The moment her fingers touched the hidden weapon, the main-gauche behind her right thigh, she drew and stabbed out in a single motion. The goddess evaded by turning sideways, thrusting her right hand forward. It wasn't so fast that Marguerite couldn't dodge. Her fist was slower than when she'd been moving at full tilt.

Marguerite evaded, leaving only a paper-thin margin between them, and the two magical girls crossed paths with their backs touching. Marguerite tried to pull away for a moment, but her head was yanked back to remain in place. The goddess's fingers were bent jointlessly to catch Marguerite's ear.

Before Marguerite could understand what had happened, her ear had been grabbed. She tried to rip her own ear off by yanking her head forward, but she staggered and failed, and when she thrust out with her main-gauche, it cut weakly through air.

Marguerite's body wobbled and swayed at the core, and the goddess stepped on her foot. Marguerite crumpled, and the goddess gave her a light knee in the gut, bending her over to spit blood—then there was a palm smack on her back, knocking her to the ground. Every single one of the gestures was light as a stroke, but the damage was so much heavier and deeper than what you'd imagine from seeing them.

The goddess released her ear. Or maybe it was just that it had been ripped off, but Marguerite couldn't even tell that right now. Either way, she was no longer caught. Facedown on the ground, Marguerite ran her fingers along her dagger, activating her magic on multiple places on the blade at the same time, transfiguring it into a shape bent like a lightning bolt.

◇ **Nephilia**

For a while, she just focused on breathing. She was panting hard, and it wouldn't settle down. As was obvious from places that were injured, her lungs hurt. Worst case, maybe they were even punctured.

If she tried hard not to think about Ren-Ren, then Ren-Ren came to her mind, no matter what. So she didn't try to not think about Ren-Ren. She thought about Ren-Ren, hoping that her feelings would give her a little strength. There had even been a magical girl who had come back to life because she'd heard the voice of someone asking for help. So you could totally turn the memories of the deceased into strength.

Nephilia agonized, and as she was continuing to gasp away, the earth went on shaking, and a bursting sound hit the air. Little rocks came flying to hit her back, and a thick tree stuck in the ground not even three steps away, tossing up dust all around. Even so, Nephilia didn't move, waiting patiently, and by the time she finally got herself up, the sounds were gone.

The back of the goddess, who was walking off into the darkness of the forest, caught her eye. From what she could see, she was horrifically wounded and staggering so much that she'd fall over with a push. But that never made Nephilia think she could win.

Nephilia stayed completely still until the goddess was gone—and that included her breath. Once she could no longer see her and her presence was gone, she finally started moving again. She moved gradually, cautiously, staying silent as she crawled to the place where the goddess had been. The first thing she noticed was the knee sticking out of the thicket, and from there, she approached the woman lying on her back. She was covered in blood, but the long T-shirt was what Miss Marguerite had been wearing pretransformation. Fallen at her side was a short sword that had been wildly transfigured into zigzags. What would you have to do to break it like that?

She was bleeding from the mouth, and her internal organs were probably damaged. Her chest was moving up and down. She was still breathing. Nephilia took a grayfruit in her hand and brought it to the woman's mouth. But the woman brushed aside the grayfruit with her right hand. Nephilia wondered if she was so dazed, she'd mistaken Nephilia's movement for an enemy attack, and she examined her face. But the woman was looking back at

Nephilia with firm will in her eyes. That wasn't the expression of a dazed person.

Nephilia shifted around, eyebrows coming together. "You have...to eat..."

"No, I can't eat now." She said it in one breath, without her voice catching.

"But..."

"The problem is my leg. One of my legs is broken, so I can't walk. I want you to lend me your strength."

As asked, Nephilia lent the woman her shoulder and helped her into a sitting position. Touching her body, she was certain. Her bones were broken, and she had internal injuries. She should be in enough pain to make her go crazy.

But in spite of that, Marguerite's voice was calm, and her words were cold and quiet. So long as the adrenaline was numbing her pain, then she could afford to speak more passionately.

"I used my magic as much as possible right before I could be fatally wounded, aiming to forcibly undo my transformation by running out of power... It barely made it in time," Marguerite explained. "So it's true that she can't perceive a magical girl who can't transform anymore due to running out of power."

"But...then at that rate...die..."

"Once the enemy can no longer perceive me, I'll move to her blind spot and eat a grayfruit to take her by surprise... Or rather, that was my plan, but I was naive. Without my leg, I can't even move around."

"You need to transform...or in the end...impossible..."

"There's...still a way. You threw that staff? I thought if the one who'd thrown it was here, they would come."

"Stop talking...better...lungs...throat..."

"There was a strangely shaped sword thrust into her left shoulder, right? She...the goddess most likely does not like that knife. If she'd known where it was fallen, then she should have just used it as a weapon, but she used it as a trap. It was as if she wanted to avoid even using it..." Marguerite held her breath a moment.

Maybe that sound from her throat was the sound of her swallowing blood. "She must have been in enough trouble that she had to use something she didn't want to as a trap. That sword thrust into her body with no resistance at all. Even as a human, you should be able to stab her with it."

Marguerite coughed and spat out blood dramatically, and Nephilia supported her from the side. She was going past her limit.

Marguerite didn't even try to wipe away the blood, glaring in the direction in which the goddess had disappeared. "Lend me your shoulder. Once the goddess notices, shove me in her direction. Then I'll lean on her body and pull out the sword in her shoulder."

"Reckless…"

"Even if it's reckless, I have to do it. She's headed to the main building. We have no time. How many have died already? Everyone she's killed has wounded her bit by bit, and it's because of them that we have this chance now. We have to make this chance count, or all their deaths will have been meaningless."

Hearing Marguerite's words, Nephilia remembered something she had to ask. Before she could think that it wasn't the time to be asking that, her mouth moved. "Ren-Ren…"

"Ren-Ren was also killed by the goddess."

Nephilia supported Marguerite, carrying her on her shoulder. That way had to be less of a burden on her. Supporting each other, the two heavily wounded magical girls started walking off in the direction in which the goddess had left.

CHAPTER 22
THE END HAS COME

◇ **Ragi Zwe Nento**

He was going to build a basic gate in the rear garden of the main building.

If that were all, it would be the simplest plan, but this actually required methods that were not simple.

In order to make a path from within, you would have to touch Sataborn's barrier, which secured the island. Ragi knew all about the Sataborn-style barriers in public circulation, from the formulas to their composition. But of course Sataborn himself would not use a generic barrier. There had definitely been nasty modifications made, and Ragi would have to do all the analysis, hacking, falsification, and readjustments himself. There wasn't enough time for a thorough preliminary investigation, and it was really almost like a performance with zero preparation.

There was a mountain of other problems, too. They did not have enough casters or enough tools, and, most of all, there was not enough time. You always had to make do with what limited time and resources there were in the field, but this time was going over the line.

Ragi tugged on the brim of his hat and readjusted it to bring it lower over his eyes. Even the light of the sun was irritating.

"We'll use the trees where the grayfruit grow," he said.

"Shall I go gather fruit?" Yol asked him.

"There's no need to eat the fruit—actually, that would be harmful. Not the fruit—we use the roots. The trees that bear the fruit are in fact all the same body connected underground on the island through the roots they put down. If we have one single root or stem, we should be able to suck up power from that. We will divert all that into our ceremony."

Ever since they'd come to this island, there had never been a moment when they had not been tormented by those grayfruit. He wouldn't say this was for revenge, but if he could use them, then he should do so as much as possible. Sucking up the power of the trees and making them wither would stop the weakening of the mages and magical girls, so you could call it killing two birds with one stone.

"The roots are laid out underground all over the island…," Yol said, "so, then, if they all dry up at once, then won't the ground fall apart?"

"If we open up a hole in the barrier, all space aside from the ground will warp a little regardless. But there's no landlord here to complain. Don't you worry. We'll be all right so long as we get away from the buildings, just in case."

Even if he did connect the force field and the roots and suck up power, it wasn't like that would solve everything. The number one priority should be to shorten the time spent, and he would expend power on that.

Ragi moved just his eyes to look around the area. 7753 and Touta were on hole digging, and Pastel Mary had set about mass-producing sheep. Yol was looking up at Ragi with a serious expression.

His plan to have all the people here escape at once was not going to work. They didn't have enough time or casters. He would get Touta and Yol out and have them seek help. Even if Yol's family appealed to send help, as to whether they would make it in time or not—they would not. Before they came, all the survivors on the island would meet their miserable fates and get killed by the incarnation base.

If he could somehow try to work out just a little more, then would he be able to add one more person to get out? If he wasn't including anyone not here right now in the calculation, then 7753 or Pastel Mary? Right now Mary was drawing sheep so intently, you wouldn't believe she'd seemed so dim-witted before. 7753 was giving instructions to Touta, and she was acting just like a magical girl with a long service record and strong leadership skills.

He felt like if he were to ask either of them to sacrifice themselves for the kids, they would tearfully agree. But he had no desire to sacrifice a magical girl who would agree with tears in her eyes.

Ragi's thoughts were pushed further ahead by the sounds of explosions in the forest. It was clear there was no time.

"I found a root! It's extending that way!" Yol called out.

"Hurry! Just hurry!"

◇ Nephilia

Nephilia loved nasty people. She liked people of just the right amount of nasty, those who weren't too nasty, who had a human weakness influenced by their emotions. Nephilia was of course aware that enjoying observing that sort of nastiness made her nasty, too.

Marguerite never lost her fighting spirit even when injured, trying to follow the enemy. Helping her out, joining her in heading into danger, was not nasty. You could even say that it went against Nephilia's principles. Had Marguerite's spirit affected her, or was she angry because the pleasingly nasty Agri and Ren-Ren had been killed? A nasty person was a nasty person because they'd set aside all of that to prioritize their own safety. Pushing through her wounds and lending Marguerite a shoulder to walk with her was in fact the polar opposite of nasty.

In that sense, it was fair to say that Nephilia was very much wavering in her convictions. However, having no fixed axis and no consistency in your life was plenty nasty. In other words, that meant that right now Nephilia was still nasty after all, and she could relax.

It was important to confirm that she was feeling normal. When a magical girl was about to die, she was often in an abnormal mental state, whether a good or a bad one.

The sound of footsteps on earth and dead leaves sounded in the forest at a fixed tempo. In the state Marguerite was in, it wouldn't be strange for her to die at any moment, but her feet were firmly moving forward. There was a strong light in her eyes. Her lips were soundly closed. She didn't look like someone who was about to die, and she didn't even look like someone who was prepared to die.

No, Nephilia mentally corrected herself. Nephilia should be the one prepared for death. If the goddess couldn't perceive a magical girl who could no longer transform, then the one she would attack would not be Marguerite, but Nephilia.

Maybe Marguerite had calculated as much. If that was the case—Nephilia stole a glance at the face of the woman walking at her side and laughed *ksh-shh*.

It would be best not to make conjectures using the logic of a nasty person. In any case, from here on out was not territory where a nasty person could work behind the scenes as such. If a battlefield in the true sense of the word awaited Nephilia ahead, then she had to get through this first.

◇ **Miss Marguerite**

Nephilia glanced at Marguerite's face and gave that giggle of hers. Marguerite couldn't understand what was so funny, but her support alone made Marguerite feel a wealth of gratitude. She digested these feelings but didn't ask the reason for Nephilia's enigmatic smile. In the first place, there wasn't the time to be thinking about anything but the goddess.

The goddess's steps were sound, not at all giving a sense of how badly wounded she was. But if she was leaving clear traces, then she wasn't using the Inspection Department's way of walking. Was she struggling that much now, or was it because she thought it best to walk a different way while she was heavily wounded?

Blood flowed from Marguerite's body—rather, it poured out of her, chilling her to the point that the heat of Nephilia's body felt feverish. But the blood loss didn't dull Marguerite's mind; in fact, she was more alert than usual. At the very least, it felt like that to her.

The goddess had two special characteristics that ordinary magical girls did not have.

The first was that she couldn't perceive those whose magic had completely left them.

The second was a capacity for learning so incredible, it rivaled her unique magic.

That first thing was a clear weakness. The second was also bound to become a weakness. When she fought like Dreamy☆Chelsea, she was less scary than the original because she lacked the spirit and philosophy, and since magical staff technique didn't take her toughness into account, it had made her oversensitive to attacks. She couldn't make good decisions about where to use the things she had learned. That was from a lack of experience.

Marguerite carried out a simulation in her head. The enemy didn't have a weapon. She wasn't going to be swinging her axes. If she attacked barehanded, she would copy Marguerite, Chelsea, or Clantail. It would be impossible to evade that as a human, so you would have to grab her and keep her from attacking. Marguerite would have Nephilia push her forward, while Nephilia would circle around to restrain the goddess from behind—after thinking that, Marguerite realized something. It seemed she had been meaning to use Nephilia as bait.

The more she thought about it, the more she realized she needed bait. Even if the magical girls at the main building were to draw the goddess's attention, if she headed over that way, then Marguerite would no longer be able to reach her.

There was no time to think about it. Marguerite drew in a breath and pulled back her chin. "I'm sorry."

"…About…what?"

"I want you to act as bait…and draw her attention."

Nephilia didn't reply, quietly laughing *ksh-shh*.

◇ **Touta Magaoka**

"I've found a root! It's extending that way!"

"Hurry! Just hurry!"

Everyone was trying their best to do what they could do. Driven onward by the wafting burnt smell, the strong sunlight, the occasional rocking of the ground, and the loud sounds hitting their ears, they moved around, carried things, gave instructions, discussed, and drew pictures.

They were all doing work that only they could do: Pastel Mary was scrawling with her pastels to continue to create sheep, 7753 was taking on the heavy work with a strength that was unimaginable from her appearance, and the old mage Ragi was giving Yol a lecture on the ceremony.

Because he was not a mage or a magical girl but just a boy in elementary school, there was no special work that Touta had to be the one to do. But he couldn't be getting sulky or mope about it. At this point, it was enough for him to just be able to do odd jobs. They really didn't have time.

There were so many things he wanted to ask the others about that had happened, and he also had a mountain of things he wanted to talk about, but they didn't even have the time for that sort of exchange of information.

A sheep passed by in front of Touta. It was about half a size bigger than the others, with a thick and bulging overall musculature. The sheep was carrying without complaint a big metal cabinet that seemed like it would be difficult for Touta to even lift.

If you weren't paying much attention when you looked at them, the sheep would all appear similar as clones, but they had unique features. Some were straightforward, like a large frame, while other differences were subtle, like sharp fangs peeking out from a sheep's mouth, or wool that sparkled in the light, or facial features that looked smart, or snorting a lot.

Touta was working with the sheep. He wasn't identifying their traits for no reason. He would give the sheep instructions that matched their size and temperament, like *"Bring that over here,"* or *"Carry this over there"*—basically, he was working as the leader of the sheep squad, so he had to look at the sheep. Their master, Pastel Mary, was busy creating more, but you'd worry about having the sheep work alone. So basically, he was a sheepdog.

"Oh, carry that over there. It seems like they have to open up some space there."

The sheep with sharp fangs gave a little nod and dragged off a plastic container bigger than itself.

They did properly understand words and would listen to what you told them. Apparently, the sheep that would go against orders or didn't understand would go out on their own into the forest to begin with. Or rather, since about nine out of every ten sheep Pastel Mary created would do whatever they wanted, only the good and competent sheep stuck around to help out with these tasks.

Working together with the sheep, Touta suddenly noticed one sheep wandering in from the forest. It didn't seem like it was going to help, and it was watching the others diligently working like they were silly. It had goggles on its head.

Touta had just been kind of looking that way, but now his eyes caught on the goggles. Narrowing his eyes, he looked at 7753. She wasn't looking at the sheep, and she was making a lot of clanking noises as she separated a cabinet into parts.

If Touta's memory was correct, those goggles were 7753's. But if 7753 wasn't mentioning that herself, then maybe they just looked similar and were actually something else.

Without stopping at his task, Touta repeatedly looked at the sheep and at 7753. He would never say so to the woman herself, but 7753 seemed rather inattentive. It seemed plausible that she was just failing to notice that her goggles were within reach.

And Pastel Mary seemed even more thoughtless than 7753. What if she'd forgotten she'd been holding on to 7753's goggles, forgotten that she'd put them on the head of a sheep, and had left them like that? It seemed likely.

The more he thought about it, the more likely it seemed that their inattention had combined here. Though he had only just met these magical girls on coming to this island, and he hadn't talked to them that much, they were bad enough that it even seemed that way to him, so it surely wouldn't be strange for such a thing to happen.

Touta struck his knee with an "All right" and headed over to 7753 at a trot, avoiding the coming and going sheep as he went. 7753 didn't turn to look at him approaching, looking instead at the stuff that had been in the cabinet.

Even if Touta stood in front of her and said, "Pardon me," 7753 didn't stop, so he called out a notch louder, "Pardon me," and when he put a hand on her shoulder, she finally looked at him.

Touta pointed at that sheep. "That sheep over there…"

7753's eyes widened and her mouth opened wide, and she yelled, "Ahh!" in a surprisingly loud voice. Ragi and Yol looked over at her. Pastel Mary didn't lift her head from her sketchbook.

7753 wandered over to the sheep with the goggles. The sheep raised its back legs, but 7753 was unconcerned with the sheep's behavior, calling out, "Ahh!" again. It was even louder than the first time.

"I was wondering where they'd gone…" 7753 took a step closer, and the sheep ran a step away, and 7753 took a step closer, and the sheep took a step away, and Touta thought that it would get away at this rate, but right as he was about to pipe up and say so, 7753 loomed in front of the sheep, goggles already in hand. Magical girls moved fast. It was a piece of cake for her to move too fast for Touta or the sheep to see.

With trembling hands, 7753 put on the goggles. The sheep before her bleated and ran off, but she totally ignored it. Then more bleating followed from the forest as well, and a bunch of sheep dashed out. They were followed by sheep that scattered in all directions at intense speed, and then a figure lumbered out.

"Is the one you dropped the golden ax?"

Someone gasped. Ragi, Mary, 7753, and probably also Touta, everyone there was looking in the same direction with frozen expressions.

It was a magical girl like a goddess. Her hair had been sliced off and twisted up, her clothes were tattered as rags, and her body was so battered all over and smeared in blood, you could hardly believe she was still alive.

Stuck in her collarbone was something like the blade of the buzz saws used in construction, and thrust deeply into her opposite shoulder was a sword he'd never seen before, and an ax was impaling her chest, pulsing to a beat. And then there was the sword sticking out of the buzz-saw wound. When he saw the handle of that sword, Touta's heart thudded. He knew that sword. It was the rapier Miss Marguerite had been using.

If the goddess had come here, it basically meant *that*. Touta's heart pounded even harder in his chest. Though the goddess was so badly wounded that it was a miracle she was on her feet and walking, on her face was a breezy smile. Coldness and heat overflowed from inside Touta at the same time, and he clenched fists that threatened to shake as he glared at the goddess. She didn't look at him at all, stepping forward with a sliding gait, footsteps nonetheless firm as she approached.

Ragi started chanting something, and, a second or two later, Yol followed.

"Or is it the silver ax?"

With a thud, the goddess took a big step forward.

◇ **Pastel Mary**

The goddess took a big step forward, and at about the same time, the sheep all dashed out. Going in the opposite direction from the sheep that had run out of the forest, they gathered around the goddess. They moved as sharply as a razor, and the sound of their hoofs was as powerful as heavy machinery. These were the elite of the elite sheep Pastel Mary had created, after all. They were at a high standard in all areas, with the intellect to understand human language, the kindness to consider others, high physical capabilities, bravery that ran counter to the image of a sheep, sensitivity like a psychic's, fluffy wool like cotton candy—and that was why they acted immediately to kill the enemy on sight.

And were flung away in all directions.

The opponent no longer had her ax. The weapons that she did have on her person were stabbed into her, so she couldn't wield them. In other words, her only means of attack was her bare hands, but she knocked away the sheep so violently, it was like she was blowing them away with explosives. One, two were destroyed like paper being ripped, and though the other sheep were not discouraged and surged in, the future that awaited them did not change.

It was no use with just sheep. Even if she was so heavily wounded and weakened she looked like she would fall, the enemy was still a magical girl, and a monstrously strong one. To go against her, you had to throw a magical girl at her.

Pastel Mary was a weakling with basically no fighting experience, and even if she did actually fight, she definitely wouldn't be any good. But she was still a magical girl. If it were Dreamy☆Chelsea, even if she'd been as weak as Pastel Mary, she'd still have acted before her head could even think. And then, after she'd done it, she would have thrown out her chest in pride. She'd be saying, *If you don't take action here, then you're no magical girl.*

Pastel Mary moved half a beat after her sheep. It wasn't that she was slow out of fear or hesitation—she was late because a moment before, she'd been looking at her sketch pad, drawing with pastels.

Before her, sheep exploded one after another, turning to bright-red wreckage to be blasted away, and with a literal rain of blood falling around her, she didn't stop, in fact she sped up, and right before she would have hit the goddess with a body blow from the shoulder, she stumbled. It was past the stage where she could stop herself. She lost her balance and pitched forward as if sliding headfirst.

The more she hurried, the more likely she was to fall. She knew that unbearably well, but still she cursed that tendency for coming out at a time like this. She started to despair, but then she thought, *No* and clenched her teeth. Remembering Shepherdspie and Chelsea, she thought firmly to herself that she was never giving up and shoved her arms forward.

A terrible gust of wind broke off trees and made Pastel Mary's hat go flying. By that sudden fall, she had just barely evaded the enemy's fist, and before she could realize that, the goddess's waist was right in front of her.

◇ Ragi Zwe Nento

Once Ragi saw what had become of Francisca Francesca, anger roiled up within him all at once. His rage was intense enough for every single one of his beard hairs to rise.

The fools had meant to seal the Sage inside *this*. This form, created only to cause harm, probably fit their design concept. The researchers had gone out of control, thinking that so long as she was strong, so long as she won, they didn't care about anything else, which had brought them to this. They lacked even a hair of respect for their great and divine precursor.

Ragi was angry enough for it to make his triangle hat float up, but he didn't let that interrupt his planning. Ragi was used to his own anger. Ever since he'd been shunted into the Magical Girl Management Department, it was rare for him not to be angry.

There was nothing for it but to go back to the drawing board. The one they were trying to avoid was right in front of them, so it would take too long to open a gate to escape. They would destroy the homunculus now. This would be more difficult than making a gate, but also more advantageous. They should expend the power they'd gathered on that.

While glaring at the sheep throwing themselves at the goddess and being slaughtered for it, Ragi swung his staff and cast a spell. It was a primitive and barbaric one, far from what a mage should use, but he had no time for self-deprecation or mockery. Ragi chanted along, and Yol began casting a spell as well. She'd figured out what he was doing, and, knowing she didn't have enough power herself, she was committing to support. The arts of the fine young lady were not to be underestimated—this was rather admirable, far beyond the spawn of your average aristocrat.

While he was impressed by how Yol took action, Ragi's anger never cooled. Anger was his fuel. If he could continue to put it on the fire, he would be able to keep going until he was killed, at least.

Many sheep had been crushed, but their sacrifice had not been in vain, as now Pastel Mary was clinging to Francesca. She kept a firm hold of her, both arms around her waist. Mary looked desperate, determined to never let go. Her sheep leaped in one after another, trying to knock the enemy over with their weight, but Francesca resisted the pressure and didn't even wobble. Despite being so badly injured that it seemed she would fall over from a finger's push, her legs were still firm.

But she had stopped walking. She stood firmly on both legs, bracing herself to keep from falling.

Francesca punched away one sheep, then another. A rain of blood poured down, and Francesca gradually started moving. She laid a hand on Pastel Mary's arm and leaned into it, but that still wasn't enough; she was being overwhelmed.

There would normally be no opportunity for a mage to intervene in a magical-girl fight. Thorough preliminary preparations were needed to compensate for how much faster magical girls were, and without that, you'd fail to keep up, and then the fight would be over. But if they were in a deadlock while shoving each other, that was something else.

A red glow covered Pastel Mary and the sheep. In this situation, support was better than direct attacks. If he shot a fireball into the struggle, the chances of friendly fire were high, and even if he did hit the incarnation base, he had no idea how much damage that would do.

It was just a slight assistance, but Pastel Mary clenched her teeth like this was her moment. She would have to scrounge up all the strength that she didn't normally use.

The current plan was a barbaric and violent one. They were abandoning the humane method of prioritizing the children and having them escape through the gate, instead putting together all their strength to crush Francesca.

For a moment, their forces were equal, but Francesca quickly pushed back, shoving aside a sheep to swing up her fist. Immediately, 7753 leaped on her. She clung to the goddess's arm and wouldn't let her swing up.

Ragi moved his drying tongue like a little rat to layer on further spells.

◇ **Navi Ru**

It had all started with Sataborn's death in an accident.

If you knew Navi and the Lab, you might suspect murder, but Navi knew better than anyone that his death had definitely been an accident.

Had he screwed up procedures due to unnoticed aging, or had he just handled things dangerously out of habit since he was used to it, like *"I always do this"*? Not being Sataborn, Navi didn't know what had caused it. But it was a fact he'd died in an accident, and the proof of that was the old mage lying there as if he were sleeping.

Navi wasn't happy about this at all. He'd let the creator die before the item requested—the base for the incarnation—was done, even though it was close to completion. Since Navi was supposed to be handling odd jobs as well as keeping watch on the old man, his responsibility would be called into question.

But Navi had not fulfilled his duty. In other words, he had not reported the incident immediately. Not for hopeless reasons—he wasn't putting it off to avoid having his responsibility questioned.

This accident was too great a setback for the Lab. Blame would fall directly on Navi's shoulders, and he would be made to take responsibility for it by leaving his post. All his accumulated efforts for the sake of his personal goal would go up in smoke, and he wouldn't even be given the option of starting over from square one.

It was a situation worthy of despair, but Navi had taken a pause there. While this situation was all setbacks, he wondered if, with just a bit of effort, it could actually work out well for him.

He was just getting things done by adding a sudden flash of insight and an unexpected situation to what he'd been planning already. It was nothing more than that.

As Sataborn's odd-jobs man, Navi had been the only one entrusted with organizing things in storage on the island. He also knew that Sataborn illegally possessed a legacy from the First Mage. He'd been wondering if he couldn't steal it somehow, but Sataborn was an expert among experts, and the island defense mechanism Sataborn had set up would prevent any sneaky theft. But now that the master had passed away, so long as you were willing to take the time and effort, there were two ways to go about it.

One idea was to go through the formal inheritance procedures and take the relic off the island. But if Navi showed someone the gear and they realized what it was, he would lose everything, so he was not going to use this method.

The second idea was this: The item was currently perceived as a broken gear, but if he could repair it to make it a gear, that would get around the perception code. If he could pull this off, it would be perfect. If Navi could take Sataborn's gear off the island, then his failure would be written off—in fact, it would be considered an accomplishment.

Navi also knew better where the will was than Sataborn himself. Navi took it off the shelf and quickly checked over the contents—but of course nothing written in it was to Navi's benefit. Naturally, an odd-jobs-man-slash-monitor was never going to get any leftovers. And even if it was inconvenient to him, magic had been cast on it so that it could not be easily rewritten. But Navi also knew what kind of magic that was.

It couldn't be erased or changed. But you could add things. Navi pasted on a transparent, ultrathin magic film with some additional items written on it. Of course the binding magic of the will wouldn't be applied to those additional items, but it just had to trick the readers.

Navi inserted himself and Yol among the heirs and made it a requirement that they be accompanied by magical girls, with a max of two, in order to lure out Maiya and Rareko. Rareko was necessary to repair the gear on the island. There were only two magical girls in Yol's house, so inevitably Rareko would come to the island. Maiya would also come. She had been the biggest obstruction to currying favor with Yol. If he made use of the island security installation, Francesca, then he might be able to get Maiya out of his way. With Maiya gone, he could manage a sheltered aristocratic girl somehow. And if he could slip into that house, he'd be one step—no, three whole steps closer to his goal.

That would pacify the anger at the Lab and also bring major benefits to himself. The plan would literally be turning bad fortune to good.

The plan had been going well for a while. Francesca, operating as a security device out of view of the host and guests, had been more useful than expected.

He'd taken one of the ten Francescas who'd been made to patrol the island as an operation test and changed everything about her behavioral pattern. Navi had shifted her into X mode, which shouldn't have happened in the first place. Since Navi would also be walking around on the island, he had prepared a code to keep himself from being attacked by Francesca.

Though she was supposed to be incomplete, between her skill in destroying the gate to shut in all intruders and her strength in finishing off Maiya, Navi had no complaints. If he made use of the installed feature that kept her from attacking a target in a confined space, then he could even secure the safety of those he wanted to survive. Destruction and safeguarding would normally not overlap like that, but they both fit perfectly with Navi's goal.

But he still had no idea what had caused the magical girls' powers to be drained away. It was creepy. He couldn't grasp what had happened. And on top of that, Dreamy☆Chelsea had brought down part of the main building, destroying the emergency gate—the one only Sataborn and the Lab had known about. This was an unexpected setback.

Navi had never imagined that Shepherdspie, the picture of an ordinary man, averse to conflict and constantly bowing his head, would hire a serious mercenary magical girl.

He'd have had to throw down quite a lot of money to pay for a violence specialist with those combat capabilities. There was no way he would have arranged for such personnel purely for odd jobs and waiting on people—in other words, Shepherdspie had suspected something. Or even if it wasn't quite suspicion, he might have had a seed of doubt. It was fortunate to Navi that he had been killed early on by Francesca.

Despite getting hit by two accidents—the power consumption and weakening and the destruction of the spare gate for fleeing when the time came—Navi had somehow pulled things off. Now that he'd accomplished Maiya's murder, the first of his personal goals, there was no longer anyone to attack him for approaching Yol. Then Shepherdspie, who was bound to become a problem, had died. As for Agri's death, it didn't matter if she was around or not, but, well, it was best for her not to be. Navi was continuing to put Ragi in his debt and protecting him, since he planned to use the man as a vehicle for advancement, and he was protecting Mana, since it would be a hassle if she died, while he had Rareko repair the gear in the confusion. Now he just had to have Clarissa finish off Francesca, and Navi Ru would acquire what he should and eliminate what would be bad to leave behind, shifting his post-event plans into execution—or that was what was supposed to happen.

Things were clearly not going as Navi wanted. The noise from the main building indicated that the fight was still not over. Clarissa had been formally trained, and she had what he'd call enough history in real combat. She knew all about Francesca's functionality, and if you added the tool he'd gotten from the warehouse, unforeseen accidents should not ever happen. But for some reason the fight had not quieted down—in fact, it seemed to be getting fiercer.

Had Ren-Ren and the other magical girls interfered somehow? Maybe they hadn't obstructed directly, but instead Clarissa had seen them in trouble and gone to save them and then gotten hurt herself. He didn't want to think about such a situation, but it was possible. She was hard and a pro, but she was still a young girl. He couldn't say for sure that she would never be moved by emotion, but, considering Clarissa's personality, it didn't seem likely.

Had Francesca gone rogue in some way they couldn't predict—had something happened that even the creator, Sataborn, hadn't imagined? But Francesca had been managed under so many levels of heavy security, it was a little hard to imagine her going out of control.

Or was there something Sataborn hadn't put in the documentation—did she have some hidden ability? Think about it, and either was possible. This was, of all things, a plan to create a base for an incarnation, ordered by the Lab. This wasn't just about the Osk Faction. It was no overstatement to say the whole future of the Magical Kingdom hung on such a major project, and you couldn't pull any mischief here by taking out a screw or two.

But Sataborn would do things that you thought impossible. No matter how many times Navi tried to erase the thought from his head, thinking *Impossible, impossible*, he couldn't rid himself of the bad thoughts.

Shit...

He shouldn't be speculating right now about what he should have done. Right now, at least, saying, *"I should have done this, I should have done that"* was just lamenting and regrets, it wasn't looking to the future. At first, it might sound productive to reflect on his mistakes in order to make them a lesson for the future, but that was an excuse. That was nothing more than a manifestation of emotional upset. While time was short, there were other things he should do.

He would leave Clarissa's safety aside for now. If she was safe, then he was just hurting himself worrying about her, and if she wasn't safe, then there was no point. Though he understood logically that he should immediately go with this course of action, it wound up taking a little time to actually get going.

He was going to eliminate all traces of the gate that had been destroyed and erase the input history on the warehouse.

When he was about to go from the rocky area to the forest, Navi's right eyebrow spasmed. The weight on the carpet he'd sent up into the sky had been reduced. He couldn't tell now exactly when it had been reduced, but at the very least, that decrease hadn't happened before Clarissa had gone off.

Not much could cause such a thing to happen accidentally. It was more likely someone had pulled mischief on him.

It hadn't been Clarissa. Aside from her, the only person who knew of his hiding place was Rareko, but the odds that she had survived were extremely slim, and, on top of that, she had no method of reaching the sky.

The face that came to mind as having the motivation, while also seeming like she could get the information, was Nephilia's. If she thought she could use him for negotiation, then he just had to correct her misunderstanding. He would smash her arrogance for thinking she could be the one to use him, using the law and contracts as her tools. That was the area where Navi was strongest. He was a hundred, a thousand times better at that than at reflecting, regretting, worrying, and grinding his teeth and feeling frustrated.

"Is something wrong?" Mana asked him.

He put on a smile and turned back to her. Mana's eyes narrowed as she gave Navi a long look, not trying to hide her suspicion. Normally, Navi would be thinking, *Hey, Miss Inspection Department, the more you suspect someone, the nicer you should be,* while mentally sticking out his tongue, but he had too much on his mind for that now.

"Oh well. It sounds like someone's on a rampage at the main building."

Without even a blink, eyes sticking to him as if it would be a sin to look away, she gave a little nod. Navi firmly restrained the urge to click his tongue. There was a plethora of things he wanted to get done, but Mana's eyes were just in the way.

◇ **Mana**

With her eyes locked on Navi, Mana gave him just the slightest nod.

She could hear the sounds of an intense battle from the main building. In the past, Mana would have just rushed over. That was because her standard for judgment had been Hana Gekokujou. Hana could never stand by and watch, so then Mana would also rush over, even if that meant ignoring the question of what she could do anyway.

Now, Mana was different. Hana Gekokujou wouldn't stand by and watch, but Hana and Mana were completely different people, and Mana knew well there was no point in her acting just like Hana.

Mana wanted to know if 7753, Tepsekemei, Miss Marguerite, and all the other magical girls and mages were safe, but what she should be doing right now was not giving in to her emotions and dashing off.

It wasn't that Hana Gekokujou had disappeared from her heart. She was always inside Mana. She was resting her hand on Mana's shoulder right now, telling her not to act recklessly.

"Agh, what in the hell are they doing?" Navi Ru shook his head in aggravation. Mana circled into his blind spot, behind his back, and, never letting her eyes move off him, she pulled out a grayfruit and bit into it. She chewed and continued to keep an eye on him.

Her doubts about this man were deepening even further. She'd had the sense something was off in the will, plus he'd been acting unnatural since they'd gotten separated from 7753 and Tepseke-mei, seeming weirdly unfazed by everything—everything was suspicious. But she sensed in that unfazed air she got glimpses of from his attitude that he wasn't even bothered by her suspicion. She felt like it was less like *"Who cares if someone like Mana suspects me?"* and more like his inner workings didn't see it as an issue that he might be suspected and investigated.

Most likely, either he could shut it down through political means or her suspicions wouldn't lead anywhere because he hadn't left any evidence at all. But that was just what Navi thought, and Mana wouldn't know if he was right until she actually tried. If 7753 helped out, she would be able to use her goggles to investigate. If something was going on politically, then Mana could borrow her father's power, and if she went through her father, then she had connections higher up. There was little she hated more than being accused of nepotism, but even more than that, she would hate to use that as a reason to give in.

Mana glared at Navi's back.

CHAPTER 23
TUMBLIN' DICE

◇ **Clantail**

An intense pain made her whole body cramp up, awakening her with a jolt. Clantail—Nene Ono—moaned and gritted her teeth but somehow relaxed her body again. Choking on the smell of earth, she used her elbows to lift her torso. She clung to a thick tree trunk, and a noise slipped out as she brought her body up only to fall on her bottom and send up dust. She leaned against the trunk and let out a fat breath.

Her entire body hurt. Her head in particular throbbed. She didn't have her glasses, so her field of view was blurry, her clothes were in tatters, she was smeared with mud, her hair was torn out in places, and blood was flowing down her arms to drip off her fingertips. Nene Ono moaned again, shook her head, then started crying out in pain and smothered that at the back of her throat.

She was digesting the situation, albeit only somewhat. Her head was still working. The pain was a big drawback, but having her wits about her was a plus.

Her memories came back to her. Her power had run out and her transformation had come undone right in front of the goddess. She was hazy about what had happened after that. Unable to keep up with magical-girl speed once she'd gone back to being Nene Ono, she'd gone from a battle participant to just a victim and had been blown away. That normally would have killed her. But someone had helped her out, so she was still alive. When she'd regained consciousness, she'd been lying under a tree. Oh, that was it. Someone had laid her down.

Had it been Miss Marguerite? Nene doubted there had been enough time for that. If she had already defeated the goddess, it wouldn't have been strange for her to have come here.

Suddenly, the ground rocked. Nene grabbed the tree trunk with her right hand, bearing the pain as she supported her body.

The sound and vibrations continued. The fight wasn't over yet. Withstanding the pain, she slowly got up by leaning against the tree trunk. She wasn't going to let it end like this. She had to do it. The fire in her heart hadn't turned to embers. It was still burning as hot as before. Her soul was still yelling to *never let it go out, like hell I'm letting it go out*. No way could she let the faces of her old friends—angry faces, smiling faces, frightened faces—become just memories.

But if she went on like this, she would just get blown away again, and it would be over. There was no point in that. If she was going to go, then transformation was vital, and for that she needed grayfruit. But when she searched her pockets, she had none on her person.

Weren't there any growing anywhere? Hadn't any fallen anywhere? She looked around the area and finally noticed. She wasn't the only one who had been laid down here. There was someone else. Sucking up the pain, she bent over and looked closely. It was a woman in a bathrobe.

Though her vision was blurry, she managed to tell who. It was Dreamy☆Chelsea's human form. She was unconscious, and for some reason posed weirdly as she lay there. Her bathrobe was speckled with blood—in other words, she was injured.

Nene squatted down and groped along to take Chelsea's wrist. Her pulse was weak. She opened the chest of the bathrobe. The wound there looked like it was closing, but it was big.

Nene found a color that shouldn't be there between Chelsea's breasts and reached out. It was a grayfruit stem. Most of the fruit had been bitten off.

It wasn't like Nene had an accurate grasp of what medical benefit it might have, but at the very least the grayfruit had been useful when she'd nursed Marguerite. She didn't know how useful this amount would be, but using it was better than not. She mashed what was left of the fruit up with her fingers and dripped the fruit juice into Chelsea's mouth. When she brought the crushed flesh of the fruit to her lips, Chelsea's tongue reached out weakly, and she took it in stem and all to munch on it.

Clantail brought her mouth to Chelsea's ear and called out encouragingly to her over and over, rubbing her body to warm it and making her drink water from her plastic bottle, then took her pulse. It was stronger and more stable than before. Her body warmth was slight, but seemed better. She still needed proper treatment, but she'd improved a little. Nene let out a sigh, then used the handkerchief in her pocket to wipe Chelsea's face and body clean.

She didn't notice that she had used up all the grayfruit Chelsea had, all she possessed, until after she'd arranged her bathrobe and laid her down on the ground with a fallen tree as a pillow. Before Nene could feel regret, she started looking for grayfruit again, but she didn't find any aside from the one Chelsea'd had.

◇ **Dreamy☆Chelsea**

Her memories and thoughts were hazy, as if she were looking at things through cotton candy. Her physical condition wasn't great, and her legs were wobbly, as if she were walking atop fleecy clouds.

The sky was gray, clouds spread all over everything. It was dim around her, and she couldn't tell if it was morning, afternoon, or evening. And there was a river flowing in front of her, filling the air with the smell of water. The river was just as big as the many famous rivers she'd seen in elementary school textbooks, such as the Ganges and the Yellow River. She couldn't see the opposite shore. Even if she looked upstream, she couldn't see the end, and when she looked downstream, the river continued to the horizon.

There was no sign of anyone but Chelsea. The river and the beach that paralleled it were incredibly barren, with none of the cuteness that Chelsea liked. If there was any cuteness, it would be on the other side of the river.

Chelsea picked up a few rocks from the beach, gripping them, crushing them, smacking them, hardening them, and forming them into star shapes. She made a star a size bigger than her palm float in the air and rode on top of it. Now it would be possible to cross the river without getting wet in the water, and also she had more cuteness now. It was killing two birds with one stone—she hadn't used just one stone, but anyway it was two birds with one stone.

She didn't know where she was, and she couldn't remember what she'd been doing until now, and everything was vague and hazy aside from the fact that she was the magical girl Dreamy☆Chelsea. But she didn't worry about any of those things. All Chelsea needed right now was to fill up on cuteness, and that was what she was crossing the river for. Chelsea struck a pose to say, *"Okay, let's go."* Right after she flew her star to the river, a loud sound hit her ears, and she stopped her star and turned back.

There was a single deer. It looked a little bigger than the kind of cute little deer you'd see in really old anime—basically the point was that it was very cute.

The deer looked up into the sky and cried out, throat vibrating. This cry was the loud sound that had made Chelsea stop. It was as if it were calling her, as if it were encouraging her, saying, *"Don't give in, you can do it."*

The deer flipped around nimbly to point its cute bottom and tail at her, then raced off in the opposite direction from the river onto a vast plain. The cuteness right in front of her was trying to run away. Chelsea panicked and ordered her star to follow the deer. This was no time for crossing the river.

Picking up speed, she caught up to the deer, and once she was close enough that she could almost reach, the deer evaporated like smoke. Before she could be surprised, her field of vision opened and she hurriedly sat up, and she clunked foreheads with the girl who was looking down at her, and both of them cried out, moaned, and writhed in pain, curling up with hands on their foreheads.

◇ **Nephilia**

Even once they heard sharp cries and bleating sheep, Marguerite still did not rush. She continued along dispassionately, at the same pace. Nephilia sensed she was not moving on impulse, but by strong will. She was not drunk on emotion. She was doing this because she should do it.

All the disturbing information transmitted to them by sounds quite unsettled Nephilia's heart, but the way Marguerite moved helped her regain her calm, and they made their way forward at the pace of a three-legged race.

A magical girl was stronger than her human form in both body and mind. Even Nephilia, who normally joked around, was equipped with enough heart to be able to walk to her possible death if the time came. But Marguerite was detransformed. Her heartbeat indicated that her calm was not from acting or a strong front. Nephilia shivered on the inside. Were the pros among the pros like this, even in human form?

Regardless of how Nephilia felt about it, they moved onward, and the powerful sunlight pouring down beyond the trees drew closer. They were at the edge of the forest. Once they passed through here, they would be at the main building. And the sounds were getting louder and louder. As they approached, the sights changed. Fallen trees, dirt, and the corpses of sheep were scattered around. Stepping over the gruesome-looking bodies of the sheep, destroyed almost past recognition and torn into pieces and scattered, they proceeded.

The trees came to an end. They could see the goddess. There were magical girls there, too. Her heartbeat came harder and faster.

It was Pastel Mary. She was grappling with the wounded goddess, and the sheep were gathering around her. The goddess tried to swing her fist at Mary's back, and 7753 clung to her arm to stop her. Both the girls and the sheep were vaguely glowing—was that a spell from Ragi and Yol?

With the violence of numbers and strengthening magic in addition to the goddess's wounds, it seemed they had somehow reached a balance.

Sheep corpses, broken trees, and dirt were scattered around, plus random items like cabinets, shelves, books, and medicine bottles. There was a circular translucent thing floating about seven feet from the goddess—was that some kind of magic?

Nephilia really didn't get everything that was going on, but it was far better than the worst she'd imagined—actually, it was close to the best. Marguerite heaved a particularly large sigh, and Nephilia could kind of sense her relief. She sighed as well. Everyone was doing well, working together.

But Nephilia knew that though 7753's help had just barely saved Mary's life, that was just buying time. Even if the goddess was heavily wounded, some grappling from a combat amateur wasn't enough to pin her down.

At this point, they needed further help—in other words, Nephilia and Marguerite. First, Nephilia carried Marguerite on her back. This was the best idea, with the goddess caught grappling now. Then Nephilia swung up her scythe and leaped out from the forest.

Nephilia came three steps out of the thicket at the edge of the forest where she'd been hiding and brought her scythe down toward the goddess's neck. The goddess didn't even bother looking at her, stance low as she yanked the clinging sheep and the two magical girls close to her. In an instant, their positions switched, and before Nephilia's swing could complete, now Mary's head was where the goddess's neck had been. At this rate, she would wind up slicing Mary.

Agh, shit!

It had been a mistake to casually intervene in this brawl. Even if Nephilia had gotten lessons from a specialist, she was far from a master of the scythe, and she couldn't turn the blade or stop it right before impact. It was the most she could do to slightly change the trajectory, having somewhat anticipated the enemy would evade.

Nephilia tried to adjust the direction of her scythe, but she still sliced into Mary's back more than shallowly. Pastel Mary's costume was cut open, blood spurted out, and a cry that was difficult to describe came out of her, but she still did not relax her grip. Pastel Mary was stronger than Nephilia had imagined, and that kept this from causing their loss.

While mentally apologizing, Nephilia slammed her elbow into the goddess's back, unflinching at the numbness running through her elbow as she struck the gear with a clenched fist. Nephilia's fist was hurt more than the gear, and it bled. But the goddess didn't go unscathed, either, and she spurted even more blood than Nephilia.

Nephilia could sense that the enemy was damaged. She swung up her fist for another strike, and the enemy tried to swing her arm to cover it, and then a sheep butted her, shifting the arm's trajectory slightly off, and Nephilia's fist reached first. Blood spurted out, and the goddess staggered.

One more shot—this time Nephilia swung up a leg under the cover of a sheep's body so it wouldn't be noticed. She grabbed the goddess's hair and yanked, and with that opening, she swung her fist. 7753 hit the goddess in the chin with a head-butt, and Nephilia struck again.

Nephilia's right fist was ripped to shreds. The enemy was gushing even more blood than she was, but Nephilia wasn't sure how well this was working. Even if the goddess was staggering a bit, it looked to Nephilia as if she was inviting an attack. But even if she was, Nephilia was definitely making her focus her attention on the gear.

Nephilia made it look like she was going to take another shot, then sneaked her left hand in—this time, she was reaching out to the sword like a butter knife stuck in the goddess. If she used this, even Nephilia could finish her off.

Right before Nephilia's hand reached the sword, the goddess grabbed her wrist. With strength like a vise, she tore skin, shattered bone, and crushed flesh, destroying it before Nephilia could even blink.

She had no time to be wailing from pain now. Everything was proceeding according to plan, so smiling was more appropriate than wailing, but she figured it would look more natural to yelp, so she did. It was important to keep the goddess from figuring out what she was after.

Miss Marguerite, detransformed, was on Nephilia's back. She would be able to reach out to the sword without the goddess catching her. This time for sure they would pierce a weak point, either the brain or the pulsing ax, and then it would be over. Even if the goddess figured out that Nephilia had been trying to make her focus on the gear and now was quietly reaching out to her real goal, the magic sword, the goddess couldn't perceive Marguerite, and they just had to hide her—their—*actual* goal.

A human hand reached out from behind that crushed wrist. She was frustratingly slow because she was a human, and also because she was wounded badly enough that it was difficult for her to walk by herself.

Nephilia howled. She was beyond lamenting about how this wasn't like her. Even the sheep howled loud in excitement, and Pastel Mary followed with a roar just like a sheep. The sheep and Mary had noticed Miss Marguerite's presence and what she was trying to do, and they were trying to conceal that as much as they could.

The goddess released Nephilia's crushed wrist, and next she brought her palm toward her face. Nephilia glared at the palm coming for her, shielding herself with her destroyed right arm as the goddess thrust at her face.

But the goddess stopped right before her hand reached Nephilia's right arm. The goddess's vaguely smiling face revealed slight shock, expressed by her eyebrows coming together just slightly.

The goddess's hand suddenly turned a different way, toward her own shoulder—in other words, in the direction in which Miss Marguerite's hand was reaching. She took Marguerite's arm without hesitation, and before Nephilia could cry out, she flung Marguerite aside.

Marguerite was thrown into the forest, breaking branches as she flew, and she came to a stop when her back struck a tree and she fell to its roots. You couldn't even tell if she was alive or dead.

◇ 7753

7753 also understood what Nephilia and Marguerite had been trying to do. After all, she'd also experienced being unable to transform into a magical girl, and so she hadn't been perceived by the goddess.

The strategy had been going well for a while. Nephilia had distracted the enemy, making the goddess focus on blocking to create space for Marguerite to act. But for some reason, the goddess had detected Marguerite's presence, and Marguerite had been tossed into the forest.

7753's goggles were presently operating at full throttle to make up for the time she hadn't had them. She rapidly switched the display, continuously gathering any information that could be even a little bit useful.

She already knew that Marguerite had been wounded badly enough that it had been difficult for her to stand. Thrown aside with wounds that bad, she might easily have lost her life this time. Normally, 7753 would have had to run straight to her, but the situation wouldn't allow that.

"Everyone, refuel! The power consumption is going fast!"

She had to deal with things, respond even before she could understand all the information that kept coming and coming. Her head felt like it was about to pop, but it could wait until this was all over for that.

The magical girls were all close to their limits. Any of them could lose her transformation at any moment. By comparison, the goddess still had reserves before her energy bottomed out. 7753 didn't have the time to look into whether that was due to the goddess having better material to refuel or due to a difference in constitution.

While clinging to the goddess's arm with one hand, 7753 bit into a bottle of liquid medicine, swallowing the contents along with the glass fragments. Opening the bottle with one hand would take even more time than using both hands, and they couldn't spare even a second more than they had right now.

Nephilia pulled out a grayfruit and swallowed it whole, and Pastel Mary put one hand in her pocket and rummaged around, then opened her mouth slightly and closed it immediately. She was the only one who had no replenishment.

It would be rather harsh to tell her she should have gotten something beforehand. The attack had been too sudden. But if they lost Mary now, and all the sheep went away, the tides of battle would be decided all at once. Even with the mages backing them up, just 7753 and Tepsekemei alone would be flung away without difficulty.

7753 thrust her hand into her pocket, hoping for something, and when her fingers touched something, she pulled it out. It was a grayfruit.

She'd only had one bottle of the medicine. And she shouldn't have had a single grayfruit. But still for some reason there was a grayfruit in her pocket. She had no idea why, but right now she didn't have the time to be digging deep into it. 7753 threw the gray-fruit at Mary.

The goddess reached out her hand and snatched the grayfruit from the air. Both 7753's and Pastel Mary's mouths froze in the shape of "ah" as the goddess swallowed the stolen grayfruit whole.

This might have been the first time 7753 had seen the goddess eat a grayfruit. It was as if she was imitating Nephilia from a moment ago—even the way she opened her mouth and used her hand was identical.

She tried to think of what to do and found no answers. Despair crept up from below, and she clenched her teeth and resisted it. Even if she didn't know what to do, she had to do something.

The goddess smiled like it tasted good, and then her expression immediately turned serious. Her eyes widened, her mouth contorted, and she vomited up the whole grayfruit she'd just swallowed with some stomach acids, then put a hand into her clothing with a pained look, as if she was searching for something. 7753's goggles were telling her the goddess was in a bad state.

The body heat drained from the arm of the goddess 7753 was clinging to. 7753 suddenly remembered, *Oh yeah.* That was the grayfruit that had been growing on the bog island. Since Tepsekemei's transformation had come undone after she ate some, 7753 had put one in her pocket and left it there, thinking later she should ask one of the mages what it was.

◇ **Touta Magaoka**

Marguerite was flung away. Touta was about to race to her, but he skidded to a stop.

He didn't stop because he was afraid. It had been way more frightening for Touta to be the one person standing there with nothing to do when Ragi and Yol were chanting spells and the magical girls and sheep were clinging to the goddess. Just what was so scary about circling around the battlefield where everyone was continuing to grapple with a fearsome enemy to go to Marguerite?

When Touta saw the rapier stabbed into the goddess, he thought Marguerite was dead. But she was alive. She was injured, and she'd been flung away, but she was still alive. So then there was nothing to be scared of.

What brought Touta to a halt was that there was something unnatural, strange about the situation.

7753 yelled something. She'd said something, but the words had come out so startlingly fast, Touta had no idea what she said. She yelled and pulled out a medicine bottle and bit into it. Nephilia took a grayfruit out of her pocket and swallowed it.

7753 was wearing her goggles now. She'd said before that stats windows popped up when she looked through them. In other words, 7753 had checked people's status through the goggles and given everyone a heads-up because their magical-girl power was starting to run out, prompting them to refuel. When he figured out this much, an "Ahh!" slipped out of him.

He basically got what was strange here. He hadn't understood why Miss Marguerite was in human form. Nephilia had come with her, and she'd been transformed into magical-girl form while Marguerite was human. It wasn't that they had been left without a choice because there were no grayfruit. Hadn't Nephilia eaten a grayfruit just now? At this stage of the fight, there was no way they would scrimp on grayfruit and make it so just Marguerite wasn't transformed, not when this was a final showdown with her life on the line.

As Touta was thinking, the situation was developing frighteningly quickly. The grayfruit that 7753 threw to Pastel Mary was stolen by the goddess, and after the goddess ate that, she seemed kind of strange and groped in her pocket, and when she tried to pull out something, Nephilia hit her and the sheep head-butted her, and fine debris like pills or something scattered everywhere.

The scattered pills fell to the ground, or into the sheep's wool, or into Pastel Mary's still-open mouth. Many of them bounced off the goddess, some touching the ax handle stuck in her chest, and then disappeared with a *shloop* as if they were sucked in.

While the goddess was rummaging for the medicine, the magical girls were pushing, and after the pills were scattered, the goddess's energy seemed down, and she was moving slower. The pushing and jostling moved from right to left as it came closer to Touta. The sheep bleated pitifully, and 7753 yelled something else rapidly.

Touta didn't blink. His breathing had stopped. He was just thinking.

Marguerite was strong. Normally there would be no reason to keep her from transforming into a magical girl, to make her fight as a human instead. There had to be some reason she hadn't transformed. Now that he thought about it, the goddess had been moving in a strange way overall. It seemed like she'd been slow to react to Marguerite compared to the other magical girls.

Touta's mind leaped from one thought to the next so fast that he didn't even understand them anymore, going dizzyingly around and around. Touta drew in a big breath and held it, tensing his stomach, and took one step toward the goddess.

◇ **Miss Marguerite**

She still had a hold on her consciousness—and her sanity. After being thrown away, even with the tree stopping her descent, her battered body had become even more injured, and the damage to her organs was reaching fatal levels. It was only that her heartbeat and breathing hadn't stopped, and at this point, her inevitable death was looming.

Mysteriously, her consciousness was clear. Maybe her sense that she had a mission to complete was moving her body and mind. The Inspection Department was generally that sort of place. Swallowing the blood that was overflowing in her mouth, she considered why the goddess had sensed her presence.

The goddess was not able to detect a magical girl who had used up all her power, or a human who didn't have any magic power to begin with. So she shouldn't have noticed Marguerite reaching out for the sword—but she had actually noticed Marguerite before she'd touched the blade and had flung her away.

Now the goddess was pushing and shoving against the sheep and the three magical girls. Swallowing the grayfruit stolen from 7753—there must have been poison in it or something—had weakened her, and though she'd been the one pushing before, now they were at about equal force. But this way, things would never end. If they just pushed at each other, it would only continue to wear the magical girls down.

They needed the sword after all. For that, Marguerite needed to think about what had caused her failure.

The sheep struggled and the magical girls strained to push the goddess down, but the goddess bent her knees and resisted. The ones who tried to hold her back got dragged along instead, their feet carving tracks in the ground, and though they tried to dig in, they couldn't stop her.

Ragi let out a little cry, and Yol took medicine bottles in both hands, bringing her right hand to Ragi and her left to herself to drink some green liquid, and the glow on the magical girls grew stronger.

Marguerite inhaled, planning to ignore all the pain in her lungs, respiratory tract, and mouth. She thought she'd taken a deep breath, but she hardly felt any pain at all. It seemed she was finally close to her time limit.

She basically understood how the goddess had known where she was.

When the goddess had dropped the pill-shaped things that she'd pulled out of her pocket just now, every single person around, sheep and magical girl, had reacted to them—probably medicine—and watched where they went. Marguerite thought that everyone had reacted similarly during her try as well. Either the goddess had seen the reflection of Marguerite in the sheep's eyes, or she'd seen the sheep's reactions and used them to anticipate the presence she hadn't been able to detect herself.

After guessing that it was one of those two, Marguerite drew in another breath. Was she hearing a sound like wind blowing through cracks because she had torn something and her breath was leaking out, or because she couldn't breathe properly, so her gasps sounded nothing like ordinary ones?

She'd managed to figure out the problem, but a further issue loomed. At this point, never mind walking under her own power, even standing up was difficult. The goddess had managed to refuel, though imperfectly, while on the other hand she didn't know how much the magical girls had in their reserves. And even if Ragi's magic had conferred a small amount of energy on them, the question was whether they could maintain it or not.

Swallowing the blood pooling in her mouth, Marguerite moved just her eyes to check the area. None of the group—not Pastel Mary, Ragi, Yol, 7753, or Nephilia—was looking at Marguerite. Just like the trailing black smoke beyond the trees, even if it was important, they saw this as not the time to be giving attention to it. Just like before, the attention wasn't on her—in other words, this was an opportunity. But her legs did nothing but tremble, and they wouldn't stand.

Marguerite drew in a breath and blew it out. She felt like she had to focus everything just to breathe, or everything would be taken away from her. Sending oxygen into her lungs, she picked up on the single thing in her awareness she had overlooked. Her eyes locked on Touta Magaoka, who was slowly and cautiously making his way forward.

◇ Navi Ru

"I believe we should also hurry to the main building," Mana proposed, but Navi definitely didn't want to do that.

"No, no. If we went without magical girls guarding us, we'd be nothing but a burden," he told her.

He anticipated the main building was a scene of carnage right now. Who knew whether you'd live or die there? He couldn't bring someone he didn't want dying to a place like that. If Mana died, then her father might get serious, and if that happened, the entire Inspection Department was bound to turn hostile to them, and then if the Caspar Faction or some such played nice guy and started meddling, then things really would be out of control.

Navi wasn't going to go. Though he could make Francesca settle down comparatively safely if he used the code, using the code where other people could see would make his own involvement obvious. That would make everything he'd done on this island come to nothing, with no guarantee that he could avoid leaving witnesses and keep everyone's mouth shut. That was exactly why he'd sent Clarissa, but there was still no word from her.

If Clarissa was safe, then there was no need to go, and if she wasn't safe, then Navi couldn't take the risk to his life. Heading over to Francesca without using the code was risking his life, and it was a risk with pretty bad odds. If he died, it was over. No matter how a heroic death might be advertised, the dead received no benefit. He could only achieve his goals if he was alive. He didn't mind losing his fortune. He'd made that contract thinking that he'd be fine giving it all to Agri if he had to. But his life was something else.

It really made him uncomfortable to have to leave things be for now, for the sake of his future. He couldn't be letting Yol die, he wanted Ragi to be safe, he wanted 7753 to die, and Touta should die—but it would be hard to actualize everything he wanted. Assuming that it would be possible to get rid of people after leaving this island, then the issue was safeguarding Ragi, but Navi might be forced to abandon him. Nephilia, who was supposed to be on his side, had moved the gear without permission, and now he had no more pawns. It was deeply regrettable to abandon Ragi, since he was supposed to have been useful in the future. But when Ragi's life was compared to his own life, there was nothing for it but to give up on that. Since he was giving up on Ragi and he also couldn't guarantee Yol's safety, that made Mana valuable as a surviving witness. That would make it even worse for her to die.

Navi turned away from Mana and glared at the main building as he plucked a leaf his hand happened to touch.

He had no one. At this point, he found himself wondering if bringing only Clarissa to the island had been a mistake. Navi himself had added the proviso that you could bring up to two, so he'd also had the option of bringing two magical girls. But Clarissa was the only one he could trust with everything. If he'd borrowed someone from the faction, he'd never be able to trust her, he didn't have the funds or the status to own a Shufflin series, and even if he were to hire a mercenary, there was no way he could tell them about everything. The only conspirator he could share it all with was Clarissa.

Navi's younger sister was, unlike him, a mage of great talent. Even a spawn of the lower classes, the type an aristocrat would snort at, could move up if they had the talent. But his sister had failed to realize that aristocrats would never value such people in the true sense.

Incarnations were the concentrated essence of the technology of the Magical Kingdom. They also made use of materials that couldn't be made public. The Lab wasn't the only place where the goals at the job site would transcend ethics. Navi had heard that even the offspring of the upper classes would be made into human sacrifices, if needed. And that was even more likely for someone of low birth who had succeeded on pure talent, someone who would be the target of jealousy.

His sister's husband was a common mage with a typical sense of values—in other words, he was a coward. Just a workplace with slight benefits and decent conditions had been enough to make him keep his mouth shut about his wife's whereabouts. No, maybe he would have shut his mouth even without a payment. Ordinary mages were afraid of the Magical Kingdom.

Navi Ru was no ordinary mage—he was far baser and more dastardly. Even if her husband had been satisfied, Navi wasn't going to just let his only sister get stolen away. Clarissa, who shared the same dastardly genes, sympathized with his thinking, and the two had worked together to ensure they could be involved in the business of developing the incarnation.

If Francesca was out of control, Clarissa was gone, and Navi couldn't act freely, then this wasn't the time to be standing around. Navi plucked a new leaf, and, feeling something was off about it, he opened his hand. The leaf was a dull brown and completely dried up.

The thicket around them was dry. When he looked around,

he saw other places here and there that had turned brown. He'd thought just a minute ago that the whole forest was annoyingly green.

Navi turned around and looked at Mana. She was also gazing at the brown leaves in bafflement. "They just suddenly lost their color... What does this mean?"

"Dunno. The hell is going on here?"

"Is this...a tree where grayfruit grow?"

Everything about the grayfruit had been unexpected. Navi didn't understand what was happening, but something was definitely happening. He clenched his right fist behind his back so Mana couldn't see and muttered, "Who knows, really."

CHAPTER 24
LIGHT AMID CHAOS

◇ **Ragi Zwe Nento**

Right now, they were at a disadvantage.

Though Francesca had been deeply wounded, she had the life force of an incarnation. It still wasn't enough to disable her. On the other hand, it was difficult to say that the magical girls had a wealth of forces, and Ragi and Yol's support in physically strengthening their allies with their magic was too slight to end the fight. The grappling and struggling was an ongoing back-and-forth. Marguerite had tried some kind of plan and failed, while Francesca had succeeded, though imperfectly, at refueling, so at this rate, they would be gradually worn down.

As this was going on, suddenly brown mixed with the green in Ragi's field of view. Some of the trees had withered up.

The sheep didn't seem to care at all about the color of the forest as they bit at and weighed down the enemy. Their master, Pastel Mary, was too busy to look over at the change in the trees; she probably had no clue. 7753 called out something, and Nephilia went on guard for it, but she didn't stop attacking, either.

Francesca's head seemed to be moving about restlessly, as if she was checking around the area for something. Did she think this abnormal situation was the sign of something to come? If that was the case, she was almost right, but she still probably couldn't fully predict what was about to happen.

It was about ten steps from Ragi and Yol to the magical girls, and five steps from that floated a translucent circular disc. It floated at the height of Ragi's waist and was about an armful in size. It was slightly oval, and if it had been shaped a little differently, it would be like a full-length mirror or a tapestry. The disc was ten steps away from Ragi. The magical girls, the disc, and the two mages were at the three points of an isosceles triangle.

The disc was the magic force field. It was manifesting in a more distinct form. It was also larger.

The spell had been proceeding automatically, and as soon as it had completed, it sucked up power in one go until it dried up the trees. The force field had changed shape, becoming larger, denser, and thicker, taking in everything.

It was clear at a glance where it had gotten this much power from. Brown now dotted the trees that had been green just moments ago. Power had been sucked up through the roots of the trees to the force field. The mages' and magical girls' power that had been being robbed all this time was now being taken back by force. Now it was actually a great thing that they were locked in a shoving match, and if they could maintain this situation a little longer, Ragi could move on to the second stage.

He would take the magic power they'd originally gathered in the force field in order to make a basic gate and send it flying at the goddess to hit her with it. Even if she was a deluxe-quality Sataborn-made magical girl, she wouldn't stand a chance.

He switched the incantation. Yol picked up on Ragi's intentions and followed along with his chanting, both spells overlapping to aim toward completion. The wavelengths combined, and the alignment of power focused on Ragi. It was coming. And he would take it. All his senses sharpened, his exhaustion eased, his hand clasped his staff more firmly, and the flow of time became slow like mud, making his movements quicker in inverse proportion. His whole body was brimming with power.

Though Francesca did seem a bit confused, like she was wondering what was going on, she still had that smile that he was sick of by now, looking down on the sheep and magical girls with a seemingly gentle gaze as she made a fist.

Ragi sped up the pace of the chant. Yol followed immediately after.

The switched chant meant the magical girls lost their strengthening. One or two of them would get hit by Francesca before the plan was complete. But while they were being hit, he would complete the spell. He would take the great volume of power sucked up from those miserable trees that were rampant all over the island and slam it into one point. It was simple and violent, but potent. This didn't need a long chant, a ceremony, or magical tools, and two casters were enough. Ragi's physical strength had been bolstered by the power, shortening the time of the chant even further.

Francesca swiped one arm through the air. A shrill sound rang out, and Ragi's eyes went wide. Something caught in his throat. His chant was cut off. Liquid dripped from his beard. Ragi held his throat. His voice wouldn't come out. All that came out of his mouth was the sound of bubbles popping.

When he staggered and started to fall, Yol caught him. She switched to chanting healing magic. Even if he wanted to yell, "*I don't need healing! Switch to attack,*" all that came from his mouth was warm fluid.

Smeared in blood, Ragi glared at Francesca. She was smiling. He felt weak. His staff, broken in the middle, slipped from his wrinkled hand and fell to the ground.

Had it been a pebble, or a fragment of some weapon? She had thrown something small at him. Ragi had reflexively raised his staff as a shield. His staff had broken, but that still hadn't stopped the momentum of the item she'd thrown, and it had hit him in the throat. If he hadn't been connected to the force field, then he wouldn't even have been able to react in the first place, and he would have been killed, his head flying off his neck. He had kept his life, but it didn't seem like he would be saved. At this rate, the spell would not be complete fast enough. Not only that, things would get even worse.

How much had she even been thinking about him? The goddess didn't even try to look at him, as if she had already lost interest. She deemed him not part of the fight. Francesca's smile seemed to be mocking the old mage.

The force field rippled. With the sudden loss of its creator, it couldn't maintain stability. Its settings were still active, but that on its own was dangerous. It was holding too much power.

A dazzling light covered the whole area.

It was merely emitting excess power as light—the safety valve was operating as intended, adjusting the output to a controllable amount—but right now was the worst possible moment for that. Ragi had been getting power from the force field, so he was just slightly dazzled, but if an ordinary mage or magical girl were hit by it, it would cause a short-term visual obstruction. To those with no magical ability, it would potentially be fatal.

Touta was diagonally one or two steps behind where Ragi stood. Right now, just moving his head made Ragi wind up literally spitting blood. Even as he stayed still, blood continued to spill from him, and moment by moment, his vision was getting narrower and dimmer. So he could only judge by sound, but he couldn't hear anything like falling, screaming, or crying. Touta was still standing. It seemed the silver lining in this situation was that Ragi hadn't caused his death.

Yol's chant did not stop. She had to hardly be able to see, but she was still going. But the magical girls' lives would end before her treatment did. Ragi tried to yell and spat more blood than before. He pointed his trembling fingers at Francesca but didn't go further.

Francesca didn't stop moving. Perhaps because she relied less on her five senses, she was ignoring the powerful light.

The magical girls could not see how Francesca moved. They took on her attacks, unable to do anything else. Francesca's smile became stronger, deeper. She swung up her fist, readying it to slam it down like a hammer on Pastel Mary's completely undefended head.

The sound of a dry clap rang out. The smile remained on Francesca's face as she looked at her repelled fist, and next she looked up at the sky. A dancer-style magical girl who flew in the sky with the sun at her back was pursing her lips to blow air, and again the sound of a clap rang out. Francesca's hair was shredded and blood flew, and the third air bullet made a direct hit on the gear stabbing her, and her smile disappeared, and she used the arm she'd raised to cover the gear.

Tepsekemei was a size larger than before, and she had just slightly more color. Even her expression looked more imposing.

◇ **Mana**

There was a flash. Despite how far away the light was, Mana couldn't help but squint and shade her eyes with one hand. It was so dazzling, it made her close her eyes for a while, and then she slowly opened her eyelids.

Just as before the flash, trees here and there were dried up and brown. Was there some kind of connection between these two strange events that had happened one after another, the withering and the intense light?

The light had probably come from the main building. It was certain that something had happened, but right now Mana didn't know what that was. Thinking back on the faces of every single one of the magical girls on this island, including the killer goddess, she knew none of them had magic that could have made the trees where the grayfruit grew wither up all over the island, then emit a powerful flash at the main building.

If this wasn't a magical girl, then it was an installation on the island or a mage. Either was possible, but the way it dried up the trees didn't suggest an installation on the island, so it seemed 60 or 70 percent likely it was a mage. Probably Ragi.

Mana looked at Navi's face again. The withered leaves had whittled down his fake-looking composure a bit, but he'd still had his mask on. With inexplicable phenomena occurring one after another, now that mask was falling off like the hair had fallen off his head. She could start to see what he was really after.

While his face was turned toward Mana, his body was turned the other way, his toes pointed at the main building. He held his left elbow with his right hand, his middle finger tap-tapping. The red on his cheeks was strong, and the wrinkles around his right eye were deeper than those around his left.

The direction his toes pointed indicated he had strong feelings about the main building, and the details of his gestures and expression hinted at what was going on inside. Back when Navi had been calm, he would have been able to hide all of this.

He was impatient. He was worried about the main building. He was thinking he wanted to go over there. She couldn't tell if he was worried about Clarissa or if there was something else bothering him.

After a beat, Navi turned his whole body toward Mana. He put on a look that was composed, for an impatient man. "I thought I was gonna go blind. That was a hell of a flash. Just who—?"

Before Navi could finish, Mana raced off. She swallowed two pills, melting them under her tongue as she cast a spell to strengthen her legs. Since it wasn't like she wanted physical abilities on the level of a magical girl, she wasn't going to use the ampoules. She didn't want Navi catching up, but neither did she want him falling so far behind that he couldn't follow her.

"To the main building! Hurry!" she told him without letting him reply. Navi said something to try to stop her, but she made like she couldn't hear it and ran.

Before, Mana had thought leaving Navi and running alone to

the main building would be out of the question. It would be very bad to no longer have a watchful eye on him.

But the withering and the flash had made Navi's mask come apart, and his attitude and reaction had given her a hint. He didn't want to abandon Mana. It was natural to assume this wasn't out of a simple desire to protect her—he wanted to watch her. It wasn't just Mana—Navi was also worried about what she would do.

So he wouldn't want to let her head to the main building on her own.

One more reason for her actions, and in a sense the biggest one, was that the odds were high that over there was an environment where mages could fight, and there was probably a mage fighting there. Even if Mana rushed over, it wasn't a given that she'd just get pointlessly killed. The bet didn't have bad odds.

That was why Mana ran. She used the medicine so Navi couldn't easily catch up with her.

Hearing Navi's footsteps as she raced down the hill, she prayed for the safety of whoever was at the main building.

If it were just Ragi, then there wouldn't have been the sounds of continuous destruction. If it were the goddess, then she would have ended a mage in one attack. In other words, aside from a mage, there were also magical girls. Mana thought that if her magical girls were safe, then that was good, and if they were doing excellent work, then that was even better—and then she smiled wryly at having thought *my magical girls* so automatically.

◇ Tepsekemei

Tepsekemei had become like faint haze wafting around. Feeble as a dead person climbing up the spider's thread and ephemeral like Toshishun struggling in an illusion, she had been unable to intervene in reality at all, unable to see or hear, and had been forced to just wait to store up even a tiny bit of power.

But then an opportunity came. The little pellets the enemy carried had spilled out everywhere.

Tepsekemei was drawn by the delicious smell. In a ghostlike state where you couldn't really tell if she was in this world or not, she screwed up her strength and leaped on it. The pill that came rolling toward Tepsekemei tapped her and melted into her. The nutrients seeped into every part of her being like fruit held out to her when she was starving, and now it made sense: *I see. So this is congee with sweet potato.*

Even if she wasn't completely back to normal, she had regained some of her power. She flew smoothly into the sky, and by the time she could look down below, she'd managed to get back half of her magical-girl form.

Below, friend and foe were all fighting in a confused mess. Seeing a magical girl with goggles on, Tepsekemei was glad to have finally gotten herself back. It made her happier to feel glad for someone other than herself.

Tepsekemei fired air bullets from above to help her friends. Just like that time against Pukin, she'd failed once at her special technique, getting into a wound to fill it up with air and burst it open.

Magical girls were smart, and Tepsekemei was also smart. She would not make the same mistake again. She continued to shoot air bullets tirelessly from high in the air, aiming for the enemy's injury.

◇ **Nephilia**

Something burst. The vibrations came to her not just as sound, but also through skin. It was the goddess. Something had hit the goddess. Another burst. Something was hitting her continuously. The goddess twisted around. She didn't like it.

She was being attacked. Nephilia couldn't see, and she had no choice but to judge based on sound and feel. Someone was attacking the goddess and succeeding somewhat.

She started to think about what was happening and immediately turned back. Right now she should just back them up without thinking about anything. For some reason Marguerite's hopes had failed to pan out, and the big plan to defeat the goddess had easily crumbled to pieces. But of course, that didn't mean it was okay to give up. At the end of the day, Nephilia had to do one thing. Her very best.

First, she let go of her scythe. It was too difficult to use this close, but if she tried to back away to make it easier, she would be dead this time for sure. She grabbed the goddess's collar with her free hand and used the arm with the crushed wrist to elbow the enemy. She slammed her elbow in once, feeling it go numb as it bounced off. Before trying a second strike, she beat her forehead against her. That bounced off, too.

She got the feeling that it hurt more to hit her now. The enemy wasn't getting stronger—Nephilia was getting weaker. Oh yeah, the magic Ragi had been casting had come undone. The slight strengthening of her body was gone.

That made her realize—Ragi's chanting had stopped. It was just Yol.

Something had happened to Ragi. There was another burst of sound. It was coming continuously.

Whether it was natural or man-made, if it was nonmagical light, then a magical girl would be resistant to it. It was probably fair to assume that the intense light earlier had been magic. It had seriously affected Nephilia, completely blinding her.

Was that somehow connected to how some of the trees had withered up before the flash? Had that light not been Ragi's doing? What was Ragi up to?

Nephilia swung her head up and swung it down. She struck not with her forehead, but with her nose. She wasn't holding back. Fireworks flew inside her eyes from the pain, and her nose gushed blood. Tears leaked out with it. Tears streaming from her eyes, she blinked two, three times, so she could blurrily see what was around her.

She didn't know what had happened to Yol or Ragi. It wasn't clear who was firing things from the air, but that had to be

Tepsekemei. Silhouettes that looked like sheep, Pastel Mary, and 7753 were struggling. And the goddess—before Nephilia could see, she was startled by the sound that came to her ears.

Nephilia hadn't just heard it before, she had sung it before. A sort of fear had carved it deep into her heart. It was Dreamy☆Chelsea's original theme song.

The goddess was singing. Her intonation was accurate as a machine's, and her voice was so clear, as if they weren't surrounded by the stench of blood and organs. It was masterful singing. Nephilia was confused. She didn't understand what this meant. Dreamy☆Chelsea had been singing on the verge of death. The goddess must also have heard her. But there was no reason for her to sing now.

As if to shatter Nephilia's thoughts, the goddess's flesh held heat.

Why?!

Nephilia was assaulted by further confusion. Was this akin to a sports team performing better when cheered for? Was she using the song like a battle cry to try to raise morale? Or was it that—she had an emotional attachment to this song, as a magical girl?

Just humming a song with no attachment or anything would not bring a magical girl's energy welling out. For a magical girl to be cheered by a song, she had to feel enough emotion for it to generate power.

It was impossible to imagine what the goddess felt, so Nephilia just had to imagine—admiration, envy, rivalry, jealousy. Some strong feelings had passed between the two as they fought, which had led to Chelsea's theme song becoming special to the goddess as well, making her spirits rise—Nephilia clenched her teeth and struck with her elbow, bashing with her forehead.

There was no way. That was impossible. Even if it was possible, just how much strength could she gain from that? It was a misunderstanding that everything could be resolved with feelings, an idea fans of old magical girls tended to fall for. It would take more than ten figures to count up all the magical girls who'd died believing in that idea, even just counting the ones Nephilia knew.

Even if the goddess got a little power back, it wouldn't fully heal major wounds. The sheep bleated as if trying to drown out Chelsea's song. Nephilia beat down with her forehead and elbow over and over, and, her vision blurry, she reached out for the gear.

The goddess raised one leg and slammed it down. The ground rocked. Nephilia's body rose in the air, and she clung to the goddess, determined not to get shoved away. She could hear a sound like cutting through air. The wind was blowing. It was blowing toward the goddess's face. She was sucking in air as hard as she could.

Nephilia remembered. Before the flash of light, the goddess had dropped her container of medicine and scattered the tablets inside all around. With the strength she'd recovered from the song, the goddess had stomped, using the shock to make the little tablets rise from the ground and then sucking them up with her fearsome lung capacity. But by the time Nephilia realized what the goddess had done, the goddess's body was filled with so much heat that she sweated just from touching her.

◇ Pastel Mary

She had no idea what was going on. There was a powerful light and sounds she didn't really get, and also for some reason she could hear Dreamy☆Chelsea's theme song. Everything was so far from her understanding—just how incomprehensible could you get?

But Mary still had to do something, though what she could do now was limited. She firmly wrapped both arms around the goddess's waist and, instead of locking her hands together, made the shape of a heart. She was imitating the strongest magical girl she knew.

She didn't know just how much of an effect it would have. Maybe doing something like this would have no point for anyone but Chelsea. But even so, even if it was just feelings, if Pastel Mary could do something like Dreamy☆Chelsea, then surely she could also have more power than normal. She believed that.

The goddess's body temperature went up, and the force with

which she was pushing Mary away was getting stronger and stronger. But Mary still couldn't give in. In a voice she couldn't say was pretty, not really knowing the lyrics, she sang loudly and poorly along with the Dreamy☆Chelsea song someone was singing.

◇ **Touta Magaoka**

All the skin that faced outward, on his face, neck, and arms, all stung. His eyes hurt the most. They didn't sting—they felt damp. Maybe the warm fluid that was flowing from his eyes to his chin wasn't tears.

Even if he couldn't see anything, even if it hurt so much he couldn't take it, Touta's legs didn't stop. In his head, he replayed the scene that he couldn't see anymore. About ten yards away, everyone was stuck in place pushing and shoving at each other. There was nothing for it but to believe that the situation was still the same and go. While taking care not to stumble over any rocks or holes, he continued to move forward at the same pace, sliding his feet slightly.

If it just hurt, that couldn't be as bad as what Marguerite had suffered. She would do what she had to, even if it hurt. She had actually been fighting while covered in wounds. A normal kid would be forgiven for crying, *"It hurts, so I can't." "He's just a child, so what can you do?"* they'd say. But Marguerite wouldn't cry. And Touta, who was Marguerite's student, was the same. That time in second grade when he'd jumped off the jungle gym and dislocated his shoulder had hurt even more than this. If it wasn't as bad as that, he could suck it up.

He decided to avoid thinking as much as possible about what had happened and why things had gotten like this. Thinking wouldn't get him any answers, and it wouldn't improve things. So then he should think about what he should think about, and do what he should do. Touta didn't have anything, he was just a child, but it had to be good for him to have something he could do, too.

Aside from the pain, not being able to see made even just walking around really tough. He felt like he would lose his balance over the littlest thing, and not just that—he sometimes almost lost his balance even though there was nothing at all. He could hear the sound of something bursting, and the earth shaking, and some kind of song, and even as events like these made him stagger, his feet never stopped, and he kept walking.

Ragi's spell had stopped at some point, and it was just Yol. Touta was worried about Ragi, but at the very least, Yol had enough energy to cast a spell. That was a good thing.

And he could hear two of the magical girls singing. He didn't think about why they were singing—he could just hear the sound, and so he walked toward that; that was enough.

Touta didn't stop thinking. Thinking was very important. If he were to stop thinking, then surely his legs would fall from under him from the pain and fear. And he had to know how Marguerite had failed, or he might make the same mistake. He really didn't want to do that.

He was starting to get a vague idea of what Marguerite had been trying to do.

Even though Nephilia had had grayfruit, Marguerite had gone with her without transforming.

The goddess had reacted differently, too. Despite having easily crushed Nephilia's wrist and trying to finish her off, when she grabbed Marguerite's wrist, she had tossed her away. It had looked as if she was trying to place something she didn't understand away from her.

The goddess was really beaten up now. Marguerite's sword and lots of other things were stabbed in her, and Touta figured the battle must have been really intense. Clantail, who had yet to return, had cornered the goddess along with Marguerite, and they had not won. But Touta thought that was strange. Marguerite was even more beaten up than the goddess, and she'd even returned to human form. But she hadn't been killed and had been following the goddess. Why hadn't she been killed as a human?

Yes, the key was Marguerite. The Miss Marguerite Touta knew would not charge at the enemy in desperation, knowing she would be killed. She'd face the goddess as human because she had some kind of plan.

With all this material in his head, his brain was working hard enough to boil as he forced out an answer.

Maybe the goddess magical girl couldn't perceive humans—more accurately, humans who had completely lost all magic power. But 7753 had confirmed that Touta had no magic power to begin with. Touta should be able to do what Marguerite had been trying to do.

But another part of him inside was trying to put on the brakes.

This wasn't the time to be testing if his idea was truly correct. If he was wrong, he would die for no reason. Even if he was right, he couldn't see, so the chances were high that he would fail. This was completely different from just having his eyes closed. He really didn't understand what was happening. He had to concentrate hard just to walk, and he could easily fall at any moment. Even if he did somehow reach his goal, after that was the hard part. Since he couldn't see. He had no choice but to rely on the others, to trust that someone who was there would give him instructions in a way that wouldn't give it away to the enemy.

In addition to that, Touta hadn't figured out the reason Marguerite had failed. Though his legs moved forward, and the sound was approaching, and the smell of blood and sheep was getting closer and closer, he hadn't figured out the reason for her failure. At this rate, he might meet the same fate as she, or maybe he would meet an even worse fate. But it was still better than stopping. If he stopped, then he would surely never be able to get going again.

It was very painful that his eyes couldn't see, but maybe it was a good thing. He couldn't help but think that maybe if he'd been able to see, he would have been too scared to walk. But maybe it was even crazier to walk even though he couldn't see. He thought he might have lost his mind, but then switched the way he thought about it—if that was true, it was fine, he figured.

He bit, smashed, crushed, and swallowed the fear in his heart, putting on as much of a brave face as he could as he took one step at a time in the direction of the sound.

◇ **Miss Marguerite**

Marguerite had had many opportunities to guide others, ever since she was a child. Many years of homeroom teachers had said, "I can feel at ease when I leave it to you, Rokugou," and all her classmates had said, "Kaoruko is so reliable." She'd been in trouble for the sake of someone else more often than because of something she'd done, and that hadn't changed even after she became a magical girl. Even without Annamarie, in the end—

Her consciousness had been fading away, but now it came back. She opened her eyes and examined those around her.

The sound of something bursting was from Tepsekemei's air bullets. The singing voice was—the goddess's, and also Pastel Mary's? Were they doing it to cause confusion, or did they have some other reason?

When she saw Touta heading her way, she almost lost her mind. She remembered wandering between dream and reality and then getting hit with intense light. Perhaps her weakness had been lucky, as her eyes had been closed before the flash. For that reason, her eyes hadn't been burned directly.

Before long, everything in her view regained clear form. Pastel Mary had her arms firmly around the waist of the goddess, 7753 was clinging to her, too, and the sheep were doing their best, despite decreased numbers. Nephilia was striking at the goddess with an expression of desperation, Ragi was pressing his bloodied throat, Yol was supporting Ragi and chanting a spell, Tepsekemei was continuously firing invisible projectiles from the air, and the goddess magical girl still would not fall, despite being covered in wounds.

And then there was Touta, whom Marguerite had been looking at right before closing her eyes. His vision had not recovered. Blood was flowing from his closed eyelids, and though he was swaying on his feet, he was clearly making his way forward. He was close to the magical girls.

Marguerite was startled, and then worried, and at the same time shocked. He had such incredible guts, it was regrettable that he was just a child. With that kind of character, if Marguerite were in service, she would have wanted to pull him into the Inspection Department. She tried to breathe out and choked on warm blood.

She started counting all the wounds on her body and quickly gave up trying to finish—and trying to move.

So what could she do? Touta was walking. There hadn't been enough time to tell him about the goddess's senses—had something led him to figure it out? All the magical girls aside from Tepsekemei were still blinded. No—the goddess alone had recovered. She was looking right at Tepsekemei. She had to be thinking about how she could reach her up in the air, or about eliminating the others in the way first.

Why was it that even though Marguerite was just seeing her from behind, it seemed the goddess had regained some energy? Was there anything that could have caused that? This was beyond just being energized because she'd sung. Something had happened. She had tried to take out and swallow those pill-shaped things, probably medicine, and had failed. It didn't seem she could have gained much energy from that.

Marguerite spat up blood, and a sigh came with it.

No, that wasn't it. There were fewer of the spilled tablets lying on the ground. She was sure there had been more on the grass and ground before. Now there were almost none.

Had she retrieved the medicine somehow? If that was the case, they had no more time. Marguerite's gaze crawled around the ground to stop on one point. A little tablet had fallen just two-thirds of her own height away. She couldn't reach that far casually. But it was lying there.

Touta was reaching out to the goddess. But his fingers weren't at the right position to reach his goal.

If the reason Marguerite had failed was that the others' attention had been on her, leading the goddess to deduce the presence of an invisible assassin, then right now, when everyone was blinded, was their chance. Touta might fulfill his goal without anyone noticing. But at this rate, he wouldn't be able to grab the hilt of the sword. Did he even understand correctly which weapon he should use to begin with? Marguerite's rapier or the gear would be no good. It had to be the strange sword like a butter knife, or he wouldn't be able to pull it out and stab with the strength of a human.

Marguerite once again confirmed her own state. She was dying. She had no strength left. She had no confidence that she could speak in a properly audible voice. But if she transformed into a magical girl, that would be something else. You could even call it the special skill of a magical girl, to wring out the last of your strength at the very end.

She pushed herself off the tree she was leaning against and fell forward. The impact and pain of contacting the ground just about made her faint, but she bit her lip and bore it, crawling like a caterpillar and then extending her tongue to push against the little tablet and stick to it. She swallowed it along with saliva and blood. She couldn't be fussing over this splitting pain now.

She felt strength. It passed from the inside of her mouth to her throat and disappeared inside her body. Its strength was mild. But right now, she was grateful enough for it she could cry.

The powerless dying woman—Kaoruko Rokugou—had transformed into the magical girl Miss Marguerite. She drew in a breath, and, while splattering blood, she yelled hard, making sure everyone there heard, "Two inches right! Three inches up!"

Everyone looked at her, including the goddess. That meant the position of the sword stabbed into her changed when she moved, but that was just what Marguerite had anticipated. Just according to Marguerite's instructions, Touta corrected the position of the hand he was reaching out. He understood.

"Straight ahead like that! Four inches ahead!"

While giving instructions, she used all her remaining strength to balance on her knees. *I will take you down*, she thought, shredding her lip with her teeth in her determination to kill as she faced the goddess. The goddess had an exceptional capacity to learn. She should be able to sense Marguerite's killing intent, having been hit with it many times before. And if her awareness was on that, then she would not notice Touta, whom she couldn't even sense to begin with.

"And with that sword! Stab her!"

She got her voice out. She thought it was loud enough. The sheep, Pastel Mary, 7753, Nephilia, Yol, Ragi, all their attention was on her. Not a single person was paying attention to Touta as he sidled toward the goddess.

Struck as she was with Marguerite's killing intent, the goddess's hair stood on end. She pulled out Marguerite's rapier, making a large volume of blood gush out of her, and, ignoring Tepsekemei's air bullets, she threw it. It wasn't originally a throwing weapon, but Marguerite no longer had the strength to avoid it. It hit her in the chest. Her hat fell and she bent back, nailed to the trunk of the tree she'd been leaning on. Her head dropped.

Marguerite's eyes were almost closed, but she could sense it. Touta pulled out the sword and stabbed the goddess. As she praised him in her heart—*"You did well"*—Marguerite's mouth twisted up.

She could see some things, even with her eyelids closed. Annamarie was standing next to her with an apologetic expression. Marguerite smiled, and then, figuring it wasn't like her, she put on a more serious look.

◇ 7753

With her eyes that could now see blurrily, she saw what happened.

First, the boy pulled out the sword. It was as if he'd appeared there suddenly. 7753 was surprised and panicked, but the goddess was beyond that.

The goddess reacted when he touched the sword, but a sheep bit her, and Pastel Mary pushed, and Nephilia clung to her left arm and 7753 to her right with all her strength, and on top of that something invisible exploded against the gear, and the goddess stopped moving for just an instant. That something invisible—that was Tepsekemei's air bullets.

The result of all of this was that before the goddess could swing her arm, the sword was swung down. Touta moved so slowly it made 7753 impatient, but with the sword pointed at her, the goddess also moved slowly, like a frog under a snake's glare.

The sword thrust into and was buried in the head of the goddess, which had taken attacks from the magical girls like they were nothing. Blood gushed from her eyes and nose, and the sword thrust through her eye socket all the way to come out the back of her head, and blood glugged out from her mouth, open wide, as she made a sound like a strangled chicken.

The strength left her. Her body temperature went down. The pulsing ax in her chest stopped moving, and her skin paled. Someone heaved a great sigh.

Nephilia ran toward Marguerite. Ragi was on his knees, but he pushed Yol in the back. Yol ran to the fallen Touta, helped him up, and started casting a spell.

Pastel Mary was still clinging to the goddess and wouldn't come away. She still had her eyes closed and was singing loudly, so she didn't understand the situation. The sheep gathered around her, grabbing the hem of her clothing in their mouths and tugging it to peel their master away.

7753 didn't let go of the goddess. This was because the goddess's information was coming to her through the goggles. Everyone thought it was over, but it wasn't over yet.

That time with Pukin, she had assumed that it was over, but it actually hadn't been over at all. If 7753 had kept her guard up until the end, maybe Funny Trick and Kuru-Kuru Hime would have lived. Many, many times she had thought she wanted to go back to that time, she wanted to go back and do things the right way until the end, she wanted to tell everyone that the villain was still alive.

She would not make the same mistake again.

"She's still—"

Before she could yell, the goddess ran. Nobody could react. The sheep were sent flying. Pastel Mary still had her arms around her, but she'd already gone slack, and she wasn't any more useful than a weight.

If they let her go now, there would be no point. Just how many people had been killed on this island by the goddess? It would wind up the same as the incident that had once happened in B City. Many people had died that time, too. 7753 had lived holding that regret. She'd sworn in her heart that she would never let things get like that again.

7753 was moving. Still grabbing the goddess's arm, she was ahead of her.

From all the information pertaining to the goddess—the location of her wounds, her behavioral patterns, the skills she'd learned, the land around them, the enemy position—7753 predicted her movement. It was mainly her upper body that was wounded, but if she covered her wounds as she moved, her right leg moved slowly. And further, it would be less likely for a counter to land from that side. With a glance, 7753 figured out her weakness and the timing, and slammed her shoulder at the goddess's left side, which was a blind spot because of Pastel Mary's position.

The goddess lost her balance. Her wounds were too severe for her to recover easily. 7753 strained with her right leg, then her left, twisting her body. She fell together with the goddess and Pastel Mary, and ahead was the glowing energy disc. Ragi had gathered power there for the ceremony. It had exploded into a flash of light, but it was still there in the same shape.

The goddess's right hand scrabbled through air. 7753 leaped off the ground with her right leg. All tangled up, the three magical girls hit the disc of accumulated energy.

◇ **Ragi Zwe Nento**

It was natural to assume that destroying the brain would make it cease functioning.

Pastel Mary hadn't let go because she hadn't been looking around her, and 7753 likely hadn't let go because she could see Francesca's status through her magic goggles.

It was just like a nightmare become manifest. Francesca's head was pierced with the sword, but she was still moving. 7753's sharp cry made Nephilia stop and turn around, but she wouldn't be in time. Pastel Mary, who still had both arms around her waist, was swung around, and 7753 drew the goddess's collar toward her with her right hand and slammed her shoulder into Francesca. All three of them in a tangle hit the disc and were instantly absorbed.

Nephilia reached out to the force field but stopped before touching it. She gave Ragi an entreating look that didn't suit her, and Ragi spat blood as he waved his right hand, sending her to run to Marguerite.

Though Yol's healing magic had helped him to recover, Ragi was still in a dangerous state. But he was still doing better than Marguerite. Even if he was seriously injured, the dregs of power that he'd gotten from that gathering of it were still lingering in his body. This wasn't going to kill him right away.

And Marguerite was not the only one heavily injured. There was also Touta. He was looking so pitiful, you wouldn't think he'd accomplished such distinguished service. As soon as he'd stabbed Francesca, he'd hit the ground and curled in a ball, and he was still like that.

Ragi left Marguerite to Nephilia and sent Yol to Touta. If not for this boy, they wouldn't have been able to defeat Francesca. They'd made him shoulder a heavy responsibility he shouldn't have had to and gotten him badly wounded. The boy's injuries were all due to Ragi's incompetence. He had to get him completely healed of all injury, or even seppuku wouldn't be enough to make up for it—to say nothing of letting him die. Then a dozen knives in the gut wouldn't be enough.

Yol took Touta in her arms and held up her right hand. Cards were stuck between each of her fingers, and with an incantation, each pattern vanished. Her choice of formulas and the speed and smoothness of her chanting all passed with flying colors.

The problem is over here.

Ragi pressed his throat and swallowed blood, and, while fighting the pain, he turned his whole body in another direction. The force field was still there, unchanged. No, it wasn't unchanged—it was thicker and denser. Sucking in two magical girls as well as the incarnation base had made it stronger.

Sheep gathered around the disc to bleat sadly. Ragi tried to push through the sheep and stumbled on the first step, and since

338   MAGICAL GIRL RAISING PROJECT, Vol. 15

the staff he was trying to cling to was broken, he went down on his knees and hung his head.

He had to deal with that gathering of energy. They'd only just gone in, and Ragi had been the one to create this disc, so he might be able to scoop out the two magical girls. Just like Touta, they were both heroes. If not for them, they couldn't have defeated Francesca. They should be rewarded. At the very least, it wasn't okay for them to die here.

But Ragi's feet wouldn't quite move. He somehow got to his knees, but it was still a long road after that. And even if he got up and approached the gathering of energy, his throat had been crushed. There was a limit to what he could do with basic formulas using an abbreviated chant. But he couldn't give up just because of his limits.

Ragi put force and anger into the outer corners of his eyes. He would do what he should do. There was nothing for it but to use up this one mage and somehow manage with that. He had lived too long to begin with. There was no need for him to live on in decay any longer.

He moved carefully this time to keep from falling, sweeping aside the sheep with his hands. Standing in front of the disc, he raised his broken staff in front of him—

"The enemy! Where is the enemy?!"

Then Mana and, a beat after her, Navi appeared from the forest.

The taut thread of his heart now suddenly relaxed. Ragi staggered, but Mana rushed forward with inhuman speed to catch him. She put a tablet in his mouth and pasted some kind of plaster on his throat. That reminded him that she'd said her specialty was pharmacy.

Mana chanted a spell, and Navi echoed her magic with a self-important look on his face. Though Ragi thought, *I don't want to get saved by someone like you,* he wouldn't say it. It wasn't just that he couldn't talk because his throat was crushed, but also that right now, he had to move onward no matter what sort of power he used.

"7753 and Pastel Mary have been absorbed into the gathering of power! I'm saving them! Help me!"

Spraying blood, he gave instructions.

◇ **Nephilia**

Nephilia figured she'd stood there for less than a second—since her challenge to do her best wasn't over yet. Even if she couldn't understand what had happened, it was enough for her to know that now the enemy was totally gone. Under Ragi's instruction, she turned around, and, with the self-deprecating thought that she looked like she was going this way and that in confusion, just like a clown dancing, she headed for Marguerite.

The rapier, broken not far from the hilt, was thrust into Marguerite's torso. Even intact, it wouldn't have been suited for throwing. She was even impressed that the enemy had thrown it with such force and accuracy. The rapier penetrated Marguerite through to the trunk of the tree behind her, nailing her to it as she sat there. Nephilia drew the rapier out of the tree, but in consideration for the bleeding, she didn't pull it out of Marguerite's torso, and she laid her down on the spot. Taking a grayfruit from her pocket, she crushed it and dripped the juice into Marguerite's mouth.

Marguerite's mouth was relaxed, with no trace of the dignity that was always there whether she was transformed or not. Nephilia bit her lip and pulled out a second grayfruit, crushed it, and added more juice.

Marguerite didn't move at all. Nephilia was about to take her wrist, then scowled. Her dominant hand was crushed. Being aware of it made it hurt more. She pretended not to notice it and took Marguerite's wrist with her opposite hand.

There was no pulse. Nephilia's thumb moved rapidly, rubbing her wrist.

"And with that sword! Stab her!"

She looked at Marguerite's face with widening eyes. She wasn't moving at all. Her voice had come out of Nephilia's mouth just then. Her magic was activating.

"Straight ahead like that!"

Her voice was sharp and strong, and it carried well. It made the tall grasses sway and passed through the dense forest, and maybe you could hear it on the other side of the forest. As far as Nephilia knew, nobody else could call out so powerfully right on the verge of death.

"Two inches right! Three inches up!"

After that call came out of her, she invested another grayfruit.

Marguerite didn't move at all. Nephilia ran her hand over Marguerite's cheek. Her body heat was leaving. Nephilia already understood that she was dead. Translucent fruit juices leaked from the corner of her mouth. She wasn't drinking it. It was just going into her mouth.

Nephilia blew out a long breath.

Just a little while ago, a certain magical girl had been completely dead and then had come back, returning from the state where Nephilia's magic would activate. According to Nephilia's experience and knowledge, that was the exception of exceptions. But even though she knew that had been beyond logic, she found herself thinking, *Maybe.* It wasn't as if she and Marguerite had been close, Marguerite wasn't even to her taste or preference—if they had been in the same class, Nephilia doubted they could have been friends. That was the sort of person this was, but she still found herself wishing this was some mistake, wanting her to come back.

She placed her head on Marguerite's lap, put her hand to her cheek, and looked at Marguerite's face once more. The lips she had felt had gone lax looked as if they were smiling.

Don't be satisfied, you stupid magical girl. There's still work left to do, so how can you go? She cursed quietly so only she could hear, and then she smiled, thinking that she'd finally gotten her nastiness back. Nephilia laid down Marguerite's corpse and stood up, rubbing the eyes with the base of her wrist. Nephilia's challenge to do her best wasn't over yet. She turned around and ran to where everyone else was. Sticking her hand in her pocket, she rubbed Ren-Ren's feathers, and, hearing Ren-Ren's words coming from her own mouth, she laughed.

Ksh-shh.

CHAPTER 25
ENDING

◇ **Mana**

Perhaps it was the season, but she couldn't escape the strong sunlight, no matter where she went on the island. Especially here in this room, renovated from a storage shed on the estate. It had been chosen because it was well lit, so the sun would come in during the day.

The line of light coming in from the window lit the man's face from diagonally above. The man squinted in the brightness, but didn't hold a hand up to shade his gaze, nor did he draw the curtains or complain to the person in charge of this room, Mana, the smile staying on his face under the light.

A peaceful disposition could be seen in the little smile lines around his eyes, his softly hanging eyebrows, and his narrowed eyes. He wore the smile of someone who would not kill an insect, and his mage robes looked well tailored and well loved, used to a pleasant degree.

The peaceful impression given off by all these things was ruined by the mark of the Lab, which she glimpsed under the casually rolled-up sleeve of his robe.

The fact that he worked for the Lab of the Osk Faction and that he wasn't trying to hide his affiliation made it clear that he was not a mage who looked like a good person, but a villainous mage who could act like a good person.

"The incident…no, the accident? It's been a week since then." With a demeanor meant to look reserved, the man made his request for the third time that day. "Too much time has passed already. How about it? Couldn't you manage something?"

Mana's answer was the same as the previous two times. "In my position, I cannot bend the rules."

When a villain chose to flaunt rather than hide his villainy, that was to his advantage.

If you lived an honest life, you would fear the outrageous. And villains are outrageous. That's why the more honest you are, the more you fear villains. And the more a villain is feared, the easier that makes their job.

So the world is made convenient for villains. Much is made of stories emphasizing kindness and consideration because everyone knows the world is set up for villains to benefit. That's why you cheer and applaud for values opposing villainy—so Mana thought. Though she would call herself still green, the more she was faced with reality, the more she was forced to believe that was the case.

The word didn't only refer to villains who lurked in the darkness. The villains among villains, the nastiest kind, publicly sat in high positions where they could devote themselves to illegality with no one to crack down on them. With mastery over power and violence, they would slip through the net of the law and occasionally change the law itself. They thought that they could move a mere employee of the Inspection Department with a simple "please."

"As I said, I was hoping you might be able to do it regardless."

The man was smiling the whole time. No matter how nice he was and how much he smiled, knowing that he worked for the Lab made his smile seem empty. He'd probably noticed her feelings but wasn't concerned about them, keeping the smile on like a formality. Maybe it was a habit of his to smile at times like this. Normally, there would be no need to be so friendly with Mana.

And there was no reason for Mana to smile back at him, either. She thought she must be wearing quite the displeased expression as she glared at the person across the table. "No matter how many times you ask, the answer will always be the same. I can't bend the rules."

"There is no need for you to do anything special for us. All I would ask is that you pretend that you never saw us. And if you could just provide an attendant..."

"We have someone who is unable to leave this island. Our investigations into that and other matters have yet to be concluded."

"But this island was originally Osk Faction land. So isn't it strange for our activities to be restricted here? It seems questionable to be unable to act freely in your own house."

"An incident has occurred on this island. Without doing a proper investigation, we cannot repay its owner. You don't need to ponder it to understand that."

"As I've said, if you use your field judgment to make it like you never saw it, just doing a quick confirmation and nothing more, then we'll leave."

He had to be aware that he was asking something outrageous, but she could also see he had the confidence to be able to push it through. No matter how unreasonable he was being, his friendly attitude never changed, and the three magical girls who stood behind him just focused their emotionless gazes on Mana.

The three magical girls stood in the shadow of the man lit by the sun. No matter if Mana spoke harshly or glared at them, they stood there without moving at all. Neither did they complain about the cramped dustiness of this modified storage room, the heat of the sunlight, or how long the conversation was going on.

The magical girls were like the card soldiers from that story. Wearing the costumes of the ace of spades, ace of clubs, and ace of diamonds, they looked like triplets. They held the sinister-looking weapons of a spear, a club, and an unholstered stun gun, respectively, ready to wield them mercilessly at any time against any subject at the order from their owner.

Basically, this was extortion backed by violence from magical girls. If Mana were to tremble in fear and obey, then good, while conversely, if she got angry and tried to grab him by the collar, then he could bring out prearranged excuses like *"I had to do it in order to protect myself,"* or *"The magical girl judged it was dangerous and suddenly took action,"* and after eliminating Mana, he would leisurely accomplish his goal.

They underestimated the Inspection Department. Because she'd wanted to be an investigator of the Inspection Department for as long as she could remember, nothing could make Mana angrier than this. Before, she would have reflexively laid a hand on them, even knowing what they were scheming.

When Hana had been around, Mana hadn't had to think about the hard stuff. The presence of Hana Gekokujou, the top ace of the Inspection Department, the magical-girl investigator who would go one-on-one with Archfiend Cram School graduates, made it so hardly anyone had tried to intimidate her, and even when they did yell, Hana had gently mediated or, if their behavior warranted it, immediately beaten them down.

With Hana gone, Mana could no longer take advantage of that. But it wasn't like she had to do this alone. If Mana stood up without thinking, Hana would lay a gentle hand on her right shoulder. Nobody could see her—Mana herself couldn't see her—but she could feel Hana's hand there, keeping her in check.

And right now, there was a hand laid on her left shoulder as well. She had worked as an instructor for the Inspection Department for many years, sending off many excellent investigators, and even after leaving her position due to a student's misconduct, she had never stopped protecting the weak. On this very island, she had never taken a step back against a strong foe, continuing to fight with a burning spirit right up to the verge of death. Mana hadn't directly seen Miss Marguerite fighting, but she could understand plenty just from what she'd heard.

Even standing before a mage who would try to carry out any form of evil for the sake of his goal, the palms of Mana's two predecessors helped her heart regain calm. And that calm would lead to preparation and counterstrategy.

Mana placed her right hand on the table. It was a careless gesture. If you weren't paying attention, you might overlook it. But this was a signal.

"Is the one you dropped the golden ax?"

Behind Mana, from a space where there had been no presence at all, could be heard a voice. The three magical girls immediately went on guard, and the man's narrowed eyes widened, face twisting as he looked up at the source of that voice.

"Or is it the silver ax?"

Nobody had noticed. Even Mana hadn't picked up on her presence. The questions were followed by the sound of metal sliding against metal. She'd probably rubbed together her axes.

The Ace of Spades' eyes never left that spot behind Mana as she brought her mouth to the man's ear. She whispered a few words, and the man's expression soured before their eyes. Then he put a hand to his mouth with an intentional-sounding cough like he was trying to hide his darkened expression as he said things like "pardon me," "sudden business," and "another time," briskly standing from his seat to bow and then leave.

The eyes of the three magical girls never left that spot behind Mana until the end, following the mage with an air of tension about them, and after the door was closed, Mana blew out a *phew*.

From behind, she could hear a bigger sigh. "Agh, I thought I would be killed, geez."

"Come on, *you'd* be killed?" Mana shot back.

Mana drew the chair she'd been sitting on to the right and turned toward the voice. A magical girl with long golden hair, a white toga, and a large ax in each of her hands shrugged her shoulders in an exaggerated manner.

Mana sighed even more deeply than before and stuck up the index finger of her right hand to point at the magical girl. "What was that about dropping axes? I told you to come if you saw the sign, but I don't recall ordering you to ask that strange question."

"Well, the words just came out on their own. I can't stop myself from doing it." She bowed her head apologetically. Her expression and gestures were all humanlike, and though she appeared to be just like the magical girl Francisca Francesca who'd gone on a wild rampage on the island, she gave a completely different impression. Well, of course, what was inside was different. "But I've been useful, right? Those people were bad guys, right? Geez, when they saw me, I got so startled. It seems like they got completely chased off, right?"

"If you have the time to chat, then work. Master Ragi never has enough help."

"Oh, yes. Pardon me." The magical girl like a goddess bowed her head slightly, and then, turning around, she clasped the doorknob.

Mana started to open her mouth, and after a slight hesitation, she expressed her gratitude. "Thank you. You've been a help." When the goddess turned around with an expression of surprise, Mana waved to her with a "Get going already," and a full ten seconds after she heard the sound of the door closing, she blew a big breath out her nose and leaned back into her chair. The wooden chair didn't seem that sturdy, and it creaked under her weight, and then, as if copying it, the wooden floorboards also made a nasty sound.

They said a veteran inspector could smell a criminal. Mana hadn't reached that point yet, and she didn't think she'd ever get there her whole life long. That was why she thought with her head.

She thought back on the things Navi Ru had done. He must have used the magic carpet somewhere. He had done something. He'd probably hidden something. Had Navi Ru collapsing and moaning on that island been him pretending to be another victim to accomplish his goal? Or had the mages' poor condition due to the grayfruit been an accident he hadn't predicted?

Francisca Francesca and the grayfruit had both come from the island. This land was owned by the Lab, so it wouldn't be strange for someone from the Lab to know something about them.

Now that she thought about it, hadn't he nursed her because he'd wanted to keep her in sight? Had she gotten that shock to the head she'd felt right before passing out because she didn't have enough magic power? Hadn't Navi Ru been right behind her then? The more she thought about it, the more suspicious it got, and she couldn't help but get the feeling that he was working in tandem with the Lab, which had been far too quick to move after the incident.

He would come again, anyway. Before then, she had to find what she could find.

◇ **Pastel Mary**

Mana had said thank you. She'd definitely said it. That was very rare. Even if she wasn't as bad as Ragi, Mana was stubborn, headstrong, always in a bad mood, and endlessly angry. She was basically a small and cute Ragi. She'd never expressed gratitude before, no matter what Mary did.

With the forest on her left, circling the crumbled wall of the main building clockwise, Pastel Mary rubbed her chin. True enough, maybe she had done something to be thanked for. There had been three strong-looking magical girls with that mage who was probably bad. As soon as Pastel Mary had called out to those four in total, they'd panicked and made a commotion and run out. Just remembering it made her lips pull into a smirk.

That time, 7753, the sheep, Pastel Mary, and the goddess had all tumbled together into the disc of power, and then Mary had lost consciousness. But Mary's being hadn't been destroyed. Though it had taken time and effort, the old man Ragi, who had created that disc of power, had salvaged her from it. Though she'd unfortunately merged with the goddess, it still seemed she'd been pretty lucky. Thinking about 7753, who'd fallen in with her, made her heart hurt.

Though it wasn't as if Mary had always been able to look at this so coolly. She'd gotten the body of a killer, of all things, and on top of that, it was extremely creepy how she would unconsciously ask whether people had picked up an ax. It wouldn't be at all strange to even have her mind taken over at some point, and it wasn't like this didn't feel bad.

But there were lots of people who couldn't even feel bad anymore. Shepherdspie must have wanted to cook more, and he must have wanted to eat more and more cooking.

Pastel Mary was unlucky. But comparatively speaking, she was happy, and thinking of it that way, she came to see things she hadn't been able to before.

She walked with two axes in one hand, sticking her dominant hand into her pocket to pull out her sketchbook. There were sketches of Ragi, Yol, Tepsekemei, Mana, Chelsea, Touta, and Nephilia, drawn with a softness of touch that increased with each page. Her drawing rehabilitation was proceeding decently enough.

She wasn't making any progress with her magic, though, and that process remained stuck. When she tried to make sheep, they would become strangely shaped, or get into a strange frenzy and attack Mary. But then if she tried to put her mind to transforming the axes, they would just wobble while wafting a stimulating stench, and it never worked.

Putting away her sketchbook, she took an ax in each hand once more. Just waving her arms as she walked tossed up wind and shook the leaves on the surrounding trees. These axes were so heavy that it would have been the most she could do to lift them before, but now she carried them lightly, with about as much strain as holding a pencil or a pastel.

The goddess's face was reflected on the dew that had accumulated in the indent of a tree leaf. The foliage shook in the wind, making the dew drop down, and the reflected face was scattered and disappeared.

Though she was beautiful, her facial features were kind of, like, a lot. Her features were too defined overall, and her nose was too prominent. Her costume didn't have enough of a soft and fluffy feeling and was not to Mary's taste. Her hands wouldn't quite get accustomed to pastels, and she would often crush them.

But it wasn't all bad. Her legs were fast and strong. "Bad guys" would be startled just to see her, like just now, and they would skitter off without opposing her. No one had ever been afraid of her in her whole life, even after she became a magical girl. There wasn't really anything good about being feared, and it would be much nicer to get along. But she couldn't deny that seeing bad guys trembling in fear over her presence brought up a refreshing feeling in her heart. Right now Mary was so powerful that evil would fear her. Maybe, if she wanted, she could do as much as Chelsea did.

Mary came to a stop and, bending her elbow and wrist, posed and lifted one leg.

"Leave it…to Pastel Mary."

It wasn't like she'd looked in a mirror, but it seemed to really fit right. She wouldn't just be protected by Chelsea—she could stand, jump, and leap at her side.

Satisfied, she relaxed from her pose, and when she was about to walk again, she sensed a presence and turned around. This sixth sense for when people were there was another thing she hadn't had with Pastel Mary's body.

A magical girl was standing there, hiding behind a tree. It was one of the playing-card magical girls Mary had thought had followed her master back, the Ace of Diamonds. She was looking at Mary with a blank face.

Had she just seen her make that pose and say that catchphrase? No, no matter if she had, Mary shouldn't panic. Getting embarrassed would make her even more embarrassed.

Making it seem like she wasn't bothered at all, Mary cleared her throat once before asking the girl, "Is the one you dropped the golden ax?"

The simple question *"What do you need?"* was replaced by that creepy one. The Ace of Diamonds did not flinch at that inscrutable remark, still expressionless as she came out from behind the tree and stepped up to Mary, holding out something. Characters Mary had never seen before were lined up on a rectangular piece of paper about the size to sit on one's palm.

The Ace of Diamonds bobbed her head in a bow, and then, without having shown any emotion the whole time, she ran off. Mary watched her back grow distant for a while, and then, after she was out of sight, her eyes dropped to the little piece of paper she'd been handed. She didn't know what was written on it, but she could kinda guess. It was probably a business card. It had to have some method of contact on it.

She stuck the business card into the sketchbook she'd pulled out with one hand and dropped the whole thing into her cleavage.

Mary hummed a tune while walking, keenly feeling that her mood was on an upturn. As for what this card meant, someone was probably trying to solicit Mary. She'd often sought work as a freelance magical girl and a minor artist, but it was rare for work to come to her.

An important mage like Ragi was researching Pastel Mary, so she would surely be able to go back to normal. So one way to be positive in the meantime would be to try to accomplish great things while she was borrowing this body for the moment. First she would show Ragi the business card and get him to tell her what was written on it. Then it might not be so bad to see whether she could be a magical girl who could stand at Chelsea's side rather than just getting protected.

◇ **Ragi Zwe Nento**

When Pastel Mary brought him, of all things, a business card from the Lab's client relations, he scolded her severely. From a week's worth of careful treatment, he'd completely recovered from the wounds he'd gotten from Francesca. Now nothing of his injury remained. Feeling grateful that his throat didn't hurt, Ragi was able to yell as much as he wanted.

After seeing Mary-on-the-inside-Francesca-on-the-outside let her eyebrows and shoulders droop as far as they would go, he ordered her, "Go outside and help Tepsekemei" and chased her out.

Ragi sat down in a poorly cushioned chair, snorting at how uncomfortable it was as he stuck his elbow on the writing desk, supported his chin with the back of his hand, and snorted again.

Over many years, anger had been Ragi's driving force. Indignation, fury, and chagrin had been an energy source for him, supporting the old mage after he retired from service. These days, everything the Magical Kingdom and the Osk Faction did irritated him.

But he took a step back to think. Was it really fair to call the anger he'd just vented at Pastel Mary justified? Pastel Mary had just taken that business card without really understanding it, and there was no reason to get angry at her without even any consideration. If she were thoughtlessly causing problems at the drop of a hat, he could understand scolding her for that. He often thought that magical girl must be living on her spinal reflexes. But in this case, she'd just taken out the business card and asked Ragi what was on it. You couldn't say she'd pulled something bad.

With swift self-analysis, he decided he was just taking his anger out on her. It was a very simplistic analysis, not really enough to even call that. This was ridiculously easy to understand.

Something unpleasant had happened, and he had vented his irritation at Pastel Mary. For her it had been quite the disaster, but since this magical girl was a flub dressed in clothes and walking around, if she would take this as a lesson and act a little less thoughtlessly, then that was enough. And if he also raised her pay or added an item to the dinner menu for her, that should work instead of an apology.

That was fine for Pastel Mary. The issue was with Ragi. The words "something unpleasant" made Ragi feel morose. He was disgusted with himself for being sentimental enough to find this unpleasant.

Right now, Clantail was not on this island.

There were many things Ragi was obliged to do, such as 7753's search and rescue, the division and reconstitution of Pastel Mary, and the organization of the inheritance, and there were also a mountain of things he wanted to do that were not obligatory. Mana had sought technical help from him, and Ragi had requested from her the support of the Inspection Department.

Clantail had been hired by Ragi. Her original contract, to attend him for the inheritance, had functionally been canceled, but Ragi wanted to keep her on. He didn't have enough hands for anything. Even if she didn't have magical knowledge or technique, just the fact that she was a magical girl worthy of trust made Ragi need her presence badly enough to feel desperate for it. Clantail was not only worthy of trust, she was also a highly capable fighter, and the most important thing was that she was quiet and not annoying.

But Clantail had rejected Ragi's request. He remembered every single word of that exchange. The memory of her looking out the window alone in Sataborn's living room echoed through his mind.

"Why was it, back then…when the magical girls were caught in Keek's game, you didn't show Snow White the documents?" she'd asked him.

Because he could not let documents from the Management Department get out without going through the proper procedures.

"If Keek had been defeated a little earlier, just a little earlier, then some lives might have been saved."

Neither Ragi nor Snow White was the one to make that decision. If you bent rules and principles and prioritized your emotions over the law, order would fall apart, all would turn to chaos, and the world would be destroyed.

"If lives are lost, they'll never come back. There were two magical girls who died protecting me. In that game, and on this island as well…" When she talked about Love Me Ren-Ren, Clantail's face contorted like she was in pain. Her fists were clenched, hands trembling, teeth clenched like she was holding something back. Ren-Ren had made deep inroads into the softest parts of her heart, and even just being there was hurting her and making her bleed.

Even witnessing her pain would not change what Ragi should

say. The law must be valued over everything. Even if it was a bad law, that was no reason not to obey it. Or at the very least, back then—when facing Snow White, that's what Ragi had thought.

No matter what legitimacy Ragi's words had, to Clantail, they must have been nothing more than sophistry. That's what emotion was. It wasn't about right or not right.

As one of those people who'd been dragged into the fracas that had happened on this island recently, Ragi thought that if there had been someone, somewhere off the island, who had said, "*I can't interfere because of the rules,*" and had just let things happen, then even if that was legally correct, he would have felt angry about it. He wouldn't have been able to help but think, *If you had bent in your conviction and reached out, lives might have been saved.*

Clantail had shaken off Mana's and Pastel Mary's attempts to stop her and had left the island. Ragi had not stopped her. He couldn't feel like he had the right to stop her.

The sound of knocking on the door cut Ragi's train of thought for a moment, and he prompted the visitor to come in. Even after Ragi called out, the door did not open. Smoke blew in through the crack under it, which was about half a pinkie finger joint wide, then formed a person.

"Pukin fell and knocked over a pot."

"Again...?"

"Pukin" was what Tepsekemei called Pastel Mary. The way she played the fool, even if he asked her where that came from, he doubted he would get an answer that would satisfy him, so he hadn't questioned her as to why.

"There's only bread for lunch," Tepsekemei said. "Mei is hungry."

"Then have Pastel Mary go shopping."

"Congee with sweet potatoes..."

"Go buy whatever you like, congee or taro stem soup or whatnot."

"What will happen to you, geezer?"

Tepsekemei called Ragi "geezer." Unlike that example with

Pastel Mary, this was definitely rude, so he'd asked her why. She'd told him, "Mei has to call you by your name so Mei won't forget it," which was difficult for Ragi to comprehend, but it was clear to him that probing into this would just be a hassle, and he also thought it would be faster to tell her owner Mana about it than to scold Tepse-kemei, and he let her be.

"You need not worry about my meals," Ragi told her.

"Also."

"What?"

"There's a guest."

"Tell me this before concerns about food. Who is it?"

"It's that guy."

Ragi knew who Tepsekemei meant. Ragi replied, "I see," and took off his hand and placed it on his desk. He got sort of bothered by its position and shifted it over by the spellbook sitting on his desk, folded his fingers, and muttered, "Bring him in."

Tepsekemei disappeared under the door the same way she'd come in, and in her place a mage came into the room—properly, by opening the door.

"Aw, it's been a long time. It's great to see you looking healthy."

His greasy smile was no different from before. It was Navi Ru.

◇ **Navi Ru**

Navi didn't want to keep coming back here, but it was the nature of employment to be forced to go to even the ends of the earth if there was some reason for it. Navi put on as friendly a smile as possible, wiped from his forehead to the top of his head with a handkerchief, and grabbed the round chair that had been next to the bed and placed it in front of Ragi to plop himself down. If he waited until he was offered a seat in this room, he'd never be able to sit. There was nothing for it but to secure a chair himself.

Making it look a little bit deliberate, he wiped his handker-chief over his head a second time and turned his eyes resentfully to the window. "It's getting damn muggy out there. That old man

Sataborn should've adjusted this place to make it a bit easier to spend time here. This sort of seething heat has to be tough for an old man in convalescence."

"Who are you calling a convalescent?" Ragi snapped.

"You were hurt pretty bad, weren't you?"

Navi had helped to treat Ragi's injury. At the time, it had really seemed like no time to be helping with a healing spell, but it had been useful in putting the old man in his debt. Even if it wasn't enough to say he owed him his life, if it kept him from getting booted at the door, then great.

The sunlight was just getting stronger as they headed into the afternoon, while by contrast the inside of this room was strangely dark and damp. When Sataborn had been there, he'd probably never opened the curtains, so it was somewhat better compared to then, but Navi thought it wouldn't kill him to open the windows, at least. But it seemed Ragi had no intention of freshening up the room, as the locks on the window were shut, the air was stuffy, and dust hung in the sunbeams. Everything about this place was gloomy, taciturn old mage included.

"What do you want?" Ragi demanded.

"Just checking up on you."

"There's no reason for you to check up on me."

"You've been working in here all this time, haven't you? It seems your guests who've come to the Management Department are having some trouble. They say they can't have important talks, since the boss isn't there, no matter when they visit."

"None of the guests are anyone decent, anyhow."

"You're going to keep staying here until you salvage 7753? You've got such a sense of duty. These days, you know, the ones to succeed are those who don't care how much you exploit magical girls."

Even while talking, Navi never stopped observing.

As far as Navi knew, Ragi was always angry. He wasn't in a good mood right now, either, but he looked less angry and more wilted. Normally he was more youthful—or, to put it another way, immature—but now he was just like an old man.

The words "like an old man" made Navi think, *I see*, the corners of his lips twisting. The wrinkles on Ragi's face were deep, his beard was long, and his hair was white without a single speck of color. He was the picture of an old mage, and Navi hadn't hesitated to call him an old man before, but he hadn't thought of him as just the old man he appeared. This realization was funny, in an indescribable way.

"Well, I didn't come today just to check up on you," Navi said.

Maybe it wasn't a bad thing that Ragi was unusually lacking in energy. In his current sad state, maybe he'd at least listen to talk that he'd immediately reject if he were feeling hale and vigorous, with lots of energy. If Ragi would just hear him out, then after that, Navi's skills would do the work.

Ragi was even more important now than before he'd come to the island. Since the gear that had been stuck in Francesca had been absorbed by the force field, in order to acquire it, he absolutely needed Ragi's cooperation, as he was responsible for the salvage work.

"My boss thinks a lot of you," said Navi.

"Nonsense."

"Your accomplishments on this island have been quite impressive. Even if we'd taken some casters who work for us now, just how many out there woulda done as great a job as you? I don't think any would."

"Flattery from you will make my ears rot."

"It's not flattery, so you don't need to worry about your ears rotting. So then couldn't you meet up just once? C'mon, just one meeting doesn't mean anything's gonna happen right there and then. Just sit down together. It's enough for you two to have an exchange of opinions as specialists. Look, since the boss is a fan of yours."

"Nonsense."

"Don't write it off with that one word. I think you'll get along. Maybe you hate the Lab, but it's not a monolith. Any department anywhere is gonna have its own factions. Well, I do get your feeling that this stuff is all nonsense. But I think you can get along with my boss. Since the boss has been against the incarnation system."

Ragi leaned forward slightly, eyes moving to glare at him. Underneath his full white eyebrows, his sharply shining eyes captured Navi. If Navi had had a weaker heart, that flash in Ragi's eyes would have made him want to run away, but Navi was privately cheering in joy. He might have caught him.

"You don't think well of the incarnations, either, right?" he continued. "Like even with the incident that happened on this island, it's fair to say it was caused by the hubris of trying to make vessels for very important people like the Three Sages. My boss thinks the same way."

"What do *you* think?"

"Me? My opinion doesn't matter. If my boss says white, then a crow is white," Navi lied smoothly.

Navi was not apathetic about the incarnation. His boss's negative stance toward the incarnation was the reason Navi had gotten his current post and was doing dirty work.

Navi would risk his life as much as he had to in order to win points. That was also the reason he'd tried to sneak into Yol's house. Falsifying the will to include himself and Yol as heirs, making it a rule to have two attending magical girls, inviting Maiya to get eliminated and Rareko to repair the gear, and arranging it so Francesca could operate and cause confusion on the island had all had one goal in common. That was for Navi to gain power and a position.

If a mage who didn't approve of the incarnations gained status, then they would try to affect the system itself. And if Navi could get in a position to insert a remark or two, then he could keep them from just disposing of the base. Just like with Pastel Mary here on this island, who was going around wearing Francesca's skin, he would give the order to try to separate the material from the base. He would turn his sister, Clarissa's mother, back to normal, and then finally he would be able to apologize to the departed Clarissa.

Clarissa's death was the one matter of regret that he would

be unable to fix. Because of the grayfruit, the weakening of the mages, and Francesca's abilities that hadn't been in the manual—all Sataborn's excessive fiddling—Navi's plan had not been able to handle everything perfectly.

That old man had been trouble in a different sense from Ragi; he was a hopeless eccentric. It felt bleak just to think about him not dying in an accident.

Ragi blew a breath out his nose, beard swaying. He must have been bothered by something, as he didn't try to look away from Navi, just staring at him without a single blink. It wasn't as if this overwhelmed Navi, but he couldn't say it felt comfortable.

Navi held his smile and tilted his head. "Is something wrong?"

"Tell me what you really think."

"What I really think? Hey, I'm an open book."

The bigger the lie, the more smoothly it came out of his mouth. What he was really thinking would never leave his mouth. Speaking badly of someone he shouldn't or making pathetic complaints wouldn't benefit Navi in any way—so he should just keep what he really thought in his head. Clarissa had been his sole accomplice, the one person he could share his true feelings with, and she was gone. Now he was the only one to listen to such thoughts.

Even if he were to throw himself on Ragi's mercy, saying, *"It's to save my sister, she's been used as material for an incarnation, please save her,"* what point would there be in that? Navi had long since stepped over the line where he would be forgiven with a sob story. Whatever his reasons were, a villain was a villain, so he should engage in his villainy proudly.

Navi looked at Ragi once more. He really did look different from usual. Normally, Ragi would never try to ask what Navi was really thinking. He didn't have that much interest in him.

Ragi's beard swelled again and went back to normal. There was unspoken dissatisfaction in his sigh. "So you won't tell me."

"I'm telling you I always say what I think."

If he said what he really thought, then nothing but complaints would come from his mouth. He couldn't let Ragi hear that.

Clarissa was gone. She had lost her life, never again to feel her mother's embrace. Navi had fucked things up, and you could call it putting the cart before the horse to kill his niece for his sister's sake, but you couldn't take back what was done. He decided there was nothing for it but to move forward, grovel to his sister once she was back to normal, and apologize to her about Clarissa. There was no going back.

Navi did not speak his feelings, instead putting on a smile like he wasn't thinking anything, and Ragi looked back at him with dark eyes. The old man and the middle-aged man gazed into each other's eyes like a boy and girl at puberty. Ragi was the first one to look away.

Ragi sighed like he was wringing air out of his lungs, muttered the few words of a spell, and made a sign with his fingers. In the space where there had been nothing between Navi and Ragi floated a palm-sized black circle, which slowly rotated to the right as it grew larger, reaching one-third of Navi's height, where it stopped.

Instantly, a tea set appeared: an antique teacup with steam rising from the black tea within, a matching saucer, and a snack bowl holding cookies.

Ragi indicated the set with his upturned right palm and pointed his dark eyes at Navi once more. "If you insist on not speaking your thoughts, then that's fine."

"I am telling you what I think, okay? So then I can have some of this?"

Ragi closed his eyes and nodded. Gesturing with a palm at the tea set, he spat out "Please eat" in a way that clashed with the politeness of his words. Ragi looked stricken, and the words that came out of his mouth sounded like a declaration of surrender. Maybe this actually was a declaration of surrender.

A declaration of surrender was just what Navi wanted. But he couldn't have Ragi going old on him yet. There were still a lot of things he had to have Ragi do for him. While mentally putting together plans to somehow console him later, Navi took the teacup in his hand with a "Thanks" and squinted with one eye.

Picking up the saucer, he brought the cup to his face. There was a little blade affixed to the inside of the handle, less than half a pinkie nail in size, and it was stabbing into Navi's hand. Despite having been hurt by its blade, he wasn't bleeding. This blade—it was a piece of an arrowhead.

Navi placed the teacup on the saucer and looked at Ragi. Ragi's expression went beyond dark to completely melancholy. His voice was heavy, as if it were oozing from the bottom of the earth.

"Using illegal means against the illegal disturbs order. That's what I've always believed. I still believe that. But the law cannot bind you. You'll avoid any legitimate methods. You won't let anyone catch you. If there is something that can get ahold of you, it's the unlawful…but you will dodge ordinary unlawfulness, after all."

Ragi's words just went in one ear and out the other. He didn't understand what they meant. The workings of his mind wouldn't turn to them.

"You held me in contempt, but at the same time you also trusted me—that no matter what you did, I would not dirty my hands with illegal activity. You trusted how I've always observed the law and gotten angry at the unlawful, and believed no matter how angry I am, I would not step outside the law. You were invited into this room without a guard and picked up a cup I offered. Without even being aware of it, you were thinking, *Ragi Zwe Nento would not break the law, so I'm not in danger.*"

Navi scratched his arm. It was shaking. He couldn't be here. He shouldn't be. He tensed his knees to get ready to stand.

"I gave instructions to Tepsekemei beforehand," Ragi said, "telling her to make contact with Nephilia as soon as you came. She'll be here soon."

Hearing Nephilia's name, Navi breathed a sigh of relief. If Nephilia would come, if he could meet Nephilia, who was his one and only family, there was no hurry to get up. He relaxed his knees and leaned back into the chair.

"If Nephilia were the one to approach you with this scheme, you wouldn't have let your guard down. You wouldn't trust someone who would make a contract with you. She's different from a stubborn and old-fashioned old man who has been obstinately rejecting you."

At this point, he was just listening to Ragi's voice. He didn't try to follow the meaning in his head. His whole mind was dyed the singular color of Nephilia, and that seemed obvious to him.

"You have lost. But this is no victory for me. The law should be protected, no matter what. My feelings on that matter still have not changed. Saying that lives that would have been lost might be saved is a poor form of self-aggrandizing pretense."

Saying just that, Ragi let out a long breath. It was as if even his soul fell out with it.

◇ **Nephilia**

On the right side of the path, tall trees and plants grew dense and luxurious, while on the left side, little new leaves budded from the junctions of the trees that had survived the fire. The fire that Ren-Ren had started had burned up to right around this line. Look up, and you could see the top of the main building beyond the trees. It would have been dangerous if the fire had come a little farther.

Nephilia giggled and spun the scythe she carried in her right hand, swiping away the vines that dangled from a tree branch with the back of the blade. The vines, which had been hanging so that if she kept walking, they might hit her head, were tossed upward onto the branch, and Nephilia walked under them.

From using her magic on Clarissa's nail, Nephilia had managed to get a general grasp of what Navi Ru had been doing, but it was still difficult for her to interfere directly. As she was wondering what to do, the two candidates who came up were Mana and Ragi Zwe Nento.

If she were trying to simply carry out justice, then she should talk to Mana, who worked for the Inspection Department, but Navi seemed to be wary of Mana. So Ragi was the better choice.

Nephilia came to the conclusion that the old mage was perfect for the job of catching Navi.

Ragi had abhorred unlawful conduct his whole life, and even when his allies had been cut through by bribery and intimidation, even when he was driven to a do-nothing position, the old mage had stubbornly turned his back to illegal acts—therefore, even a villain like Navi would wind up unconsciously trusting him.

Nephilia told Ragi what she'd experienced on the island and her hypothesis about Navi, and she replayed Clarissa's words using her nail for him. When she got the answer she wanted, Nephilia pumped a fist in her heart with an *All right!* She didn't have to ask why such a foolishly honest and spotlessly upright old mage had had a change of heart at this point. Obviously, the information Nephilia had given Clantail during the turmoil—that the incident had taken so long to resolve because the Management Department chief had not swiftly offered information on Keek—was involved.

A single old man would see a friend he could trust as a rare and valued item. Losing that would make his faith waver.

The old man was not nasty, awful, or bad, and there was nothing praiseworthy about using him. Nephilia didn't want to do it. But if Navi Ru was going to pull something, then she had to hit him from a direction he wouldn't expect.

"Hope…Agri…satisfied…little…revenge…"

Nephilia put a hand in her pocket, reaching for the feathers there to rub them. When she'd first started this, it hadn't gone really well, but now she could smoothly connect one word to the next to make a conversation. The trick was to drop the volume of the voice for the parts she didn't need.

"No / matter / whose / sake / it's / for, / I / think / it's / best / not / to / do / bad / things." Ren-Ren's voice came out of Nephilia's mouth.

"If it's to…beat…bad guys…," Nephilia replied.

"It / seems / like / you're / pushing / yourself, / Nephy."

When she was in a really good mood, she would chat more with Ren-Ren. Clantail had transferred her the money, as promised. If she used Navi combined with that money, she should surely be able to do some interesting things.

"I'm...all right..."

Ren-Ren fluttered her wings, bobbing up and down as she flapped. Though her face was the picture of concern, lately she had been constantly trying to curtail Nephilia's risky behavior. Thinking maybe the way she flew was a little wrong, Nephilia made the feathers move in a more relaxed manner.

"There / should / be / a / better / way."

"This is...the best way...for the family."

When Nephilia brought up family, Ren-Ren closed her mouth apologetically. It was an unfair move to pull, but Nephilia had always been unfair, so she would apologize in her heart to gain forgiveness.

Ren-Ren's bobbing up and down spread to shifting from side to side, and Ren-Ren circled Nephilia in the shape of a V. She folded her arms and legs and seemed to be thinking about what to do about this.

Nephilia was aware that Ren-Ren was dead. So was she was hallucinating Ren-Ren worrying? She couldn't say that for sure.

After the incident, her feelings toward Ren-Ren had grown stronger with the passage of time, and she'd searched her body and found a little wound that looked as if she'd been pricked by an arrowhead. She wasn't sure when it had happened, or whether it had happened accidentally or deliberately, but she'd spent that whole day smirking to herself, making the mage from the legal office whom she'd met with that day over a contract think she was quite creepy.

Did she still keep a degree of control over her heart because Ren-Ren was already dead, because Nephilia had an aptitude for it, or because Ren-Ren hadn't been using her magic seriously? Whichever it was, Ren-Ren was still the favorable type of nasty, so just having her at her side let Nephilia laugh *ksh-shh*. And besides, they were family no matter what, so it was far better to have her there than not.

◇ **Dreamy☆Chelsea**

Chie had expected nothing other than a firm scolding from her mother, Fuchiko. But despite Chie's having predicted even the details of her carping, like *"It's because you did magical-girl work without listening to what Mom says that these bad things happened to you,"* her mother didn't make any accusations and just cried.

The story of Chie's life was sponging off her mom while continuing as a magical girl, but even she got hit in the heart by those tears. She started to cry, too, and, remembering what had happened on the island, she cried even harder, and mother and daughter made the bed at the hospital quite damp together.

But still, her mother was her mother, in the end. Though she did cry, it wasn't like she'd become a meek person, and by the next day, she was already nonchalant about it, and nagged Chie as expected: "It's because you did magical-girl work without listening to what Mom says that these bad things happened to you," followed by "I'll stop you if you try anything similar again, even if I have to punch you to do it."

Normally her father would mediate and say something like, *"Now, now, calm down,"* or *"I'm sure Chie has her own ideas about things,"* but now he just smiled with a sad expression and wouldn't butt in, and even Chie felt remorseful, thinking, *I guess I did something that bad*, and after leaving the hospital, she didn't consider *I'll work as a magical girl!* like before.

If you put it into the words "earning money as a magical girl," then it was no more than that, but having actually experienced it for herself, she knew there could be nothing more brutal. Of course, it couldn't be that tough every single time, but if you could assume half or a third of that bloodshed, then it would be impossible for Chie to make a living as a magical girl.

Even Chie's mother, whom she saw as very talented, kept being a magical girl as a hobby and had become a housewife—couldn't you say that proved how harsh the work was? With hazy thoughts about how not everything in life could go well, the day Chie was released from the hospital, she sat in her designated seat at home on the veranda and gazed at the garden without doing anything.

Chie had given up on being a career magical girl. But if you asked if that equaled giving up on being a magical girl, she would cutely tilt her head, and then there would be Dreamy☆Chelsea, puffing up her cheeks even more cutely and saying, "I don't think so."

For starters, if magical girls were water, then money was oil. Thinking about them together made things weird. Wanting to continue as a magical girl and wanting to make money should be thought of as separate things. Chie Yumeno was just the pretrans-formation human, and her scheming to make Dreamy☆Chelsea into a tool for making money would be lacking in due respect. That would be obviously deserving of punishment.

In a corner of the garden was the persimmon tree that she had planted as a seed when she was five years old, branches extending like long arms. The fruit was sweet and juicy. There were also wooden stakes, piles of rocks reminiscent of cairns, and a stone lantern upside down in the earth. Every single item here was a page in Dreamy☆Chelsea's history. A lot of her "training" she'd been dragged into, but she'd also really enjoyed some things as games, and there were one or two things she thought she might have even taken to the level of a sport.

Chie groaned under her breath. It was because she'd noticed herself thinking that maybe she could make money from putting those "sports" out in the world. This was wickedness.

If labor didn't suit a magical girl, then was it good or bad to try to gain an income without working? Even if it was fine now, her mother wouldn't stay silent forever. She would start saying again to get a job, earn some money, get out of the house, get married.

If she had to get a job, in the end, would it be best for her to work as a magical girl? She had the feeling that her thoughts were going in circles. When she thought about what had happened on the island, she didn't want to work as a magical girl.

Chelsea totally hadn't had enough cuteness. Even though there had been lots of sad things, painful things, tough things, awful things, she hadn't been able to accept it all. Lives she'd had to protect had been lost, and even just remembering made her feel like her body would be torn up.

Becoming a career magical girl would mean feeling the same thing, and in the course of doing that over and over, she would probably even lose her own life. Chie covered her face with her hands. She didn't want that.

She spread her fingers. The persimmon tree peeked into view between them.

No.

Even if Chelsea didn't become a career magical girl, it wasn't like the sad, painful, tough, and awful would go away. She just wouldn't see those things anymore because she wouldn't be there. In fact, wouldn't there be a future, then, where the people who could have been saved had Chelsea been there were not saved?

Just remembering the incident that had occurred on that island made her feel so terrified she couldn't stand it. She never wanted something like that to happen to her again. But did Dreamy☆Chelsea think that? Thinking that since it was sad, painful, tough, and awful, she wanted to look away, no matter what happened off where she wasn't looking, it didn't matter since she wasn't looking—that wasn't Dreamy☆Chelsea.

Even if Chelsea felt regret, she wouldn't run away. Those feelings of *I should have done this, I should have done that* she would have made use of the next time to do great in the sequel. That was way more Chelsea than sneaking around and sniffling and crying to herself in bed.

Chie brought her hands away from her face and crossed her hands. She moved just her arms to make a pose, and in a tiny whisper so that nobody could hear, she muttered, "Leave it to Dreamy☆Chelsea."

Smacking her knees, she stood up and yelled to the kitchen, "Hey, Mom. There was ground beef in the fridge, right?" This small wooden house was thirty years old—yell a little loud and it would go all the way to the other end.

Her mother poked her head out of the beaded half curtain to the kitchen. She looked suspicious. "There's some stuff I froze. What do you want to do with ground beef?"

"Do you have celery, carrots, potatoes, onions, and tomatoes?"

"Like I said, for what?"

"Cooking. I was thinking I'd bring it as a gift to a friend."

"Huh. This is a rare turn of events... You're going to cook yourself?"

"That'd be kinda hard, so help me out. I think I can find out how if I search for it. It's a delicious pie called shepherd's pie."

◇ **Touta Magaoka**

The 126th Card Shop Hinapiya Magical Battlers Open Tournament was total chaos. The Battlers open class had been made to go out of control readily to begin with, with the laxest restrictions of all the different regulations, and cards that were forbidden under other regulations could be used at a limit of one. But the regulations weren't the reason that the tournament had gone out of control.

The tournament was usually all the same faces, but this time, an unknown powerhouse duelist stormed in. Really she did just apply normally to participate and then showed up, but to the regular participants, who were totally used to tournaments being as peaceful as lukewarm water, it was like she'd stormed in.

The regulars at the tournament at Hinapiya were only guys, from youngsters with single-digit ages to senior players in their forties, and she was a rarely seen female participant. And it wasn't simply that her sex was female.

She had fluffy sausage curls spun in spirals, a one-piece dress decorated with golden embroidery and gems, an aristocratic and elegant bearing, and a charmingly handsome face, fluent Japanese with even a mastery of the game slang despite looking like she was from some unknown country, a wham-bam combo deck packed with expensive cards that cost thousands of dollars, and masterful skills, as she followed the combo route called "solitaire" without a single error in judgment.

This girl who was just like a character out of anime or manga easily beat down the regulars.

When it seemed like she would go on to win the tournament, standing in her way to face her at the finals was the elementary school dueler Touta Magaoka. Though from game one he let "solitaire" happen initially, starting from their second game, he threw in all the meta cards from the sideboard, investing everything to prevent a combo, and overcame it. In the third game, his aggressive sideboarding caused the girl to change her deck type from combo to control, and, amazingly, Touta returned the cards he'd pulled from the side to abandon his resistance to combos, winning a victory by a monster offensive with an emphasis on maintaining the battle line.

They say all participants offered a thunderous round of applause at his skill in foretelling even the deck type change made by his opponent.

And then, after the tournament was over, Touta and the girl—Yol—had hamburgers at a nearby fast-food restaurant. Yol was paying. It felt pathetic to say so, but Touta's wallet couldn't even spare the money to pay for himself.

"I was surprised when you said you wanted to join the tournament," said Touta.

"I've been wanting to participate in public tournaments for some time. The date just happened to come at a good time, so it was a good opportunity, right?"

The latter half of Touta's memories from the island were incredibly vague. He'd been very badly hurt, and he'd heard that his eyes had been in a particularly bad state. He hadn't been able to see at all for a few days, and his eyelids hadn't opened. His aunt, Yol, Ragi, and Mana had brought in mages who kept trying many treatments, and finally he was able to see.

When he was finally able to see his aunt again, she was thin and relieved to the core as she took Touta's hand and told him, "I'm sorry." Touta, on the other hand, felt like he was the one who'd done something bad, but he figured he hadn't had any other choice at the time. Besides, Touta wasn't the only reason his aunt had grown thin. Even if a child couldn't really understand what it was like to have an old friend pass away, it had to be tough for an adult. Touta hadn't known Marguerite as long as his aunt had, and even he'd cried on finding out, cried like he was wringing all the fluids out of his body.

It had been a month since the Touta medical team had dispersed, but even after that, Yol had come to visit him once a week. She would give him medication and examine him, and play some games with him while she was at it. But she'd never once participated in a tournament before.

"They didn't get angry at you?" Touta asked her.

"This is actually my chance. Since they haven't decided on new attending magical girls for me..." Yol hesitated, and Touta automatically hung his head.

"Ohhh, I see... Maiya and Rareko..."

Maiya and Rareko had lost their lives in the incident that had occurred on the island. Of course there was no way he could forget. And Marguerite, too—Touta's gloomy thoughts were cut off by the tap of Yol's cup being placed on the table, and Touta lifted his chin to look back at her. Her expression was back to the way it had been before. Strong, and bright, and cute.

"Besides, there are things I wanted to speak with you about as well."

"You wanted to talk about something?"

"I talked about how I don't have the aptitude to become a magical girl, didn't I?"

"You said they did a test or something for it, right? And there were 7753's goggles."

"Yes, yes. And you don't have the aptitude, either, right?"

"Yeah..."

Maybe it had been a joke, and maybe she'd just been saying it, but Miss Marguerite had called Touta her student. At the end of the end, when Touta had burned up the little courage and energy he had to leap on the goddess, Marguerite had gathered attention to herself by yelling out loud. Knowing what Touta had been trying to do, she had helped him out.

That was the last time he'd heard Marguerite's voice while she was alive. She would never be able to tell him whether she'd actually recognized him as her student, if he'd managed to live up to that title or not.

He'd met a lot of magical girls on that island. There had been scary magical girls. There had been strange magical girls. There had been cool magical girls. And all of them had been strong.

Touta thought that he'd like to become a magical girl, too, but you couldn't become one if you didn't have the talent.

"Don't you want to become a magical girl?" Yol asked him.

"Yeah, I do. Of course I do." He didn't say, *A magical girl like Miss Marguerite.*

Yol drew back her chin, saying, "I'd like to become one, too," then leaned out over the table. "So listen." Her voice got one or two levels quieter. Touta brought his face close to hear. "I found out there's a secret way to become a magical girl, even if you don't have the potential."

"Really?!"

"Shhh… Keep your voice down. I told you, it's a secret."

"Oh yeah…sorry. But really?"

"It's called an artificial magical girl. They're apparently canvassing for them now… Hey, do you want to try it together?"

There was no room for hesitation. Touta nodded enthusiastically.

◇ **7753**

7753 read through the letter from Mana once, read it again, and sighed. It said that for reasons relating to an incarnation of one of the Three Sages occupying ruins or something, she would be busy for the time being and wouldn't be able to come to the island. Circumstances aside, this was sad and trying news for 7753 right now. It was too miserable to not be able to go anywhere and to have no one to talk to. To be more precise, maybe she did have enough people to talk to, with Tepsekemei, Ragi, and Pastel Mary, but Tepsekemei wasn't suited to conversation, Pastel Mary's current appearance had wounded 7753's heart too deeply, and Ragi was always in a bad mood. Without Mana around, there was nobody on this island she would enjoy chatting with.

No, she reconsidered. If she thought about when things had been at their worst, then this was just losing one person to talk to. A few weeks earlier, 7753 had been smack in the middle of real isolation.

◇◇◇

7753 had awoken from a very long sleep to find she couldn't move or use her voice. She could neither see nor hear, and it had taken her quite a while until she understood her situation. After some confusion and verification, she realized she'd become a single, incredibly large tree with roots that penetrated every corner of the island. It seemed like it had to be another dream, but quite unfortunately, it was not a dream, but reality.

It was a single tree on a little hill, just a swelling of earth in the center of the island, right at the edge of the fire. If it had been positioned slightly lower, it might have been burned up. From there, it was connected to the other trees through the roots. In other words, all combined it was one tree, but the ends of the roots were outside of her consciousness, and the farther away you got, the darker it was. Generally, she could only perceive herself and her surroundings, and she couldn't move or talk. Her bark was hard, her leaves were thick, she grew fruit full of juices, and she was just there. Even if she didn't have ears, she could feel the wind and the sound of leaves rustling, and even without eyes, she could actually perceive what was there, and even its motion. But when it came to moving herself, it wouldn't go like before, and she couldn't do it no matter how she tried.

After a desperate body blow to the goddess, 7753 and Pastel Mary had tumbled into that disc of power. She'd lost consciousness after that. Waking up to find yourself a tree was just too much. 7753 had been the one to connect the gathering of power to the tree roots, under Ragi's instruction. Even if she had a vague idea as to why something like this had happened, this was still clearly way too cruel. If this was divine punishment, wasn't there some better way?

Her hard struggle continued for some time. She had an idea of the area around the tree, but since she couldn't see or hear, that idea was ultimately vague. She just tried everything, seeing if she couldn't extend her senses somehow, or call out and move, and even when she couldn't do it, she didn't give up right away. She kept changing how she did it and how she thought about it as she went through repeated trial and error. Of course 7753 had no experience turning into a plant, to say nothing of knowing what a magic plant could do and what it could not. She would take anything, so there was nothing for it but to just try.

As she was testing out things, willing to take anything, she came to gradually spread out what she might call the net of her senses. As she did that, she came to grasp the situation on the island bit by bit. She was relieved to find that Mana and Tepsekemei were safe, but she had no way to communicate her own will.

7753 carried out further trial and error. Though it was great she'd managed to sense the presences of Mana, Tepsekemei, and Ragi, there was no point if she stopped there. They were probably doing something to try to save her. If she could at least tell them where she was, that would dramatically change the situation, and maybe they could save her right away.

She tried lots of things, wondering if she could somehow regain the physical senses she'd had as a magical girl, but it just didn't work out. Her roots wouldn't move, her leaves wouldn't move, and her branches wouldn't move. When she gave up, thinking this wasn't going to go anywhere, she realized one thing. She had managed to bear fruit.

It seemed really difficult to make them realize her presence via fruit, but she had no other options. 7753 focused on just the fruit of the tree where her consciousness was trapped, making them grow. She wasn't doing it because she wanted to attract small animals and insects. Her target was something else.

On the fourth night after 7753 had begun her fruit concentration operation, a vague floating shape approached her through the sky. In her heart, 7753 cried out in joy. She had already considered that the glutton Tepsekemei would come for the grayfruit.

The issue now was how to communicate her own presence. But Tepsekemei just furrowed her brow suspiciously and gazed at the 7753 tree. She didn't even touch a finger to the grayfruit before flying off somewhere. When she came back after some time, she brought the two mages.

Ragi's face was solemn, Mana's was happy, and Tepsekemei's was inscrutable. Those other two aside from Mana wore the same expressions as always, and 7753 was relieved they were all safe, and confirming her own humanlike feelings of relief made her relieved again.

"It's here," said Tepsekemei.

"Indeed, there is a reaction," said Ragi. "This is it. It seems Tepsekemei was right."

"To think she's stuck inside a tree... That would have been dangerous, if Mei hadn't noticed," said Mana.

"Mei did good?"

"Yes, good, good, you're amazing. How could you tell, Mei?"

"Smell and atmosphere."

"It doesn't matter how," said Ragi. "Let's just begin the task."

They knocked on bark, dug up roots, and cast spells, until at the end they peeled off the bark by force to expose what was inside. When they showed 7753 herself in the mirror, she was shocked. She looked like a plant and human combined and split in two, like a dryad out of the stories, half-buried in the tree. She'd been stuck with her face inside the tree, her upper body and face just barely poking out. Her goggles were carefully hanging from her neck.

"The parts sticking out are one thing, but inside has fused with the tree," said Ragi. "We can't rip you out by force. You'll be like this for the time being."

7753 was disappointed, but the plant 7753 in the mirror had no expression—she didn't even move.

A few days after that, Ragi tried a number of spells, enabling her somehow to speak.

"Just what on earth happened?" 7753 asked.

The story they told her was not a happy one. Hearing of Marguerite's death had made 7753 despair. Clarissa, Rareko, Agri, and Ren-Ren had all been killed by the goddess.

But there was also some good news. Though Ragi and Touta had been in danger, Mana had rushed to them with medicine and first aid, and with Navi helping to treat them, their lives had been saved. Mana said Clantail and Dreamy☆Chelsea had also survived somehow.

Ragi explained to her that 7753 was no longer 7753, but it seemed that she was still more or less 7753. He said being shoved into the disc of power had caused various things to get mixed up, and 7753's self had gone through the roots to become one with the tree that bore grayfruit—or rather, she'd functionally taken it over.

Her concerns over whether she was actually 7753 started treading into philosophical territory, but all the mages, including Mana and Ragi, were just glad that she was safe, and they didn't seem to think that her state was a misfortune that couldn't be undone. Although she wasn't totally convinced, she did think vaguely that if all the mages were thinking that, then maybe that was how it was.

Apparently, Pastel Mary had fused with the goddess magical girl, and now she had the body of a killer, and she'd started asking against her will about the whereabouts of axes. So 7753 decided to be positive about things—she figured that her own state was preferable to that.

Tepsekemei, Mana, Ragi, and Pastel Mary stayed on the island, taking care of 7753 while searching for a way to turn her back to normal. She couldn't waste their consideration. While she still felt fuzzy about it, she decided to do her best to live, and started looking for what she could do.

Even if she couldn't move, it wasn't like she couldn't do anything. In a sense, she was a being like the essence of magic. Magic made the impossible possible. In other words, right now 7753 was a crystallization of the impossible.

The speed of her thoughts increased, and she came to be able to sense the state of all the trees on the island around her, and every day she continued to evolve as a magic tree.

◇◇◇

"I'm done now, Tepsekemei."

Tepsekemei folded up the letter that had been open in front of 7753's face and tucked it into her pocket. 7753 gazed at the letter until the moment the cute puppies bordering the stationery disappeared into Mei's pocket, and after it went out of sight, she breathed another sigh.

"Why are you sighing so much?"

"Ohhh, sorry. It's not good to sigh in front of people, is it?"

"The letter is not the only event today."

"Oh, really?"

"There are guests."

"Guests? For me?"

"A scary magical girl and one more, a loud one, are here."

Tepsekemei went to go call the "guests," and when she came back, she had brought two magical girls. One was someone 7753 didn't know. Her expression was hard, and you could see she was tense. Her motif was that of a wolf, and she had a rifle over her shoulder, but it looked like a toy, not a real gun.

And there was one other. 7753 was acquainted with her, but they weren't close. In fact, what 7753 had been scared of was her persona and her reputation. She was scared right this moment, wondering why on earth she had come. But not seeing her would be scary for other reasons, so there was no choice but to see her.

"It's been a long time. I've come here today with business with you, 7753."

"Ah! Oh, yes."

"This is Uluru."

"…Nice to meet you."

"Nice to meet you, Uluru. My name is 7753. Also…well, yeah. I'm glad you've come. I'm sorry I'm like this, but…I'm glad I could see you, Snow White."

Afterword

This is the afterword for *Magical Girl Raising Project: Breakdown* parts 1 and 2, a project that took many years from start to conclusion. It's been the fruit of a long serialization, with breaks taken along the way. To everyone who has been eagerly looking forward to this: I'm sorry for the wait. Please do enjoy it.

But still, I'm sure the majority will say, "'Please enjoy it'? I've already read the book." Since it's called an afterword because it comes after the book.

But don't you worry, there is still more after the afterword. The end-of-book fan pages that were also in part 1 feature a continuation of the magical-girl interviews, with even more volume this time. And those are also followed by evaluations from 7753 of the magical girls who appear in *Breakdown*. Please do take a look at 7753 as a professional, a side of her rarely seen in the main story.

And what's more and more, there is one more thing related to the afterword. Those people who have been following the web serialization might know, but there is an online-exclusive afterword published in the *Breakdown* section of *This Manga is Amazing! WEB*. It's the longest afterword in my history of afterwords. The information and such that I couldn't put in the main story is there, so please do read that if you like.

And what's more and more and more, recently I made a Twitter account. Aside from ramen and mahjong, *Breakdown* sometimes does and sometimes doesn't come up. A little while ago I made a string of tweets related to Maiya, leading to some excessive work being thrust upon me, like, *"You can write that much just about Maiya, so this will be no trouble for you."* Anyone who is interested, I would be happy if you would check out @asariendou.

Also, there is this afterword. You might think that what with having the online afterword and doing things on Twitter, I must have nothing to do here. I thought so, too. But I quickly reconsidered that.

Though I have done many things thus far, it's not as if I've done everything I can. I figure there is still more. And so in this afterword I will touch on things I think I've still not spoken about. Saying "I think I've still not spoken about" is just in case I forgot that I mentioned it somewhere and have wound up repeating myself, but I will pray that doesn't happen.

◇ The Great Magical Girl Athletic Meet: Beef Broth–Flavored Rice Balls Included

This is the event where Ragi met Clantail. It was originally a very small sort of thank-you-party-type event, but the one in charge of announcing the event gave it a strange name as a joke. And then that announcement caught the eye of the Archfiend Cram School graduates, who were starving for events, and it turned into a disaster. It was chaos: not enough food, not enough staff, too many participants, someone wanted by the law walking around over there.

Ragi, who was one of the guests, thought, *This is no good*, and so he worked to get the confusion under control. And since it was difficult for him on his own, he got help from three of the participants who had good sense, comparatively speaking: Clantail, a magical girl who loves ramen, and a magical girl whose personality changes when she's on her lawn mower. They resolved all the problems.

◇ **The Magic of the Sataborn Estate**

A convenient spell is cast on the estate so that things come flying when you snap your fingers. When things come flying when you snap your fingers, a child's prank can turn that into a big disaster (and Chelsea's mischief actually did kick off a big disaster), so there has to be magic in the snap or it won't activate.

Mr. Shepherdspie can still sort of use it, even though he has no confidence in his magic power at all, so it's not like that much training is needed, but when your power is so weak, you tend not to get the item you want. Since Sataborn didn't consider that his nephew would be in trouble when he used it, it seems it would be quite difficult for him to use.

◇ **Magical Battlers**

This is a card game that Touta and Yol both love. It's not only very popular among elementary and middle schoolers, but also a fad among magical girls. They even say that the number of players continued to increase, thanks to a pretty girl showing up to cosplay at Magical Battlers tournaments.

Depending on the regulations, you might have to use expensive cards, so it's known for being unkind to the wallets of children. It's not uncommon for magical girls' wallets to be similar to those of children, and sometimes they will go bankrupt for cards, or get caught with fake cards.

There has been a collaboration with *Cutie Healer*, and there are whispers of plausible-sounding rumors that there exists a limited-edition Archfiend Pam card that some Archfiend Cram School graduate made.

◇ **Magical Girls' Regular Clothing**

One of Archfiend Pam's teachings is that "a magical girl should not undo her transformation in front of people." This refers to how, since the difference between magical-girl and human reflexes is as great as the division between heaven and earth, even if she thinks she could transform again, she might be killed before she could do it, so watch out. And it would expose her, and it would be bad if she were to be tracked. It's a scary world.

Professional magical girls all keep in mind something like this idea, to a greater or lesser extent. And so the more professional one of them is, the more often she'll transform from an outfit she can't show to others. Leisure wear and pajamas are on the better side, and apparently some will be in their underwear or in tracksuits from middle school. There's also the rumor that when a certain famous magical girl detransformed she was naked, but whether that is true or not remains unknown.

◇ **Magical Gates**

These are transfer devices used daily by people who work for the Magical Kingdom. They are extremely convenient devices that enable going from one gate to another in an instant, no matter how far apart they are.

But since the way they are used changes every time technicians develop a new version, or in the first place a different series of gates will look and be used completely differently, there are apparently a lot of magical girls who struggle with these systems. There was a short story where Filru had a really bad time trying to use them, and that is not because she's bad with machines. There's a special rule at the Department of Diplomacy that Archfiend Pam, who is truly incompetent with machines, is forbidden to use gates.

◇ **Tepsekemei's Parts**

She can send off parts of herself to act independently. When the parts are away from her, if her main body gets wiped out for some reason, then the parts will return to the main body.

You might say doing all this is beyond becoming one with the wind to go anywhere she wants, but since Mei believes, *My magic should be able to do this* and she actually can do it, nobody can complain about it.

They say animal magical girls tend to be powerful, but there is also the theory that the reason for this is that they don't have human common sense, so they don't perceive crazy things as crazy.

◇ Children with No Magical Potential

The children of mages will generally become mages themselves, but rarely there are some who have no magical talent. If they are incompetent like Mr. Shepherdspie, then, well, it can work out somehow, and if they have magical-girl aptitude like Clarissa, then they can make a life for themselves in that direction.

If they lack even incompetent talent and can't become magical girls, either, then you have something not very good for a reputable family. I will omit specifically what happens.

In common mage families, well, they can do decently enough, in the way of someone with no expectations of success. Since there are always nasty people who will demean them incessantly, it seems it's not uncommon for them to live in the human world as humans.

◇ Chelsea Power

When she was straining against Francesca, the un-magical-girl-like remark, "The hell are you?" popped out of Dreamy☆Chelsea's mouth. There is one reason that she panicked: She'd never before encountered a magical girl stronger than she was.

She can't beat her mother in wrestling, but that's due to experience, technique, and magic, and at the very least, in a pure test of power, Chelsea had never lost before. All her mother's friends are also quite the lineup of fierce fighters, but she's never lost to them, either.

That she can manage to have a shoving match against an incarnation base is incredible on its own, but Chelsea wasn't aware of that. Her confidence in her strength, which she hadn't even been aware she had, broke during that stage of the fight. Of course something un-magical-girl-like would pop out.

◇ Nephilia's Life at School

It's not unusual for magical girls who get on the track of freelance activity young to quit their studies early and ultimately live their lives without going to high school. Nephilia is a magical girl who got on the track of freelance activity young, but she is going to high school. Since it's a university-oriented school, it's hard to get into, and just keeping up with her studies takes quite a bit of effort.

Nephilia is busy to begin with, so why did she go to high school?

She likes nasty people—so, when you get down to it, she likes people. She loves school, it being a place where lots of people gather to live their lives. Also, she doesn't want to make her parents worry, and, well, since schoolwork isn't much different from memorizing laws, she went to high school.

The truth is that of the magical girls who went to that island, the most sociable one might be Nephilia.

◇ Mary the Artist

Aside from those who go freelance because of the agency, there are also people who do the work aiming for an official hiring contract.

Pastel Mary is the type who does have dreams for the future but is freelancing for money. Her dream, however, is not to make a living as a magical girl, but to make a living with art. And not just art, but pictures of the sheep that she loves. Her room is filled with pictures of sheep, and though her friends tell her it's like the room of a psychopath, she still loves them so much.

To make it on just sheep pictures alone is pretty difficult. Actually, it's crazy. Pastel Mary does know how society works, and so she's accepted that making a living using magic that creates sheep from pictures is also in a sense making a living off drawing sheep, and she is working hard as a freelancer again today.

◇ **Marguerite and Death Prayer**

It's been brought up in this story many times that Miss Marguerite is in charge of teaching at the Inspection Department. Death Prayer calls herself her partner, so where does she work?

The answer is accounting.

To those who think, *Huh? An accountant is the partner to a teacher? Isn't that funny?* you're entirely right. Death Prayer just decided that she's her partner because she felt like it at the time. The staff at the Inspection Department can't come down hard on accounting, so there is rarely anyone who will deny her proclamation. Marguerite had already quit Inspection, so she could deny it, but this sort of thing is kind of nostalgic for her, and it was too much hassle to shoot Death Prayer down every time, so she functionally ignored it and let it be.

Well, even saying she was in accounting, the Inspection Department never has enough hands, and people get sent out to all sorts of places, so maybe it's not necessarily wrong.

◇ **Love Me Archer**

It was mentioned in this story that Nephilia took classes from a specialist in order to learn how to use a giant scythe. So as for Ren-Ren's archery—she's entirely self-taught.

Nephilia is actually the unique one here; most of the time a magical girl who possesses a special weapon as a part of her costume will be able to use it well even without education. It's not like Nephilia couldn't use the scythe, but she wanted to take it to the next level or two, and she sought the opinion of a specialist for that and got some education.

Ren-Ren has also practiced the bow on her own, but it wasn't like she had nothing to base it on. She copied bow skills from manga and anime. It's common for a magical girl to be able to re-create even an incredibly bizarre special technique, and normally this sort of study would never work, but it actually went well for her.

Ren-Ren sometimes did and sometimes didn't use reference material for her various techniques in this book. While Love Me Ren-Ren is the messenger of love, when it comes to manga and anime, she loves action stories.

◇ The Bald Magical Girls

The bald magical girls who tried to raid the Management Department while Chief Ragi was out had the tables turned on them. The defense functionality of the Management Department will be a bit reduced when the master is out, but it still cannot be easily conquered.

Now, the truth is this scene isn't inserted in chronological order. And some people might have thought, *That felt sudden.* That's because it is.

I wrote that scene upon coming back from a fairly long break in serialization. It restarts from a scene you can read on its own, so that people who are like, *"This is the first time I've read this in months"* can slip right into it.

That background aside, those girls were sealed in for a few days until Chief Ragi came back, and upon his return, he gave them a full lecture before finally releasing them. However, if that would teach them a lesson, then they never would have tried extreme information theft to begin with. With this practice behind them, the girls are stronger, and they might yet attack the Management Department again.

◇ Magical Girl–Style Staff Arts

Although many people practice these, there is no head school, and their origin is unclear. I figure there was some Minmei

Shobou–type episode, but there are no magical girls to talk about it. The general theory is that some magical girl with martial expertise created it.

◇ **The Secret Techniques of the Inspection Department**

That the ear-grabbing technique that isn't supposed to leave the department is actually known on the outside is depicted in the short story "The Fairy of the Inspection Department." There was no time to use it in the story of *Limited*, but the ace of the Inspection Department, Hana Gekokujou, can also use this technique.

She may have had an advantage in mock battles, since she made her opponents worry about just which set of ears they should grab. Just what is there in the position where her human ears should be? Or is there nothing? That's a secret even Mana doesn't know.

◇ **Relics of the First Mage**

They're apparently dug up in quite a lot of different places. They're generally broken.

They can be repaired with magic, but once you've repaired them, it's difficult to restore the shape they took from before they were broken, so if there's no business in using them, they're often just left as they are. At the end of the day, the First Mage is the god of the Magical Kingdom, so part of the reason is that you can't mess with these just because what God left behind is broken.

And now the page count is about to reach its limit. I am still brimming with the urge to write, but I think I will leave it here for today.

Thank you very much to Meru for submitting Dreamy☆Chelsea, Lapis Nyamuriinu for submitting Nephilia, Kujira Hebi for submitting Pastel Mary, Nottsuo for submitting Miss Marguerite, and DQR@N for submitting Love Me Ren-Ren. It's thanks to all of you that I have been able to continue *Breakdown* until the end. They have all been cute, strong, and exceptional magical girls.

Thank you to everyone else who applied as well. You stimulated my muses quite a lot. They still continue to burn as fuel for my heart so I can do my best on *Magical Girl Raising Project*.

To all the people from the editing department who have guided me, and Corrections S-mura—or rather, my lifelong rival S-mura, who has been forced to clash opinions with me every month, thank you very much.

Marui-no, thank you very much for your wonderful illustrations. It becomes quite the job when you're already busy with not only magical girls but also even human forms and mages. These convincing designs, and some more-than-convincing designs, have satisfied me so much, as a fan. The ones I personally like are Maiya and human Chelsea and also Mr. Shepherdspie. They just feel totally convincing.

And to all my readers, thank you very much for sticking with me for this long. Let us meet again in the continuation of this story, *Cerulean Blue*.

I think it felt like there were more characters than usual in this volume because it was so packed with images of mages and human forms for me to think about and draw... This was truly a dense book. I was impressed by all the characters with such mental fortitude even in their human forms.

Thank you very much!

Marui-no

With character evaluations by a Magical Girl Resources Department veteran!

Celebrating the novelization!

Breakdown: Magical-Girl Interviews & Profiles

※ The following pages include some spoilers, so please read the rest of the book first.

Magical-Girl
Interview No. 1

Dreamy ☆ Chelsea (Part II)

According to the documents I have here, you tend to break things.

"I hardly do that at all lately! There might've been more of that a long time ago."

By "hardly," does that mean you still fail to gauge your own strength?

"I guess it's like there's a bit of a gap between the ideal Chelsea and the real Chelsea… But you know, that's basically why Chelsea works hard to be her best self!"

How do you cope with breaking things?

"Can we not talk about this?"

I think people might be very curious about how a cute, clumsy magical girl generally deals with her mistakes. I'm sure new magical girls would find it useful as well.

"You think…? Eh, fine. You just write

(Continued from Part I)

What sort of magical-girl activities do you typically do?

"Chelsea rides a star and patrols the town at night. If Chelsea finds people in trouble, she zips over on that star to help them out, or she gets off the star and lends them a hand."

Do you make mistakes?

"Oh, you know, only sometimes, very rarely…"

a letter of apology saying, like, *'I'm sorry.'* It depends on how bad the destruction is, but sometimes Chelsea sends money, too."

That sounds fairly realistic.

"Chelsea's mom was like, *'You're old enough now, so get serious about these sorts of things…'* Wait, who cares about that? It's Chelsea's job to help people who are hurt or in trouble. So Chelsea does what she can. There's nothing wrong with that."

I see. Now for the last question: What is a magical girl to you?

"Hup! Hya! Spin, spin, spin, spin…smaaack! And stick the landing. How's that?"

Um, I'm not sure how to respond…

"That was supposed to convey Chelsea's idea of a magical girl."

Since this is an interview, do you think you could put it into words?

"It's not something you can verbalize that easy."

I understand. Thank you very much for your time today.

"Huh? Wait, hold on, Chelsea's not done talking… I mean, you don't fully understand, surely. Like, you've gotta have a firm basis in the overall history of magical girls and Dreamy☆Chelsea's thirty-year background and everything. Mm-hmm, and since Chelsea's so nice, she'll explain it for you. First we start when Chelsea was born, and this is a great story—"

Magical-Girl Profile

Magic	Can freely control stars.
Real Name	Chie Yumeno
Age & Profession	34, unemployed

Magical-Girl Stats

Destructive Power	♥ ♥ ♥ ♥ ♥
Endurance	♥ ♥ ♥ ♥ ○
Agility	♥ ♥ ♥ ♥ ♥
Intelligence	♥ ♥ ○ ○ ○
Assertiveness	♥ ♥ ♥ ♥ ○
Ambition/Desire	♥ ♥ ♥ ○ ○
Magic Potential	♥ ♥ ♥ ○ ○

Likes
Magical girls (Showa era), convenience store sweets, old-school games

Dislikes
Violence, hassles

Resources Department Comments

Her physical stats are extremely high, and her love for magical girls is astounding.

A serious veteran with a thirty-year history, she hasn't been resting on her laurels; instead, she's been hard at work this whole time. Her magic to control stars was mere child's play at first, but she's taken it to new heights by honing her accuracy and speed.

You'd be wrong to assume she's the type to seek power—she hates violence. She's also not a member of any organization but instead works hard as a local magical girl. Such a great person.

Magical-Girl Interview No. 2

Nephilia (Part II)

Celebrating the
novelization!
Breakdown
Magical-Girl
Interview

②

(Continued from Part I)

The first thing that comes to mind when people think of you is likely your characteristic laugh.

"Ksh-sh-sh."

Yes, that's it. Why do you laugh like that?

"It's natural… Establishes character… Indicates listening… Lots of things…"

So it depends on the situation.

"Ksh-sh-sh."

But enough about your laugh. I hear you've been involved in a number of incidents due to the peculiarities of your magic.

"Unintentionally…"

You don't like touching corpses— was that right? But you need to suck it up for work, huh? Is there any particular incident that sticks out in your mind? Like a murder, for example.

"Murders…not really… Lately…we catch the culprit…pretty quickly…"

I suppose it would be rude to call that disappointing. So, any other

incidents?

"Fans of…deceased…singers… and voice actors…"

Yes, of course. They want to hear the voices of people who are gone.

"Stole…mementos… Got caught after…"

I thought we were going to get a sad story, but it ended up being a scary one instead. Anything else?

"Explored some ruins… Wondered what ancient people talked about…"

Oh-ho. So what were they saying?

"All in an ancient language…so I didn't understand…"

Ah, right. But of course. Is there anything further of note?

"The incident…Keek caused…"

The one where she imprisoned multiple magical girls in a cyberspace, right?

"Helped…investigate…lots of things…"

Did you make any new discoveries?

"All sorts of…interesting things…"

Such as?

"They said not to…tell anyone…"

Understandable… Now, to wrap things up: What is a magical girl to you?

"Ksh-sh-sh."

That sounds deep… Thank you very much for today.

Magical-Girl Profile

Magic	Can hear the voices of dead people.
Real Name	Iria Funada
Age & Profession	16, high school student

Magical-Girl Stats

Stat	
Destructive Power	♥ ♥ ♥ · ·
Endurance	♥ ♥ ♥ · ·
Agility	♥ ♥ ♥ · ·
Intelligence	♥ ♥ ♥ ♥ ·
Assertiveness	♥ ♥ · · ·
Ambition/Desire	♥ ♥ ♥ ♥ ·
Magic Potential	♥ ♥ ♥ · ·

Likes
Decently scummy people, interesting things

Dislikes
People rotten to the core, death

Resources Department Comments

Physical abilities are fairly average, but she carries a scythe and knows how to use it. Very strong mentally, and smart, so she's a quick thinker. She's the type who's hardier than her physical stats indicate.

Her magic lets her hear the voices of the dead. Although not particularly convenient, it can be indispensable in criminal investigations, or to families looking to remember deceased loved ones.

Has some difficulties with communication. And those difficulties aren't so simple—her biggest problem is that she enjoys struggling to communicate.

Pastel Mary (Part II)

Magical-Girl Interview No. 3

(Continued from Part I)

How long have you been a freelancer?

"I think it's been about two or three years. I haven't counted, so I'm not quite sure."

You say you've never run out of work that entire time.

"Yeah, more or less."

According to our investigation, 70 percent to 80 percent of your clients' reviews of your service involve you screwing up. They claim you fall a lot, your sheep go out of control, or all the shedding makes them cough.

"Why are you looking up stuff like that?"

I think it's natural to look into your interview subjects. I always do. So how is it you don't run out of work when you do nothing but mess up?

"Well, um… How indeed?"

Don't ask me.

"Now that you mention it, I feel like I don't have many repeat clients…or rather none at all… Maybe my mess-ups were the cause."

Like I said, don't ask me.

"But my work still doesn't dry up..."

That's exactly what I'm talking about. I'm asking for the reason why your work doesn't dry up.

"Hmmm, I don't know. Luck...I guess?"

...When you think of Pastel Mary, you think of sheep. Is there a limit to how many you can create?

"Probably."

Wait—you don't know yourself?

"I draw what I need. I've never thought about trying to see how many I can put out."

You draw what you need? There are a number of sheep walking around in this very room, and I saw some in the hallway, too. Were all those sheep necessary?

"I thought it'd be nice if things were a little busy."

How terribly considerate of you. To finish: What is a magical girl to you?

"Now, how should I put this? It's difficult. I feel like it's tough to describe in a word, or to give, like, one example. Hmmm... I think maybe if I could have some time to come up with an answer, then—"

Thank you very much for your time.

Magical-Girl Profile

Magic	Can materialize the sheep she draws with her pastels.
Real Name	Yoh Tanada
Age & Profession	Around 20, art school student

Magical-Girl Stats

Destructive Power	♥ · · · ·
Endurance	♥ ♥ · · ·
Agility	♥ ♥ · · ·
Intelligence	♥ ♥ · · ·
Assertiveness	♥ · · · ·
Ambition/Desire	♥ ♥ · · ·
Magic Potential	♥ ♥ ♥ ♥ ·

Likes
Drawing, sheep, being relied on

Dislikes
Gym class, aggressive people

Resources Department Comments

Physical stats are on the low side. Personalitywise, she doesn't seem suited for combat or disputes. A sweet, easygoing girl.

There doesn't appear to be a limit to the number of sheep her magic can create, so she could probably manage in a fight by compensating for her low stats with lots of sheep. However, given her personality, I doubt she would even want to do that.

Her biggest problem is that she's a klutz. It's impressive that she's gotten this far as a magical girl. She's a dangerous individual who means no harm.

Miss Marguerite (Part II)

(Continued from Part I)

So you were an instructor with the Inspection Department.

"You could say that, yes."

I hear things are pretty brutal over there.

"It's certainly very risky business, and having a criminal slip through your fingers leads to even greater damage. All that strict training is par for the course for the Inspection Department, I'd say."

That's amazing.

"Although perhaps, as someone who left her position with the department, I shouldn't act so high and mighty."

That's not true at all. Doesn't your training live on, even now?

"I wouldn't know."

Were there any students who left a strong impression?

"…Well, sure, I suppose there were."

If you wouldn't mind telling us about them…

"I wouldn't say that information is classified, but I'm not sure I should discuss it in an interview."

Yes, you're right. Pardon me.

So, have you picked up any pesky work-related tics, or rather, any habits because of this job?

"I now evaluate people upon meeting them for the first time."

That is, whether they seem like they would be a good student?

"Whether or not I'd be able to fight them off if they were a criminal who attacked me."

I see. That's certainly a pesky work-related tic.

"I knew there were a lot of strong magical girls among the ones who've starred in anime, such as Cutie Healer…but I had no idea that even a journalist with the Public Relations Department would be this powerful."

Huh? A journalist?

"Even as we speak, I can tell that you are highly athletic. The way you sit lightly in your chair, ready to move at any moment, the way your gaze is so nonchalantly alert to your entire surroundings—"

Wait—me?! Please stop!

"Tee-hee."

Huh? What? Were you teasing me? Oh, don't do that.

"But it's true that you're powerful."

Um, so, for our last question: What is a magical girl to you?

"It's all about strength. Depending on how you use it, it can be a blessing or a curse."

It sounds like you're speaking from experience… Thank you very much for today.

Magical-Girl Profile

Magic	Can bend straight objects.
Real Name	Kaoruko Rokugou
Age & Profession	27, freelancer

Magical-Girl Stats

Destructive Power	♥ ♥ ♥ ♥ ·
Endurance	♥ ♥ ♥ · ·
Agility	♥ ♥ ♥ ♥ ♥
Intelligence	♥ ♥ ♥ ♥ ·
Assertiveness	♥ ♥ · · ·
Ambition/Desire	♥ · · · ·
Magic Potential	♥ ♥ · · ·

Likes
Quiet places with nice scenery, rose-scented candles

Dislikes
Complicated relationships, pushy people

Resources Department Comments

Her physical stats are high level across the board. However, this is not where the basis of her strength lies—I would say it's in her technique and experience. She has the skill and courage to face powerful opponents.

The conditions for activating her magic are quite limited, so you'd think it would be difficult to wield in battle… and yet she makes full use of her technique and experience there, too.

She's also mentally strong, and has a lot of perseverance. But constantly bottling things up will add stress. I think she should let off some steam from time to time.

Love Me Ren-Ren (Part II)

(Continued from Part I)

It sounds like you'll take any work related to families.

"Yes. That's partly because the importance of family is what led me to become a magical girl."

Doesn't it bother you when the work takes up a lot of your time, or when the pay isn't up to snuff?

"It's not about the money. Also—this might sound a little like I'm showing off, but…"

Yes?

"I think the smiles from people after I've resolved their problems are the biggest reward."

I don't think you're showing off.

That's very magical girl-like.

"That's so kind of you to say."

But isn't it a real burden, taking on anything and everything and not being able to choose your jobs?

"Magical girls are built to tolerate things, even if they push themselves a bit."

I've heard stories that some families' relationships soured again after you resolved their

problems. How does that make you feel?

"That sort of thing happens, but then I just resolve things again."

Ah, so you do thorough follow-ups as well.

"A family does not break. Though it might crack and seem broken, it can be fixed. Does that ring true for you? In terms of family, I mean."

Huh? What is this, a reverse interview? I don't have a family.

"…You don't?"

That's right. My parents died young, so if I'd had siblings, then I wouldn't have wound up all alone in the world. As a child, I used to pester my mom and dad for the impossible, saying I wanted a big sister.

"You want…a big sister?"

Oh, I did when I was a child. I don't anymore.

"Not anymore… So you're not a little sister…"

Umm…? Is it okay to continue?

"Ah! Yes, pardon me. I'm quite all right."

Finally, what is a magical girl to you?

"Someone who will save you when you're in trouble and protect those who are dear to you… That's what I want to be. That's my ideal."

Yes, I see. Thank you very much for your time today.

Magical-Girl Profile

Magic	Anyone she shoots with her magic bow will fall head over heels in love.
Real Name	Rei Koimizu
Age & Profession	17, high school student

Magical-Girl Stats

Stat	
Destructive Power	♥ ♥ · · ·
Endurance	♥ ♥ · · ·
Agility	♥ ♥ ♥ ♥ ·
Intelligence	♥ ♥ ♥ · ·
Assertiveness	♥ ♥ ♥ · ·
Ambition/Desire	♥ ♥ ♥ ♥ ·
Magic Potential	♥ ♥ ♥ · ·

Likes
Families that get along, friends, lovers, going for a stroll in the sky

Dislikes
Discord, breakups

Resources Department Comments

True to the standard that winged, flying magical girls don't have much power—although in this girl's case, given her use of projectiles and the nature of her magic, she doesn't really need power. Speed and technique are more important, and it's in those aspects that she excels.

Her magic is powerful. The conditions for its activation are straightforward, and its effects are simple and strong. However, her magic becomes harder to use as time goes on. After the second activation, it gets more complicated.

A gentle girl who values family, although I have a slight nagging feeling that there's something off about her.

Magical-Girl Profiles

Clarissa Toothedge

Magic	Knows the location of any object she's bitten.
Real Name	Lu
Age & Profession	10, Lab employee

Magical-Girl Stats

Destructive Power	♥ ♥ ♥ · ·
Endurance	♥ ♥ · · ·
Agility	♥ ♥ ♥ ♥ ♥
Intelligence	♥ ♥ ♥ ♥ ·
Assertiveness	♥ ♥ ♥ · ·
Ambition/Desire	♥ ♥ ♥ ♥ ·
Magic Potential	♥ ♥ · · ·

Likes
Bread with lots of butter, exercise, conspiracies

Dislikes
The people who stole her mother, quirky girls

Resources Department Comments

Just like other animal-type magical girls, she possesses the abilities of the animal that is her motif. Quick and nimble, with a strong jaw and legs. Not as powerful as big cats like tigers or lions, but second to none in agility. She's quite clever, so I believe she could beat some big names. Her magic isn't half bad in terms of utility; in battle, it can help keep her alert and search for enemies. Otherwise, she could bite every single thing she owns and never lose a thing, which is nice. Regardless, she's incredibly talented for her age.

Magical-Girl Stats

Destructive Power	♥ ♥ ♥ ♥ ♥
Endurance	♥ ♥ ♥ ♥ ♥
Agility	♥ ♥ ♥ ♥ ♥
Intelligence	♥ · · · ·
Assertiveness	♥ · · · ·
Ambition/Desire	♥ · · · ·
Magic Potential	♥ ♥ ♥ ♥ ·

Likes
Singing, fighting

Dislikes
Grayfruit

Francisca Francesca

Resources Department Comments

Her physical stats are highly unusual. I've been doing this job for quite some time, and I've never seen anything like this. If there were a magical-girl Olympics, then she would be a gold medalist.

Her magic makes direct use of her physical abilities and is also powerful.

Conversely, her emotions have yet to be developed. I imagine that aspect depends on her future growth. Her physical abilities and magic pack an extremely lethal punch, so I'd like to take special care in developing her ethics and morals.

Magic	Fights with the mysterious axes she carries in both hands.
Real Name	Francisca Francesca
Age & Profession	0

Magical-Girl Stats

Destructive Power	♥	♥	♥	♥	♥
Endurance	♥	♥	♥	♥	·
Agility	♥	♥	♥	♥	·
Intelligence	♥	♥	♥	·	·
Assertiveness	♥	♥	♥	·	·
Ambition/Desire	♥	♥	·	·	·
Magic Potential	♥	♥	♥	·	·

Likes

Staff technique, sincerity, a master worthy of service

Dislikes

Frivolity, lack of discipline, villains

Resources Department Comments

She was strong to begin with, but training seems to be her hobby; she's been aiming for new heights to just get stronger and stronger.

Her magic staff has a special effect on liars, so its force varies depending on the opponent. Since almost everyone lies, the staff is sturdy enough to be used like a regular one. Combined with her combat skills, it's quite an impressive item.

She has a magnificent disposition. I just feel that people tend to misunderstand her.

Maiya

Magic	Fights with a magic staff that beats liars.
Real Name	Maya Mutou
Age & Profession	44, butler

Magical-Girl Stats

Destructive Power	♥	♥	♥	·	·
Endurance	♥	♥	♥	·	·
Agility	♥	♥	♥	♥	·
Intelligence	♥	♥	·	·	·
Assertiveness	♥	·	·	·	·
Ambition/Desire	♥	♥	♥	♥	·
Magic Potential	♥	♥	♥	♥	·

Likes

People you can rely on, overly long sleeves, pot-au-feu

Dislikes

Weaklings, useless people, garlic chives

Resources Department Comments

Her physical abilities are decent, and it seems she herself has gone through some training that's made her fairly strong. She still has room to grow, so I'm looking forward to seeing where she goes from here.

Her magic is genuinely powerful. Given how user-friendly it is, I bet many people would want it. I imagine she's in high demand.

However, despite all these elements in her favor, she somehow has low self-esteem that's apparently dragging her down. She's truly talented, so I'd first like to give her a confidence boost.

Rareko

Magic	Can fix things that are broken.
Real Name	Arare Mutou
Age & Profession	23, maid

HAVE YOU BEEN TURNED ON TO LIGHT NOVELS YET?

86—EIGHTY-SIX, VOL. 1–11

In truth, there is no such thing as a bloodless war. Beyond the fortified walls protecting the eighty-five Republic Sectors lies the "nonexistent" Eighty-Sixth Sector. The young men and women of this forsaken land are branded the Eighty-Six and, stripped of their humanity, pilot "unmanned" weapons into battle...

Manga adaptation available now!

WOLF & PARCHMENT, VOL. 1–6

The young man Col dreams of one day joining the holy clergy and departs on a journey from the bathhouse, Spice and Wolf. Winfiel Kingdom's prince has invited him to help correct the sins of the Church. But as his travels begin, Col discovers in his luggage a young girl with a wolf's ears and tail named Myuri, who stowed away for the ride!

Manga adaptation available now!

SOLO LEVELING, VOL. 1–6

E-rank hunter Jinwoo Sung has no money, no talent, and no prospects to speak of—and apparently, no luck, either! When he enters a hidden double dungeon one fateful day, he's abandoned by his party and left to die at the hands of some of the most horrific monsters he's ever encountered.

Comic adaptation available now!